DEATH MOVED QUIETLY TOWARD THEM.

Closer. Closer...

He reached the bed just as the woman cried out, her breasts thrust upward, her nipples erect and glistening. The man under her groaned, long and low and deep, his chest pumping with the frantic beat of his heart.

"Aren't you glad I waited up?" she purred, running her hands up his chest to brush several long strands of hair away from his face. "Did you like it?"

"Like it?" he asked incredulously. "Shit, I think I'm dead."

"No," Death whispered as two heads swiveled toward him, two pairs of delightful blue eyes alight with shocked recognition. "Not yet anyway."

Other *Leisure* books by Kimberly Rangel:
SHADOWS

THE HOMECOMING

KIMBERLY RANGEL

LEISURE BOOKS NEW YORK CITY

A LEISURE BOOK®

February 1998

Published by

Dorchester Publishing Co., Inc.
276 Fifth Avenue
New York, NY 10001

ISBN 0-8439-4352-1

This is dedicated to Nina, Gerry, LeeAnn, Donna, Mica, Jan, Bonnie and Marian, a wonderful group of writers and friends. And to Donna Meins for never being too busy, or too optically impaired for a final read. Y'all are the greatest!

I would also like to say a special thank you to Larry Fitzgerald of the Texas Department of Criminal Justice, for lending me his expertise and answering even the most trivial questions. Your help was invaluable!

The line that separates Life from Death is shadowy at best.
Who shall say where one ends and the other begins?

—Edgar Allan Poe

THE
HOMECOMING

Prologue

I'd always wondered what death would feel like.

I knew what it looked like—a milky white corpse sprawled in a pool of red, lips blue, bloody holes where the precious eyes had once been.

I knew what it smelled like—the strong, pungent aroma of sweat and fear and excitement. The scent as inviting as the blueberry cobbler Granny used to set on the windowsill to cool. I could stand for hours, sweat pouring off me from the hot summer sun, just drinking in the smell and thinking about savoring the first bite.

That was always the best part in everything I did—the thinking about it. The doing was good, too, but never quite good enough. That's why I had to start over and try again. And again. And again.

I knew what death sounded like—a shrill scream, a choked gurgle, a final rasping breath. God, I loved that last sound. I would always lean just close enough so that my ear was right there. The chest would heave, rise one last time. Then there it was, loud and clear like the end-ing buzzer on *Jeopardy!*. So final. So absolute. So damned perfect. For me, there's never been a sweeter sound.

I even knew what death tasted like. I know it sounds a little morbid, but when it's right there in front of you, all over you, so warm, like hot strawberry syrup, you just can't help yourself. I would gather a little on the tip of my finger. Only a few drops, but it was better than strawberry syrup. Warmer. Richer.

Actually, I didn't even like the taste at first. For a few seconds, I almost puked, but it's kind of like eating lima beans when you're a kid. You don't want to. The thought of it repulses you, but once you make yourself do it that first time, then again, hell, you start to like those suckers. Crave them, in fact.

But no matter how I many times I'd seen death, heard it, tasted it, I never really *knew* what it was like. Oh, I could imagine, all right.

In the early days of my career, I used to climb into bed at night, pull the covers up over my head and hurry to sleep. I didn't want to think about what I'd done, what I'd seen, least of all dream about any of it.

But after those first few times, I couldn't sleep so easily anymore. It was just like the time I'd walked in on Cheryl Ann Chambers when she was in the girl's toilet, taking a piss. I'd just stood there, staring at her . . . you know, all those soft, fuzzy curls *down there*. I'd never seen a girl like that, just my granny, but she was all old and wrinkled, and *down there* had been an overgrowth of coarse gray hair that made me think of the sewer rat I'd cornered in the shed one time and beat with a tire iron. But Cheryl Ann wasn't anything like Granny. At thirteen, she had creamy white skin, the whitest I'd ever seen, smooth young curves, and a patch of wispy blond hair.

She'd screamed so loud when she caught me staring that I just knew every single student at Nostalgia Junior High had heard. Scared the shit out of me, she did. I turned and ran as fast as my cheap, hand-me-down gym shoes could carry me. I was only twelve, and at twelve you didn't think of sticking your dick in when you saw pussy. No, you thought, *Ugh!*

Anyhow, one of the teachers saw me running out of the girls' bathroom. The old witch gave me a paddling and two weeks' worth of detentions, but at least she didn't send home a note. I was grateful for that. I certainly didn't want Granny finding out. She would've beat my ass but good. Even worse, she would've hauled me to church, stuck me on my knees in front of God and everybody, and had the reverend and the whole damned congregation praying for my soul for doing such a sinful thing. Fornicating, thinking about fornicating, even saying the *F* word out loud, were at the top of Granny's sin list. Next came lying, I think.

Funny how sex ranks higher than murder on the sin scale. I always wondered about that, but I never said anything to Granny. She was a God-fearing Christian woman, after all. Who was I to tell her she had her priorities screwed up? Besides, it was that initial ass-whipping fear getting the best of me again.

Anyway, I did feel ashamed at spying on Cheryl Ann at first. I climbed into bed that night and closed my eyes real tight, and tried not to think of that triangle of little blond curls. If I didn't think about it, maybe God would forget what I'd done, and so would I.

After a few nights of feeling guilty and forcing myself to sleep, I just couldn't do it anymore. I would lie awake, stare at the June bugs bumping into the overhead bulb and think of Cheryl Ann on purpose. Think of what it would feel like to touch her *there*. And lo and behold, I didn't wake up castrated, or blind, minus my baby blues, or any of the other things Granny said would happen if I grew up to be a sinner like my daddy. So you see, I stopped listening to Granny pretty early on.

The killing was just like that incident with Cheryl Ann Chambers. After that first time, I pulled off my ruined Halloween costume, crawled under the sheet and closed my eyes real tight until I fell asleep. I was a teenager, so young and naive. Once I got a taste of the anticipation that came with thinking about what I was going to do, what I'd already done, I grew up really fast. That's when I stopped sleeping most nights and started planning. In those days, you had to have a plan. Details meant the difference between doing what you wanted—needed—to do, and getting caught. It wasn't like it is now—homeless people on every corner, runaways camped in every vacant doorway, criminals walking the streets just waiting for a nice, attractive, mild-mannered Joe like me. Nowadays people can just disappear and it doesn't make any difference. Nobody misses them. In fact, society's better off without them. Granny always said the world was going to hell in a handbasket. She was right about that, but back in the old days you had to be careful.

Not that I ever really worried about getting caught, but I did give it some thought. After each killing, I often wondered how it would be for me in the end. I spent hours and hours and hours watching June bugs and just thinking, anticipating. Surely I would get as good as I gave? I thought so, you know, Granny's "Do unto others" firmly branded into my mind.

In those last few moments when they stretched me out on that table and strapped my hands and feet down, I couldn't help but giggle. I mean, this was it. What I'd been waiting for, dreaming of for ten years, since my first killing. Now I would know firsthand what death was really like. No more wondering. No more envying those who'd already found out because of my creative genius.

I took a deep breath and filled my lungs with antiseptic-laden air. I could feel the eyes of those people in the witness chamber, though I couldn't turn my head enough to see anyone. It didn't matter, though. Just knowing that they were there, watching, seeing what I'd seen so many times in the past, heightened the anticipation.

The warden and the priest stood next to me in the

death chamber, one on either side of the table. The priest mumbled some prayer while the warden looked solemn. He nodded toward the chemical room, and the medical technician came in with two IV hookups. One for each arm, the second in case the first should fail. I giggled again, every nerve in my body alive with anticipation. This was really *it*.

Then it came. Just the slight prick of two needles. The technician disappeared. The first chemical pulsed through me and my eyelids grew heavy, my thoughts slowed, my excitement calmed. I don't remember much after that. It was all over in a matter of seconds. *Seconds*. Then I was finished. The end.

I can't tell you how mad that made me. I mean, an amateur could have done a better job than those morons, damn them. I was deserving of a far better end. Every witness in the damned witness chamber knew that. The media, too. They'd wanted to see some blood, some suffering, *something*. Even that cable television lady had told the world I should be strung up by my balls and skinned alive. She had the right idea, though she could have come up with something a little more original. I mean, that was one of my earlier exploits when I was still experimenting, before I'd gotten my routine down. Toward the end I'd gotten so much better.

The families of all those pretty young girls—they knew I deserved more, too. Hadn't they picketed for weeks on end, written their congressmen, rallied for a more painful punishment? Hell, yes! They begged for everything from castration to burning me alive. But do you think the government listened to one word? Hell, no! Not that it surprised me, but it did piss me off. Royally. I mean, we elected those bastards, right? But that's justice for you. They'd fried Ted Bundy down in Florida and he hadn't been half as deserving as me. He'd had that first moment of electrifying contact. The sound of sizzling flesh. The acid taste in his mouth.

And what did I end up with? Old Blue Eyes, himself?

Not a shittin'-ass thing, and this was Texas where they're supposed to do everything bigger and better. Right. Those pansy redneck bastards ended ten years of hard work in a matter of seconds. No sound. No smell. Not even a measly taste. Just a slip of two needles, a swift, deadly injection, and it was done. So quick and painless. So damned unfair.

So, you see, when another chance presented itself, I couldn't ignore it and go away, nice and quiet like, as Granny used to say. I deserved better, and I'd show those bastards just how deserving I was. I was still in my prime. Still thinking, planning. Still craving. I had at least another ten years left. At least.

It was only fair that I get a second chance.

An eye for an eye, as Granny always used to say. An eye for an eye . . .

Chapter One

It was a particularly bloody night.

Darby Jayson yanked open the pantry door and rummaged inside. Her fingers closed around the neck of a bottle and she pulled the Jack Daniel's from its hiding place behind a box of Cheerios. Moonlight filtered through the kitchen blinds, casting slats of shadows into the room. Holding up the bottle, she stared at the deep gold liquid. Half-full. That should get her through the rest of the night, but she would have to restock first thing in the morning. Before tomorrow night. Just in case it happened again.

She clutched the bottle in the valley between her bare breasts. The glass was warm, soothing to her chilled skin, but it did little to thaw her insides. Hopefully the whiskey itself would do that.

Darby left the kitchen and went to fetch her robe from the bedroom floor. She shrugged into the thick terry cloth, belted the waist and pulled the ends tight, before snatching up the bottle again and heading for the living room.

17

The hardwood floor was like ice to her bare feet and she wished she'd thought to put on a pair of socks. She would've gone back, if her need for the JD hadn't been so fierce. That and the fact that she knew no matter how many pairs of socks she pulled on, it wouldn't be enough to ease her chill.

Anxious feet ate up the distance to the entertainment center that covered nearly an entire wall of her cluttered living room. Slivers of moonlight touched everything, the silver mixed with swirls of blue neon from Come As You Are, a small beer joint next door where the music was loud, the booze cheap and the women even cheaper.

She squinted and rummaged through a mountain-high stack of cassette tapes before she found the right one. With trembling fingers, she popped in the tape and shoved the volume up. Sound exploded as a guitar wailed and drums beat a frenzied rhythm that did nothing to calm her nerves, and everything to distract her from the images racing through her mind. But the music wasn't enough.

She grabbed the remote control, punched the on button. A big-screen TV lit up the room and a familiar talk-show host sparked to life, her voice drowned in the music blaring from the speakers. A caption at the bottom of the screen indicated that this was a rerun of the day's episode on mothers who date their teenage daughters' boyfriends. From the argument occurring on screen, Darby knew the mother had done much more than date the pimply faced teen sitting beside her.

Remote control in hand, she walked over to the sofa, past the makeshift desk that sported her laptop computer and printer. A stack of clean paper sat to one side, maybe an inch of used paper on the other. Barely an inch. Her inch-high Great American Novel. She had no doubt the publishing houses would be beating down her door any second. Right. She was more likely to walk away with a news award for her review of The Morgue, a new club on the east side that had an honest-to-goodness embalming table at the center of the dance floor.

No, Darby didn't have aspirations of being a great novelist. She wrote to clear her head, to get her thoughts out of her mind and down on paper where she could deal with them. Though she couldn't actually remember when she'd last written anything. She gave another puzzled glance to the finished pages and headed for the sofa. She could sort through that inch of paper later, after she'd thawed out.

Shoving aside several old newspapers, two half-empty Chinese takeout cartons and a week-old empty pizza box, she sank down onto the battered sofa. Even through the thick terry robe, she felt the cold leather against her backside. A chill worked its way down her spine, but she knew it didn't come from the sofa. It came from the inside, as always. After nights like this, she always had a hard time warming up. An impossible time. It could take three, four days, even a week or two before she'd start to feel normal again.

It would take a lot longer after tonight.

She tucked long legs beneath her, folding the ends of her thick robe over her feet. The temperature outside was fairly warm for San Francisco in October. Around sixty degrees. But it might well have been below freezing as far as Darby was concerned. It was cold. So very cold. Especially tonight.

Hot air swirled through the apartment, the heater blasting full force. But it did little to ease the gooseflesh covering every inch of her body, or to warm the ice water pumping through her veins.

A demo from one of San Francisco's hottest grunge bands screamed at her from across the room, and the Jack Daniel's called from her lap. *I'll warm you up, Darby. I always do. . . .*

She unscrewed the bottle of JD and took a long, deep swallow. Liquor burned a vicious path down her throat, but she welcomed the feeling. Her saving grace. This would warm her when all else failed.

She took another long drink as a shiver rippled through her.

It had been one hell of a bloody night. The worst she could remember, and she had plenty with which to compare. The television sent colored shadows playing across her skin as Darby stared down at her hands. They still shook, but not from the cold. It was crazy. Insane. Her entire body felt as if she'd been thrown into a deep freeze, all *except* for her hands. She could still feel the warm blood spilling over her fingers. . . .

She rubbed her hands together, desperate to erase the sensation. When that didn't work, she took another drink, then another, as always.

And as always, the dream pushed its way into her consciousness, fighting the dulling effects of the alcohol, refusing to be forgotten so easily. As if she could ever forget. Not when the bizarre, distorted dreams revisited her every few months or so.

This one had come only a week after the last. Just *one* week, a record since they'd started nearly ten years ago. Since that night back in Texas when she'd opened her eyes to find her friends butchered.

Darby and her friend Katy had been the only witnesses left after a Halloween slumber party had resulted in the unexplained murders of three of the five partygoers. Katy had been so freaked out by what she'd seen, she'd wound up in a catatonic state at a nearby sanatorium, still her home the last time Darby had checked a couple of years ago. That left Darby as the only sane witness—a witness who didn't remember a damned thing. She'd blacked out, completely forgotten those few hours during which some lunatic had hacked away at her three best friends, then disappeared without leaving a trace of evidence behind.

That was why she had the dreams, because she couldn't remember. Katy hadn't been able to forget, to deal with what had happened. It had been too traumatic and she'd snapped, but Darby's protective instincts had kicked in. Her brain had simply blocked out that which was too difficult to deal with. Whether she consciously remembered or not, however, she'd still seen the killings, and those images were buried somewhere deep inside. Every now and then they shifted closer to the surface and she'd have the dreams—gruesome, macabre dreams of blood and killing that had her leaning over the toilet, puking her stomach out before she even fully woke up.

The kicker was, she didn't simply dream about some man chopping up people. She wasn't a silent observer. No, she *felt* him. In the dreams, she was actually inside his head, feeling his feelings, thinking his thoughts. . . .

She touched a hand to her still-queasy middle. Tonight had been no different. Worse. She'd sat on the cold tile in the bathroom for a good hour, her head resting against the toilet seat, leftover visions running rampant through her mind, making her retch over and over until she'd had nothing else left inside.

As always, the victim had been a woman. This one had been young, slender, with jet black hair and large, sapphire eyes. Maybe that was what had freaked Darby out so much. She'd actually seen distinct features this time. Usually the dreams were so distorted, so fuzzy, she couldn't see clearly. For whatever reason, this time had been different.

The woman had been so pretty, with her flawless skin and wide blue eyes. So pretty and so perfect, until she'd opened her mouth to scream. Her face had changed then, her eyes lit with terror as she watched death close in on her.

"Please, please, please," she cried over and over again. Her dark, ruby lips trembled, the one word tumbling over itself as she sank back against the graffitied wall. No escape.

He liked that. A thrill of excitement went through him, like a jolt from a worn-out electrical cord. A smile tugged

21

at his lips and he lifted the knife. There was nothing like the feel of hot, pulsing blood when it spurted from that first slice. A giggle vibrated between his lips. No, nothing like it at all. It was heaven.

The closest he would ever get, as Granny had once told him, God rest her dry, shriveled-up soul. But he didn't need her silly, overrated notions of heaven. He knew better than to believe in heaven and hell. There was only life. Death was just the beginning of another life, another chance. He knew that firsthand.

"No," the woman said, the word a choked, shocked whisper as the knife arced down. Then there wasn't any more pretty face, no lying blue eyes gazing back at him. Just blood. So much sweet, intoxicating blood . . .

"No!" Darby wedged the open bottle of Jack Daniel's between two sofa cushions and rubbed her hands frantically back and forth on the thick terry cloth of her robe until they were raw, her wrists aching from the effort. Finally, she slumped back to the sofa and downed more of the Jack Daniel's. Her hands throbbed and stung, but she welcomed the feeling. Anything was better than the blood.

She stared across the room, into the bright, watery eyes of the talk-show host as the woman pretended to sympathize with her pathetic guests.

Concentrate! her mind screamed. If she could just concentrate on what was in front of her, she could forget what was in her head.

A single tear slid down the talk-show woman's cheek, and disgust forced Darby to grab the remote control and change the channel. She hated seeing anyone exploited. She'd had her fill of it after the murders. The media had swarmed all over her hometown, spreading accusations, demanding answers she didn't have. They'd been almost as bad as the police. It was no wonder Katy had lost it.

Another station, another pathetic talk show. She finally settled on CNN. A group of soldiers marched across the screen as a reporter went live to some Middle Eastern country caught in the midst of a bloody conflict. A battered soldier pleaded his cause in a foreign language, and Darby thought about the first time she'd seen a real, live soldier on television. She'd been maybe four or five and Nixon had been in office. They'd filled the screen with propaganda. But no matter how they tried to hide the truth, it was there, inside of the men who were supposedly overseas fighting for democracy. And when those men had come home, they'd brought the truth with them.

She'd done a lot of thinking, and had finally concluded that her dreams were like those flashbacks so many Vietnam vets had after the war. The flashbacks were suppressed memories. The men had subconsciously blocked out the ugliness, but it was always there inside them, eating away. What they'd seen. What they'd done . . .

"Goddammit," she hissed, wiping a hand over her eyes and taking another long, shaky drink, then another, until she'd downed the last of the bottle.

A guitar gave a final, ear-shattering screech; then the tape went silent, and a news anchor's voice filled the apartment.

"Now we go live to San Francisco, where a grisly discovery has been made."

Darby stared at the bottle, then shot a glance at the clock. Four A.M. Too late to buy another bottle, but maybe Rudy might have something in his liquor cabinet. Just enough to warm her up and knock her out for a few hours. She had a lunch meeting today with her editor at *San Francisco Harmony*, the Bay City's number-one music magazine, which ran her weekly "What's Hot In the Music Scene" column. The column featured reviews of local bands and new clubs, and had been a huge success since she'd taken over the position nearly two years ago, much to her delight. After a three-year stint as an assistant music reviewer for a mediocre New Jersey rag, she'd been burned out and ready for a chance at her own column.

". . . due to the violence of this particular crime, police have only just now identified the murder victim found early yesterday morning as District Attorney Mike Morgan's daughter, Tracey. Now we go live to the scene with Doug Miller down on the Bay Area's east side, where the body was discovered less than twenty-four hours ago by sanitation workers. Doug, tell us what's going on."

The male reporter's voice droned on and Darby stood, empty bottle in hand. She would tiptoe down the hall to Rudy's apartment. Surely he'd be home from his gig by now, probably eating or drinking, trying to wind down. That was one thing about her friends: they were night people. Most were musicians or club owners, or into the music scene in some way. Rudy played guitar for a successful local band called True Grit.

". . . after last week's murder of young Trina Wilson near the waterfront, investigators are saying it could be the work of a serial killer in the San Francisco area, though police have yet to confirm this. There is no known connection between the two young women. Trina Wilson was a waitress in a small diner near Thirty-sixth Street, divorced with two children." A cheap snapshot of a pretty blond flashed on the screen. The woman was smiling, clutching a child on either side of her, the tiny faces pressed so close to hers it was impossible to distinguish her features. About the only thing evident from the picture was that she had blond hair, and two gorgeous kids who were crazy about her.

A pang of sympathy shot through Darby. It was such a shame. Violence was so senseless. Those kids would have to make do without a mother now, and all because some lunatic had decided to get his rocks off and cut loose on some poor defenseless woman. Her stomach did an involuntary flip. Her hands tingled and she tried to stab the off button on the remote. Her trembling fingers wouldn't cooperate and she hit the volume instead. The reporter's voice blasted through the room.

"DA Morgan's daughter was a senior in college, from the upper west side, a top student with a bright future ahead of her. Out for a night barhopping with friends at some of San Francisco's trendy nightspots, she was last seen at Ramone's around one A.M. Police can only speculate what happened after that."

Another picture flashed across the screen and Darby stopped dead in her tracks. The bottle of JD slipped from her suddenly lifeless fingers, and glass shattered around her. A scream burst from her throat as she found herself face-to-face with a young, attractive woman with jet black hair and brilliant blue eyes.

For the second time that night.

Chapter Two

"You're shittin' me, right?" Rudy Travers scooped up the last of the shattered bottle of JD and dumped the glass into the garbage can he'd pulled from Darby's kitchen.

"It was her," Darby insisted.

Rudy gave her an incredulous look and wiped his hands on his faded jeans. He still wore his stage clothes— tattered jeans ripped in all the right places and black cowboy boots. No shirt. That would have ruined his rock-star image. Dark, silky swirls of hair covered his lean, lightly muscled chest. He had a good body, though his face could have used some work. His jaw was slightly narrow, his lips thin, his pale blue eyes watery. Eyes that were very bloodshot at the moment, undoubtedly from too much smoke, too much liquor and too much of something else, if the speck of white powder beneath one nostril was any indication.

But no woman in her right mind really noticed anything about Rudy except the curtain of dark, thick, luxuriant hair that hung nearly to his waist. And, of course, his ass. He had one of the best Darby had ever seen, though that was the last thing on her mind at the moment.

Pain pulsed up her calf, sending slivers of heat through her body. She sucked in a breath and cradled her bleeding foot. A large chunk of glass protruded from the ball area, just below her big toe.

"Maybe you saw her on the news before or something, then dreamed about her," Rudy said. Pushing several long strands behind his ear, which sported a small gold hoop, he popped the top off a bottle of beer and took a long swig. "Every night after I watch Baywatch, I'm usually going at it hot and heavy with that blond with the big—"

"This is different, Rudy. I never saw that girl before last night. Ouch," she cried, when her fingers accidentally touched the glass. White-hot pain lanced through her foot. Her toes started to throb a vicious tempo reminiscent of the angry music she'd been listening to earlier.

"Gimme," Rudy said, plopping down on the coffee table in front of her and motioning with his hands. When she hesitated, he said, "Come on, Darby. I know you've got this shy thing going on and all, but I'm here and I'm willing, and I'm not going to jump your bones, at least not without your consent. I've seen bare legs before— yours included, with those short little skirts you wear— and I've managed to control myself."

At his disarming look, she smiled, just a slight tilt of her lips. That was all she could manage with her entire body still shaking, her foot blazing. She clutched the edges of her robe together, stretched her leg and rested her injured foot on his knee. His skin was warm and hairy through the rip in his jeans. Oddly comforting.

"You probably saw the chick before and you just don't remember." He grabbed the gauze and antiseptic he'd retrieved from the bathroom.

"Maybe."

"This is gonna hurt," he warned.

"Just do it." She clenched her teeth and braced herself as Rudy reached for the protruding piece of glass.

An excruciating moment later, he held up the result of his efforts. Through watery eyes, Darby stared at the blood-smeared glass. A single drop of red wound a path down the glass, and her stomach clenched. The dream pushed its way back in bits and bloody pieces and she doubled over, holding her stomach.

"Hey," Rudy said, kneeling beside her, his hands going to her face. He tilted her gaze up to meet his. "You okay? I didn't mean to hurt you, but that glass was really deep."

"It's not that." She shook her head, then grappled for control a long, silent second, before mumbling, "Maybe I did see her before. Hell, I don't know." But she did know. Deep inside she knew she'd never seen Tracey Morgan before . . . before she'd seen her killed, her throat slit, her eyes carved out. She'd even heard her voice.

No!

"Shit, Darby. You're shaking." Rudy gathered both of her hands in his. "Just take a deep breath and relax. Whatever you saw, whatever you thought you saw, it's over." He gave her hands a quick squeeze, then dropped them to her lap. Snatching up the lit cigarette he'd stuck in the ashtray before starting on her foot, he took a long, deep drag. His stance was so relaxed, they might have been discussing Billboard's Hot 100, rather than life and death—mainly death. The irony struck her and she would've laughed if her throat hadn't been so tight from all the vomiting she'd done earlier.

"I'm sorry, Rudy. I guess all of this must seem pretty silly to you. I mean, me freaking out over a news report."

"Jan loses it watching Barney." He gave her a lopsided grin meant to ease her fears. "Something about the system being screwed up when they'll put a purple dinosaur on the tube and pay him big bucks when he can't sing for shit. And here Jan is, the next Melissa Etheridge, and she can't even find a job waiting tables, much less get a record exec to listen to her demo."

Darby rubbed her hands over her arms while he proceeded to bandage her throbbing foot. Her mind raced, searching for plausible answers. "Okay, so maybe I did see her somewhere before and just projected her into my dream."

"Sounds good to me. Hey, didn't you say she was at Ramone's the last time someone saw her? Didn't you do a review of their headlining band last week?"

"Yes. Yes, I did." Hope flared, but along with it, dread churned, slow and unnerving, in the pit of her stomach.

"There you go, then. Maybe you saw her there, then dreamed about her for whatever reason." He took another quick drag on his cigarette and pointed a finger at her. "Or you know what? Maybe you're right about never having seen her. Maybe you had some sort of weird psychic experience instead." At Darby's skeptical look, he added, "I know it sounds freaky and shit, but Jan's got this friend who's into all that kind of supernatural stuff. She used to date Lenny Beaver, the drummer for Small Fortune. Anyway, besides having access to some top-of-the-line snort, this chick actually has visions into the future. She even predicted the date when Small Fortune would sign their contract with that new independent label out of Cincinnati. Swears to Lenny that she saw it one night after they'd been going at it pretty hot and heavy. She was just lying there, Lenny asleep right beside her. Then—bam, this vision starts to roll through her head just like a videotape." He took another drag, then ground the cigarette into the ashtray. "Maybe that's what happened to you."

Darby frowned. Things would be so much easier if she really were psychic. So much easier, in fact, that she couldn't keep from asking, "You really believe that could be the reason for the dreams?"

"I've seen stranger shit happen." He cut a final strip of first-aid tape and wound it around the fresh bandage.

"Like me over here cleaning up after you when I could be down the hall balling my brains out."

"That is kind of strange," she said, summoning her courage and a smile. "Thanks, Rudy."

"Just remember, sweetheart. You owe me."

"Name your price." She struggled to one foot, then stepped down gingerly on her other. Pain lanced up her calf and she tilted. Rudy caught her easily, hauling her up against him, his arms solid around her.

"I don't think you're ready to pay out what I'm asking." His blue gaze caught hers and she didn't miss the hungry light in them. She stiffened, putting a few safe inches between them.

"One-track mind." She averted her gaze, eager to ignore the unease crawling up her spine. "If you don't behave yourself, I'm liable to tell Jan."

"Jan? Honey, she and I are just friends." When she flashed him a look that said, "And I'm the pope," he added, "*Good* friends, but still just friends. Cross my heart."

"I wouldn't bet my money on that promise."

He feigned a hurt look. "I'm wounded, Darby. Truly wounded."

"You will be if you don't hurry home. I bet she's waiting up."

Her words must have hit home because his smile died and he glanced at his watch. "Damn, it's after five." His gaze shifted to hers. "Will you be all right by yourself?"

"Fine."

"You sure?"

She eyed him a long moment, his arms so warm and comforting that she wanted to melt against him. Just for a few minutes. Just long enough to chase away the chill that still iced her insides. "And if I'm not?"

He seemed to consider her words; then a grin split his face. "Well, I've got a double bed with plenty of room for an extra person. You can squeeze in between me and Jan."

The thought actually brought a chuckle to her lips. Jan was Rudy's unofficial significant other, and every woman's nightmare. She was jealous and bossy and, from the hell Rudy put up with, probably great in bed. It was obvious to anyone that it was a loveless match, but Jan was territorial.

"I don't think that's such a good idea. Didn't she threaten to cut off your—" She cleared her throat, her gaze dropping to the object of her statement. "*It*," she finally said, "if you didn't start showing her a little devotion?"

"You heard that, huh?"

"Hard not to. She was screaming at the top of her lungs."

He shrugged and gave her a wicked smile. "She has got quite a pair of lungs."

"I'm sure that's what first attracted you."

"No, I'm more a leg man, myself." His gaze swept the length of her, fixating on the tiny sliver of leg revealed where the edges of her robe had come loose.

"Forget it, Romeo. I'm really tired."

"In that case"—he rummaged around in his pocket and pulled out a small medicine bottle—"I've got exactly what the doctor ordered. Take one," he said, pushing the bottle at her. "It'll help you calm down and get some sleep."

She shook her head and pushed his hand away. "I don't do that anymore."

He gave her a knowing look. "The booze do just as good?"

"Yeah," she admitted. "Yeah, it does, and it's not illegal."

"Illegal?" He looked offended. "This stuff is prescription."

"Whose prescription?"

"Okay, you made your point. But with one little pill you can forget a hangover the morning after. You'll sleep like a baby and be ready to go the next day."

"Only with a little pick-me-up, right? A little coke chaser to pull me back up after this thing buries me?" She held up her hands and pushed away from him. "It's a vicious cycle, Rudy."

"Hell, you sound like one of those commercials. 'This is your brain. This is your brain on—' "

"I don't do that stuff anymore," she said again, hobbling around the couch, snatching up trash as she went. "And if I take a little drink every now and then, it's my own business."

"Except when I have to come down here at five in the morning."

"Nobody asked you to."

"No," he said. "Nobody asked."

She hadn't asked. She'd screamed, and he'd barreled down the hallway, nearly kicking in her apartment door to come to her rescue. Good old reliable Rudy, who was always ready to lend a hand, drugs, or a little something more. He'd hit on her for two months after she'd moved in, trying to talk her into bed. But Miss Shy and Mighty wouldn't be talked into anything. She'd listened, smiled, even thought about it, but nothing more. Rudy wasn't really her type. He was everyone else's type, going through woman after woman after woman. All really *good* friends, she felt certain. But there was never anything more than sex.

Did she want more?

She'd never given it much thought. Commitment and all the traditional notions that went with it—house in the suburbs, kids, nine-to-five job—had never entered Darby's mind.

Hell, who was she kidding? Rudy *was* her type. That was the trouble. They had more in common than she cared to admit, and seeing him, being with him, reminded her of just how much.

"I was just trying to help," he said, his voice cutting into her thoughts.

Guilt churned inside of her and she stopped her mad

hunt for a stack of mail that had slid between two sofa cushions. "I'm sorry," she said, turning to him, an old newspaper trembling in her hands. "I appreciate everything, Rudy. I really do. I didn't mean to be such a bitch. I'm just . . . I don't know what's happening to me anymore. I've always had the dreams. I've even seen glimpses of faces before, but nothing really distinct. Not a real face. No one who had a name, a life. No one really *real*. Until tonight." The paper slipped from her fingers and she clasped her hands together, tears filling her eyes. She blinked furiously, and shrugged away when Rudy reached for her. "I'm fine. Really." When he didn't look convinced, she wiped at her eyes and forced a smile. "Really."

"If you're scared, I'll stay," he offered, but Darby could see the dark circles under his eyes, the exhaustion making the tiny lines around his mouth deeper. He'd barely gotten home from his Friday-night gig at Monte's when she'd screamed. He was probably dead tired.

And as much as she liked his company, as much as she needed it, she couldn't risk Rudy taking the invitation to mean a lot more than just her need for a friendly face. And, bottom line, she felt nothing more than friendship for him. No heat flooding her senses when she talked to him, not even a little twinge of her nipples when they pressed up against his chest. No physical reaction, let alone an emotional one. She gave a firm shake of her head. "No, you go on home to Jan. I'll be fine."

After she'd reassured him at least a dozen more times, she finally shut and locked the door behind him. Then she turned back to the chaos of her living room. In the bright light of all the lamps Rudy had switched on, the room was an even bigger mess than her life.

She sank down onto the edge of the sofa and stared at the television screen. The same female news anchor who'd reported the murders filled the screen, her mouth moving rapidly. But Darby couldn't hear her voice. The word MUTE flashed in red print at the corner of the screen. The only sound other than her own breathing was that of the hot air pumping from the central heating unit.

Sweat trickled down her temple, but she didn't feel the heat of her skin. Just the cold deep, deep inside her. It wouldn't go away: she knew that just as she knew the dreams would never go away. Not until she made them go away.

She fingered the piece of glass Rudy had pulled from her foot, part of the bottle's emblazoned *J* still visible beneath the smear of blood. Yes, her life was a mess, all right. A big, uncontrollable mess that only she could put in order. There were no friends who could offer a comforting shoulder, no family to come to her rescue. Sure, she had friends, but no one really close. Rudy was probably the closest person to her, and she kept him at arm's length. As for her family, they were completely out of the picture. She had no brothers and sisters, and both her parents were dead. She was alone, as always. Alone and scared.

The truth weighed down on her like a ton of bricks on a very rickety foundation. She could keep on living her life, drinking herself into oblivion whenever she had a particularly bad dream, just as she'd been doing for the past nine years.

Or she could face her demons and try to lay them to rest.

Her gaze shot to the bottle of Valium Rudy had left on her coffee table. The urge to reach out, to swallow a couple, sent a tremor through her. Her fingers burned, twitched. She tried closing her eyes, but it didn't lessen the temptation. Her body knew what the effects would be, but still craved the numbness, even after three years of being straight.

She leaned forward, her fingers closing around the bottle. At that moment, an image flashed on the muted television screen. The bottle slipped from her hands. The pills scattered. Tracey Morgan's face stared back at her

again as the station did another follow-up on the late-breaking story.

Somehow, the sight gave her the strength to stand up and walk away from the pills. Short of taking an overdose, nothing would make her forget. She could numb her mind now, but when the feeling returned, so would the dreams. The memories. The nagging question—Why her?

Deep down inside, she knew the answer waited for her hundreds of miles away, in Nostalgia, Texas, in the house where she'd watched, and forgotten, the murders of her best friends.

Watched, or *committed* those murders.

She already knew she was more than capable of taking another life. The bastard who'd been her father lay six feet under, testimony to that fact. Yes, she knew how to kill, all right.

But her best friends? The only people who'd made her miserable life bearable?

Maybe.

That maybe escalated into an irrefutable yes when Darby bent to scoop up a piece of trash and spotted the bloody footprint near the front door. Her body went hot, then cold, her gaze riveted on the sight. Her heart slammed against her rib cage.

Reason kicked in after a long, painful second. It could be Rudy's footprint. There'd been blood all over the floor, he'd stepped in it, tracked it to the door—

But he'd been wearing boots, and this was clearly a print from a different sort of shoe. A much smaller shoe.

Possibly one of her own shoes, only she hadn't been wearing shoes. She'd been barefoot when she'd cut herself. And she hadn't put on a shoe since she'd dropped the bottle of JD. Not since then, and there was no explanation for a bloody footprint before then. Unless—

For sanity's sake, she cut the speculation, limped to the kitchen and retrieved a dishrag. Then she returned to scrub madly at the telltale print.

Her footprint, but not her blood, a voice whispered.

No! But even as denial raged in her head, her gaze went to the hallway. She knew if she went to her closet and rifled through her shoes, she would find a match for the print. She knew, and that knowing spurred her to rub harder at the hardwood floor, as if she could erase the knowledge as easily as the blood. She couldn't, she realized several heaving seconds later as she struggled for a breath and tried to swallow against the tightness of her throat.

A psychic couldn't leave a bloody footprint.

But a killer could.

No! There could be a logical explanation for the footprint. There was one: she just had yet to identify it. It was there—a reasonable, obvious excuse. It was there and she would realize it sooner or later, but not now while she was so worked up.

Despite the fear swirling around her, making her throat tight, she forced herself to her feet, hobbled to the bedroom and pulled two battered black leather traveling bags from the closet. Without glancing at her shoes, she scooped up the six pairs she owned and dumped them in one of the bags, before starting on her clothes.

Maybe Rudy was right, she thought as she stuffed several outfits into one of the bags. Her jerky movements sent pain shooting down through her calf and she grimaced. She *could* be having some sort of psychic experience.

But maybe, just maybe, the dreams weren't dreams at all, but actual experiences.

The last thought drove her faster. She packed in a matter of minutes and rushed around the apartment, picking up trash and making a halfhearted attempt to straighten the mess. At the dining room table, she slammed the lid shut on her laptop, grabbed the stack of unused paper and the inch-high stack of finished work and shoved everything into her other suitcase. The six A.M. news was just coming on when she sat down on the sofa, grabbed the telephone and punched in her editor's number.

"This is Vivian. I'm not bloody well here. You know what to do at the beep."

"Viv, this is Darby. I hate to call so early, but I've got sort of an emergency. I won't be in to work today. I'm taking my three weeks' vacation—"

"What?" A groggy British accent came over the line. "You can't," Vivian snapped without waiting for a reply. "Mitchell is already on vacation, and the temporary service can't even get me a decent receptionist to fill in for Joyce, who's out having twins, and Megan's on indefinite leave trying to regroup. If it isn't babies, it's damned bloody nervous breakdowns."

"I know this is short notice, but I'm not leaving you high and dry. Steve's my assistant. Give him a chance to assist."

"He's not half as good as you, Darby. The BAMMIES are coming up next week and there are two brand-new club openings this Friday on Halloween. That's only six days away. Don't do this to me."

"Please, Viv," Darby said, her voice desperate, her fingers clutched around the receiver. "Just be human for once and don't give me a hard time."

"Are you in some kind of trouble? If it's money—"

"No, no. I just need to get out of here for a little while, get my head together, sort through some personal business, that sort of thing. Please."

A long second later, she heard a heavy sigh. "Fine. I'll speak to Steve, but I can't let you go for three weeks. You've got one."

"Three," Darby insisted. "That's the time I've accumulated."

"Two," came Vivian's firm reply.

"Agreed."

After Darby hung up, she grabbed a sheet of paper, wrote a quick note to Rudy asking him to look after her place. Then she folded the letter, slipped it in an envelope with her spare apartment keys and headed down the hall.

She slid the letter beneath his door, pausing for a long second as she heard Jan's high-pitched squeal, followed by a man's long, deep moan. There was no mistaking the familar timbre of Rudy's voice, and heat flooded Darby's cheeks. Feeling like some sort of peeping Tom, she turned and bolted back down the hall. Back in her apartment, she made flight arrangements, called a cab, and poured herself a cup of strong black coffee. She sat in the kitchen and waited for the first few rays of pink to creep over the building next door. Soon, though, her eyelids began to drop.

An hour later, she jerked awake, sober and still every bit as frightened as when she'd been downing the Jack Daniel's. She hurriedly gathered her things; locked her apartment and climbed into the waiting cab.

Oddly enough, a strange sense of peace crept through her as the driver sped them toward the airport. For better or worse, she was going back to Texas, to find out the truth once and for all. Whatever she discovered, she would deal with it when the time came. She was through running from the past, trying to forget.

Darby Jayson was finally going home.

Chapter Three

She'd been watching me again.

I should have been afraid. I never liked witnesses. I was always careful to make sure there were never any witnesses. Then Darby showed up, and bam, my plans were screwed.

I mean, she'd always been there, close to me. So close. She could've watched anytime she wanted to, but at first she didn't want to. She kept to herself, always so shy. So afraid. That was my Darby.

I made her even more afraid. She could feel me, and it was always the same routine. I'd go out, go to work, and Darby knew what I was up to, though she would never admit it. No, she would turn a blind eye and crawl into a bottle. That was all right by me. Perfect, in fact. Like I said, I never liked witnesses.

Then there she was one day. I don't know what made her watch, but she did. She probably realized what a great show she was missing. What can I say? My handiwork is quite a sight to see, and, of course, I've always been a people magnet. Women, in particular, have always flocked around, never able to resist me. Darby resisted as long as she could; then she couldn't help herself. Curiosity got the best of her and she watched. So much for shyness.

Anyhow, as much as I like people, I didn't like Darby nosing around. I gave her a good show, thinking to scare the holy shit out of her. That would send her running for a bottle of whiskey and keep her from hanging around, poking her nose where it didn't belong.

Like I expected, she went for the booze, all right, but then she came back. The next time I went to work, there she was. I was pissed. But I'm a true professional, and that means adjusting to any situation. Darby was there, hanging over my shoulder, and I had to get used to it. No matter how I tried to cut myself off from her, when the time came and the knife was in my hands, my concentration was elsewhere and Darby would just creep in to spy.

After I got over the initial shock of having her there, I actually started to like her watching me. Just knowing she was there, seeing what I was seeing, what I was doing, made the whole thing even more exciting. I'm a sucker for voyeurism. I know I'm usually the one who does the watching, but it was kind of nice having the tables turned.

Besides, later on, I knew she didn't really remember what she'd seen. She would watch me, but what I was doing never really registered in her head. I've always known about the dreams, you see, but they were never very threatening before. She never *really* saw me the way I've always been able to see her. She would remember bits and pieces, no pun intended, of what I did to my victims, but only after the fact. Usually the dreams came days, even weeks after one of my performances.

But last night . . . Last night was a first. The dream came sooner this time. Just hours after the show.

It had been only a week since my last victim, but I

hadn't been able to stop myself. This particular one had been so pretty, and so deserving when she'd smarted off to my face. "Take a hike," she'd said. "I'm not into that kinky shit. I'd rather die than drink with you."

I smiled when she told me that. Thou shalt not lie, as Granny used to say, but there the bitch was, lying to my face, telling me she'd rather die. Die? And I'm next up for sainthood. This bitch was so alive. She didn't want to die. She's just lucky Granny couldn't hear her. She would've taken a switch to those long legs for sure. Granny wasn't there, but I was, and I had to punish her. For her own good.

For mine, too. I could feel myself getting impatient, greedy. This may come as a surprise, but I hate to wait. I know patience is a virtue and all that, but I was never very virtuous, not in the face of someone like my latest masterpiece—a female so spoiled and conceited that you know some sorry SOB spared the rod long ago, and now society's paying for it.

She made me so mad that I didn't want to wait.

Now, I don't usually get angry. Excited, yes, but angry, never. Not since that night in the attic. I'd been so steamed, I'd sliced up three pretty young things before I'd spent enough energy to realize what I'd done. It was a shame. Three fresh, young lives, and not a sliver of pleasure from any of them.

I promised myself then and there that I would never let anger rule my actions again. Forget spontaneity. Planning is everything. It feeds the fantasy, as all those prison shrinks who came to visit me used to say.

But this time . . . Well, at least I waited an entire week. I was tempted to slice the bitch up right then. I wanted to cut out those pretty lyin' eyes and swallow them whole. But I waited seven whole days. Then I threw caution to the wind, and what do you know? Careful, meticulous, not-a-spontaneous-bone-in-my-body me actually enjoyed it. Every second. It was my best yet, and I could tell Darby was really moved this time.

Unfortunately, it'll be her last time.

She's getting too close to me, too observant. As much as I like knowing she's there, it's kind of creepy in a way now that she's so close. I know if I don't put a stop to it now, she'll eventually distract me. I'll get sloppy, and that I can't afford. No, as much as I came to like Darby being there, as much as it excited me, I can't risk it again. What if she saw more the next time?

That wouldn't do. Not at all. Watching from a distance is fine, but she was practically breathing down my neck last night, and I can't risk her getting in my way. I won't allow that. If I didn't let Granny interfere, I sure as hell won't let Darby.

Not that I would do anything to hurt Darby. I could never do that. I love her. I've loved her from the first moment I saw her, *felt* her. She was so young, so innocent, so very afraid. No, I could never hurt Darby.

That's why I can't let her watch me again. The only problem is, I think Darby's finally getting some ideas of her own. Spineless, weepy, alcoholic Darby. Will wonders never cease?

Not that it's really a problem. I'll just teach Darby that it's not nice manners to spy on someone. Yes, I'll teach her real good.

The air conditioner cycled on; cool air streamed through the vents. It was cold, so cold inside the small apartment. And dark.

Not that he needed a light. He could walk blindly through this apartment and know every twist, every turn. He'd done it time and time again.

He moved down the hallway, his footfalls silent, before stopping in a doorway at the far end. Neon light from the beer joint across the alleyway flooded the bedroom, illuminating the creature that writhed on the bed.

It was two people actually, he knew, yet it looked like some sort of two-headed monster with extra arms and legs, the skin a rich blue rather than the color of flesh. The thing glistened with sweat, the arms and legs moving together with no particular agenda. Low, throaty moans floated the distance to him, and he smiled.

This was better than he'd thought. He knew the thing on the bed was guilty, but somehow seeing proof of the sin made the punishment all the better.

She and I are just friends . . . Cross my heart . . . The lie echoed in his head and excitement bubbled inside him.

There was no shirking his duty now, even though it was a guy and he usually didn't do guys. Not usually. But responsibility was responsibility. Spare the rod and spoil the child, as Granny always said.

Throaty moans filled the air, the sounds almost pained, and excitement sizzled through him. As much as he'd liked to shrink back in the shadows and watch for a while, listen, he couldn't. Time wasn't his friend. He had to move quickly, to tie up this last loose end and do his duty before dawn awakened.

His hand tightened around the large butcher knife he'd retrieved from the kitchen, and he barely caught the giggle before it burst from his lips. He loved using a knife. Even one as old and battered as this one. The handle was worn and faded, but sturdy. A good grip, he decided as he clenched and unclenched his fingers to the same rhythm that the man, faded jeans down around his ankles, pumped in and out of the woman spread beneath him. The man's curtain of dark hair obliterated both their faces.

Holding the knife up, he ran the tip of his finger against the blade. A drop of blood beaded, sliding down the mirrorlike surface to drip-drop toward the cheap carpet covering the floor.

He caught the bloody tear in midair with his other hand, the warm crimson sliding over his knuckle, gliding around his palm. Then with a quick flick of his tongue, the evidence was gone, and he was hungry, so very hungry after tasting that one, bittersweet drop. He wanted to feel the heat on his hands, the power as it covered his skin, seeped *inside of him and sent a tingling rush to his brain and another vital part of him.*

Yes, it was time to feed the fantasy.

He stepped closer, the couple on the bed completely oblivious to him, to Death, who moved closer and closer to their sweat-soaked bodies.

They rolled, shifting positions. The female moved on top, her head thrown back, her body arched toward the blue neon sign flickering outside the window. The man held her thighs and worked her up and down in a fierce, frenzied rhythm. In and out. Harder, harder . . .

Death moved quietly toward them.

Closer. Closer . . .

He reached the bed just as the woman cried out, her breasts thrust upward, her nipples erect and glistening. The man groaned, long and low and deep, his chest pumping with the frantic beat of his heart.

"Aren't you glad I waited up while you played nursemaid to that bitch down the hall?" she purred, running her hands up his chest to brush several long strands of hair away from his face. "Did you like it?"

"Like it?" he asked incredulously. "Shit, I think I'm dead."

"No," Death whispered as two heads swiveled toward him, two pairs of delightful blue eyes alight with shocked recognition. "Not yet anyway."

Darby bolted upright. The jacket she'd been clutching slid past her bent knees to puddle in the small area of space at her feet. Wildly, she stared at her hands.

No splashes of blood marked her pale flesh. Still her fingers trembled. Worse than seeing the blood, she could feel it. So warm and liquid, rushing over her hands like hot fudge over an ice cream sundae—

She slammed her mind shut as nausea roiled in her stomach. Her gaze darted frantically and she drank in her surroundings—the puzzled-looking old man sitting next to her, sipping a martini from a plastic cocktail glass, the petite, redheaded stewardess offering him another cocktail napkin, the brightly lit window to her left. Brilliant sunshine streamed through the window, and Darby glanced out to see a blanket of cottony clouds beneath her.

She sank back against the seat. She was on a plane bound for Dallas. It was barely noon and she'd merely dozed off. The dreams had her so screwed up, she'd even had one during her brief nap. But she could take comfort. This time it had really and truly been a dream. No flashback. No actual experience. The certainty of that last point sent relief flooding through her.

Rudy and Jan had been in this dream, and she knew for a fact they were both alive and well, and as Rudy so delicately put it, probably still balling their brains out. It had only been hours since she'd slid the note and her spare keys under his door. She could still hear the muffled grunts and groans. Yes, they'd been having quite a time.

Heat swamped her face and she took a deep breath, cutting a sideways glance at the man next to her. He gave her a sly smile and Darby's face flamed hotter. She silently cursed herself. As if the old man could read her thoughts! On top of everything else, now she was starting to get paranoid.

She busied herself with retrieving her fallen jacket and smoothing it over her legs before settling back into her seat. The vibration of the jet seeped through her, begging her muscles to relax. If only her heart would slow its pounding. If it kept up this pace, she'd die of cardiac arrest. Not that the notion didn't have its appeal. Then she certainly wouldn't have to worry about any damned dreams, much less the truth.

Calm. Breathe. Swallow.

The commands echoed like a silent litany in her head and she closed her eyes and signaled for the stewardess.

A few minutes later, she'd downed two small bottles of bourbon and was busy working on her third. The shaking in her hands subsided and a slow warmth seeped through her. This was better. Much better, she decided. With the liquor clouding her senses, she could rest and not worry about any damned dreams.

Not that she had to worry anyway. Rudy and Jan were alive and well and she was just being paranoid—

The thought ground to a halt when she raised her glass to take another drink. Her gaze caught something she'd missed before, a tiny sliver of red that ran from the tip of her index finger, down about a quarter of an inch. Her heart stopped beating altogether. Her drink crashed to the tray. Ice and liquor flowed into her lap and soaked her jeans. The dream rushed at her, surrounding her, filling her consciousness, and the breath caught in her chest.

She saw the knife, large and menacing, reflecting death and blue neon. The blade sliced into her finger. The small drop of blood slid down her skin.

No!

But even as she rejected the truth, the cut stared back at her. Proof.

Proof of what?

That Rudy and Jan were dead?

No. She'd heard them, alive. Very alive, judging by the moans and groans still ringing in her ears. Her imagination had to be working overtime.

That, or something really had happened to her friends since she'd left the apartment, and she'd actually connected with the killer on some sort of psychic level. The possibility pounded through her head and Darby downed the rest of the third bottle, stuffing the fourth bottle, still full, into her purse for later. She signaled for the flight attendant.

"Another please," she said when the redhead leaned down to her.

"Sorry, but we're about to start our descent. You'll have to put your tray up and fasten your seat belt."

"Just one more. I'll be quick," Darby promised, but the woman simply shook her head.

"We'll be landing in Dallas in about fifteen minutes. There's a lounge in the airport."

But it wasn't the lounge that Darby headed for the minute she walked off the plane. It was a pay phone.

She dialed Rudy's number with trembling fingers. The phone rang once, twice, a third time before the machine finally clicked on and Rudy's deep voice rang in her ear, followed by a beep.

"Rudy, this is Darby. Just calling to let you know I made it all right. I'll try back again later."

She couldn't help but wonder as she left the message, if Rudy was there to hear it. Or was he lying in a pool of his own blood, the bed soaked, Jan butchered next to him? Had she finished the two of them off before she'd left the apartment?

Stop it!

She slammed the receiver down. She had to get ahold of herself. Worrying and wondering wouldn't solve anything. The cut on her finger could have come from any number of sources—a wayward vegetable peeler, a sheet of computer paper. Yes, that was it. She'd shoved a whole stack of computer paper into her bag before she'd left. A sharp edge must have sliced into her finger. The cut was small, inconsequential. It was natural she wouldn't have noticed it. And if not the paper, there'd been all the glass from the broken JD bottle. She could have cut herself while picking up the mess.

And the bloody footprint?

There had to be a logical explanation for that, too.

There is. You're a killer. A killer . . .

No. She wouldn't convict herself without first collecting all the evidence she could. She'd file the footprint away, the small cut, and concentrate on reviving her memory. Nostalgia was a little over two hours away. She glanced at her watch. She should be able to make it by early afternoon. Sunset wasn't until after six o'clock.

That would give her plenty of time to get a good look at the house.

If she was really and truly a cold-blooded killer, it would have started there, on Halloween night, with her three best friends the first victims in her long and bloody career.

Chapter Four

Two hours and fifteen minutes later, Darby steered her rental car, a brand-new black Mercury Cougar, off Interstate 45 onto Highway 161, the main strip through Nostalgia, Texas. The small, hole-in-the-wall farming town had barely been a speck on the map ten years ago, and wasn't any more than that now.

Time had obviously slammed on its brakes that Halloween night. The road was still the blacktopped nightmare she remembered, gutted with potholes, gravel lining the shoulders. There were no familiar convenience stores, no chain restaurants, not even a McDonald's. The same rusty gas station sat at the corner of the first red light, the pump one of those old-fashioned kinds with a bubble head. The only thing remotely new about the station was the shiny silver screen door. Darby watched as an ancient man clad in greasy overalls, a shock of silver hair on his head, shoved open the screen door and headed around the side of the building. Old Man Waltrip, the oldest resident of Nostalgia. No one knew his age exactly, though speculation had been the topic in the high school cafeteria more than once. The old fart claimed he'd been baptized right alongside Jesus, and few in town would argue it. Except for Reverend Masters, that is.

Her gaze shot to the small, one-story church that sat a little farther down the road. The brilliant Texas sun blazed down, glinting off the small white sign that hung out front—FIRST PRESBYTERIAN CHURCH OF NOSTALGIA. The good reverend's name was still emblazoned across the bottom. She'd have to see him while she was in town. Not that he'd be too anxious to see her. He'd looked almost relieved the day Darby had packed her bags and walked out of his home, out from under his care, fifty dollars and a bus ticket to Houston in her pocket. She couldn't really blame him.

He'd tried to do right by her, but with nine of his own children and three foster kids, he'd had his hands full. Too full to deal with a sixteen-year-old walking poster girl for troubled teens. The reverend had enough responsibility trying to console the town's citizens after the tragedy of that night. Console them, and help them forget.

But no one could forget with Darby walking around. She'd been a constant reminder, and so she'd spared him and everyone else the trouble of asking her to leave. She'd walked away on her own. Run away, to be more exact.

In all honesty, she'd wanted nothing more than to forget that night herself. But she'd been young then. It had seemed so much easier to run away from her troubles and hope they wouldn't catch up with her. She'd actually thought that maybe, just maybe, if she ran far enough, they would disappear altogether.

They hadn't, and she was still running away—only now she ran into a bottle every chance she got. Like the town, she hadn't changed much.

No more, she promised herself. She couldn't run anymore, Otherwise she'd be heading straight for a nervous breakdown. Or suicide. Or both.

By coming home, she might be that much closer to Huntsville Penitentiary and Death Row, but at least she would know. She stiffened, her fingers tightening on the steering wheel. For once, Darby didn't want to be clinging to the pendulum, waiting for fate to swing for or against her. She wanted to know which way she was going, wanted to have some say in it. She was through being manipulated by circumstance. She wasn't running from the truth anymore. She was ready, and eager, to face it. For better or for worse, she reminded herself, and gunned the engine when the light changed to green.

As she headed down the strip through town, she drank in her surroundings, her gaze going to every building, every sign. She might have been cruising with her friends in the old beat-up blue Chevy pickup that had belonged to her best friend, Linda Tucker.

Her *dead* friend.

The thought sent an icy shiver through her, to land directly in the hollow pit of her stomach. She braked for the next red light, and her gaze went to the motel on her left. The place consisted of a single-story stretch of rooms situated in a half moon around a half-full swimming pool, the water a murky green. A giant-sized pink flamingo stood next to a worn sign that read *Tropicana Motel*. The bird's eyes had faded, and the end of the beak was still missing. The bird resembled a blind, maimed ostrich more than the beautiful flamingo she remembered so well. But then, it was partly her fault. She and Linda had climbed to the top of that flamingo on a dare. Linda had slipped and that was when the beak had broken off. They'd done twenty hours of volunteer maid service at the hotel for that incident, not that Darby had minded. Back then, she'd much preferred spending her evenings with Linda instead of with the reverend.

Her eyes teared and she blinked, turning her attention to the opposite side of the street. Jimmy Joe's Diner stared back at her, the windows still hung with checkered curtains. Next door stood Proctor's Grocery and Feed.

Both buildings looked the same, maybe somewhat older, the signs a little faded, but still the same.

The light changed and Darby drove on. Beyond the few signs of civilization, land stretched in both directions, the landscape dotted with cows. She spotted several farmhouses, most of the homes old and worn, exactly where she remembered them from her childhood. Still others were brand-new, with freshly paved driveways cutting a path across the land.

Another half a mile and Darby reached a fork in the road. Gravel spewed against the underside of the car as she veered left. Dust billowed behind her wheels. She crossed the railroad tracks and drove through a maze of dirt roads, the rolling fields surrounding her quickly giving way to a forest of oak trees. After a good fifteen minutes, she finally spotted the house peeking past several gigantic trees up ahead.

But the house wasn't what drew her attention. No, it was the huge trailer parked alongside the dirt road near the driveway. A pickup truck and several cars lined the opposite side. Several roadblocks had been set up to prevent entrance to the driveway. A six-foot-high chain-link fence glinted in the afternoon sunlight, cutting off access to the three acres surrounding the house.

"What the hell?" she muttered, pulling over and killing the engine. She read the emblem on the side of the trailer—the insignia for a local television network in nearby Dallas.

Darby shoved the car keys into her pocket and covered the distance to the driveway's entrance on foot. The canopy of trees overhead soon gave way to blinding sunshine as she reached the blockade. Shielding her eyes, she stared across the yard to the house.

The two-story structure looked ready to collapse. She remembered that the house had been blue, but not much of the color was left. The paint had cracked, peeled, until the entire structure looked unfinished. The first-floor windows were boarded up. The upstairs windows yawned back at her, vacant black holes where the glass had once been. All except for the very top window, which was still intact. The attic.

The courage she'd built up during the drive from the airport vanished. A chill crawled up her spine and her mind traveled back. . . .

"Come on, Darby. Don't be a chicken!" Katy Evans climbed from the front seat of the old blue Chevy and bounced across the yard, her ample chest jiggling beneath the Nostalgia High sweatshirt. Perfectly ironed jeans molded to her figure, the ends stuffed into polished black ankle boots. "It's just a big old house. There ain't no bogeymen inside."

"My pa says there is," said the redhead who climbed from the pickup's cab after her. Jane Wallis dusted off the seat of her jeans, old and worn and not nearly as perfect as Katy's, before turning to retrieve a portable radio she'd stashed in the bed of the truck. "He says there's pure evil in that house."

"And your pa drinks too much of that apple wine he brews," Trish Walker said, jumping down from the tailgate where she'd been perched during the ride.

"Amen," added Linda Tucker as she crawled from behind the wheel of her daddy's old blue Chevy. She turned and stared back inside the cab at Darby, who sat motionless, her hands clasped in her lap, fear swirling through her like water in a whirlpool. "Ain't no such thing as evil places, Darby. Evil's inside of folks. This is just an old, broken-down house."

"My pa does say a lot of stupid shit," Jane said, clutching the radio as she headed after Katy, who'd already reached the porch steps. Trish, with two bags of groceries in her arms, followed.

"That's what I've been telling you." Katy's perfectly manicured pink nails dove into her jeans pocket and came up clutching a large pocketknife.

"What in blue blazes is that for?" Trish asked.

"Cutting the screen, silly. And anything else we need it for. I got it from Paul Russell. It's his daddy's hunting knife." She bent down to make a large slice in the bottom of the screen door leading to the porch. "Grab the ice chest and come on," she said over her shoulder to Linda and Darby.

"Give me a hand, Darby," Linda said, a smile on her face. "And stop worrying; old Reverend Masters won't know you came out here. He thinks you're at my house. He's got enough to do keeping track of those monsters of his to worry about you. Relax. You, me, Trish, Katy and Jane— we're all here together. The five musketeers. Don't be so jumpy."

Darby pushed her fear aside and climbed from the pickup. They were all together, and there was nothing to be afraid of. She'd given up fear three years ago when she'd buried her mother, and the bastard they'd called her father. She was here, with her best friends in the entire world, and she was going to have a good time if it was the last thing she did. Besides, Linda was right. Evil lived inside of people, not places. Darby knew that all too well, and as for worrying about Reverend Masters's belt should she be caught . . . Well, he probably wouldn't even know she was gone. The term monsters didn't even touch the reverend's hellacious brood.

"What did you tell your folks?" Darby asked Linda as they each grabbed an end of the ice chest and headed for the front porch.

"That I'm spending Halloween night in the abandoned house of Texas's most notorious serial killer, upstairs in the very same room where he slaughtered his first victim."

At Darby's shocked expression, she added, "Right. And Katy was just voted most virtuous in the freshman class." She laughed. "Get real. I told them Reverend Masters was having one of his all-night youth prayer meetings. Graham would blister my ass if he knew I was here, and I don't want to even think what Mom and Dad would do. They're all for burning this place to the ground. Wanted to do it *tonight when they slip the guy the needle down at Hunts-ville and send him to hell like he deserves. But Mayor Bakey vetoed the idea. If he thinks he can make a buck, he's all for turning this place into a shrine to the late great Samuel Blue, the Earl Campbell of serial killers."*

"Don't you think it's kind of creepy?" Darby stared up at the old house, the paint chipped and peeling, the windows dark.

"Of course," Linda said matter-of-factly. "What better place to spend Halloween?"

Darby could think of at least a dozen places, especially when she and Linda reached the attic where Katy, Trish and Jane were already unloading bags and lighting lanterns.

The wind whipped at the house and wheezed through the cracks. Darby's skin prickled. She rubbed at her arms, then busied herself arranging sodas in the ice chest.

"Perfect," Katy said as she adjusted the glow on one of the lanterns. An eerie yellow light filled the attic, pushing back the shadows, but not nearly enough to calm the chills creeping over Darby's flesh. "You're always such a wet blanket, Darby. Don't be so jumpy."

"Yeah," Trish added, adjusting the radio until a rock ballad drowned out the silence. "You look as pale as that ghost they say lives up here."

"Yeah," Jane added, coming up behind Darby. "Boo!"

Darby whirled, giving her friend a glare. "I'm not jumpy," she insisted. "Would everybody stop saying that?" She glanced around and tried to calm her rapidly beating heart. It was just an attic. A big, old attic with a coat of dust covering the floor and a stagnant smell in the air. No dead body. No blood. Nothing to even clue them in that someone had actually died here.

A creak sounded on the staircase and Darby bolted to her feet. She whirled, only to find a grinning Paul Russell be-hind her. The senior running back for the Nostalgia High Giants gave her a wide grin, and an embarrassed heat *rushed from the tips of her toes, to the end of each and every hair on her head.*

Okay, so she was a little jumpy. A lot jumpy, but then they were standing in the very same room where someone had died, for heaven's sake.

"Gotcha," Paul bellowed before turning to catch Katy, who flew into his arms.

"Katy!" Linda's angry voice doused Darby's initial panic. "This was supposed to be a private party. What the hell did you go and tell Paul for—" The words seemed to stick in the girl's throat as she stared past Paul, at the figure who materialized in the doorway.

Graham Tucker looked ready to blister his little sister's ass, all right. His usually bright blue eyes were as dark as a rain-filled sky, his expression thunderous. The dark scar that bisected his cheek—a souvenir from an opposing team's running back who'd been wearing his class ring during a vicious tackle—made him look all the more deadly. In fact, Graham looked ready to blister each and every ass there, Darby's included. She inched backward, all the while ignoring the nagging voice in her head that said that wouldn't be such an unpleasant experience. Graham's big, strong hand on her—

"An all-night prayer meeting, huh?" His deep voice slammed the door shut on her thoughts. He stepped into the room, his large frame making what had earlier been a monstrous, empty place seem very small now. His accusing gaze shot to the soft drinks and chips, the radio blasting Bon Jovi's "Living on a Prayer," the Ouija board Katy had placed on the floor near the window. "If I were you, I'd drop to my knees and start praying really fast, Linda. You'll need divine intervention to get out of this one."

"We're just having a slumber party," she said, her voice flip, but Darby could see the wariness in her eyes.

"So why didn't you tell that to Mom and Dad?"

"Come on, Graham. They wouldn't let me come within a mile of this place." She moved forward, her eyes wide and pleading. "Please don't tell. It's only for tonight. Besides, I *didn't say anything when you came in at three in the morning last Friday night with Patsy Martin's panties in your pocket—"*

"Outside," he said, one big hand reaching out to grab her sleeve. Then he hauled her out the door and down the stairs. Raised voices carried from the first floor, but Darby couldn't make out what was being said. Or rather, shouted.

"What'd you bring Graham for?" Katy demanded as she turned on Paul.

"How the hell did I know Linda would lie to him?"

"She always lies. He'd keep her hog-tied in the garage wearing an iron chastity belt if she didn't."

He smiled. "Don't be mad. Besides, I brought the beer." He held up the brown paper sack.

"Ugh," Katy said. "You know I hate beer."

He smiled, then produced another paper bag containing a four-pack of wine coolers. "Am I forgiven?"

Katy glared at him a few seconds more before she smiled and let him put his arm around her. "This time." He tried to plant a kiss on her cheek and she shrugged away. "If Linda gets to stay. But if Graham drags her home, you can go to the movies next Saturday night by yourself, buster."

The jury came in a minute later when a smiling Linda crested the top of the stairs.

"Well?" Katy demanded.

"He's mad as hell."

"But?"

"He said I could stay. Besides, he's picking up Claire Marlboro in an hour and I told him I'd tag along if he made me leave. He sure as hell doesn't want me killing his chances of scoring, so here I am."

"Looks like it's you and me next Saturday, baby." Paul moved in for another kiss, but Linda's next words stopped him cold.

"He said if you're not down in thirty seconds, you can hitch all the way back to the Dairy Queen to meet the other guys."

"Shit," Paul muttered. "I never get to have any fun."

"You will next Saturday night," Katy promised. *"Bye, honey."* She blew him a kiss, then grabbed the sack of wine coolers from his hands. *"And thanks."*

Trish followed her lead and confiscated the beer. *"Double thanks,"* she added.

Another *"shit,"* and Paul turned to stomp down the stairs and out the front door.

"Let's get this party on the road," Katy said, glancing at her watch. *"It's almost midnight. Halloween is nearly over and we haven't even played one game."* She twisted the top off one wine cooler, plopped down in front of the Ouija board and motioned for the other girls to follow. *"I'll go first."* A quick gulp of wine; then her fingers touched the game piece. She closed her eyes and recited the first question.

Then—

"Hey lady!"

Reality jerked Darby back to the blinding sunlight and the crunch of gravel as a very formidable security guard made his way around the side of the dilapidated house. He shooed her away with his hand, then went about his business walking the yard's perimeter.

Then—

Then nothing. Absolute zero. She remembered everything so clearly, as if she'd lived it only moments ago, but what followed the start of the Ouija game was a complete void. The next conscious thought she had was of opening her eyes to see Police Chief Maggie Cross leaning over her, fear and terror and dread reflected in the woman's deep-set eyes, a room of carnage surrounding them.

"I guess what they say is true." The deep voice came from behind her, so cold and angry and achingly familiar. "The criminal does return to the scene of the crime."

Darby turned to find herself staring up into Graham Tucker's stormy eyes. Indeed, he was mad as hell. Madder, even, than the last time she'd seen him that Halloween night. Not that she could blame him.

He thought she'd murdered his sister.

And Darby herself was beginning to think he might be right.

Chapter Five

"Graham," she said, her heart slamming against her ribs as she faced him. "It's been a long time."

"Too long." His deep voice slid into her ears, resonated through her body. "Much too long."

But Darby had the distinct feeling it hadn't been long enough. Despite the years, the sight of him still scrambled her thoughts and pushed her hormones into overdrive. Crazy! She wasn't some young, love-starved kid. She was a grown woman.

Yet here she was, feeling the same way she'd felt fifteen years ago when she'd first set eyes on Graham Tucker. He'd smiled at her—a fleeting flash of brilliant white teeth and boyish charm that hadn't meant anything. She'd been nobody to him. Invisible.

She certainly wasn't invisible now, not that he was smiling. But it didn't matter whether he smiled or scowled. The effect on her was the same.

God, he'd changed.

He was still good-looking, but that all-American, ap-

ple-pie wholesomeness that made girls rip off their panties and jump into the backseat with him was gone. In its
place was a cold, threatening air that suggested he'd be
the one ripping off the panties.

His shoulder-length black hair had been cut short,
cropped close to his head, almost military style. A day's
growth of stubble covered his once clean-shaven jaw,
making the scar on his cheek seem deeper. Full, sensuous lips that had always been curved into an easy grin
were now drawn together in a grim line.

He wore a white Dallas PD T-shirt and faded jeans that
hugged his thighs a little too closely for Darby's peace of
mind. He had the same muscular body she remembered,
but it was harder, leaner, a man's body, not that of a
teenage quarterback. The shoulder holster he wore over
his left shoulder, a very deadly looking gun peeking past
the holder, only added to his maturity, his hard edge.

Yes, everything about him was hard—his features, his
body, his eyes. Especially his eyes. Those bluer-than-blue
eyes had always sent a tremor of awareness through her.
Only now she felt something else.

Fear?

Or anticipation?

For as much as Graham Tucker had changed, the feelings he'd always stirred in her had not. Not one little bit.
She wanted him.

She always had.

"I knew you'd come back," he went on, his deep voice
scattering her thoughts. "I just didn't think it would take
this long. But then everyone else is crawling out of the
woodwork for this, so it stands to reason."

"I . . ." Words failed her and she swallowed. *I'm sorry.
I missed you. I never forgot you.* . . . She forced the
thoughts aside. "What's going on here?" she managed to
ask as she turned to stare past the chain-link fence, her
gaze sweeping the yard before settling on the house.

She felt his gaze, so damned hard and penetrating, and
something inside her twisted.

"The tenth anniversary of Samuel Blue's execution," he finally said. "You know the house was boarded up right after the police investigation. As soon as the physical evidence unit finished their sweep, Old Man Dawson had the place shut up, and he's been holding tight, guarding this place ever since." Disgust edged his words. "Nobody's been inside for nearly ten years. These television people came along and offered him a nice check to let them do a walk-through on Halloween. The station's hyping it as an exclusive. See the house where Blue committed his first murder. The show should up their ratings considerably. Hell, the station's probably hoping they'll find some new undiscovered evidence. That would really draw the viewers."

"What could they possibly find that the police didn't?"

"You tell me," he said.

"If the police couldn't manage to find any evidence, I'm sure a TV reporter and camera crew won't come up with much."

"You'd better pray they don't; otherwise, you might find yourself sitting on Death Row where you belong."

She turned to face him, despite every alarm blaring for her to turn and run. She didn't need this confrontation with Graham. Didn't need to stare into those eyes of his, eyes that stared into her, through her, it seemed, and saw much more than anyone had ever seen before.

The same eyes that had watched her at the police station during the long hours of questioning after the slumber party. Eyes that had convicted her even when the police had released her due to lack of evidence. Those eyes knew the truth. They knew what she didn't want to admit. That she was a killer.

No! She didn't know that for sure. Not yet.

"I know what you think of me, Graham, and you may be right." She shook her head. "And you may be wrong. I just don't know. I can't remember what happened that night."

"Still the same old lie? I didn't believe it then and I don't believe it now."

"I don't blame you for being angry," she said, her throat nearly closing around the words. She swallowed, begged some unseen entity for strength, and wished the entire time that she'd had a few extra drinks on the plane. "I'm angry myself for what happened that night. For losing Linda. I know what you must feel—"

"Come off it!" He stepped toward her, murder blazing in his eyes, and she thought for a split second that Graham Tucker might pull out his mean-looking gun and put her out of her misery. "You have no idea how I feel," he hissed. "I lost my sister that night. My family. *Everything.*"

Something inside her made her take a step back, then another, until the fence bit into her back. "I know that, Graham. I'm not trying to belittle your pain. You have every right to hurt and to hate—"

"You want to know about hurting?" He leaned down, his face inches from hers, his breath heating her face. "My mom does a couple Valium every night just so she can sleep a few solid hours without waking up to go into Linda's room to make sure this isn't all some bad nightmare. And my dad, he got tired of watching my mom kill herself with the pills, so he just took off to Fort Worth. So don't talk to me about hurting. You don't even have a clue."

"Like hell I don't," she said, the words coming from someplace deep inside, the small part of her spirit so close to the edge of madness.

"*You* want to know hurting, Graham Tucker?" She held her hands up. "It's not knowing if these hands are the hands of a killer. It's drinking myself into oblivion because I can't escape my nightmares any other way. It's living for nearly ten years wondering and worrying and nearly going crazy because I can't remember that night." She shook her head and fought for a calming breath. "So don't tell me I don't have a clue. I know hurting, and I'm sorry that you've been hurt. I really am."

"No, you're not." Just when she thought he would grab her, he forced himself away to lean against the fence beside her. "You're not sorry. Not yet." His gaze went to the house. "But you will be, Darby. You and whoever else was involved in my sister's death. You'll all be sorry."

But she was already sorry. So very sorry for what had happened that night. For her part in it, if any.

But there was no *if*. Darby had played a role in those killings; she just wasn't sure which part she'd played. Witness or killer?

Killer.

The word echoed in her head and her attention dropped to her hand and the tiny pink sliver of healing skin. Her fingers trembled, heated, and she closed her eyes, forcing the sensation away.

Maybe Graham was right.

And maybe not.

"They won't let anyone inside?" she asked. "Just for a few minutes?"

He slanted a glance at her, his eyes shuttered. Only his voice revealed his bitterness, his pain, his rage. "So anxious to relive old memories?"

"Anxious, no. Determined, yes."

"Why?"

"I told you. I want to remember." Frustration and fear and the god-awful not knowing swirled inside her. "I need to know what happened that night. Whether or not I did have something to do with those deaths. I know you don't believe me, but I *don't know*. That's why I'm here. I thought maybe seeing this place again, being here, might trigger something in my memory."

He looked thoughtful for a long moment; then his lips twisted into a half smile. "You want to know what I think? I think you're here because you're drawn to the attention this place is getting. Like I said before, the criminal always returns to the scene of the crime. Your type thrives on the attention, the danger of being so close to discovery. And now with the TV station doing all this hype, the place is swarming with people. You're here to soak it all up and pat yourself on the back for being so clever while all the chumps around you sit on their asses and wonder if any new evidence will be found. If the murderer will finally be caught and put to justice, or if the whole damned investigation was for nothing and it was Samuel Blue's ghost who sliced and diced those girls." He laughed then, a harsh sound that grated across her nerve endings and forced her blood to pump faster.

"Ghost?" The notion wriggled its way into her brain. If only things were that simple, that easily explained. "You mean people actually think a ghost may have killed Linda and the others?"

"Some people. Desperate people. No one wants to believe a person could do something like that and get away with it, so they look for any excuse to explain what happened. A ghost seems like a pretty convenient one. Then they don't have to admit that the same monster who did this is walking around loose among them, living in their neighborhood, shopping at the same stores, going to the same church, standing next to them on the street. . . ."

His words smacked of insinuation and she stiffened.

"What do you think of the ghost theory?" she finally asked.

He turned on her then. "A ghost didn't pick up that knife." He stepped closer, urging her backward. "A ghost didn't keep stabbing and stabbing until my sister was unrecognizable." The words flew at her, sharp and stinging. "Until there wasn't much left but a bloody piece of meat." He stood toe-to-toe with her, towering over her, and Darby felt the anger holding his body rigid. A fierce anger that rolled off him in waves, slamming over her, beating her down until she wanted nothing more than to sink to the ground and slither away, straight into a bottle of liquor. "A sick bastard did that. And either you're the bastard, or you watched. Whichever, I'll find out. I promise you that. I'll find out." And with that, he turned and strode for his worn pickup parked on the opposite side of the road.

"Hey! Ain't nobody allowed on this property. Move away from the fence, miss." The security guard's voice rang in her ears and Darby let go of the fence, turned and walked to her car, her heart pumping, every nerve in her body keenly aware that Graham watched her from his place behind the wheel.

"I'll find out," she promised herself, pushing back the urge to hightail it back to her car and down the tiny bottle of bourbon she'd slipped into her purse on the plane. "I will."

Graham Tucker was an asshole, but then he had a right.

More than that, however, he liked being an asshole.

Nobody liked an asshole, and that suited him just fine. He wasn't out to win any popularity contests, or make friends, or be a nice, likable Joe. He was out to catch killers. One in particular, at the moment.

Few people liked him, except J. C., but then the Dallas PD shrink had always had an interest in hard-ass cops. That was why she'd married three of them and was busy working on number four. J. C. liked to get inside their heads, find out what made them tick, what kept them ticking when other cops buckled under the stress of the job.

Of course, she'd done a little more than simply crawl inside his head. She'd crawled into his bed in between husbands two and three. A bad move he'd immediately regretted, except for the three hours he'd spent humping his brains out. They were colleagues, and he'd wanted to keep a strictly professional relationship. But then he hadn't been thinking with his head. Not the one on his shoulders, at least.

Not many liked Graham at all, but most respected him, and that was enough. He stared through the dusty windshield of his beat-up Chevy pickup and watched Darby Jayson climb into her car.

His gaze followed the curve of her slender legs as they folded into the front seat. She wasn't a tall woman. Actually, she was short by most standards, but she had a great pair of legs. Curved just right. She'd certainly grown up. He searched his brain for some memory of those legs, but found none.

When he thought about Darby, prior to the killings, he remembered little, except, of course, that she'd followed his sister everywhere, doing everything she did. The two had been inseparable. Linda's shadow. That was all Darby had been to him. Until he'd watched her the morning after the killings, stared into her face as the police had cuffed her.

Yes, she'd become more than a shadow then. She'd turned into a real person—a scrawny, shy teenager, a little too short, too quiet, too plain.

Too damned deceitful.

Her image had burned into his memory then—dark, frightened eyes set in a pale, blood-spattered face—to haunt him for the rest of his life.

Hell, the moment he'd seen her standing at the gate to Samuel Blue's house, he thought he'd been having just another nightmare. It couldn't be her. She hadn't walked away from here, free and clear, only to come back. It didn't make any sense.

Yet it made perfect sense.

He knew some killers thrived on the attention, the media coverage, and damned if there wasn't a hell of a lot now. His mother had called him, begged him to take a few days' vacation from his detective position with the Dallas Police Department, to come home to Nostalgia. The press was pestering her and she needed him to fend off reporters. He'd been here only two days and already he'd turned down interviews with six television shows, including *A Current Affair* and *ET*. The town's sole motel was nearly filled to capacity. The diner was packed at all hours of the day. Jimmy Joe, the owner, had even decided to extend hours to accommodate the rush of business. The ordinarily quiet little town had turned into a zoo.

Perfect for Darby's long-awaited homecoming.

As much as Graham knew that, he'd still been surprised when he'd walked out of the diner and seen her sitting at the stoplight, her shiny black car catching winks of sunlight.

He'd thought he was crazy, imagining things, his brain mush from sleep-deprivation or the hellacious Texas sun. But then he'd followed the car, and lo and behold, he'd hit pay dirt. It had been her.

His sister's killer.

At the very least, an accomplice.

What about witness?

He forced the thought aside. Darby was guilty. He'd come to that conclusion a long time ago. She was the most likely suspect. She was capable of killing. The whole damned town knew that.

Witness was out of the question. Darby was a killer or an accomplice, and either way, her hands were bloody.

Red seeped across his consciousness, distorting his vision, and he closed his eyes. There'd been so much blood, splattering the walls, turning the hardwood floor a deep, dark red. . . .

His eyes snapped open and focused on Darby. She sat in her idling car, staring at the house. Probably remembering.

Yes, her coming back now made perfect sense.

Despite her small size, he knew it was her. Somehow, some way, she'd killed Linda and Trish and Jane.

It wasn't Katy. He knew Katy like he knew his own sister. She didn't have a vicious bone in her body. She was just as much a victim as his sister, only she hadn't died. She'd gone crazy. Completely crazy. She had to be to have passed a lie-detector test while claiming the Devil had killed his sister.

But Darby . . .

Everyone knew Darby Jayson was more than capable of killing someone bigger and stronger than herself. She'd done it before. And, of course, she'd failed her lie-detector test. He knew that in itself wasn't incriminating. Many people failed under duress. But couple the failed test with her old man's death, and that was enough to convict her in Graham's mind.

Then, of course, there was the final nail in her coffin. Katy had run away from the carnage, straight to the nearest farmhouse. But the police had found Darby upstairs in the attic, the lone blood-spattered survivor. If she wasn't the killer, why hadn't she been murdered right alongside his sister and the others? Why would the killer leave a witness?

No killer would, unless the killer *was* the witness.

Darby was guilty. He knew it in his gut, even if all the hows and whys didn't quite connect in his head. Yet.

Graham had spent the past eight years with the Dallas Police Department, two years doing patrol duty, and the last six in Homicide, working his way up through the ranks to detective. He'd spent his time training, learning to think like a killer. To crawl inside their heads, walk and talk and *be* the killer, so that he could catch them. So he could mete out justice, the justice he'd never had the chance to see imposed on his sister's killer.

Until now.

Graham had another chance, one sitting in the front seat of a black Cougar not more than twenty yards away. The anniversary in six days was stirring up a lot of old hurt. Maybe it had stirred Darby's bloodlust again. Graham didn't know. He only knew that he intended to find out the truth this time.

He didn't buy her forgetful act for a second. She was lying. He could see it in her eyes, and the eyes never lied.

Darby had lying eyes, as well as a lying mouth. A soft, full, trembling mouth that no doubt tasted as good as it looked.

And Graham had one hell of a hard-on.

A quick glance down at the bulge straining against his jeans sent a wave of disgust rolling through him.

Yes, he was an asshole, all right.

A horny asshole, though it didn't surprise him. His dick never failed to betray his better judgment. Not that night nearly ten years ago when he'd left his little sister at Samuel Blue's house so he could go screw his brains out in the backseat of Claire Marlboro's brand-new Plymouth.

And certainly not now, even though the object of his lust was most likely a killer.

Correction—*was* a killer. Darby Jayson was guilty, and Graham intended to prove it. One way or another. Hard-on or not. She wouldn't walk away from Nostalgia this time.

Not this time.

The room smelled even worse than Darby remembered.

She wrinkled her nose and stared around her. Her gaze touched the orange shag carpet, the scarred nightstand, the narrow bed with the abstract orange-and-yellow spread. The entire room was stuck in a sixties time warp.

"Sorry I had to put you way at the end here, but it's the only room we got left." The clerk's voice drew her attention and Darby turned around. "I got a reporter from the *Morning Star* right next door due to check out tomorrow. I can move you over, if this one don't suit you well enough."

"No, no. This will be fine."

She watched Pinky Mitchell scratch his bald head, then dangle the room key between meaty fingers sprinkled with curly black hairs. He wore an orange-and-blue bowling shirt buttoned only halfway, which gave an unhindered view of his chest and the top of a substantial beer belly. Black hair furred his white skin, crept toward his neck. The same hair that covered his milk white arms. He had hair everywhere, except on his head.

"You look awful familiar, sweet thing. Do I know you?"

He knew about her. Everybody in Nostalgia did. She'd been the scandal that rocked a small town, not once, but twice.

And she knew about him.

Pinky Mitchell had once been Pete Mitchell, before he'd had one of his little fingers chopped off in a bar brawl with an angry trucker. He'd had the piece of amputated flesh stuffed and mounted so he could display it on the dashboard of his car. From then on, he'd been called Pinky. The only child of Myron Mitchell, the hotel's owner, Pinky was an out-of-work high school dropout whose idea of success was a night out drinking without pissing on his boots.

Yeah, she knew about Pinky, all right.

She could remember him hanging around the hotel, lusting after Linda that time they'd been stuck doing community cleaning service. It hadn't mattered that he'd been twenty-five and Linda had been fifteen-year-old jailbait. Linda had been pretty, the kind of pretty that made even the finest, upstanding, God-fearing Christian man look twice. She hadn't so much as smiled at Pinky. In fact, she'd told him to go straight to hell on a couple of occasions when he'd passed her a little too closely, or stared at her a little too long, but no amount of cursing or insults had stopped Pinky.

He stared at Darby, his mouth open slightly, a collection of saliva pooling at the corners. Obviously, like the room, Pinky Mitchell hadn't changed at all, with the exception of ten or fifteen extra pounds around his middle. Still sloppy, lazy, and willing to drop his pants at the first sign of encouragement.

Darby pulled self-consciously at her sweater.

"You know, I'm sure I know you." He scratched his head again before clapping his hands together. "I got it. Mickey's Pool Hall last Saturday night."

She shook her head.

"The VFW dance two weekends ago."

"I'm afraid not. I just flew in from San Francisco."

"Hell's bells, you're one of them TV reporters. That's where I've seen you. I shoulda known. Why, I got a lady from one of them ritzy cable shows a few doors down. Next to her are a coupla fellas from *Dallas Prime Time*, that news show. The rest is newspaper and magazine people. Hot damn. So which station do you work for?"

"I'm not a reporter."

"But I've seen you somewhere. I never forget a pretty face, and yours is about the prettiest I've seen in a long time." He kept staring at her and she turned to drop the key onto the nightstand and reach for her bags.

"Where's the ice machine?"

"Down the walk, just outside my office. If you ain't no reporter, what are are you doing in Nostalgia? Your folks here?"

She shook her head. "I'm just in town looking up a few old friends."

"Old friends, huh?" His gaze roved from her head to her toes and she got a disgusting vision of all that hairy flesh pushing down on top of her. "Might be nice to add a new friend to your list."

"Maybe, but I've got enough friends already."

He laughed. "Ain't nobody got enough friends, sweet thing. Always room for one more."

"How much do I owe you?" she said, eager to change the subject.

"First night is due up front."

"I'll pay for the first week." She rummaged in her bag, pulled out several twenties and handed them to him.

He licked his thumb and counted out the money. "Nice doing business with you, sweet thing." He stuffed the money into his front shirt pocket and eyed her once more. "Real nice."

"Yeah, a pleasure," she mumbled, turning away to busy herself arranging her suitcases on the bed. When he made no move to leave, she glanced up. "I can manage from here."

"Yeah," he said with a leering gaze. "I see you're managing just fine."

So much for subtlety. "I really would like to get unpacked and maybe take a nap." Her gaze slid past him to the open doorway. Metal winked as a car pulled into a parking slot a few doors down. "Do you think we could finish this conversation later?" The slam of a car door punctuated her question.

"Right now seems pretty good to me—" he started, his words dying a quick death when a man's tall form appeared in the doorway. Pinky glanced over his shoulder. "Say, Tucker. This ain't your room."

"It isn't the office, either, Mitchell."

"Just seein' to my guest's comfort."

"Yeah, I bet. I saw that reporter from room nine banging on the office door. Maybe you'd like to see to her comfort?"

A smile brightened Pinky's face at the prospect. "Duty calls," he said, before turning to leer at Darby a full second more. "But you just come on over to the office if you need anything, sweet thing. And I do mean *anything*."

"She'll remember that," Graham said waving the open door. Pinky took the hint, winked at Darby, then left. Graham slammed the door in his wake.

"Thanks. I thought he would never leave."

"No thanks necessary. I wasn't protecting you from him."

"Oh." Heat crept into her face and she turned away from him to busy herself unloading one of her suitcases. Glass clinked, and her hand closed around a nearly empty bottle of Jack Daniel's. She ignored it and retrieved the rest of the suitcase's contents. "If you're so dead set on the fact that I'm guilty, and a danger to the good citizens of this town, what are you doing here?" She scooped up an armful of lingerie and shoved it into one of the drawers. "Got a death wish, Tucker?"

"Yeah, but it isn't my own." His voice came from right in back of her and she jumped. How had he made it across the room so fast? And without her hearing him?

"All my death wishes are reserved just for you," he said, holding up a pair of slinky black panties she'd dropped.

Snatching the panties from him, she tossed them into the drawer and slammed it shut with her hip. Then she turned back to her suitcase, intent on ignoring him.

Fat chance. Even if she could have tuned him out mentally, his physical presence was something else altogether.

He was too close. Too male.

And she was entirely too sexually deprived.

"You saved Pinky Mitchell," she muttered, suddenly angry with him for thinking the worst of her. Crazy, she knew, because the worst could very well be true. But then she wasn't operating completely rationally. Not without a drink in her hand. Her gaze lingered on the suitcase that held a bottle of Johnnie Walker, before zooming to the next one. "Your duty's done."

"Not yet," he murmured. He hefted her second suitcase up onto the bed and flipped it open.

"I can do this by myself," she insisted, moving in to pull a handful of CDs and a CD player from the newly opened case.

The leather bag housing her laptop joined the suitcase on the bed. "Just helping out."

"Well, I don't need your help." She grabbed the leather bag and busied herself unloading the laptop and her inch-high novel.

"What's this?" he asked, fingering the stack of neatly typed pages. "Keeping a diary of your exploits?"

"Yeah." She stacked the laptop and printer on a small table in the corner, slapping the paper down next to it. "I'm sure the world is waiting with bated breath for the life and times of Darby Jayson, music reviewer and columnist. They'll market it as a new sleep aid."

"Don't sell yourself short. I'm sure the world would love to read about you. Sex and violence sell big, and with your background—"

She turned on him. "Get out. Please. Just get out."

His eyes glittered with something close to triumph or smugness, as if he'd been trying to yank her chain. "Sure thing. I've got some unpacking to do in my room next door."

"There's a reporter next door. The *Sun* or the *Star* or something like that."

"There *was* a reporter next door. She checked out early. I'm the new guest."

"Comforting."

"Convenient," he corrected. "I want to be nearby when you show your true colors, which I'm willing to bet is soon."

Soon . . . The word followed her into the shower long after the door had slammed behind Graham Tucker and the sound of his boots had faded on the walkway outside.

She stared down through a stream of water at the cut on her hand, so pale, already healing and fading.

Graham was willing to wait for her to slip up, but Darby couldn't wait. She had to help things along. *Do* something.

The prospect had her desperately craving a drink. The bottle of Johnnie Walker called to her from the bedroom, begging her to pick it up, down a long, soothing drink. That was certainly doing something, drowning her troubles, hiding away inside a liquor bottle where the truth couldn't get at her.

But when she came out of it, woke up, when the dulling effects of the booze wore off, the truth would still be there in the form of another dream, another tormented face, another slice mark on her hand, or her arm, or wherever she lost control of the knife when the killing frenzy fell upon her—

No! She couldn't let her thoughts get carried away. She was here to jar her memory, to remember that night. Nothing else. Nothing more. Not yet. Somehow, she knew that night held the answer. If only she could unlock the door to her past and see for herself.

Once she knew the truth, then she could worry about the DA's dead daughter back in San Francisco. And all the other victims, some faceless bodies, some merely flashes of blond or red or black hair, light or dark skin. Yes, then she could worry about the rest. For now she would take one thing at a time: remembering the slumber party.

Five minutes later, Darby sat down on the bed and reached for the telephone book. There was only one other living person who knew the truth about that night.

"The Devil," Katy Evans screamed, kicking and lashing out at the men who held her, hauled her to the ambulance. "I swear, the Devil did it!"

The Devil.

Katy had seen, just as Darby had. So why blame the Devil? Why not tell the truth?

To protect a friend.

But Katy hadn't been Darby's friend. Not really. Not a good enough friend to see herself committed to an insane asylum for Darby's sake.

That was exactly what had happened.

And now? Where was Katy now? Still locked in the sanatorium, spouting the same nonsense about the Devil, protecting a friend that wasn't really a friend?

There was one person who would know.

A quick skim of the listings, and Darby found the number. She reached for the old-fashioned rotary phone on the nightstand. After listening to five rings, she was about to hang up when the line clicked.

"Blessings to you!" came the recorded greeting. "You've reached Myrna Evans, psychic extraordinaire, the key to your future, your past, to fame and fortune. Unfortunately, the key is indisposed at the moment, but if you leave your name and number, I'll return your call. Wait for the beep—"

But Darby couldn't wait. She slapped the phone book closed, then dressed in a T-shirt and jeans.

While she slipped on her boots, her gaze fell to the slice mark on her hand. Her thoughts traveled back to Rudy and Jan and the blue neon–lit apartment. As she tied the laces, her fingers trembled.

Call, a small voice whispered. A quick phone call could ease her worrying. She would know for sure they were all right, that it had just been another death dream.

With a shaky hand, she reached for the phone.

She fingered the rotary dial, her index finger going to the first number in Rudy's area code. *Call*, that small voice whispered again, and she started to dial. First one number, then the next, then—

A knock sounded and her hand stopped three numbers shy of completing the call. Relief surged through her. Saved by the bell, she thought. Or rather, the knock.

"Forgot to give you an ice bucket," Pinky said when Darby hauled the door open.

"Thanks," she said, taking the scarred white plastic container he held out to her.

"No problem," he said, glancing back over his shoulder. "Course, if you're really grateful, I can think of something I'd like to have a lot better than a measly thank-you—" He stiffened at the sound of a door closing several rooms down. "Hell's bells, that man is wearing my patience thin. What the hell does he think he's doing? I told him to wait, for Chrissake! At least let the maid get in there and clean the dadblamed room before he hauls all his shit inside." He spun on his heels and lumbered down the walkway.

She tossed the container to the bed, snatched up her purse and left the motel room before chancing another glance at the phone. She could call later. No hurry, especially since she was worrying over nothing.

Nothing, she assured herself once again as she climbed into her car. Pinky and whoever he'd been cussing were nowhere in sight, she thought thankfully. She'd had her fill of Pinky Mitchell.

Minutes later, she steered the rental car down the main
strip through Nostalgia, her gaze searching for the right
street that would lead her to Myrna Evans. To Katy.
To the past . . .

Chapter Six

"Mrs. Evans?" Darby pounded on the door of the small, wood-frame house. Okay, so she'd known Myrna Evans wasn't in. The answering machine had said as much. Still, she'd hoped.

She gazed at the large window to the left of the door. The curtains were drawn. The word CLOSED had been scribbled across a piece of cardboard and propped against the glass.

She turned and glanced at the large sign that stood in the yard, a giant purple hand with the letters of Myrna's name on each fingertip. The palm area offered readings, astrological charts, séances—a one-stop shop for all your supernatural needs.

Her gaze swept the slightly overgrown yard, the weed-filled flower bed that lined the walkway, before going back to the small wood-framed house. The structure was the same, a little older certainly, the white paint peeling at the corners, the rain gutters sagging from age and weather. The same, yet different.

KIMBERLY RANGEL

Katy's ten-speed was no longer propped against the side of the house, the window to her room no longer open, her lacy pink curtains no longer blowing in the breeze. The window had been closed, a shade added to block out prying eyes. Darby could only speculate what lay in the room beyond.

Sunlight winked off the glass, blinding her. She closed her eyes, and a memory bubbled and floated to the surface of her mind.

Cotton-candy pink wall paper covered the walls. Prince and Bon Jovi posters hung in uniform precision along one wall. A pair of red-and-white pom-poms hung from either side of the dresser mirror. Pictures lined the corners of the mirror, but not with the usual haphazardness. Katy's pictures had been placed with the utmost care. So neat and perfect, just like Katy.

The sounds of the nearby highway grew muffled, replaced by the plunk of a needle dropping onto an album. Madonna's "Like A Virgin" seemed to fill her ears.

"Geez, Katy. Do you have to play that again?" Linda *whined, tossing the latest issue of* Teen Beat *onto Katy's perfectly made bed, the sheets and spread so tight an army sergeant would have beamed with pride. She plopped herself down on the bright pink coverlet, despite Katy's squeal.*

"Geez, Linda. Move your big butt. You'll wrinkle my bed."

"So what? You're giving me permanent brain damage playing the same song over and over." She covered her ears and stared in frustration at the small record player in the corner. "We've heard it eighteen times."

"And we'll hear it nineteen, right, Darby?" Katy shot her a pointed look that said take-up-for-me-would-ya?

Darby shrugged. "Whatever you say."

"Can't you ever take a stand?" Katy demanded. "Whatever this, whatever that. Can't you just say what you think?"

"She does," Linda jumped to her defense. "She thinks whatever, so get off her back."

THE HOMECOMING

"Nineteen," Katy said sullenly, turning the volume on high. *"And if you two don't perk up and stop being so boring, I'm liable to bring the record player and the record to Blue's house tonight, just to torture you guys."* She collapsed in a nearby beanbag chair to stare at the rain splattering against the windowpane. A typical, boring, rainy Saturday at Katy's house. Ah, but tonight, raining or not, that was when the fun would start. . . .

The wail of a passing diesel pushed into Darby's thoughts and jerked her back to reality.

Shielding her gaze from the sun, she focused on the house from her past, a house she'd visited time and time again. Every Saturday afternoon with Linda to listen to records on Katy's stereo. Sometimes after school. Always with Linda, though. She never would have dreamed of coming on her own.

Linda had been Darby's buffer. Her friend. The one person who'd accepted Darby the way she was—shy, quiet, withdrawn, *boring*, as Katy had called her—and liked her anyway. Despite what she'd done.

Poor, frightened Darby. She had no choice.

It was self-defense, plain and simple, Your Honor.

Self-defense . . .

Self defense or not, choice or not, she'd shed another person's blood.

Worse, she hadn't been repulsed or sickened, or even frightened.

She'd been glad. Relieved.

A shiver gripped her and she rubbed her arms despite the warm temperature. She knew what it was like to draw blood, knew that she was capable of it, and so she had to remember the truth about the slumber party. *For better or worse.*

Darby pounded on the door again and fought back the disappointment. Finally, she turned back to the gravel-lined driveway.

"Hold your horses. I'm coming. I'm coming."

The muffled voice brought her back around.

"Hell, a woman can't even sit down and have herself some lunch and a little peace and quiet these days."

Locks clicked, wood creaked and the door swung open.

Darby found herself standing face-to-face with Myrna Evans. *Jezebel.* That was what Reverend Masters had always called Myrna, and Darby had always thought the term fit. Myrna Evans had always been a loose-moraled, do-what-you-please woman, despite all the church busybodies who'd made it their business to save her heathen soul.

Her red lipstick, black eyeliner and vivid blue eyeshadow were just as thick as Darby remembered, her hair still jet black, though Darby suspected the color had more to do with a bottle of Clairol than with Myrna's Gypsy heritage. Big hoops hung from her ears. A bright emerald scarf held her hair at the nape of her neck. She wore a muumuu the same vivid purple as the hand standing in her front yard.

Like the house, Myrna had changed little, with the exception of a little sagging here and there. Well, a lot of sagging.

She'd looked like a flamboyant, exotic Gypsy in her younger days. Now she simply looked like an old woman trying to look like a flamboyant exotic Gypsy.

"Didn't you see the 'closed' sign?" she demanded, wiping at a smudge of mustard at the corner of her red mouth.

"Yes, but—"

"Closed means closed, missy," she said in between chews.

"But it's really important."

The woman looked ready to close the door in her face, before a spark of recognition lit her eyes and she swallowed her mouthful. "Don't I know you? Aren't you the new woman that moved into town with Hershell Crempkin?" She waved a finger excitedly. "Yeah, it is you. Pretty young thing with dark hair, dark eyes. You were runner-up in the Miss Grant County pageant last year."

Darby shook her head. "Sorry. I don't even know Hershell Crempkin. I just checked into the motel today—"

"You're one of them TV people." A smile brightened the older woman's face as she slapped her palms together. "Well, why didn't you say so? What can I do for you? I had that woman from the *Star* here just yesterday to have her chart done. That and talking. She sure liked to talk."

"I don't need my chart done. I need to find—"

"Said she didn't need hers done either, but I'll tell you like I told her, answering questions don't pay my bills." She reached behind her and flicked the sign from CLOSED to OPEN, before rubbing her hands together. "So what'll it be, hon? A chart? Or I could do a palm reading. That doesn't take as long, if you've only got a couple of questions. Then again, if you're like that writer fella that came out here last month for research, I could give you my special New Level Consciousness package, which includes a full astrological chart, a palm reading, two psychic experiences with the deceased loved one of your choice—"

"Actually, your daughter is the one I'd like to speak with. Is she still at the hospital in Point Bluff?"

"Ain't been there for nearly a year now, and she don't talk to no TV people. Newspaper either. They been hounding her, but she slammed the door on every single one of them. Even that lady from the *National Enquirer* who offered her ten thousand dollars for an exclusive story." Myrna shook her head. "Never should have let that girl out of the hospital. I told that doctor she ain't got all her gears working right. Imagine anybody turning down ten thousand dollars for something as simple as talking. Crazy, I tell you."

"Where is she now?"

"She ain't gonna talk to you."

"She will."

"And what makes you so sure?"

"I'm not one of the TV people, or the newspaper, or

any magazine. It's me, Mrs. Evans. Darby . . . Darby Jayson."

Darby watched as the color faded from the woman's already pale complexion.

"Oh, my Jesus!" She snatched the glasses from her pocket and shoved them onto her face. "Why, it is you," she exclaimed after a quick perusal. No gasp of horror, no glittering fear in her eyes. At last someone who hadn't tried and convicted her.

"I'm in town for a few days and I really need to see Katy."

The woman pulled her glasses off and shoved them back into her pocket. "It's nice of you to look in on her, Darby, but I can tell you right now, she ain't fit company, especially when it comes down to the subject of that night. She don't want to talk about it, or see anybody associated with it. You'd do better to stay away while you're here."

"I need to see her, Mrs. Evans. It's really important." When the woman looked ready to refuse, Darby added, "If you don't tell me where she is, I'll find her on my own. I will."

Myrna simply stared for a long moment; then finally she turned and disappeared back inside the house. A few minutes later, she emerged with a crumpled piece of envelope, an address written in blue scrawl on the back.

"She's here in Nostalgia, living just on the other side of town." She looked wistful for a long second. "Don't get over there as much as I should. Not lately, anyhow. Business has been good. Lots of folks in town for the anniversary, everybody wanting to ask questions."

"And get their charts done?"

"Hey, a woman's got to make a living. Besides, I like to talk while I work."

"Thank you." Darby reached for the address, but Myrna hesitated before letting go of the paper.

"She's changed, Darby. That night, something happened to her." The words sounded more like a warning than a statement of fact. "She ain't been the same since."

"Neither have I," Darby replied. Myrna let go of the paper, and Darby slipped it into her pocket. "Thanks."

She walked to her car and climbed in, all the while conscious of Myrna's dark brown eyes following her. Katy had inherited her mother's eyes, though her blond hair had come from her father. Darby thought the craving for perfection had come from Katy's father, as well. But nobody, including Katy, knew much about him except that he'd been blond and good-looking.

Big brown eyes . . . Darby suspected that much about Katy hadn't changed. But the rest?

What had happened to the fun-loving, blond-haired girl every boy in school had lusted after? The picture-perfect Katy whose clothes had always been ironed and starched, her makeup just right, not a wayward strand of lustrous blond hair out of place?

Darby didn't know. She remembered Katy only the way she'd been the night of the killings, those brown eyes wide, frantic, her tanned legs and arms flailing wildly as the paramedics forced her into the back of a waiting ambulance despite her screams of protest.

Darby hadn't seen Katy since then.

While Darby had spent her time at the police station, Katy had been hospitalized, sedated "for her own good," everyone had said. Katy was delusional. Sick. No wonder, after what she'd witnessed.

Now, it seemed, those same people thought she was well enough to live on her own.

But how was she living? Was she haunted by the same dreams as Darby? Did Katy climb into a bottle every night in order to escape, to forget, to appear sane when she was all screwed up inside? Or was she really better? Sound of mind now because she remembered the truth?

Either way, Darby would find out.

And so would Graham Tucker, she realized as she turned onto the main strip through town, and spotted Graham's pickup in her rearview mirror.

He was following her.

An odd rush of fear went through her. Crazy, she knew. She had nothing to hide. She'd openly admitted to him why she'd come to Nostalgia, the fact that she just might be a killer.

It wasn't her own discovery she feared, she quickly realized as the pickup drew closer until he followed at an unmistakable distance behind. No, she wasn't afraid *of* Graham Tucker; she was afraid *for* him.

If she was, indeed, a killer, then he could be in terrible, terrible danger. Her fingers tingled and she gripped the steering wheel tighter, her gaze drawn yet again to the tiny sliver on her finger.

Her mind rushed back to the bloody footprint in her apartment, the face flashing on her television screen, the same face from her dreams. . . .

She willed the images away. It was broad daylight; pavement separated them, not to mention the metal of two vehicles. Nothing was going to happen now. Here.

And later? When the sun set and the dreams came and Darby found herself lost amid the blood and death?

Not then, she assured herself.

But Graham's image rose in her mind to shake her determination. She saw him so clearly—his shadowed jaw, his short dark hair, full lips, his rich blue eyes. The bluest eyes she'd ever seen. So cold and blue and all-knowing.

With a quick glance in her rearview mirror she could have sworn she saw those eyes distinctly. His gaze fixed on her, held her entranced for a long moment during which her determination crumbled and her courage fled.

Get away! a small part of her begged.

The part of her that remembered the death and destruction of that night, and knew who was responsible.

She had to be at the wrong place.

She glanced again at the address on the crumpled paper on the seat next to her, then at the crooked letters scratched on the side of the old trailer.

This was it.

The right place, yet it was all wrong.

There wasn't a trace of Katy's beloved pink anywhere in sight, just a run-down piss yellow trailer, sheets of aluminum serving as a roof. A TV antenna rose like a twisted antler from one corner of the roof. The shell of a refrigerator, door unhinged and propped next to it, sat beside the trailer door. The outside of the fridge was rusted, the inside dirty, filled with a collection of rainwater and slime. Similar items junked up the front, from several old tires to a rickety TV stand, the legs twisted and rusty.

A junkyard. Pink and perfect Katy lived in a piss-yellow junkyard.

This couldn't be the place.

"Hold it right there."

Darby whirled to find herself face-to-face with a deadly looking tire iron. The hand gripping it trembled and the weapon shook threateningly.

But it wasn't the weapon that sucked the air from Darby's lungs and stopped her heartbeat.

It was the woman holding the weapon.

Katy.

Darby could have passed her on the street and she never would have known her. Gone was the sparkle in her brown eyes, the healthy tan she'd always spent all summer perfecting. No pink lipstick outlining her luscious mouth. No apple-blossom cheeks.

Katy's once glorious mane of blond hair had been chopped off short, nearly ear level. Her eyes were a dull, mud color, her face pale. Too pale. Her mouth was pulled into a severe line.

She wore a plain black skirt and a wrinkled brown blouse—*wrinkled*. Her shoes were black and clunky, the kind their freshman math teacher had worn.

The hideous kind of shoes Katy wouldn't have been caught dead wearing.

But this wasn't Katy. Not the Katy Darby remembered. The vivacious, picture-perfect, do-anything and dare-anyone Katy who'd pulled out the Ouija board that Halloween night . . .

"Come on, everybody. It's almost midnight," Katy said, *settling down in front of the Ouija board. "They're about to do it."* She leaned over and turned the volume up on the radio. *The music had paused. A reporter's voice crackled over the airwaves.*

". . . ten minutes and Samuel Blue will be the first serial killer in Texas history to die by lethal injection. Blue, convicted of twenty-nine counts of capital murder, has been sitting on Death Row in the Ellis unit for three years now. With his appeals exhausted and the governor's public rally against violent crime, Blue will pay for his crimes tonight, in the most humane of execution methods—"

"The bastard should be castrated!" came a shout in the background, followed by a string of other suggestions.

"Hang him!"

"Fry him!"

"We're live outside the Walls unit," the reporter's voice broke through the shouts, *"where the execution is scheduled to begin in approximately six minutes. A sizable crowd has gathered here, including several of the loved ones of Blue's victims."*

"My baby girl is dead because of that monster," came a tear-filled voice. *"God forgive me, but I hope he burns in hell for what he's done. . . ."*

"Why don't you turn that off?" Linda plopped down across from Katy. *"And blow out the candles. The lanterns we brought give off plenty of light."*

"It sets the mood."

"It's creepy," Jane said, flopping down next to Linda.

"Exactly. It's Halloween." Katy took a long drink of wine cooler, then reached for the pointer, a triangular piece that stood on three felt-tipped legs. *"Come on,"* she said, motioning to Darby and Trish. *"It's almost time."*

"Do you really think we should be doing this?" Darby asked, handing a bag of potato chips to Linda. *"I mean, it*

doesn't really feel right." She glanced around at the shadowy attic. *"It feels weird."*

"So nobody's making you play," Katy said, positioning the pointer at the center of the board. She guzzled another drink of wine, then placed her pink-polished fingertips on the edge of the cardboard. *"We'll play without you."*

". . . carved out the eyes of his victims in a slow, torturous process before killing them," the reporter's voice droned on.

"Maybe Darby's right," Jane said, swallowing a mouthful of potato chips and slanting a nervous glance around her. *"It's creepy up here."* The loud crackle of the radio punctuated her sentence and she jumped.

Katy laughed. *"Lighten up, silly."*

"Well, it doesn't bother me." Trish reached for a chip, but her hand shook visibly.

". . . one minute till midnight," the reporter's voice announced.

"It's almost time," Katy said excitedly. *"Come on, Darby. Don't be such a wet blanket. It's Halloween. It's supposed to be creepy up here. That's why we came, to set the mood to summon my grandfather."*

"You really think it'll work?" Linda asked, staring skeptically at the board. *"I mean, it's made by a toy manufacturer, for heaven's sake."*

"Of course it'll work. Mom calls Granddad all the time, and people pay her good money to call loved ones for them," Katy replied.

"My mom says your mom's a crackpot," Linda retorted.

"She's just jealous 'cause your daddy used to have it bad for my mom. He probably still does."

"Does not."

"Does too."

". . . the stroke of midnight. In sixty seconds, a full minute after, the injection will begin."

"Hurry!" Katy squealed, motioning for the rest of the girls to place their fingertips on the cardboard pointer.

Cardboard, *Darby reminded herself. Linda was right. It*

was just a stupid game, a toy. Just wood and cardboard made in a factory right alongside baby dolls that could actually pee and water pistols that glowed in the dark. Just wood and cardboard, and this house was just wood and concrete. There wasn't anything creepy about it. It was just old and run-down. Dusty. Neglected.

And her fear was totally irrational.

She sat down, Indian-style, and touched the pointer, her fingertips between Linda's and Jane's.

"Close your eyes," Katy instructed. Her voice grew somber. "Granddad, we know you're listening. I'm here with my friends and we've gathered to talk to you. Can you hear us?"

The radio hit a high crackle and a tremor swept through Darby. A gust of wind whispered across her skin and her eyes snapped open. She watched in stunned amazement as the pointer started to tremble, then move.

Katy was doing it. She had to be. Darby's gaze flew to the girl who sat, eyes closed, head thrown back, a small smile on her lips as she felt the movement at her fingertips.

"Yes. I knew you were here. Mama said you'd come if I called. Do you miss me, Granddad?"

The pointer trembled again, slid across the smooth wood, again indicating YES.

"Shit," Linda exclaimed, jerking her hands back.

"Cripes," Jane followed suit, and so did Trish. Until Katy was the only one touching the cardboard.

"I miss you, too. Do you know how long it will be before I see you?"

The pointer trembled, sliding across the alphabet.

"Holy shit," came Jane's stunned voice. "It's really moving."

"No, it's not. It's Katy," Linda insisted as they all stared in amazement at the pointer.

"Sssshhh," Katy hissed, eyes closed, hands still touching the pointer. "You'll scare him away. Go on, Granddad. Finish."

The pointer trembled, slid an inch more to hit N, *then stalled.*

"Come on," Katy chanted. "When, Granddad? When will I see you again?"

Another gust of wind swept through the attic, strange since the window was barely cracked and the trees outside didn't so much as stir.

A strange shiver crept up Darby's spine. Someone was here. Or something . . .

She glanced to her left, her right, behind her.

Nothing. Still she felt it, something watching her, breathing over her shoulder. A coldness, an evil.

"Answer," Katy pleaded, and the pointer slid slowly toward O, *then headed for the last letter. "When will I see you?"*

The pointer settled over W.

N-O-W.

The candles flickered.

The radio crackled and buzzed, the sound grating across Darby's nerves. Through the chaos she heard the faint voice of the reporter.

". . . one minute after midnight . . . just received word the execution has started . . . Samuel Blue is finally getting his due . . ." The voice faded into the static of the radio.

The candles flickered, then died, plunging the attic into darkness.

"This isn't funny," Katy said. "Okay, which one of you blew out the candles? Who—" Katy seemed to choke on the word.

"Katy?" Darby said, straining to see through the darkness.

"What the hell happened to the lights?" Linda asked frantically from next to Darby.

"This isn't funny," Jane said, her voice shaky. "Not a damn bit funny."

Then as quickly as they'd died, the candle flames sparked, flared, pushing back the darkness.

Darby stared across from her at Katy, who sat with her

hands still touching the pointer. Katy's wide, frightened brown eyes sparkled. Then the color brightened, faded and . . .

The image vanished as quickly as it had flashed in Darby's mind. That was the last thing she'd seen before she'd escaped into the blackness of her own mind and cut herself off from the carnage that followed.

Chocolate brown eyes lightening, changing, firing a vivid *blue . . .*

Impossible! Katy didn't have blue eyes.

She had brown eyes. Watery, red-rimmed, slightly glazed brown eyes that blazed with suspicion, then recognition as Darby held up a hand and said, "Katy, it's me."

Then the eyes blinked, shuttered, and Katy Evans sank to the muddy ground at Darby's feet.

Chapter Seven

Darby knelt down and leaned over the unconscious woman. "Katy?" She pressed her ear to Katy's chest.

Okay, her heart was still beating.

Breathing, Darby thought. She had to check her friend's breathing.

The moment she leaned forward, her face inches from Katy's, the woman's eyes snapped open.

"You." Katy gasped, one hand shooting up to grasp Darby's wrist.

Startled, Darby jerked away and Katy's grip faltered. Her gaze didn't. Unblinking, she stared at Darby, suspicion and fear fighting a battle in the murky brown depths of her eyes.

Brown. Darby stressed the word to herself. Certainly not blue.

"You're real," Katy said incredulously.

The statement might have seemed odd, but Darby knew all too well what Katy felt. Disbelief. Doubt that whispered that Darby was merely an image from the past come back to haunt her.

93

"Yes, I'm real." Darby touched Katy, only to have the woman shrink away from her.

"This time," Katy stated, as if there had been other times when Darby hadn't been real.

"What do you mean—"

"What are you doing here?" Katy cut in, climbing to her feet. She didn't bother to wipe at the mud that clung to her ugly skirt. The tire iron lay submerged in muck. She reached down for it, her pale white fingers plunging into the mud without a second's hesitation. Only when she stood facing Darby again, muddy tire iron in one hand, did Darby notice the worn Bible she clutched in her other.

"I came to talk to you." Suddenly every nerve in Darby's body tingled and a chill rolled through her. She glanced around at the trashy yard. "So this is your place?"

"Yeah." Katy's suspicious brown gaze darted around her before homing in on Darby once again. "You're here because of all those TV people."

Darby shook her head. "No, I didn't come for the anniversary. I had no idea they were going to do a live broadcast from the house."

"Crazy people, all of them. They should stay away from that place. Far away."

"Have you been there since you got out of Point Bluff?"

Katy shook her head frantically. "I won't go back there. It's better to let that place alone. To forget."

"I thought so, too," Darby said. "But it isn't." A pleading note crept into her voice. "I'm going crazy, Katy. I have to remember that night. I have to know what happened—"

"Jesus will help you forget." Katy clutched the Bible to her chest. "He'll help you. Just give all your troubles to Him."

"He can't help me on this. I have to help myself. I have to remember. That's why I'm here, Katy. I know you saw what happened that night. I know you remember."

"No, no. I gave it all to Jesus. He took it away, all the

memories, the pain. He washed me in forgiveness."

"Forgiveness?"

Katy's glazed eyes collided with Darby's.

"He forgives everyone."

Will He forgive me? a small voice whispered inside of Darby. *Will He wash away Linda's and Jane's and Trish's blood and give me back my sanity?*

Jesus wasn't the answer for Darby. The truth was the only answer. The only salvation from going completely and totally mad.

Killer or not, she could face the future if she knew the truth, whatever that future might be. Prison, Death Row, death itself, or a life of sobriety, listening to the music she loved, writing her column and her novel. Whatever, she would face it *after* she remembered.

"You remember, Katy," she prodded. "You know what happened that night. You can tell me."

Katy shook her head frantically, as if a fly buzzed around her and she tried to shake it away. "I don't have anything to say about that night. Talk to Jesus. He knows. I gave it all to Him."

"Please, Katy. I need you to talk to me, to tell me what happened." Darby stepped forward, and Katy stepped backward. Katy, who never shied away from anyone or anything.

She hasn't been the same since that night.

Since that night . . .

"Talk to Jesus, Darby. Just talk to Him."

Darby blinked back a sudden bout of tears that sprang to her eyes. "I . . ." She swallowed. "I know you don't want to talk about that night, but I really need to ask you some questions."

"No."

"Please. I need to know what happened, Katy." She leveled a stare at the woman. "I still can't remember. I came back to Nostalgia to find my memory of that night. To find out the truth about who killed Linda and the others. You know, Katy. I know you do."

"I don't know. I gave it to Jesus. He washed away my sins, took the past, cleansed me. I don't know anything now. Only He knows." Katy inched backward until her back came up against the side of the trailer. Another frantic shake of her head. "I don't know."

"You saw what happened." Darby stepped closer, her gaze drilling into Katy's. "You saw who did it. Who was it, Katy? Who?"

Silence stretched between them, disrupted only by Darby's frantic breaths, the thunder of her heart. Or maybe it was Katy's heart.

"The Devil," came Katy's breathless whisper. "The Devil came into that room that night and killed Linda, and Jane, and Trish, too. I saw him. I felt him. . . ." Her words trailed off as her white-knuckled fingers clutched the worn Bible to her chest. The tire iron slipped from her hands, thunking to the ground. "I saw him, and I ran. It was him. I know it was."

The Devil.

If only that were true. If only it had been the Devil, or Samuel Blue's ghost, or Jason, or Freddie Kreuger, or Count Dracula. But it hadn't been any of those. Graham was right. It was a real, living, breathing person who'd slaughtered Linda and the others.

It was . . . ?

She battered at the black wall in her mind, desperate to break through, to see a pinpoint of truthful light.

Nothing. Only Katy's vivid brown eyes changing color—

Stop it. It was ridiculous and she was grasping at straws, her mind conjuring images to avoid the truth that she herself was guilty. That she'd picked up the knife, plunged it into her friends over and over.

Maybe.

Her gaze shot to the newly healed nick on her finger, then back to Katy, who stared at her as if she were the Devil.

Probably.

"Was it me, Katy? Did I do it?" The questions came out in a frightened whisper. "I need to know. Did I?"

Confusion lit Katy's wide brown eyes. Then . . . Relief? But why?

"You really don't remember?" Katy asked.

"No, but I have to. Don't you see that? I have to know."

"Not you," she murmured. "The Devil. He did it. He was there. I felt him. When I was calling to Granddad, I felt him come inside the room. Inside . . ." Her words trailed off as a shout of "Hallelujah" came from inside the piss-yellow trailer.

"Inside what, Katy? What?"

But Katy wasn't listening. The fear had left her eyes, replaced by a strange panic induced by the sounds coming from the TV. "Oh, my goodness," she cried. "I'm missing it." She glanced at Darby. "You have to go. I—I never miss Reverend Ackerby's afternoon revival. Channel Fifty-one, every afternoon at four. I never miss it. It was nice to see you again, Darby." Her face broke into a quick smile, yet it didn't touch her eyes. They remained distant, glazed. "God bless you." The screen door slammed behind her, and Darby was left standing outside the ugly yellow trailer. Alone. No more enlightened than she'd been when she'd driven up a few minutes ago.

When she and Graham had driven up.

Her gaze traveled past the mailbox at the end of the drive, to the pickup parked a few feet away. Her gaze collided with his for a long second and a bolt of awareness shot through her.

He knows, a small voice whispered. A voice she quickly silenced. What Graham Tucker did or didn't know didn't mean a hill of beans to her. She was only concerned with what she herself knew. Which wasn't much at the moment.

Shouts of "Hallelulah!" and "Praise the Lord!" grew louder, rattling the metal walls of the trailer. Darby thought about knocking on the door, begging to be let in, but she knew talking to Katy was useless.

She'd changed, all right. She'd turned into a religious fanatic. A sloppy, unkempt religious fanatic, escaping into her Bible the same way Darby escaped into a bottle.

Was she trying to forget? Was that what eight years in a mental institution had taught her? To turn the past off the way she would a TV switch? To seek an escape? What about facing the past and dealing with it?

But Katy *had* faced the past. She hadn't blocked out what had happened. She knew. Somewhere beneath all the "God blesses" and "Jesus saves," she knew the truth.

Darby's gaze swept the cluttered yard, the half-rusted trailer. This was what the truth had done to Katy. It had altered her life, changed its course and sent her spiraling down the road to nowhere. It had turned all the pink to a drab yellow, dulled the sparkle in her eyes. The truth had sapped the life right out of her.

Yet Darby still needed to know. Despite the consequences and what waited for her on the other side of that black wall dividing that night from the rest of her mind. She needed to know why she'd been the only sane survivor. If someone else had come into the attic, wouldn't he have killed all of them? Katy had run away, but Darby had sat there, waiting for death. An easy target. Why hadn't she been killed as well?

Because she'd been the one doing the killing. Maybe.

Unfortunately, she wasn't going to find out for sure standing in Katy's yard listening to Reverend Ackerby give a fire-and-brimstone sermon.

Dodging puddles of mud, Darby walked back to her car and climbed in. She shoved a tape into the tape deck and turned the volume up, despite her aching head. Music roared through the speakers, blocking out the preacher's shouts. She gripped the steering wheel, her hands trembling.

Focus. She closed her eyes, ignoring the ache inside her, the craving. *Just one drink. One little, tiny drink.*

Then her head wouldn't hurt anymore. She wouldn't have to think, not about that night, about the truth, about

Katy's wide brown eyes changing to a vivid blue—

No! She pictured the DA's daughter, her smiling face, her vibrant blue eyes. *Dead.*

The sobering thought renewed her determination and she revved the car's engine. She would go back to the motel, take a nice, hot shower and listen to some music. That would relax her. She could sleep, and tomorrow she could set her mind to figuring out a way over the fence, past the security guard and into Samuel Blue's house, up to the attic where the carnage had taken place.

Then she would remember.

"She's here," Graham said as he strode into the office of Nostalgia's chief of police.

Maggie Cross finished off her last bite of tuna sandwich, wiped her hands on a rumpled napkin imprinted with bright orange pumpkins and turned to stare over the stack of paperwork that littered her desk. "Who's here?" she asked, wiping her mouth and gathering up the remains of a late lunch.

"Darby Jayson."

Her hands paused over an empty juice container. "When?"

"This morning."

"Well, I'll be a son of a bitch," she said in a hiss, tossing the container into an already overflowing trash bin. "She's got lucrative timing. I bet there are fifty newspapers and TV stations that would pay an arm and a leg for an interview with her."

"She says it's purely coincidental that she came back now. She's still telling the same story," Graham said as he paced in front of her desk. "She doesn't remember what happened."

"You believe her?"

"She was sitting right there in the attic. Shit, she was practically covered in blood." His mind traveled back and he saw her image in his mind. A killer, or a witness? He shoved the last thought aside. A killer, he told himself.

She'd done it before and she'd failed the lie-detector test. Proof enough. "It'll be a cold day in hell before I believe her bullshit," he said, the words more to convince himself than Maggie.

"Not her story. I'm talking about her coming back here. You think she's on the up-and-up about it being coincidental?"

"I'll believe it when I see Satan building a fucking snowman. She's here for the publicity, maybe the money, definitely the glory. She's gets off knowing we're a bunch of dumb shits who can't even see her guilt when it's right in front of our noses." Graham sniffed. "But I can smell shit a mile away. I could then, and my sense of smell's gotten better over the past nine years. She's here for the glory, all right."

"And?" Maggie prodded. "Come on, that's not the only reason you think she's here. There's something else. What is it?"

"Nothing."

"My sense of smell is pretty strong, too, Graham Tucker. Now tell me the truth. What do you think she's up to?"

"I think it doesn't matter what I think," he finally said. "All that matters is that she's back, for whatever reason, and I intend to keep an eye on her."

"Shouldn't you be keeping an eye on your mother?"

"She's fine as long as the reporters stay away. I thought maybe you could put a patrol car out in front of the house. Just until all this is over."

"So that's what this little visit is all about," Maggie mused. "You didn't come to warn me, only to sweet-talk me into some surveillance."

He grinned. "Is it sweet enough?"

"For anybody else, I'd say they'd just done a piss-poor job. But for you, the man who'd sooner cut off his arm than ask for help? I'm liable to get a toothache."

"Thanks, Maggie."

"Hold on there. It's sweet enough, but I'm not in a position to help. The fact of the matter is that I can't spare any men. Do you know since that TV crew set up the fortress around Blue's house, we've had over two hundred people swarm into town? Hell, that's quadruple Reverend Masters's entire congregation. I've had a stack of complaints. Reporters asking questions, strangers showing up, taking pictures, stirring up a mess of old hurt.

"Hell," she went on, "one of those Dallas reporters wanted to take pictures of the baptismal font at the church where Darby and the other girls were baptized. Masters nearly had a heart attack. Blasphemy, he called it. Exploitation. I've got my men fending off reporters right and left, checking out complaints. It's a damned zoo. And I have this sinking feeling it's only going to get worse when word spreads that she's back. Damn, this town doesn't need this. Folks here were just starting to forget, to let their kids out to trick-or-treat again. Damn, damn, *damn*."

"Come on, Maggie. My mom's been through hell. Half of the complaints coming in are nothing more than paranoid citizens overreacting. Like Lyle. The kid stole a candy bar, for Chrissake. In Dallas, that would qualify the boy as a damned Boy Scout."

"Paranoid or not, a citizen is a citizen. Lyle and his property are my responsibility, whether it's a candy bar or a television set. Around here, lifting candy is a crime."

"Yeah, I forget this place is 'Ozzie and Harriet' land, instead of hometown to Texas's bloodiest serial killer."

"Past is past," Maggie said. "Blue was executed. He's dead and gone and the people in this town deserve to rest easy now."

"And my mom is one of those people. She deserves a little peace and quiet. She's been through enough. You know that. She was a basket case when Dad packed up and walked out. You were the one who found her after the overdose, took her to the hospital."

"You should have been there, Graham." She stared at

him, a knowing look in her eyes. "But you weren't. You're never there."

"She's having a hard enough time without having to see me. I remind her of Linda."

"Or she reminds you of Linda."

His failure. He forced the notion aside.

"This isn't about me," he muttered.

"Isn't it?"

"No. It's about my mom. Her safety, not to mention peace of mind. Come on, Maggie. Show some heart. All I'm asking is for one little squad car to keep anyone from bothering her. It's only six days until Halloween. Things will cool off after that damned broadcast."

"You're a stubborn one, aren't you?"

"That's what they tell me."

She leveled a stare at him. "If I do this, you keep an eye on Darby Jayson. I don't want her presence here to upset anyone. Understand?"

"A woman after my own heart."

"You haven't got a heart, Graham. At least that's what they tell me."

"Keeping tabs on me?" he asked.

"You said it yourself. Your mama and I are friends, and you don't visit near as much as you should. Luckily, I've got friends on the Dallas PD who keep us updated on the infamous Detective Tucker. You've got quite a reputation."

He smiled, and she frowned.

"All of it bad, I'm afraid. You're one pushy asshole, Graham."

"That's what I keep telling myself." He turned and headed for the door. "Thanks," he added before leaving the small office.

Her "Keep me posted" followed him out into the corridor, and down the hall of the hub of crime fighting in Nostalgia, a small two-story structure that would have fit nicely into one-fourth of any precinct house in Dallas.

But then there was very little crime in Nostalgia.

THE HOMECOMING

Things were usually quiet, peaceful. That was the way the town had been before the slumber-party killings. The police saw little action, the highlight of the week being a Saturday night when the kids got a little rowdy and the cops had to flex some muscle.

Muscle that amounted to little more than a stern lecture, or maybe one of the patrolmen driving a rowdy teen home to his parents. It was a far cry from the crime-infested streets of a big metropolis like Dallas, particularly the drug-rich slum area where Graham lived.

"What the hell are you living in that hole for?" one of his few friends, Dr. J. C. Reynolds, had asked too many times to count. Being the department shrink, J.C. was always wanting to know everything, to dig inside his head. Always looking for a motive. Normally, Graham didn't put up with having his brain picked, but J.C. was different. No ulterior motive behind her questions. Just plain curiosity.

"I like to be near my work," he'd told her, and he'd been honest.

He walked and talked and breathed his work. He knew the streets inside and out, and they knew him.

But the reason was twofold. Penance, he told himself. Never again would a killer escape him.

Never again.

Certainly not now.

What do you think she's up to?

But Graham didn't think. He knew.

There was a murderer in Nostalgia, and it was only a matter of time before another victim fell.

Chapter Eight

Home sweet home.

I still can't believe we're here. That Darby actually had the guts to get on the plane, to drive into this shitty place after all this time.

It's my influence, I know. She's finally starting to think for herself, courtesy of me, of course. That should make me feel good, except Darby's assertiveness doesn't figure into my plans.

Don't get me wrong. I'm proud of her. She had the balls, figuratively speaking, to show her face around here, to stand up to that pussy Graham Tucker, and I admire her. She's even been resisting the booze. Bravo!

The only problem is, this new leaf she's turned over interferes with my plans, and I never let anything interfere.

I'll be damned if I'll let Darby. We'll just see how long she stays around this pissant place, how long she stays away from the booze, once she has another dream.

She'll be crawling into the nearest bottle, desperate to

escape the sweet scent of blood, the images of death. Ah, such sweet, sweet memories . . .

Memories that fade too damned fast.

Yes, we'll just see how long she holds up once I start giving her a little something to think about. Really think about.

Darby doesn't like to think, you see. Or feel. The moment a problem develops, or an emotion stirs inside her, she looks for a way to cope. A drink. It's classic obsessive behavior, and I should know obsessive.

Not that I'm obsessive, mind you. I have control over what I think and feel and do. I control the fantasy; it doesn't control me. But after that three years sitting on Death Row, letting those shrinks examine me, I learned a lot about that sort of behavior.

I mean, when you've got twenty or thirty guys spending hours and hours asking all sorts of questions, staring at you like if they stared long and hard enough, they could see inside you, you learn what obsessive means pretty damn quick.

Day after day, they asked so many questions, stupid, ridiculous questions about my family, my childhood. They wanted to understand me, to piece my personality together like a puzzle using the bits and pieces of my past.

But I'm not one of those simple puzzles. No, I'm definitely one of those thousand-piece jobs, and none of those shrinks had ever worked a puzzle so large. They couldn't figure me out. I tried to tell them there was no formula for a man like me. No tragedy of the past that shaped me. I am what I am.

I like what I do. What I feel.

I simply *am*, no rhyme or reason to it.

But I'll be damned if those shit-ass shrinks could grasp such a thing. They're like all the rest of society. They want reasons, explanations. It gives them some sense of power, as if they could recognize somebody like me, someone with the potential for greatness, for death. They don't want to realize that they have no control, no say-so over guys like me. No power.

I have the power.

I can send Darby straight into a bottle if I want to. I can drive her to the edge, make her do what I please. I always have, and I don't intend to stop just because she has it in her head to relive some stupid moment from her past.

No, I think it's time I put Darby back in her place.

I never did like rebellious women.

A woman should know her place, my Granny always used to say. God took a rib from Adam to make Eve, to make a helpmate. Not a controlling, headstrong female. I'm sure if he'd had even the slightest hint of times to come, the women's lib movement, bra-burning, affirmative action, he'd have let Adam keep all his ribs and given him a dog instead.

Not that I don't like women.

I love them. I always have. So damned pretty. So warm. So alive.

I love women, and I adore Darby. That's why I have to stop her now. Before she takes this independence thing too far. I wouldn't want to see anything come between us.

We were meant for each other. Weak, frightened Darby and strong, powerful me. We complement each other. Two halves of one whole. Of course, I'm probably more like three-quarters of the whole, and Darby's the rest. But what the hell? I'm a generous guy. I'll give her the benefit of the doubt, boost the old ego.

Yes, Darby and I go together.

What God hath joined together let no man put asunder. . . .

We belong together. Like Ben and Jerry, Snoopy and Woodstock, Jesus and John the Baptist.

So you see why I can't let Darby pry us apart. It's sinful. Wicked. My soul would burn for sure then. Not that the thought isn't appealing. But my work here isn't finished yet. There are still lessons to be taught. Fantasies to be fed, as all those shrinks would say.

Still so much work.

And, of course, Darby herself is my next job.

"*. . . aw, come on. Give Pinky a little old kiss.*"

Death stood outside the front office of the motel, near a side window that he'd raised about three inches. Just enough to hear every word exchanged between the couple inside the room.

"*I've got work to do, Pinky. Toilets to clean, beds to make, wastebaskets to empty. There's no invisible fairy who goes from room to room, ya know.*"

"*Hell, Melba. The rooms can wait. I can't.*"

"*Amen to that.*"

"*What's that supposed to mean?*"

Throaty laughter floated out the window. "*That you got a hair trigger, honey.*"

"*Not tonight,*" *Pinky vowed.* "*I'll last as long as you want. Now come on and give Pinky a little kiss.*"

"*Stop that. I told you. I got work—*" *The words ended with a high-pitched squeal.* "*Don't you know how to take no for an answer?*"

"*No.*" *Pinky grunted. The sound of lips smacking floated through the open window, along with the sounds of an* Andy Griffith Show *rerun blaring from the TV.*

Death gripped the windowsill, felt the wood beneath his fingertips. A sliver of wood punctured his flesh, slid deep into his skin. He closed his eyes, a delicious pinpoint of pain traveling through his body, feeding his brain and making him crave more.

So much more.

"*You're such a nasty boy, Pinky Mitchell,*" *Melba said, all trace of annoyance gone from her voice.*

So much for having a lot of work to do, he thought. Liars, all of them. He could almost see the maid's eyes, the flicker of deceit, the gleam of dishonesty as she went on and on about having work to do. Work. Ha! She had sinning on her mind.

A throaty moan carried through the window, into the night, into Death's ears.

His hand tightened on the windowsill, embedding the splinter deeper. Pain whispered across his senses, so subtle, so seductive, so hypnotizing. His other hand tightened around the knife he'd retrieved from Pinky's small kitchenette. Just a quick reach through one of the rear windows and he'd been the proud owner of a double-bladed hunting knife.

As if that pussy Pinky had ever hunted a day in his life. He was a wimp, a cocksucker, just like his pa.

Death had known Pinky's old man when the bastard hadn't been so old. But he'd always been a pussy. A mean, opinionated pussy. Just because he'd owned the hotel, he'd thought his shit didn't stink. That he was better than everybody else.

The man was no better than the cow manure used to fertilize the flower beds around Nostalgia Park Cemetery. And neither was his chip-off-the-old-block son.

A tingle of anticipation went through him. He could hear Pinky's piggish grunts of pleasure. Grunts that would turn to desperate cries the moment Death faced him, knife in hand. He could see Pinky's ugly, pale complexion, see the splotches that colored his cheeks darkening. He could see his eyes. Watery blue . . .

His hands trembled. Just a quick flick of the knife and those eyes would be his, in his hands, blood rushing through his fingers, the tissue slippery and wet and round.

Melba moaned, the sound floating through the window to send flame shooting through his body, straight to his groin.

It had been nearly ten years since he'd entertained the idea of more than one victim at a time. Not since the slumber party. Perhaps that had soured him. He hadn't had nearly as much fun as he should have. Ah, but he'd been angry then. Out of control. Not his usual self.

Since then, he'd never done more than one during a single kill. With one, he could concentrate on his work, make sure the details were perfect. But after doing the couple back in San Francisco, he'd kind of liked it. Of course there was risk when you challenged yourself with two, but the victory, the rush of blood, the slash of the knife, the tortured twist of their faces, was well worth it. Two for the price of one.

He kind of liked the sound of that.

Double the pleasure.

Double the fun.

He smiled to himself, remembered the old chewing-gum commercial. Of course, his idea of doubling the pleasure was probably a little different from what they'd intended. But pleasure was pleasure.

"Oh, that's nasty, honey," Melba cooed, her voice trailing into a fit of giggles. "Just the way I like it."

"And what else do you like?"

"I like it when you put it here. And here."

"And here?"

"Especially there," she assured Pinky. "Jesus, where did you learn that?"

"I was born knowing this, sweet thing."

Another commercial and the Andy Griffith tune whistled through the room.

Death stood at the window, excitement coursing through him. He puckered his lips, joining in with the tune.

"Did you hear that?" Melba's breathless voice asked.

Death clamped his lips together, stifling his anticipation.

"What?" Pinky asked

"I heard whistling."

"TV, sweet thing. Just the TV."

"Not that whistling. I heard a different whistling, higher."

"TV," Pinky said again; then his voice faded into a low, descriptive monotone of exactly what nasty things he wanted to do to her, the words obviously meant to distract her from anything and everything other than his seduction.

Death smiled to himself, his grip on the knife solid, despite the trembling in his fingers. Two for the price of one, a voice chanted inside his head as he leaned in and caught a glimpse of Pinky, and the woman, now naked, sitting astride his lap, her bare breasts brushing against his furry beer belly.

A wave of anger rolled through him, twisting, tugging at his rage.

Wicked. Sinful.

I've got beds to make.

Liars! All of them.

He held the knife tight, his other hand going to the doorknob. A soft turn and the bar clicked, opened.

A smile curved his lips as he pulled the door a half inch, then an inch. An inch and a half. Two inches . . .

Headlights flashed, tires spewed gravel, and a shiny red Ford pickup rolled into the parking lot.

"Get two rooms," the driver called to his buddy, who'd climbed out of the cab. "Your ass is too damn drunk, Clint. I'm putting you to bed; then I'm driving down to Wilda Mae's to find me a little company."

The man named Clint, a black Stetson resting at a lazy slant atop his head, black boots peeking from beneath the bottom of his black jeans, silver belt buckle gleaming, gave a crooked thumbs-up.

Letting go of the doorknob, Death shrank back into the shadows between the two buildings, the small space drawing him deeper into its protection.

The cowboy staggered by, shoved open the office door and let loose an excited whoop.

"Well damn, if this don't beat the band!"

A string of vicious curses followed, Pinky obviously upset at being interrupted, as well as several squeals from the maid as furniture squeaked and she scrambled for her clothing.

Death stood in the shadows, his fingers clenched around the knife. *Resist,* he silently chanted, the urge to lunge out, slice the cowboy's neck in two and feel the warm heat on *his skin nearly overwhelming. Then he could do Pinky and the maid. Three would be better than two.*

A bigger rush . . .

A foolish mistake, he quickly realized when the shiny Ford gave a loud honk, the noise followed by a "Hurry the hell up, will ya?" The motor revved, the smell of exhaust a keen reminder of the cowboy's buddy who waited in the truck, watching.

A witness, and he didn't like witnesses.

As badly as his hands shook, he forced himself to turn, to push deeper into the alleyway, away from Pinky and the maid, the cowboy, and the sweet, sweet promise of death.

So much work to do, but not tonight. Not now.

He rounded the back of the motel unit, to the window at the back of Pinky's kitchenette. Light pushed through the screen, casting a strange dot pattern on his hands. Death stared at the delicate fingers, the knife clenched so tight, so precious in his grasp.

Tighter, tighter, he held the handle until wood cut into his palm, sending a rush of frenzied pain to his brain. A small taste, but enough to sustain him for a little while.

For the moment.

With a deep sigh of regret, he forced his fingers open. He pulled the shirt over his head and wiped the handle free of any prints. He giggled. He was always so damned careful. So smart. Using the shirt to hold the clean knife, he reached through a small slice at the corner of the screen and placed the knife back down beside the package of bologna and loaf of bread where he'd retrieved it only minutes before. The sound of voices drifted from the front of the unit—Pinky's irritated clamor, the cowboy's slow Southern drawl. The maid was silent.

Probably embarrassed.

He wondered briefly whether or not she felt sorry for what she'd done. Ashamed.

If she didn't, she would. Soon. She would fall to her knees, beg forgiveness. Beg for her life.

Maybe he would grant her a few precious moments

more, time to feel the pain, to relish Death closing in on her. To see Death face-to-face.

To see the knife headed straight for her eyes, then the red haze of blood, then no more sight. Just feeling. Blood gushing from her eyes, drip-dropping on the floor like the spatter of sweet summer rain on a tin roof.

She would be sorry then. They all were when Death finished with them.

But then that was his job. To make them sorry. To make them pay for their sinful ways. He was Death, after all.

So much work to be done, and one particularly important job in front of him. Tossing the shirt over his shoulder, he clenched his fingers tight, driving the splinter even deeper until a drop of blood beaded on the skin.

With a flick of his tongue, he tasted the red heat, let the flavor linger on his tongue. Yes, a very sweet job, though it would have to wait a little longer—

The soft rustle of trash drew his attention. He turned to see a small black dog rummaging through the garbage from an overturned can in back of the adjoining unit. A red collar encircled the animal's neck. A silver heart-shaped tag dangled from the leather strap, catching glints of light from the bare bulb that flickered in the alleyway in back of the next unit.

He smiled, slipping his hand back in through the window to retrieve the knife.

Maybe he could get something done tonight after all.

Turning, he closed the distance to the fluffy black animal, knelt down and reached his hand out, the other clutching the knife.

The dog smelled the bologna and whimpered, inching a glistening black nose forward a few cautious inches. Closer, closer . . .

The movement was swift, not at all as slow as he would have liked. But time didn't permit any savoring beforehand. Not with so many people so close. God, he was smart, and fully in control of the fantasy.

Ah, but this wasn't fantasy. This was real. So precious and real.

Red heat rushed over his hands, filled his nostrils, and he drank in the scent. A few practiced movements of the knife and he relished the sight—empty, bloody eye sockets, red tears trailing down the furry face, the blood the same vivid crimson as the collar around the animal's neck.

Death reached out, caught a few delicious drops and touched them to his lips. Heaven . . .

Darby sat straight up, her gaze darting frantically. The motel room was dark, the only light pushing through the slats in the blinds to cast linear shadows on the floor in front of the window. A bitter taste filled her mouth and she scrambled to her feet, her terry robe tangled around her legs.

She flicked on the light in the bathroom, a bare bulb that exploded brilliant white light in the lime-tiled room. Leaning over the sink, she turned the knob on full force and shoveled handfuls of water into her mouth, desperate to rinse out the bitter taste.

Over and over, she spit and rinsed, but the taste was there on her tongue, as if it had seeped into her tastebuds and taken up residence. A bitter taste, like the god-awful buttermilk Reverend Masters used to make everyone drink at dinner, but sweeter. Bitter and sweet.

Her stomach swirled, heaved. What was left of her lunch at the diner ended up in the sink. She rinsed her mouth. Still bitter, but now more from the vomit. She splashed cold water onto her face, before sinking down to the toilet seat and holding a towel over her dripping face.

A dream. Just a horrible, nauseating dream.

No one had died. Not a person, anyway.

The dog's frenzied whines filled her ears and she clamped her hands over them.

Her trembling hands. She could still feel the warm rush of blood, not as intense as what she felt when the

113

victims were human, but intoxicating all the same—

No!

A dream. There was no dead body in this dream. Only a dead dog that wasn't really dead because this hadn't been real.

Or had it?

She stumbled to her feet and felt her way through the room, pausing a second to make sure her robe was belted before she pulled open the door.

She'd taken a hot shower, not even bothering to slip into a nightshirt. Just her panties and robe before she'd collapsed onto the bed. Her head had hurt so bad. Throbbed, to the point that she couldn't see straight anymore. Couldn't think.

Not about anything except a nice drink.

She pushed the craving away, focused on a mental picture of the DA's dead daughter in San Francisco, and reached for the doorknob. Outside, she rushed around the side of the building, into the back alley that ran behind the units.

No trash cans, not even a piece of crumpled paper anywhere. Still, she walked all the way down, until she knew she stood behind Pinky's front office. A quick glance at the shadowy ground—not a trace of blood anywhere—and relief swept through her. No dead animals.

No red heat seeping over her hands, warming her tongue.

Nothing.

She closed her eyes and slumped against one brick wall. What was happening to her? Was she really having some sort of weird psychic experience? Was she connecting with a killer, getting inside his head, seeing through his eyes, feeling what he felt, hearing his thoughts?

Not this time at least. She willed her eyes open and pushed away from the wall. There had been no killing this time. No dog in the alleyway, not a speck of blood.

Just a weird, macabre dream.

She headed back down the alleyway, her steps lighter, the taste in her mouth not as bad as before. Just a dream. Another nightmare—

Her thoughts scrambled to a halt when she heard the slow Alabama drawl drifting from a nearby window.

"I ain't drunk, I tell you."

"You're drunker than a skunk. Now shut up and hold your foot up so I can help you with your boots. Otherwise, baby brother, you're on your own."

"Yessir." The words slurred together and Darby's heart stalled in her chest for a long, breathless moment.

She knew the voice. She'd heard it before.

"What would I do without you, Hank?"

"Sleep with your boots on, you fool."

"That's all right. If I can screw with 'em on, I can damn well sleep with 'em on. . . ." The words faded and Darby knew Clint had passed out.

Clint.

She knew his name was Clint because she'd heard his voice before. Seen him staggering by her, smelled the rancid scent of beer and cheap aftershave seconds before she'd felt the dog's delicious heat spilling over her hands . . .

In her dream.

The knowledge sent her racing back to her hotel room. She couldn't know his name from a dream. Dreams weren't real. She'd seen Pinky and the maid, but she knew them. You could dream of people you knew, but not people you'd never met. Not a drunk cowboy who'd barged in on . . .

On what?

Death. The word echoed through her head and her hands started to shake. She stared at the bed, the rumpled covers, and knew she couldn't lie back down, couldn't risk having another dream or . . .

Or more than a dream. An actual experience.

No. Maybe she'd seen Clint and Hank somewhere before. Maybe that was why they'd turned up in her dream. Maybe it was merely coincidence.

Yes. Those were two possibilities that she couldn't—wouldn't—rule out.

Even so, she couldn't chance falling asleep again, not tonight. Not with death so fresh in her mind, filling her head, covering her hands.

Stop it.

Her gaze went longingly to the nearly empty bottle she'd pulled out of her suitcase earlier. Not even a quarter-inch of whiskey inside, certainly not enough to help. But there was also the tiny bottle of bourbon she'd stashed in her purse on the airplane. That would provide at least one or two drinks. Enough to help her put things into perspective.

Help her to think.

She reached for her purse, only to draw her hand away. *Get real.* That was exactly what the liquor wouldn't do. She wouldn't think; she'd lose herself in a drunken stupor. Forget.

Hell, she'd spent most of the past nine years forgetting. But it wasn't simply the bad stuff; it was the good stuff, as well. Major moments in her life. Her eyes blurred as she thought back to losing her virginity. She knew what night it had happened, how old she'd been, but she couldn't remember the act itself, what it had felt like, nor could she really remember the guy. Just a nameless, faceless somebody who'd picked her up.

And the forgetting didn't stop there. She'd lost most of the top moments in her life to a drunken haze. She'd been too numb to feel any excitement at landing her first job, renting her first apartment, winning an award for a great review of a local pub. All those precious memories had been drowned in bottle after bottle of liquor. She had nothing to look back on except an endless string of hangovers.

A tear slid from the corner of her eye and she dashed

it away. She wouldn't forget anymore. Good or bad, she would face whatever came her way.

For better or worse.

She shrugged out of her robe, slipped on jeans and a T-shirt, shoved her feet into boots and grabbed her purse. Minutes later, she left the motel room. As she turned, her attention was caught by Graham's pickup sitting next to her car. He was right next door now, probably watching her.

The knowledge sent a tremor up and down her spine. She could practically feel his gaze on her back as he waited to see what she would do next. Oddly enough, all she really wanted to do was bang on his door and throw herself into his arms the moment he answered. She wanted to bury her head in the warm crook of his neck and hide from herself, her thoughts, the damned dreams, the very same way she buried herself inside a bottle.

But just as she had to shake her addiction to the booze, she couldn't give in to the one thing she craved just as much as the liquor.

Tearing her gaze from his pickup, she climbed into her car and left the motel behind in a spew of gravel.

The truth about the slumber party waited in Samuel Blue's house, upstairs in the attic. Yet there was another truth that called to her.

Gripping the steering wheel, she stared down at her hands. Hands that could kill. Hands that *had* killed. There was no denying that. She'd picked up the knife, sunk it fast and sure and deep, felt the blood on her hands, seen death on someone's face.

Since she was in town to dig up her memories, to face who and what she was, she should start at the beginning. In the home where she'd grown up, watched her mother be beaten nearly every night, where she'd hid underneath her bed, desperate to escape the same fate.

The home that had never been much of a home, but a prison.

The place where she'd stabbed her father to death.

Chapter Nine

God will forgive you.

Reverend Masters's words echoed in Darby's head as she steered the car down the darkened streets of Nostalgia. It was a small, country town that rolled up the sidewalks at sunset. The stores were closed, the gas stations, the diner; even the Dairy Queen closed up shop at nine P.M. The only place you could find any action was out on the highway, at Wilda Mae's, a honky-tonk about a mile or so down I-45. Or Bobo's Truck Stop, a few miles further. Or Poppy's, a small icehouse just outside of town. Or out in the fields on any number of ranches, where the kids gathered to guzzle beer, toast marshmallows and make out.

She stared at the passing landscape, searching for any sign of a bonfire. Nothing but a velvet black plain that stretched in all directions. No spark of fire, no sign of civilization. It was Sunday night, after all. Hell, even J. J. Jackson, the town drunk and frequent visitor to the Nostalgia jail, kept himself in check on the Lord's day.

Nostalgia was as quiet, as peaceful as she remembered. And as smelly.

The scent of fertilizer drifted through her open windows, to twine around her like a noose, and she cranked up the window to trade the cool night air for the blast of the car's air conditioner. Still, the scent clung to the interior of the car, drifting through the vent cracks to renew her throbbing headache.

She opened her mouth, determined not to breathe through her nose, but the scent, so strong and pungent, burned her tongue, her throat. Real smart, she thought, as she clamped her lips shut and wished for a stiff shot of scotch, or bourbon, or whiskey, or even a damned soda to wash away the shitty taste. Another scent to distract her nose from the god-awful stench.

No two ways about it. It stank. Window up or down. Breathing through her nose or her mouth. It reeked. But then it always had out here on Farm Road 62. Right near her house.

She slowed the car, her gaze pushing through the darkness searching for the chicken-shaped mailbox.

As if it would still be there.

She searched anyway. That mailbox had always been the one thing to distinguish her house from the dozen or so others that lined the farm road. There were no street numbers, no streetlights, nothing but acres of grass and trees separating each house. Occasionally she spotted a jack-o'-lantern glowing from atop a fencepost, or a scarecrow with a pumpkin head. Everyone was gearing up for Halloween this Friday night.

The moment her headlights illuminated the faded white box, the chicken that sat on top, her heart skipped a beat.

Home.

Yet it wasn't her home. Not a real home. Linda had had a real home, with loving parents, a gorgeous older brother to look out for her.

A lot of good he had done. The thought flitted through

her mind and a pang of sympathy shot through her. Graham hadn't been able to protect his sister that night, any more than Darby had been able to protect her mother from her father's rage that cold lonely night so long ago.

The night she'd lost everything.

She slowed the car, searching for the driveway. A turn of the wheel, and she left the farm road behind for a narrow dirt driveway that wound for several yards to the small wood-frame house where Darby had spent her childhood.

The trees had overgrown, nearly obliterating the front of the two-story structure. She glimpsed vacant black holes where windows had once been, peeled wood where white paint had once gleamed. Abandoned.

The realization surprised her. At first.

She drove the car forward, leaving behind any glimpse of the road as she wound down the driveway, deeper into the cocoon of trees that surrounded the house. The car inched beneath an overhang of oak branches that scraped across the roof like nails on a chalkboard. A shiver worked its way up her spine. It was so dark. So vacant. Abandoned.

It shouldn't have surprised her one bit. Not considering what had happened here. Back in San Francisco, or New Jersey where she'd lived before that, or Washington before that, or Miami or Denver or Chicago before that, crime, particularly murder, was so widespread, it was impossible to abandon someplace just because someone had kicked the bucket there. The mess was cleaned up, maybe the carpet replaced, or the floors waxed, or whatever, and life continued.

But here in Nostalgia things were different. The crime rate was nearly nonexistent, and when something terrible happened, like murder, well, of course, the house was left to rot, the townsfolk afraid to drive by, much less go inside.

They thought if they ignored what had happened, it

would simply go away. The ugliness would fade and they could forget.

If only she could forget, she thought, pulling the car to a halt and killing the engine. She sat staring up at the empty house, goose bumps dancing along her skin.

She could forget. One long, slow, delightful drink and she could forget all about the night her parents had died. All about what she'd done. She clutched the steering wheel, ignoring the urge to turn the key, back out and head out to the highway, to Wilda Mae's or Poppy's for a drink. That would help her forget, all right.

But when morning followed and her head cleared, she would realize the lapse in memory had only been temporary.

Forcing herself out of the car, she walked onto the porch and tried the door. At first she thought it was locked, but then she remembered how the blasted thing had always stuck. Surely years would only make the hinges even rustier and harder to open.

Bracing herself, she shoved her hip up against the stubborn door and turned the knob at the same time. A low creak, and the wood gave, swinging back on its hinges with a grating whine.

Then she stepped inside, her eyes adjusting to the blacker-than-black darkness inside.

But she didn't need to see to find her way through the house. She knew it like the back of her hand, the layout burned into her memory, locked away like a map in the buried treasure chest of her brain. The knowledge was there in her head, just as the truth of what had happened here was imprinted on her soul. Nothing could erase it, change it. What was done was done. And she had to live with the consequences. The possibilities.

You're a killer, Darby. A cold-blooded killer . . .

She was. She knew that. Remembered all too vividly the feel of blood on her hands, the rasping sound of her father's last breath, the glazed sheen of death in his eyes.

God will forgive you.

The reverend had told her that over and over in the days that followed her parents' deaths, and she knew he spoke the truth. God would forgive her, if she asked. The thing was, Darby didn't want forgiveness, because she wasn't sorry.

Glad.

Relieved.

Disappointed that she hadn't done the deed sooner and saved her mother's life.

But not sorry, not for what she'd done that night so long ago . . .

"You call this well done?" Her father's booming voice carried up the stairs, to the second-floor bedroom where thirteen-year-old Darby sat on the floor playing solitaire. Quietly. Daddy liked quiet. He hated noise, and Darby was always careful not to do anything Daddy hated.

Not that her effort made much difference. No matter how perfect things were, how hard she and her mother tried, he always seemed to find something to hate.

"It's been cooking for over an hour." Her mother's voice was small, as always, and Darby had to strain to hear it.

"It's walking, for Chrissake!" Her father's voice cracked through the house like a bolt of thunder. A shudder went through Darby and her hands went numb. The cards fell in a pile to the hardwood floor.

"I cooked it longer than all the others," her mother said, her voice louder as Darby crept down the staircase. "Really, Vince. I did. There isn't an inch of pink anywhere."

"Are you blind, bitch? Look right there!" Dishes clanged, shattered, and her mother's gasp reverberated through the house, shaking the walls, shaking Darby as she cleared the last step.

Light flooded out from the open kitchen doorway at the end of the hallway, outlining two distinct shadows, one much smaller than the other.

"Please, Vince. Calm down. I'll cook it longer. As long as you want."

122

The large shadow dominated the doorway, one big arm clutching a plate. The smaller shadow cowered in front of him.

"Can't you ever do anything I say, woman?" The large arm clutching the plate held it high and aimed.

"No, Vince. That's one of my mama's plates."

"This cheap thing? It figures," he muttered. The larger shadow twisted. The plate sailed through the air, crashed against the far wall.

"No," her mother begged as the large shadow moved deeper into the room, headed for the kitchen cabinets.

Darby inched closer, her back flat against the wall, her nerves trembling. She should turn, run, hide in her closet as she'd done so many times, but she couldn't. Her mother's voice, so small and frightened, so achingly familiar, kept her rooted to the spot, listening, watching the play of shadows in the pool of light.

"That mother of yours never could cook an edible meal." The word edible *came out more like* audible, *a slur lacing the other words. Her gaze darted back down the hallway where it opened up into the living room. A television set cast dancing colors across the room, reflecting off the brown glass of the bottle sitting on the table beside her father's recliner. Only an inch of liquid left inside, and it had been full earlier today. She'd seen it in the cabinet herself. Seen it, and resisted the urge to yank it out and pour it into the toilet.*

Fear had kept her from doing anything, just as fear kept her plastered to the hallway wall, afraid to run for fear her mother might need her, afraid to rush to her mother's aid for fear she'd feel her father's fist on her cheek, his belt on her legs, his eyes on her small, aching breasts beneath her thin cotton nightgown.

"Just a couple of lazy bitches, the both of you," he raged on. Cabinet doors flew open. More dishes shattered. "Don't know why she even passed these things on to you. You can't even cook a decent steak to put on 'em." The words slurred together, the sound sending shivers up and down

Darby's spine, dread churning fast and furious in her stomach.

"Please stop, Vince. Please." The smaller shadow fell to her knees in front of him. "This is all I have left of her," came the small cry as frantic arms tried to gather the broken pieces littering the floor. "All I have of my mama."

"Leave it and fix me something to eat, woman!"

"But I did," she cried, gathering up pieces. "I already did."

"Something else, dammit," he said, an unmistakable threat in his voice. "Something cooked right."

"Yes," she said, still gathering pieces. "Yes, I will. Just a minute—"

"Now," he boomed, delivering a vicious kick to her kneeling form.

The smaller shadow sprawled out with a whimper and Darby froze, her heart pounding furiously, anger screaming in her head, urging her to do something. Anything.

"Okay, Vince," came her mother's pained voice. "Just let me get these first." She got to her knees, her arms still clutching pieces of broken dishes.

"Dammit, I said now! Don't you know what now means, bitch? Am I going to have to teach you what now means?"

"No, no," she said with a sob. "Please just let me get the rest of these. . . ." The sentence trailed off into a cry as the larger shadow delivered another kick, and another.

"Now," he shouted, slamming his booted foot into her again. "I said now, now, now—"

"Stop it!" Darby cried, the words releasing her from the paralysis holding her body tight. She flew into the room just as her father's head shot up, his boot aimed for another kick.

Things seemed to move in slow motion then. Darby saw the shiny toe of his polished cowboy boot, saw her mother's fear-filled eyes; then her mother's head jerked to the side, the tip of the boot smashing against the side of her skull.

THE HOMECOMING

The sound echoed in Darby's head, drowning out the sound of her own scream.

"Stupid bitch," her father grumbled once more, before turning away, reaching into the refrigerator and dragging out a six-pack of beer.

Darby sank to her knees beside her mother's broken body. "Mama?" Her voice was a shocked prayer. "Mama, are you all right?" She touched her mother's shoulder, nudged her. Still. So very still.

"Get on up to your room," her father said, popping the top of his beer can and guzzling the contents, as if by consuming the beer, he could make it consume him, take him away from all this, make everything right.

But nothing would ever be right again.

"She's hurt." But Darby had the terrible, terrible feeling her mother was more than hurt. She was dying.

"She's fine." He tossed the empty can at her. It hit the hardwood floor, rolled. "She'll be up and about, giving me hell and screwing up my dinner like always, the worthless piece of—"

"She isn't fine." Her voice was high-pitched, frantic. She could hear herself, but she had no control over the words flying out of her mouth. If she had, she would have stopped them, heeded the warning that flashed in her father's alcohol-glazed eyes as he glanced at her, before turning his attention back to the next can of beer.

"Look at her," she pleaded, desperate to drag his attention away from the beer. "She isn't fine. She's bleeding. She isn't moving. Oh, my God, she's . . ." She didn't want to say it. Think it.

Instead, she simply held her mother, felt her warmth slowly seep away, degree by precious degree.

"Fix me something to eat," her father finally grumbled, as if he hadn't heard a word she'd just said. "Now," he added before chugging the second beer. Gold liquid dribbled from his mouth, trailing down his chin to drip-drop silently onto the hardwood floor, while her mother's life seeped out onto that same floor in a steady pool of red heat.

"Now!" he roared as he dropped the empty can into the sink. Darby didn't budge. She couldn't let go of her mother, couldn't let her slip away for good this time.

"Are you deaf, girl? Cain't you hear?" He reached out, gripped her upper arm and hauled her to her feet. His cold and clammy hand lingered a little too long. "Just as lazy as that bitch of a mother of yours." He yanked her around and shoved her against the stove, where the frying pan sat over a medium-burning fire, the sound of potatoes cooking sizzling through the air. "Now get to work and make damn sure it's well done this time."

She tried to turn, to raise her arms, to do what he said because she knew that if she didn't, she would wind up on the floor next to her mother.

Tears slipped from her eyes, slid hotly down her cheeks, her gaze riveted on her mother's closed eyes, a few broken pieces of her precious dishes clutched in bleeding hands.

"Didn't you hear me, girl?" Her father turned on her, staggered closer.

She backed up, the stove coming up hard against her back. Her arm bumped the frying pan handle, the skillet jumped, a little grease sloshing over the side. Flames sparked and Darby jumped.

"Or maybe you got dessert on your mind?" He smiled then, the coldest smile she'd ever seen, and she shivered. "Is that it? You up for a little something sweet, Sugar?" He licked his lips and she knew what was coming. She'd lived this moment in her nightmares, fueled by the lingering glances since she'd started to develop, the looks that made her skin crawl and her stomach feel funny.

At that moment, she would have traded anything to feel his fist on her face, the same as she'd felt it so many times before. Like the night before last when she'd failed to bring him a beer right away because she'd stopped to help her mother unscrew the lid to a jar of pickles. Or the week before when she'd stared at his soiled undershirt a little too long and he'd given her a black eye for being a smart-ass.

But tonight was different. Tonight he had more on his

mind than a few punches. She tried to tear her gaze away from his lips. She needed to bolt, to run. Her mother wasn't there to plead with him, distract him from doing whatever he pleased.

She was unconscious. Near death.

More tears slipped from her cheeks as she finally tore her gaze away from her father. She stared at her mother, her slack features, the blood pooling near her head.

"Don't look at her. Look at me, bitch! Me!" He thumped a fist against his chest. "You ain't gettin' out of here in one piece, you know that, don't you?"

"Please." She forced the word out through tight throat muscles.

"Please?" He smiled. "I like the sound of that. Yes, I surely do. Please, with sugar on top." His gaze drilled into hers. "You know I been lookin' at you, don't you? Yeah, I been lookin' at your sweet little body, Sugar, and I think I might be obliged to show some mercy, on one condition. . . ." One free hand dropped to stroke his bulging crotch. "Yeah, one great big condition. You serve me up a little dessert, with plenty of sugar on top." He reached for her and she slapped him away.

One condition. *One* great, big condition.

The words pounded through her head as he grabbed and poked and touched. Fear and anger swirled together in a frenzy that had her slapping, squirming, struggling, scratching.

Flesh ripped and she saw the bright red lines on his cheek, the blood dripping down his unshaven jaw.

"Goddammit!"

Her gaze collided with his and that was when she saw it. Gone was the lust that made her skin crawl. Instead, his red-rimmed eyes were filled with a coldness. A fierce, gleaming coldness, the same gleam she'd seen in his eyes when he'd kicked her mother. Over and over.

He reached for her. His hands grasped her throat. Darby gasped for air, her arms flailing wildly, fingers clutching the cabinet, searching, desperate. . . .

"Bitch!" The fingers grew tighter, blackness swam and she felt herself sinking into nothingness where her mother already waited. Lifeless eyes beckoned her forward, her mother's twisted and bleeding body urging her home.

She scrambled for something, anything, her fingers finally closing around the cool wood.

"Good for nothing—" Her father's voice faltered in mid-sentence. Fingers loosened from around her neck and he stumbled backward a few steps, a stunned look on his face.

He stared down at the dark red stain spreading across his soiled undershirt, then at the knife clutched in Darby's hands.

"Bitch!" he roared, reaching for her again.

She shoved the knife between them, the blade sinking fast and deep into his chest. He gasped, opened his mouth as if to call her another name. Instead, blood spurted from between his lips, dribbling down his chin the same way the beer had only moments ago.

He stumbled backward, collapsing on the table. Legs splintered, wood creaked and the table crumpled beneath his weight. He crashed to the floor, so close to her mother, arms and legs sprawled. Blood seeped from the knife sticking out of his chest.

Gasping for air, Darby sank to her knees. She grappled for her mother's hand, relaxing some when she found the limp fingers still warm. Tears burned her throat, her eyes; grief gripped her.

But there was something else, as well.

Relief.

She stared at her mother's twisted body, then down at her own hands. Her fingers were sticky with her father's blood, and she felt no sorrow, no regret, nothing but victory for what she'd just done. The hateful bastard was dead. Finally.

But not soon enough, she realized. Blood seeped from the side of her mother's head where her father's boot had landed, a bruise from two nights ago still visible on her left cheek.

Not nearly soon enough.

THE HOMECOMING

*   *   *

Darby found herself sitting on the bottom step of the staircase, inches away from the spot where her mother had lain, her blood and life seeping away. The blow to her head had rendered her unconscious, causing a severe hematoma that had put her into a coma and killed her two days later in a lonely hospital bed while Darby sat at her side, pleading and praying.

All for nothing.

Someone had scrubbed the blood away, her mother's and her father's, removing all traces of the death. Nothing for the eye to see.

Yet Darby could see.

After retrieving a small flashlight from the glove compartment of the car, she walked through the house, seeing death in every corner.

In the form of an old magazine rack, now coated with layers of dust. In her mind's eye she could see her father pick up the rack, aim it at her mother, leaving a bloody red welt across her cheek, busting her nose.

In her parents' bedroom upstairs, where the mattress lay bare and stained, the metal headboard still dented where her father had beaten her mother's head against it several times and given her a concussion.

In the bathroom mirror, the glass cracked where her father had smashed her mother's face, crushed her cheekbone on the left side, a wound that had taken weeks to heal, not that her mother's face had ever been the same. Her cheek had sunk in after that, a small indentation the size of Darby's thumbprint.

Jagged cracks snaked across the mirror, distorting Darby's image as she stared at her reflection, seeing bits and pieces of herself, but not a complete whole. As if she were scattered, separated into distinct pieces that needed to be fit together.

And one piece was missing.

She knew what she was capable of. She lived with that knowledge every day, with the memory of her mother broken and bleeding, with the memory of the satisfied rush as she'd stared at her father's dying form and said good-bye. Good riddance.

But had that one incident been enough to turn her into something monstrous? Had that one letting of blood made her crave more? Had it unlocked some dark, obscene part of her?

Or was she merely psychic?

She'd never believed in such things, even when Rudy had told her about Jan's friend. But maybe so. She hoped so. Finding out that the supernatural did indeed exist would certainly be preferable to the other alternative.

That she hadn't merely witnessed the slumber-party killings, but actually committed them.

She walked out onto the front porch and sat down. Crickets chirped their night's melody, joining with creaks and buzzes and other sounds that made her hug her waist.

Of course, it was certainly possible the dreams were nothing more than that. Just wild and crazy dreams.

That she could certainly deal with, she decided, and that was what she would think until she remembered the slumber party.

She stared at the twin pools of light glaring back at her and thought of Graham Tucker. Had he followed her out here? She'd thought she'd seen headlights behind her.

The possibility sent tremors dancing along her nerve endings.

Her thoughts staggered to a halt as she stared down at her hands, at the slightly swollen area at the tip of her finger. She bolted to her feet, rushing toward one headlight.

Standing right in front, she held up her finger, fear and dread churning into a horrible mix as she stared at the small splinter embedded deep into her skin.

She closed her eyes as memories rushed at her, Pinky's

moans and groans, the knife gripped in her hand, the wooden windowsill where the sliver of wood had worked its way into her flesh.

Into the killer's flesh.

Chapter Ten

Panic crashed over Darby like a giant tidal wave swallowing a weatherworn pier. She clutched her finger, feeling the steady ache every time she pressed the tender flesh and urged the sliver of wood deeper. The feeling was so familiar.

She pushed down on the skin and a small rush of pain splintered her brain. She gasped, then scrambled to open the car door.

Killer, killer, killer. The word repeated in her brain and she retrieved her purse, dumped the contents on the seat and rummaged around for the tiny liquor bottle she'd swiped from the plane. Just one drink. One tiny little drink and she could face this, deal with it—

Her thoughts crashed as her hands clutched the bottle and her mind traveled back. . . .

To the kitchen where her mother lay sprawled in blood.

"She's fine," her father said, reaching for the beer, his thoughts centered on getting the booze from the can into

his mouth as fast as possible. So he wouldn't have to see her mother lying there. Wouldn't have to see the blood, smell the death, acknowledge what he'd just done. So he wouldn't have to deal with reality.

Disgust swept through her, settling into her stomach and making her sink to her knees in the open doorway of the car. She was just like him. Just like the cold, hateful bastard who'd called himself her father. He hadn't turned to the alcohol to deal with his problems, but to ignore them.

The liquor could keep him from feeling. He could go numb, ignore reality and his responsibilities.

But it was different for her. She enjoyed drinking. She liked everything about it. The sounds—the slide of the cork, the glug-glug of liquor meeting the glass. The taste—the sweet hint of sugar in a really good wine, the faint bitterness of a beer, the strong bite of a bottle of Johnnie Walker Black. The way the booze made her feel—relaxed, at ease, ready to face any- and everything. She wasn't her father. The drinking was different for her. *Different.*

Even as denial raged fast and furious inside her, she knew the truth. The liquor wasn't a coping mechanism. It was an escape, pure and simple. It sent her spiraling into another world, one where problems didn't exist, where peace and harmony reigned, always eager to welcome her with that first long drink.

The peace and harmony were merely an illusion, however. A facade. She didn't really feel relaxed or happy, or anything. She was numb. No feeling. No thoughts. Nothing.

Oblivion.

Her hand started to tremble, the bottle warm between her fingers, inviting, yet for the first time she didn't feel the urge to unscrew the cap and drink as much as she could, as fast as she could.

Her father's image stayed rooted in her mind. The can at his lips, beer dribbling from the corners of his mouth, down his chin to drip and mingle with her mother's blood.

Her father.

She'd denied him for so long, not wanting to think that such a monster could possibly be related to her, yet he was. He was her father, she his daughter. Worse, she was just like him. A chip off the old alcoholic block.

The knowledge made her feel sick inside, in her stomach and in her heart. She'd hated her father for so long because he'd buried himself in a liquor bottle. The drink had made him even meaner and more hateful than he'd been sober, and she'd hated him then, too. But what she felt for him couldn't compete with what she felt for herself at that moment.

Disgust, revulsion, bitterness . . .

She tossed the bottle several feet away and watched as the liquor seeped out, turning the dust into a puddle of muck.

Pain filled her as she rested her head on the edge of the seat and thought of her mother. For the first time, Darby didn't run away, into an alcoholic haze, eager to escape. She welcomed the feeling, embraced it because she could do nothing else. No escape this time.

Not this time.

She wasn't her father.

Her father would have run from this, drowned his problems at the nearest bar, but she wouldn't do that. She was here to see things through, to find the truth, and she couldn't do that if she was stumbling around in a blind stupor. Not feeling. Certainly not thinking.

She forced herself into the car, her heart thumping a painful rhythm in her chest. It hurt to breathe, to move, yet she managed both, drawing strength from someplace she'd never known existed inside her. At least not without a good solid bottle of booze in her hand.

Darby had never been strong in her own right.

She'd been just like her father, molded and shaped by the man himself. Conditioned, as any shrink would have said. The product of an alcoholic and abusive parent.

A chip off the old block.

A killer . . .

Her gaze went to her finger as she steered the car back onto the main road. The proof stared back at her.

But proof of what?

She'd dreamed of spying on Pinky and the maid, of clutching a knife and waiting at the window where she'd gotten the splinter. Of slaughtering a poor dog in the alleyway.

But she'd been in the alley herself and hadn't seen a trace of blood. And other than the poor, crying animal, no killing had taken place. Not in this dream.

Her finger now throbbed with awareness, to the same steady tempo as her aching head. The same relentless question beat at her brain, demanding an answer she didn't have. What was she?

Dreamer?

Psychic?

Killer?

She shoved a CD into the player, cranked the music up and rolled down the windows despite the stench that surrounded her from the fertilized fields. The smell was worth the wind whipping at her hair, her face, stinging.

Penance, a small voice whispered from somewhere deep inside. From that part of her that knew so much, while her conscience knew so little.

Not anymore. Not after tonight.

She headed for Samuel Blue's house, desperation building inside her, filling her with an anxiousness that wouldn't be satisfied until she'd answered that burning question. Tonight. Before she lost her nerve, drove to the nearest bar and drank her fill.

Tonight. Now.

Even if she had to climb the fence, sneak past the security guard and break a window, she was going in.

* * *

That was exactly what she would have to do, she realized a good ten minutes later as she parked several feet down the road from the house. The front yard was brightly lit with a floodlight.

Climbing from the car, she clung to the shadows of the trees, her gaze riveted on the uniformed man walking the perimeter. She studied him, the long, slow stride back and forth in front of the house. A walkie-talkie slapped one hip with each step, a holstered gun on the other.

She almost lost her nerve, but then her gaze collided with the attic window. The black square called to her, promising the truth, promising freedom from the dreams that haunted her.

She circled the fence and walked around the house until she was out of sight of the guard. The fence proved easy work. She was small, her hands fitting in the chain links with ease. She snagged her jeans going over the top, feeling a streak of heat against her thigh, but then she was over, the pain lost in the anticipation of being on the inside. So close. So very close.

She shot across the yard toward the back porch, her gaze darting frantically as she searched for some sign that she'd been spotted. The light back here wasn't as bright. The shadows encouraged her, embraced her. She reached the back door without incident. Of course it was locked, and the window beside it was boarded up. Without a hammer or something to pry the nails loose, she didn't have an ice cube's chance in hell of getting inside.

Damn.

". . . all's quiet out here." The security guard's voice drifted to her, closer than it should have been, and she froze.

Panic charged her. He was coming. He'd seen her!

". . . lunch in about an hour." He laughed, the sound a tad softer, as if he'd taken a few steps in the opposite direction. "No, no, you're good company, Stan. Don't know what I'd do without this radio. It would be awful lonely out here without you."

She realized he was talking on his walkie-talkie and relief swept her. Short-lived, however. His voice was closer now, as if he'd headed around the side of the house rather than out front. Was he walking her way, coming around the back while she stood there panicking?

She slid silently around the opposite corner, to the other side of the house, and found a window that wasn't boarded up. Common sense told her to run. The security guard was walking the perimeter. She didn't have the time.

Yet she was so close.

With a fierce push of the window the glass slid up a fraction. Victory surged through her, quickly dispelled when she felt the icy draft snake through the inch of space to wrap around her like cold tentacles. Like her father's cold, clammy hands.

The sensation circled her neck, squeezed.

She clutched at the windowsill, desperate to hold herself steady, but at the same time, the sensation forced her away from the window and the small open inch of space. Darby stumbled backward. She lashed out, swinging her fists, fighting, but there was no attacker to fend off. Nothing save a cold draft of air and invisible, relentless fingers that refused to let her loose.

And a blackness that quickly swallowed her whole.

"What the hell . . . ?" Graham gripped the fence, squinted through the darkness at Darby's struggling figure, partially obscured by the shadows clustered at the back of the house. She moved backward, struggling, out into the moonlit backyard.

He saw her swing wildly, fighting . . . fighting what?

Just as the question voiced itself, she went down, flat on her back, knocked out cold.

The moon waxed full and silver above, enough for him to see that no one was with her. Hell, he could even make out her features.

Her eyes were closed, face passive, chest rising and

falling from her exertion a moment before.

Drugs, he thought. Schizophrenia. He'd seen it all in his eight years with the Dallas Police Department. But nothing quite like this.

Her eyes had been clear this afternoon, not those of a druggie. And she'd appeared stable enough, though he wasn't ready to dismiss the schizo theory yet.

Then what?

He gripped the fence, ready to climb over and find out exactly what was going on. At that moment the security guard came around the corner, his flashlight beam slicing through the darkness, to zero in on Darby.

Graham started to climb, only to stop after the first few steps when Darby lifted her head.

"What are you doing back here?" the guard demanded.

"I . . ." Her voice faltered for just a moment, a dazed expression on her face. She looked just as she had that afternoon—confused, scared, vulnerable.

Then something happened. A calmness seemed to settle over her, to take charge, and she smiled up into the flashlight beam. An enticing smile.

Dammit, she was a killer, he told himself. A killer. He knew that. The trouble was that his body wasn't responding to the killer, but to the woman.

Undoubtedly she had the same effect on the guard, because Graham was pretty damn sure it wasn't the flimsy explanation she gave in the next few breaths that kept the guard from calling the police and charging her with trespassing.

"I—you caught me," she blurted, giving the guard a sheepish smile. She climbed to her feet, dusted off the seat of her jeans and stepped toward him, despite his ready-for-trouble stance.

"I'll ask you again, lady. What are you doing back here?"

"My curiosity just got the better of me. I know it isn't much of an excuse, but it's all I've got." Her smile was disarming, brilliant, even more so in the direct beam of light.

The security guard glared a moment; then his expression softened. "At least you told the truth. You wouldn't believe some of the stories those high school kids have been telling me." A chuckle passed the guard's lips and he seemed to relax. His arm dropped to his side. The flashlight beam focused on the ground, encircling their legs in a small pool of light. "The last two boys I caught out here claimed they were stargazing."

She glanced up at the sky. "I love the stars, myself. So tiny and sparkling. Like a sky full of diamonds." She fixed her gaze on him. "So romantic."

The guard smiled. "Yeah," he quickly agreed. "My wife says the same thing."

"Wife? That's too bad," she purred.

She smiled, her teeth a flash of white in the dim light. She really knew how to lay it on thick. The guard seemed entranced for a long moment before finding his composure. "It's been nice talking to you and all, but you really shouldn't be back here."

She glanced around and shrugged. "Oh, well, so much for reliving old memories."

"You're from around here?"

"Sure am. I used to stand right here in this spot." She stared around her, as if searching for something, then moved a few inches closer to the guard. "Yes, right here. I would stand and gaze up at the stars for hours. Those high school kids might have been snowing you, but they were right about this being a perfect spot for stargazing. Why, on a night like this, you can even see the Little Dipper."

The security guard tilted his head back and gazed up. "Yeah, I guess it is pretty good from right here. The Little Dipper, you say?"

"Uh-huh. Right there to the left." She pointed. "See it?"

Little Dipper, my ass, Graham thought, glancing at the multitude of twinkling stars. And he was next in line for the department's Mr. Congeniality title. There might be a pretty decent view, but there was no Little Dipper. He remembered enough from his college astronomy courses to know what the damned Dipper looked like, and this wasn't it.

"Can you see it?"

The guard gazed a second longer. "Yeah, I think so. Yeah." He nodded eagerly. "Yeah, I can." He smiled, then nodded toward the house. "But I'm afraid you'll have to leave. Visitors are prohibited and the TV station will have my hide if they find anybody here."

"No problem. I was just curious. Just looking, walking down memory lane, you know." She actually looked concerned. "I don't get home very much these days and this place holds so many memories."

I bet, Graham thought.

"No harm done," the guard replied. "Just don't let it happen again. After the thirty-first, this place will be open to the public. They're gonna open some kind of killer museum or something. You can visit as often as you like."

"I'll remember that."

"Where's your car?"

"Down the road."

"Well, follow me around front and I'll let you out the gate."

She cast another long gaze at him. "Handsome and helpful. Your wife is a very lucky woman."

"That's what I keep telling her," he said, smiling as Darby took his arm so he could lead her back around the house.

Graham stood in stunned silence for a long moment, disgusted and shocked and totally pissed at what he'd just witnessed.

She'd actually tried a little breaking and entering, been caught red-handed, and now she was getting an armed escort to the front gate.

Is there any friggin' justice left in the world?

Yes, he told himself. There was justice and he would see that Darby Jayson got hers in the end.

The promise brought an unbidden image to mind—Darby's curvaceous backside beneath him, his fingers pressing into her soft skin, his cock pushing slow and deep—

He slammed his mind shut to the thought. He couldn't get sidetracked by his own lust this time. He wouldn't.

Sprinting for his truck, he climbed into the cab just as Darby appeared at the front gate several yards away from where he'd parked. He watched as she said good-bye to the guard and walked to her parked car, a little way ahead of his own.

All the while, he tried to sort through what he'd just witnessed. Not so much her snow job of the guard. She was a good liar. Hell, he already knew that. He was more interested in what had happened to her at the window, and, more important, why she'd been about to break and enter in the first place.

His mind traveled back to their conversation earlier that day when he'd told her about the live walk-through the television station intended to do.

"Do you think they'll find anything?"

Her words echoed in his mind and reality crashed down around him. She was worried they would find something. Some evidence overlooked by the police. She'd come out here, climbed the fence, tried to go in the window.

To cover her tracks?

To hide her guilt?

To remember. The thought pushed into his head before he could stop it. Maybe there was something to her amnesia story. Maybe she really didn't remember. Maybe—

No. She was guilty. The fact that she was alive and breathing, coupled with the failed lie-detector test, proved it.

His gut instinct confirmed it.

His guilty conscience prayed for it.

Darby Jayson was going to get hers. Soon.

The only thing he didn't understand was what had stopped her. She'd collapsed before the guard had rounded the corner, before she'd been discovered. Why hadn't she gone into the house?

That question niggled at his brain as he followed her back to the motel, watched her walk into her room, shut the door behind her.

He watched her silhouette on the closed shades. She slipped the shirt over her head, pushed the jeans down her legs. For a long moment he simply stared, struck by the fierceness of his want for her.

Her, of all people.

It only confirmed what an asshole he was. If she really was a killer—no, *because* she was a killer—he should fear her. Despise her. Anything but lust after her—the very woman responsible for his sister's death. Or at the very least, connected, deeply connected, to the one who was, indeed, responsible.

Disgusted with himself, he stalked toward his motel room, right next to hers. He flung open the door and stomped inside. Shrugging out of his shirt, he opened the drapes, pulled a chair up to the front window and collapsed, boots propped up on the air conditioner. His gaze fixed on the porch right outside where her car sat alongside his truck.

If she tried to leave again, he would see her, just as he had the first time.

He sat there, watching June bugs bump into the light-bulb hanging outside his door. He hated stakeouts, but he hated this one even more because he was anxious.

Anxious to catch her, to see her locked up, punished for his sister's death.

Anxious to make amends, to find peace, to gain forgiveness for his sister's death. For as much as he wanted to blame the killer, he was really the one responsible. He'd left Linda there that night. Left her to die.

He closed his eyes, seeing her mutilated body rolling

out on the gurney. The last time he'd ever set eyes on his sister. The funeral had been closed casket, her picture sitting atop.

But the picture had done nothing to replace the image in his head—her face obliterated, her eyes empty, bloody holes. The image stayed with him, reminding him what a bastard he was, what a failure.

And he hungered all the more for justice.

For vengeance.

Chapter Eleven

Blackness consumed Darby. Heavy. Thick. Impenetrable.

She fought to wake up. Somewhere deep inside her, she knew she had to open her eyes, so she tried.

And failed.

Smothered.

That was what she felt like. And that was the strange thing. She *felt*, as if she wasn't really asleep but stuck in some dark cave with no way out.

No light. Nothing to see.

Yet her other senses were alive. The stale odor of mothballs and disinfectant filled her nostrils with each deep, frantic breath. A steady *chug chug* echoed in her head. Cool air whispered across her skin, turning it to gooseflesh.

She couldn't be asleep.

Could she?

She fought against the blackness, to escape, or wake up, or both. Then it seemed as if someone stood over her, hands lifting the veils of darkness until she managed to pry open her eyes.

She expected to see the window, to find herself on the back porch of Samuel Blue's house. The sight that met her eyes stole her breath away.

Her gaze touched the scarred dresser, the rotary-dial phone, the dingy orange curtains, the window unit grinding out a steady stream of icy air. The hideous motel room. She was back at the Tropicana.

Abruptly, she sat up, the bright orange coverlet balled around her ankles. She stared down at the panties she wore. Only panties. The rest of her clothes lay in a heap beside the bed. The steady tick-tock of the clock drew her attention. Five-thirty.

Five-thirty A.M.

But it had been three A.M. when she'd driven up to Samuel Blue's house. When she'd climbed the fence, lifted the window, gripped the sill. When she . . .

Nothing.

Her mind was blank after that. She remembered the darkness, the frantic thought that she was being strangled by someone.

But how had she gotten here in bed? And when?

She rifled through her mind, searching for something that would make sense out of everything. What had happened once she'd opened the window? Why couldn't she remember it?

The last two hours were a blank, a void just like those bloody few minutes during the slumber party. She remembered nothing.

Yet three people had died right in front of her that Halloween night.

And last night?

No one had died. Only the dog, and that *had* been a dream. She'd searched the alley, found nothing.

That did little to ease her anxiety, however. She'd lost two and a half hours. *Two entire hours*.

Her hands trembled and her gaze shot to the nearly

empty bottle sitting on the dresser. But as she stared at the Johnnie Walker, she saw her father's face, his glazed eyes, and her stomach did a somersault.

Scrambling from the bed, she hit the bathroom just as the first wave of nausea slammed into her. She dropped to her knees and leaned over the toilet, but nothing came out. Just dry heaves gripping her muscles, spasming through her body until every bone ached.

Several minutes later, she hauled herself up to the sink. She splashed water onto her face before attacking the splinter. With shaky fingers, she squeezed and squeezed, until blood drip-dropped into the basin and she'd forced the sliver of wood free from her skin.

She watched the splinter disappear down the drain, along with the pink water as she held her hand beneath the faucet. Her finger throbbed, but she ignored the sensation, just as she did her damnedest to ignore the nick on her other finger where the killer had trailed his knife. . . .

No! Coincidence, she told herself. There had to be a reasonable explanation. Most likely a paper cut. An innocent accident, just like the splinter. She could have picked up the sliver of wood anywhere last night. At her old house. At Samuel Blue's when she'd gripped the windowsill. No, she'd had the splinter before then. When she'd been reliving the past at her old home.

She could have gotten it there, she deduced. When she'd opened the front door, touched the wooden banister to go upstairs. The splinter wasn't proof of anything.

And the blackout? More than two hours of unaccounted-for time where she could have been doing anything.

Killing . . .

If so, she would face the consequences later, after she remembered the slumber party. She just had to hold it together until then.

A tremor wrenched through her and her hands started to shake so badly, water sloshed onto the floor, droplets catching on the bare skin of her legs, gliding down to pool near her feet.

She caught a glimpse of her pale face in the mirror, her wide, frightened eyes, and for a second she could have sworn she was back in her house, thirteen years old and terrified, listening to her father's shouting, his footsteps moving closer to her, his threats pounding through her skull.

Terrified.

Her stomach spasmed, her shoulders quaked with the dry heaves that gripped her. Gasping for a deep breath, she forced the feelings away and gripped the edge of the sink as if it were a lifeline and she was drowning.

She was. She was drowning in her own fear, going under—

She had to calm down. She wouldn't get anywhere if she wound up a hysterical mess right there on the dingy tile floor.

Control.

The word echoed through her brain, forcing the rest of her to listen. She pushed everything away—last night, the throbbing in her finger from the splinter, the questions, the worry.

After several minutes, her heartbeat slowed. Her breathing came easier. The tightness in her chest eased and her stomach settled.

Now she needed a course of action.

She went back into the bedroom and sank down on the edge of the bed. The cool air swirled around her, chilling her body as she simply sat there breathing.

In. Out. In. Out.

Her stomach grumbled and she leaned against the headboard. Hungry. The feeling, so basic, so instinctive, so *normal*, brought a hysterical laugh to her lips.

She was thin, too thin, her boss, Vivian, had told her more times than she could count. But she'd never been into food, never dreamed of the taste, of sinking her teeth into a chocolate fudge brownie, or savoring a double-cheese pizza with all the trimmings.

Now, if that pizza had been one hundred proof, maybe . . .

Food had never ruled her like the booze. She'd never had to watch her weight, other than to make sure she didn't waste away. Toast and coffee for breakfast, whatever for lunch, and maybe some dinner.

She wasn't exactly sure what she usually had for dinner, other than a couple of scotches on the rocks. After that, she could have been eating mud pies, for all she knew.

This morning was different.

Despite the fear and dread she'd felt only moments ago, an odd sense of self-satisfaction now curled through her at the realization of what she'd done last night.

She'd resisted the bottle, opened her soul to the past, to the memories of her father's death she'd tried so hard to forget.

The feel of the knife in her hands.

The feel of the blood dripping between her fingers.

She'd faced those images—her mother's broken body as it heaved its last breath, her father's red-rimmed, liquor-glazed eyes—and they'd frightened the shit out of her, but not enough to send her running to the bottle. Not this time.

A smile tugged at her lips and for the first time, Darby felt a surge of victory, however small. She went to the closet and rummaged around for some jeans and a T-shirt, desperate to get dressed and get back to work before she lost her courage and reality overwhelmed her again.

She couldn't dwell on splinters and cuts and blackouts.

She had a slumber party to remember. Then she could face herself, and the truth, whatever it might be, and the consequences. A nice normal life, or Death Row.

*   *   *

148

"What'll it be, little lady?" Old Man Waltrip leaned down and peered through the car's open window. A mass of wrinkles spread from the corners of his narrow black eyes. Deep grooves cut into his weathered forehead and around his pinched mouth.

God, he did look old enough to have been baptized with Jesus. Though from the smell of him, a pungent aroma of beer and sweat and grease, she doubted Waltrip knew what a drop of holy water felt like.

"Unleaded, please," Darby said, pulling off her sunglasses to rummage in her purse for her credit card. "Fill it up."

He shuffled around the car, shoved the nozzle into her gas tank and started the pump. All the while, Darby was extremely conscious of those narrow eyes studying her.

"Check the hood?"

"Please." She hit the button, the hood popped, and his white head disappeared.

"About a half quart low. Nothin' to be too worried over. Radiator's fine, too." Black eyes peered at her again as he slammed the hood shut and headed for the driver's side.

He set about washing her window and Darby busied herself with arranging her credit cards in the slots of her wallet. Through downcast eyes, she could see him openly staring at her.

"Eighteen fifty," he said a few minutes later when the bell on the pump rang.

She handed him the credit card, never so glad in her life as when he disappeared through the shiny screen door, and into the interior of the ancient gas station.

He was back all too soon.

As he handed her the credit card, his leathery fingers clutched the edge and refused to let go when she reached for it.

"I know you," he said.

After Pinky, Darby wasn't in the mood for another Twenty Questions. Besides, after her run-in with Graham Tucker, she'd come to the conclusion that a low pro-

149

file was best. The last thing she needed was word of her return to leak to the visiting media.

Unfortunately, Pinky had probably broadcast the news from here to Dallas by now, thinking he could make a quick buck. Still, she had no intention of helping him out. The fewer people who knew about her return to Nostalgia, the better.

She didn't want a media circus, television interviews, a book or movie deal. She wanted only the truth.

"I do know you." His fingers still clutched the edge of her credit card.

"I just got into town yesterday." There. Maybe he would think she was one of the visiting media people.

"Yesterday, you say? Lots of people coming into town for the anniversary. Business ain't been this good since the real thing nearly ten years ago."

"Maybe you can retire when all this is over."

He smiled, letting the card slip from his fingers.

Relief coursed through Darby as she stuffed the credit card back into her wallet.

"Naw, retirement ain't for me. They'll bury me out by this old pump." He slapped a hand against the gas pump, before scratching his head.

"Thanks."

"Reverend know you're back in town, Miss Jayson?"

His words froze her hand just as she reached for the ignition.

"Naw, I don't reckon he does," Waltrip went on. "Otherwise he would have had his church ladies over at the motel, leading some candlelight vigil, trying to exorcise you and save your poor soul."

Her gaze collided with his. "I . . ." She swallowed, her throat suddenly dry. "No," she finally managed. "I—I haven't seen him."

"I don't reckon he'll be none too pleased. Tried to act all torn up about your leaving, but I could see he was mighty relieved. No offense, but I cain't say as I blame 'im none. Bein' a reverend and all, he's got a reputation to uphold, and it certainly didn't look right havin' a murderer livin' in his house, even if it was self-defense. Killin' is killin', and then there was that messy business with the slumber party and you failin' the lie-detector test and all." He shook his head. "Gave the reverend quite a bad name. Hell, it gave the whole town a bad name. You back for good?"

She shook her head, the action sending a queasy feeling to her stomach.

"Naw, I reckon not. Probably in town for the anniversary. A shame it'll all be over within another couple of days. All this stuff's been damn good for business. Take care, little lady." He flashed her a toothless smile, a speck of sunlight dancing in his narrow eyes. "If I see the reverend, I'll give him your regards."

Still stunned, Darby simply sat there, staring after him as he hurried over to another car. So much for keeping a low profile.

But she knew it was more than that that had her hands shaking. It was all Waltrip's talk about the reverend.

He wouldn't be pleased at all. He'd stare at her, condemnation in his eyes, and make her feel as if she were standing before God and everyone for Judgment Day.

That was the way he'd always made her feel. Uncomfortable.

As if he could see straight through her, past the fierce walls surrounding her memory, straight to the truth.

For all her false regrets after her father's death, when she'd stared into the reverend's eyes, she'd known he knew the truth. That she wasn't sorry. That her only regret was that she hadn't killed her sorry bastard of a father sooner.

And after the murders, she'd felt the same guilt when he'd looked at her, into her, as if he could see what she couldn't.

That she'd held the knife, plunged it into her friends over and over and over.

And if she saw him now, she feared the look in his eyes

would kill her nerve and send her running away again, before she found out what had really happened—

The blare of a horn interrupted her thoughts, and she glanced up to see Waltrip frowning at her and waving her out of the gas station to make room for another car.

Gathering her wits, she started the Cougar, pulled out onto the main strip through town and headed for the diner. No, the last person she needed to see was Reverend Masters, and hopefully with a little caution on her part, she could avoid him entirely.

Two minutes later, she killed the engine, climbed from the car and crunched across the gravel toward the door. The parking lot was full. Undoubtedly the anniversary was boosting business for everybody, not just Waltrip.

A bell tinkled as the diner door opened, and Darby found herself face-to-face with Reverend Masters. So much for caution.

He looked exactly as she remembered, with the exception of a few extra wrinkles. His forehead was a bit wider, his hairline an inch or so receded from the picture in her memory. Otherwise, he was the same, as if he'd stepped from her mind to stare at her with his dark brown eyes.

There was no accusation now, however. No hidden truths.

Shock filled his gaze, his face pale, as if he stared at a ghost.

"Sweet Jesus," he cried, the white sack he carried hitting the ground with a thud.

"Reverend." Surprisingly, her voice was working. Score one for determination. She nodded toward him, bent to retrieve the white bag she was certain carried his usual tuna on rye, the same lunch he'd had every day. She handed him the bag, stepped around him and headed for the doorway.

"Get thee behind me, Satan." His words followed her inside the diner.

As she slid into a vacant booth, her heart drummed. Surely he would follow her, demand to know why she'd returned, then haul her over to the church next door for a prayer session for her tainted soul.

Instead, he gripped the white bag and started across the parking lot, his stride stiff, as if each step required the ultimate effort. He crossed the gravel, rounded the church, and disappeared through the rear door.

For the second time that morning, Darby felt that strange tingling of self-satisfaction, as if she'd just fought an important battle and come out the winner.

She breathed a sigh of relief. At least she wouldn't waste her energy worrying and dreading what would happen when their paths finally crossed.

Another deep sigh and she turned her attention to her surroundings.

Jimmy Joe's Diner smelled of fried eggs and biscuits and homemade jam, and Darby took a deep breath. Pumpkin streamers hung from the ceiling. A jack-o'-lantern stood sentry near the cash register. Sunshine streamed in through the open blinds, reflecting off the scarred Formica tabletop. Everything was old and worn, from the round stools surrounding the soda fountain, to the ancient jukebox in the far corner. Old, and oddly welcoming, as if time had stood still for her. Waiting for her return.

A bear of a man wearing a stained white T-shirt and matching pants, a white apron draped around his beer-belly middle, pushed his way through the narrow walkway between tables.

"The special this mornin' is steak and eggs," he said, coming up to her. "Cooked any way you want 'em, honey."

"I don't know. . . ." Her gaze scanned the menu she'd pulled from its place between a napkin dispenser and a plastic cow creamer.

The man frowned, stuffing his pencil behind his ear. "Look, if you're one of them media people from out of town, forget askin' for bagels, or poached eggs, or that cappuccino stuff. We serve real food here. Coffee strong enough to peel the paint off your house, homemade biscuits with Jimmy Joe's homemade preserves canned right here on the premises, and you can forget askin' for a fat count. We ain't heart smart. If we cain't cook it up in a skillet, you're out of luck."

"How about pancakes and sausage?"

The man grinned. "That we can manage, hon. Homemade maple syrup, too. Jimmy's Joe's got a maple tree out at his granddaddy's place. Coffee?"

"The strongest you've got."

The man's smile widened. "Welcome to town, little lady."

"Oh, and some orange juice, too. Please."

She was definitely taking charge. When had she last had orange juice without something extra to give it a little kick?

Not in years, she realized, and the knowledge brought a film of tears to her eyes. She'd missed out on so much.

Not anymore. She was in control now, for better or for worse, she reminded herself yet again.

The "better" lasted all of forty-five minutes while she ate her breakfast and stared out into the sunlit parking lot of Jimmy Joe's. She watched people come and go, saw a few familiar faces, but no one else recognized her. Not that it would have mattered. After facing Graham yesterday, and the reverend today, she was ready for anything that came her way.

At least she thought she was, until the better turned to worse and she ran smack-dab into Mary Lou Wallis, one of Darby's old English teachers, and the mother of Jane, who was murdered right alongside Linda and Trish.

Darby had just paid her check and was exiting the diner when she slammed into Mary Lou, who dropped her purse and a stack of letters.

"Oh, my," the woman said, kneeling to collect her things. "I didn't see you—" The sentence drowned in her throat the moment Darby knelt beside her and their gazes locked.

"Let me help you." But Mary Lou had stopped gathering up her things. She knelt there, frozen for a long moment, before her entire body started to tremble, then shake, her face pale, frightened. As if she'd seen a ghost.

She had. She'd seen Darby, a ghost from the past, a reminder of her daughter.

Darby searched for something to say, guilt ebbing and flowing through her beneath Mary Lou Wallis's tortured eyes.

"I . . . What are you doing here?" came Mary Lou's small voice.

"I'm here for a visit."

"I . . ." The woman opened her mouth again, but no words came out this time and Darby feared she was in shock. She had a strange, glazed look about her that was quickly noted by the waiter who'd served Darby her breakfast.

"Mary Lou? Honey, are you all right?" The man leaned down and pushed Darby out of the way so he could get a better look.

"She . . . It's her. . . ." Then Mary Lou Wallis fainted dead away in the doorway of Jimmy Joe's Diner.

"Call 911," the waiter bellowed before turning accusing eyes on Darby. "What the hell did you say to her?"

"I . . ." Her voice faded when she heard the murmurs rolling through the crowd.

"It's her, I'm telling you."

"That's Darby Jayson."

"*The* Darby Jayson? The one they arrested that night?"

The murmurs floated through the crowd and the floor seemed to tilt, but Darby held on, forced herself to her feet and headed for the doorway of Jimmy Joe's, anxious to slip away, to forget the accusation in Mary Lou Wallis's tortured eyes.

"Hold it right there, miss." The voice accompanied a uniformed police officer, and before Darby could blink, she was taken by the elbow and led outside to a waiting police car.

Then she was speeding through town toward the police station, a route she'd traveled nearly ten years ago. On Halloween night after her three friends had been slaughtered.

Chapter Twelve

"I didn't do anything wrong," Darby said for the umpteenth time to the officer who'd intercepted her outside of Jimmy Joe's. As he had for the past fifteen minutes, he simply grunted and kept on about his business, which, at the moment, involved escorting her down the main hallway of the Nostalgia Police Station.

"What about my car?" she tried again.

Just the usual grunt and the tightening of his fingers on her elbow.

"This is police harrassment."

Another grunt, a quick turn, and Darby found herself thrust into one of the offices that lined the hallway.

"Here you go, Chief," the officer said, before slamming the door behind Darby and taking up guard duty right outside.

She found herself alone in a small room, facing an overweight woman sitting behind a huge desk piled high with paperwork.

"Miss Jayson," the woman said, pulling spectacles from her round face.

For the first time in the last fifteen minutes, Darby actually felt some tension ease out of her muscles. The woman could have been the poster pinup for all-American grandmothers, with her silver hair, round face, ruffled blouse. She waved a chubby hand at Darby and motioned her into the chair opposite her.

"Do I know you?" Darby asked as she sank down into the chair, then immediately regretted her action when the woman stood.

Nix the grandmother idea. The woman stood nearly six feet tall, her stature dominating the small room. She came around the desk and perched on the corner inches away from where Darby sat.

Apprehension slithered through her, settling into her bones and tightening her muscles.

"Don't you remember me?" the woman asked.

Darby stared a full minute more before shaking her head. "You look a little familiar, but I can't quite say."

"Maggie Cross," the woman said, extending her large hand. "The job's turned my hair prematurely gray, I'm afraid."

"Chief Cross," Darby exclaimed, squinting her eyes for a closer look. Yes, yes, of course. The chief had been a tall woman, though very slender, with carrot red hair. Nothing like this grandmotherly woman, yet the eyes were the same. Cool, calm eyes that seemed to miss nothing.

"So," Maggie went on, clasping her hands together. "I was hoping we'd get a chance to have a little talk. I like to know who's in my town."

Outrage fired through Darby, her arm stinging where the officer had held her. "So you send an armed escort? Have me thrown into the back of a police car just so we can have a little visit? You could've come to the Tropicana. I'm staying in room—"

"Four B. I know. And I wasn't really set on a meeting until the reverend's call. Then, of course," Maggie went on, "the 911 came in from Jimmy Joe's." She shook her head. "Your presence here is mighty unsettling. Reverend Masters was fit to be tied. He's afraid you'll open too many wounds, and I have to agree. Doc Waller's with Mary Lou Wallis right now."

"How is she?"

"She's in a state of shock. Same thing happened right after Jane's death. Husband thought she'd never get over what happened and start functioning normally again. I'm afraid she's back at square one now. Seems that seeing you stirred up all those old memories of Jane."

"I'm terribly sorry." Darby clutched her hands in her lap, Mary Lou Wallis's tortured face emblazoned in her memory. If only she could see the night of the slumber party as clearly.

"Not half as sorry as you're going to be, little lady."

"I'm afraid I don't follow you."

"It took a long time, but this town finally got over that night. Folks moved on, pushed it to the back of their minds. It's all better forgotten, as far as I'm concerned. But you people don't seem to see it that way."

"You people?"

"Television. Press. All of you are out for a hot story, a big byline, even if it means tearing up folks' lives in the process." She gave a firm shake of her silver head. "But I won't have it here in my town, and I won't have you stirring up a lot of old hurt."

"I didn't come back to hurt anyone. I have some things to get settled in my own mind, Chief Cross," she said imploringly. "I came to ease my own hurt."

Maggie stared at her long and hard. "Still," she said after a pensive moment, "your presence here is unsettling."

"Since when is unsettling against the law?" Darby glanced at the police officer standing just outside the door. "The last I heard, it wasn't a reason to arrest anyone."

The woman smiled, but the expression didn't quite

touch those calm, cool eyes. "It ain't, and you're not arrested."

"Good. Then I'll be on my way. I have a busy day ahead of me."

Maggie stood at the same time as Darby. "Make sure your day doesn't involve any of my citizens. I don't want any more calls. And I don't want the reverend calling a special revival on your behalf."

"So he's still as vigilant as ever?"

"When it comes to the Lord's work, keeping this town on the straight and narrow, yes, he is. His life's purpose is to meet up with each and every citizen in the hereafter."

"And my being here might interfere with his purpose?"

"Maybe." Maggie extended her hand for a shake. "And maybe not."

Reluctantly, Darby accepted the gesture and slid her hand into Maggie's. The woman's pudgy fingers closed around hers.

Seconds ticked by, but the handshake didn't end.

"Thanks, Chief. I'll heed the warning," Darby assured her, trying to pull her hand free.

Maggie's grip tightened and she pulled Darby an inch closer. "Another phone call could mean the difference between unsettling and harassing, and that *is* cause for arrest." The chief smiled. "Do we understand each other?"

"Perfectly."

"Good." She released Darby's hand and nodded at the officer, who opened the door and ducked his head in.

"Yeah, Chief?"

"See Miss Jayson back to her car." He nodded, and Maggie walked back around her desk to sit down behind her mountain of paperwork. Shoving her spectacles back on, she picked up where she'd left off, her attention going to the file in front of her.

Darby's fingers throbbed from the pressure of Maggie's

grip. She rubbed her hands together as she followed the police officer.

"Oh," Maggie said, glancing up just as the duo reached the doorway. A bright smile lit the woman's face and Darby could practically smell the homemade chocolate-chip cookies. "Welcome home, Darby. It's good to see you again."

The words followed her out into the hallway and sent a shiver down her spine.

"Yo, Baxter," the desk sergeant called out as the officer steered Darby past the desk.

"Not now, Murf. Cain't you see I'm on assignment?"

"I can see, all right." The desk sergeant's eyes raked Darby from head to toe and she pulled self-consciously at her T-shirt. "But you got an urgent phone call."

"Take a message," the officer barked, steering Darby around a corner.

"All right, but you know how huffy your wife gets when you're too busy to talk to her."

The officer hauled Darby to a jarring stop. "It's Doris?"

The desk sergeant nodded. "And she sounds mighty pissed. Something about you forgetting to take out the trash for the third morning in a row, and the last time she looked, being a wife wasn't supposed to be the same thing as being an indentured servant and—"

"I'm coming." He steered Darby to the nearest chair. "You stay put, missy. This'll only take a minute."

"My morning's already shot," Darby said, exasperated. "What the hell?"

He gave her a solemn nod, then headed for the nearest telephone where he said all of two words before going silent. From the sheepish expression that crept over his face, the red stain darkening his ears, Darby knew he was getting the reaming of his life. *Go, Doris.*

"Decide to turn yourself in and confess?" Graham's deep voice slid into her ears.

Darby glanced up to find a pair of accusing blue eyes staring down at her.

"Not yet." She snatched up a copy of *Field and Stream* and busied herself flipping pages, all the while wishing that she'd put on a bra that morning. "Not until I know what I'm confessing."

He laughed, a harsh sound that sparked her anger and twisted her already frazzled nerves to the limit. "Same old song and dance."

"Did you come here just to badger me?" She glared up at him.

"As intriguing as the idea is, no. I've got business with Maggie—"

"Hey, Graham!" The shout came from a uniformed officer who'd just reported in for the shift change. He stood, pulling off his hat, unhooking his nightstick. Darby recognized him as one of Graham's old high school buddies, a fellow football player.

"How's it hangin', man?"

"Good," Graham replied.

"You up to a few beers at Poppy's? I'm officially off duty in about five minutes. . . ."

The conversation was drowned out by the frantic thud of Darby's heartbeat and she knew she had to get away from Graham, or wind up passed out on the floor from heatstroke, or whatever the hell was making her so hot.

She stood, slid past him and retreated down the opposite hallway. A quick turn of the corner and she saw the sign for the ladies' room blazing like a beacon.

Shoving open the door, she rushed over to the sink, leaned forward, her forehead against the blessedly cool glass, and closed her eyes. The air conditioner cycled on, and frigid air streamed through a small vent somewhere in back of her, rustling the hair at her nape and sending a chill through her despite her sweaty skin.

She was definitely under too much stress. Enough was enough for one day.

"You okay?" a woman's voice asked, and Darby's eyes snapped open to the reflection of a petite blonde standing in the doorway behind her.

"Fine." She managed a smile and concentrated on turning the cold water on while the woman headed for one of the stalls.

A few seconds later a toilet flushed; then Darby felt the woman pass behind her again, heard the door open and creak shut.

Stress, she thought, splashing cold water onto her face. She closed her eyes against the moisture. She was definitely under too much stress for one person. The reverend she could have handled, and Mary Lou Wallis, even the meeting with Maggie. But then Graham had to go and show up, and start harassing her with his eyes—

The notion disintegrated when she felt the heat behind her. A familiar heat. And of course it belonged to a familiar body, and a damned familiar voice.

"And I thought you'd finally stopped running away."

Her eyes snapped open and she found herself staring into Graham's reflection, his face close to her own, his body partially hidden behind hers.

"You're not supposed to be in here. This is the ladies' room."

"Funny, but I don't see any ladies in here. Just you."

"Score one for Graham Tucker." She prayed he didn't notice the shakiness in her voice. He dwarfed her with his enormous size. A strange electricity jolted through her body, trailing straight to her nipples, which beaded beneath the thin cotton of her damp shirt.

Obviously, the reaction didn't miss Graham's notice. His gaze dropped, settling on the twin objects of interest.

Instinct urged her to cross her arms over her chest, but she couldn't seem to move. Her hands gripped the basin, hanging on of their own accord, and no matter how much her frantic brain issued the command, she couldn't seem to get her fingers to let go and come to her rescue.

"You're not supposed to be in here," she repeated again, hoping and praying like hell that he would take the hint and leave, since she couldn't. Not without turning around, going through him to get to the door.

"You can't run from me, Darby. Not this time."

"I wasn't running away."

"Really? That quick glimpse of the back of your head as you rounded the corner sure fooled me."

"I just needed some air. It was so hot out there. . . ."

"Looks like you managed to cool off." His gaze dropped again and she felt its searing heat on her pebbled nipples, sending a trail straight to the already moist spot between her legs. "Or are you just glad to see me?"

"You're so funny."

"I'm not trying to be." The words, so low and serious, sent another jolt of heat through her. *Absurd.*

She was definitely hard up. Here she was getting wet just talking to a man. A man who hated her.

Insane.

She would've laughed, if her throat hadn't been so tight. That one word—*insane*—not only summed up her feelings at that moment, but her whole life. Her entire existence was one big mixed-up puzzle, and she was missing a crucial piece. She couldn't begin to sort things out and put her life together until she found that piece. Until she remembered.

But remembering took a quick backseat to the heat rolling through her. Forget the stress attack. It was Graham making her hot, his breath at the nape of her neck heating her blood, his nearness making her skin blaze, and he hadn't even touched her.

Yet.

The word bounced through her head at the same time he reached around her, one large hand skimming her rib cage, his fingertips going to one puckered nipple.

What the hell do you think you're doing?

The question was there on the tip of her tongue, but her voice deserted her. Instead, a small, choked sound slid past her lips as a dozen delicious pulses spread from her nipples, through the rest of her body.

He made a *tsk-tsk* sound, his fingertip circling her aureola. "Shame on you, Darby."

"What?" she managed to ask.

"You said you were hot. You look cold, but you don't feel cold." His voice was a husky whisper that skimmed her senses and scrambled every ounce of common sense that screamed what a fool she was to allow him to touch her.

To want him to touch her.

To want him.

He was off limits. He hated her, she reminded herself. He wanted her in prison. He wanted her on Death Row. He wanted to be the one to shove the needle into her arm and send her to the hell he thought she so rightly deserved.

His fingers spread out, circling her nipple, molding the damp material to her breast. "No, not cold at all," he murmured. "You'd never know there was ice water flowing through your veins."

She stiffened, feeling more like the ice water flowed over her rather than inside. *What the hell was she doing?* She'd never let any man touch her. Not sober, anyway. And this wasn't just any man. This was *him.*

She pushed his hand away, and fortified her defenses. "And I thought my day had gotten as bad as it was going to get. Then you show up and prove me wrong."

"Not wrong, *guilty.* Of course, when I walked in and saw you, I thought maybe you'd started feeling a little guilty without my help, and turned yourself in."

"Maggie wanted to meet me. It seems my presence is a bit unsettling to certain members of the community."

"I'll bet." Sarcasm dripped from the words, sending a knife twisting inside her. She wanted to cry. To yell. To slap him. To shake his confidence. He was so damned sure of her guilt. . . .

And she was so damned uncertain.

"Look," she said, gathering her courage and wishing all the while for a stiff shot of bourbon. Then it wouldn't matter. Nothing ever did. "I didn't come here to hurt anyone. I just want to find out the truth." She pried her fingers from the basin and gathered her purse. "Then if a confession's in order, I'll give one."

"I want one now."

"I don't know anything now."

He shook his head. "Then I guess I'll have to file a report, because I do."

The question brought her head swiveling around. "What are you talking about?"

He smiled—a cold, calculated smile that sent a sliver of fear straight through her, yet at the same time, a tingle of excitement shot from her head to her toes. *Insane.*

But then Darby didn't exactly have a stable record when it came to behavior. Withdrawn and shy when sober. Wild and . . . ? And who knew what else when she'd had a few drinks. Or a few bottles.

"I saw you last night, Darby. At Samuel Blue's house. Trespassing might not be a big offense in San Francisco, but in Nostalgia it carries a pretty heavy penalty. Not to mention breaking and entering."

"You saw me?"

He nodded. "Every pathetic second. I've got to hand it to you, you're a better actress than I thought. You charmed the pants off that guard."

He released her and turned toward the doorway.

Before she could stop herself, Darby grabbed his arm. "You really saw me last night? You have to tell me what happened!"

"Get real." He shrugged loose, but she latched on to him again.

"I am real. Please. I—I don't remember and I have to know."

"I'm sick and tired of this shit—"

"I know you don't believe me, but I *don't* remember." She clutched his arm. "Tell me, Graham. Please."

He stared at her for a long moment, disbelief creasing his features.

"On one condition," he finally said.

The words echoed in Darby's head. Fear jolted her

back to the past, to the night her father died.

I might be obliged to show some mercy, on one condition. . . .

A wave of revulsion rolled through her, yet at the same time, she felt a whisper of heat against her nipple where Graham's fingers had touched her only moments ago.

This was different, she told herself, pushing away the fear and the dread that made her want to sink to her knees. She was a grown woman, not a small, frightened child. And Graham had information she needed. Desperately. She could barter.

No matter what she had to trade.

On one condition . . .

"Okay," she whispered, wondering why her voice sounded so uncertain when she'd already made her mind up.

"But you haven't heard the condition." Those blue eyes drilled into her.

"I don't need to. I know what you want, Graham. And—and it's okay." She softened her grip on his arm, tried to make her fingers move to stroke him, but she couldn't quite accomplish the feat. "Whatever you want," she said, all the while her mind screaming *No!* "Just talk to me about last night."

Graham studied her a long moment, her words replaying in his head, sending a thrum along his senses, straight to his already throbbing erection. He'd come in here to intimidate and manipulate her, to play her, but it looked like he was the one being played.

Damn it all.

"You know, you've changed, Darby."

"You haven't," she replied, her eyes meeting his, hunger blazing in her gaze. Hunger and something else . . . Uncertainty? Fear?

His imagination. She wasn't the same innocent shadow of a girl who'd followed his sister around. She was all grown up. Tainted by her past, soiled by the blood on her hands and her conscience. Spoiled by the secrets hidden inside her.

"No, you haven't changed at all," she went on. She slid her fingers up his arm in a slow gesture that might have been seductive, if he hadn't noticed the trembling. Felt it deep inside him. Uncertainty. Fear. No matter what she said, how confident, how agreeable. She was scared.

Something stirred inside him. A protective urge that warned him to keep away from her, but damned if that wide-eyed innocence he sensed below the surface didn't call him all the more.

His fingers clamped over hers. "Ah, but I have changed." He thrust her hand away. "I don't drop my pants at the first sign of a good piece, and that isn't what I had in mind as a condition."

Shock, then confusion swam in her wide eyes. Then came the uncertainty. Yes, he was sure of it this time. "I . . . But you touched me and . . ." Hot splotches colored her high cheekbones. "Then you said . . ." She shook her head. "I'm sorry. I guess I thought—"

"You thought wrong. I want to know why you're here in Nostalgia. The real reason. Otherwise, I'm going to Maggie, and that ass you're shoving in my face will be sitting behind bars before you can say 'I don't remember.' So if you want to prance around town doing whatever it is you're here to do, you'd better come clean."

"You first," she said. "I need to know what you saw last night. What happened after I pushed open the window? Then I'll come clean. I swear."

An image flashed in his mind, of Darby stumbling backward, fending off some invisible attacker before passing clean out on the ground.

But she hadn't passed out. She'd picked herself up moments later as if nothing odd had just happened.

"I saw you give one hell of a performance. Oscar caliber."

"What did I do?"

"You sweet-talked the security guard into not calling

the police; then you sauntered over to your car, climbed in and headed back to the motel to crash."

"I *drove* back to the motel?"

"No, you flew."

"Did I drive all right? I mean, no speeding, or fast turns? No weaving on the road? Nothing unusual?"

"You drove just fine. Signaled at every stop, the works."

He stared at her as she slumped against the edge of the sink, as if reeling from the information he'd just given her. As if it was brand-spanking-new to her. As if it hadn't been her he'd seen last night.

"You missed your calling, Darby."

"What?"

"A damn fine performance. The only problem is, I'm not one of your fans. I don't want your lies; I want the truth." He gripped her shoulders, shoved her up against the door, his body close. Threatening. It was a move he'd done time and time again in the past, with criminal after criminal.

But this felt different. He didn't feel so threatening in this stance. It felt right, their bodies close together, more tempting than threatening—

He slammed his mind shut to the thought. Anger bunched his muscles tight. "Tell me, dammit. What's your game, Darby? What the hell brought you back here? The media attention? Is that it? Do you need it so much, you'd risk coming back? Wasn't it enough that you sliced up your friends and walked away without so much as a slap on the hand? That you not only destroyed them, but their families as well? That you killed not just three innocent kids, but a whole fucking town?"

"No!" she shrieked, wrenching away from him. "I didn't—I mean, I don't know." She slapped at the tears that spilled from her eyes. "I really don't know." She turned, hauled open the door and slipped out into the hallway.

The door rocked shut, and Graham found himself

standing alone, mad as hell, and feeling like a heel, and that made him even madder.

He shouldn't feel sorry for Darby Jayson. Hell, he *didn't*. He felt nothing for her except revulsion.

At least, that was what he wanted to think. But the doubt that niggled at his brain told an altogether different story.

And made him all the more determined to find out the truth.

If he had the proof of her guilt right in front of him, that would kill the doubts about her innocence. And it sure as hell would kill the erection throbbing in his pants.

Or would it?

Either way, he had to have some answers and he wouldn't get them standing alone in the ladies' room. He shoved open the door and strode down the hallway, then out into the parking lot.

"Wait up," he called to the police officer ushering Darby into the backseat of a nearby patrol car. "I'll take care of this for you."

"No thanks, Tucker. Chief gave the duty to me and I like my butt in one piece, thank you very much."

"Then you'd better give your wife another call. Apparently, she wasn't through talking to you. She's on the phone now, and she doesn't sound very happy."

"But what about me?" Darby asked as the police officer looked nervously from her back toward the police station.

"It's your lucky day," Graham said, taking her by the elbow and steering her toward his pickup. "I'm headed your way."

"Well, that stands to reason, since you've been headed my way for the past twenty-four hours."

"I told you I didn't intend to let you out of my sight. I want to know what you're up to."

"I'm up to finding out the truth."

"So am I."

"Wait." She gripped the truck door. "Unless you promise to stop badgering me, I'll walk back to Jimmy Joe's." She glanced up, a stern expression on her face, as if she'd come to some sort of decision. "You want to keep an eye on me, fine. But I'm through explaining myself to you, and I'm sure as hell through arguing."

"Agreed."

She stared at him, as if deciding whether or not to trust him. A trickle of sweat slid down her temple and she glanced at the hot sun hanging overhead, then the cool interior of the truck. It was that time of year when the nights were cool, cold even, but on a cloudless day, you felt like it was summer all over again.

"I've got to be an idiot." She tossed her purse on the seat and climbed in after it.

But Graham had the feeling he was the crazy one.

Crazy for feeling so mixed up when he should be dead certain of her guilt.

Crazy for lusting after her when he knew she was a killer.

An even crazier for climbing into the cab of his pickup with her, with barely a few inches of seat between them.

She was too close.

Too pretty.

Too deadly, he realized a few minutes later when he saw her eyes turn from a deep chocolate to a vivid blue.

Chapter Thirteen

Graham blinked, and the glimpse of blue faded, deeper, deeper, back into the rich brown depths of her eyes.

Relief coursed through him, but it wasn't quite strong enough to push aside the unease that something wasn't right.

Something other than the obvious.

"I feel like I'm fourteen all over again," she said when they stopped for a red light. The nearby junior high had just let out. A stream of kids flowed across the road, headed for the Dairy Queen on the opposite corner.

"A far cry from San Francisco?"

"From most any place in the free world."

"Yeah," he agreed. "The reverend says this is the last piece of God's country, and he intends to keep it that way. I don't suppose he was too happy when he saw you this morning."

"That's an understatement. I swear he had to pick his jaw up off the ground."

"Too bad I missed it."

"I'm surprised you did." She slanted him a sideways glance. "Considering you appointed yourself my watchdog."

"Yeah, well, I overslept."

"Long night?"

"Endless." He shifted in the seat, suddenly uncomfortable. "How about you? Still manage to sleep at night?" He knew it carried a double meaning. Hell, he meant it that way, despite their truce. He would rather have her arguing with him. Talking to her was too disconcerting. She seemed too much like a real person rather than a killer.

As if she read his thoughts, she simply shrugged, annoying him further when she didn't rise to the bait. "I sleep some nights. And some I don't."

"So your conscience does bother you."

"Maybe," she replied.

"Meaning?"

"I have nightmares."

"That stands to reason."

"If you intend to keep baiting me," she said, "just pull over right there and I'll walk."

"Sorry," he said, shifting again. *Damn, but it's hot.*

"Yeah, I bet."

"So tell me about the nightmares."

She shrugged. "There's nothing to tell. They keep me up at night, scare the shit out of me. End of story." From the way she clamped her lips together, he got the impression she didn't want to talk about them.

"How long have you been having them?" he prodded.

"Too long." She turned a glance on him. "What about you? Nightmares keep you up last night?"

"Actually, you kept me up."

She smiled, just a vague tilt to her lips, but enough to send an ache straight to his groin. *Dammit.*

"Afraid I might slip away?" she asked.

Afraid I might slip inside, he thought. "Among other things." He swerved left to avoid a small kitten smack-dab in the middle of the street. The truck rocked for a split second, then relaxed.

"Poor thing," Darby murmured, turning to stare behind them. "Do you think we should stop? Maybe it's lost."

"Terry Jacob's cat just had a litter. They're all over this area. Don't worry, the mama will gather them all up come dinnertime."

She let loose a big sigh, her chest straining beneath her shirt, and Graham forced his eyes onto the road. *Don't look.* It wouldn't bother him if he didn't look.

Right. She was there in his mind's eye, chest heaving, soft lips parting for a sigh. *Aw, hell.*

"Still know everybody in town?" she asked.

"Most everybody," he told her. "I don't get back here as often as I should. There's a new vet in town now that Mr. Simpson passed on. A few new families near the outskirts of town. But otherwise, it's the same bunch. Everybody's a little older, a little more set in their ways. Nothing's changed much. It's still quiet here. Peaceful."

He started through an intersection, only to slam on his brakes when a car raced through, trying to catch the light. "Shit!" The brakes screeched and the pickup lurched forward. "It used to be quiet and peaceful until this damned anniversary thing out at the Blue place. Hell, now we've got tourists here. In Nostalgia, for Chrissake!"

He pressed the gas and started forward again. He felt her gaze and he knew she stared at the shoulder holster partially hidden beneath his faded denim jacket.

"So you're with the police department in Dallas?" she asked.

He nodded. "Homicide." He wiped a trickle of sweat from his temple and shrugged out of the jacket. "And this is my partner." He fingered the holster. "A Beretta nine millimeter. The best friend a guy can have in my line of work. The only friend," he added.

"Sounds like lonely work."

The observation prodded at something inside Graham. He shook the feeling away. "How about you? What have you been up to for the past ten years?"

She smiled, a knowing look in her eyes. "Why don't you tell me."

He had to hand it to her. She was smart. But then he'd always known that. Since she'd walked away from a multiple murder without leaving a scrap of incriminating evidence behind her. Very smart, indeed.

"Let's see," he started. "After you left here, you did some sort of field reporting for the *Tribune* in Chicago. Then it was on to Denver, where you stopped the field work and started editing some weekly homemaking column. Then Miami and a weekly entertainment column. After that, it was the same type of thing in Washington, then a bigger column in New Jersey. And finally a major column in a major local magazine in San Francisco."

She smiled at his recitation. "Impressive, huh?"

"Nope. Tiring. But it doesn't surprise me."

"What doesn't surprise you?"

"The urge to migrate," he told her. "To keep moving. That way you don't have to face what you left behind. It's called running away."

She frowned. "I thought you were a cop, not a shrink."

"One and the same. Shrinks dig into people's thoughts, and cops do the same." Hadn't J. C. told him that over and over whenever he'd been trying to crack a tough case? *Get inside their heads,* she would say. *Shrinks do it all the time, and so should cops. Good cops.* "You can't catch a criminal if you don't know how he thinks, what he thinks."

"I guess you're right. About the shrink part, but I wasn't running away from anything. I was running to something. A better job, a better life. A place where I really fit in."

"It's called home," he pointed out.

She looked thoughtful, the sunlight playing on her features, making her seem pale and vulnerable. "Maybe I was looking for home," she finally said. "You know, when I left here I thought, good riddance. There was nothing for me. No family, no friends. Nothing. But I was wrong. There is something here."

He felt her gaze as he pulled up in front of Jimmy Joe's, killed the engine of the truck and turned to face her.

"What?" he asked.

"Memories. My past is here, whether I like it or not. I can never move on and find a real home while my memories are still buried somewhere here."

"Are you sure it's just memories you're after, Darby?"

"I don't care about the anniversary, or the media, regardless what you and Maggie Cross might think."

"That's not what I'm talking about."

"What then?"

"Evidence." She had the nerve to look puzzled. "You went to Blue's house last night to retrieve a lot more than a few minutes of memories." His arm snaked out, his hand circling her neck, pulling her so close he could feel her warm, short breaths against his lips. "What's in the house, Darby? Did all those crime-scene investigators really miss something? Are those TV reporters really going to stumble onto the find of their careers? New clues to convict the slumber-party killer? You."

"Memories," she ground out. "That's the only reason I went there. The only reason I'm here now. The only reason. And I don't give a damn if you think otherwise."

Her eyes blazed anger and fury and he had the insane urge to kiss her just to wipe that frown from her face.

"You'd better start giving a damn," he said, thrusting her away from him. "Because I'm on to you, Darby. I'm climbing inside that pretty little head of yours, and I'm going to nail you to the wall, honey. That's why I'm here. Why I'm staying here, and why I'm staying on your ass until you're behind bars where you belong."

He expected her to lash out at him, to tell him to go straight to hell, to offer to send him there, but she didn't. That damned vulnerable light gleamed in her eyes, sending a niggle of doubt straight to his gut. Wordlessly, she scrambled out of the pickup, slammed the passenger door and hurried over to her car.

"Yes, your ass is mine, Darby," he said, his eyes on the object of his thoughts.

The trouble was, he wanted that statement true in the worst way, in a very physical way, and he wondered how much longer he could go on damning her to hell with his lips, when he wanted to do other, much more pleasurable things to her.

Not this time. He chanted the words silently, a desperate mantra inside his head. He couldn't let his dick lead him around, or straight into anyone as dangerous as Darby Jayson.

And she was dangerous.

He closed his eyes and pictured her—full, sensuous lips, pale face, blue eyes—

Hold on. She didn't have blue eyes. She had brown eyes. *Brown*, and what he'd seen earlier had merely been a play of sunlight. Or his imagination. Or both.

Or . . .

Crazy. He was crazy and it was hot and he was hot, and damned if he was going to start considering the impossible.

Darby Jayson had brown eyes. End of discussion.

He shot a glance at her car as she pulled out of Jimmy Joe's parking lot; then his gaze went to the squad car a few blocks away. The car swerved into traffic, staying a safe distance behind her.

Just as it had done the entire way from the police station. It seemed Maggie wasn't going to leave Darby's surveillance up to him. She had her own man on the job.

All the better.

Graham had a few errands to run, a couple of phone calls to make, and he hated the thought of letting Darby out of his sight.

But now . . .

He still hated the thought, but better to see to his business now, during the bright light of day while Darby was busy visiting various town landmarks and stirring up the townsfolk with her presence, than tonight.

He didn't know why he felt uneasy about nightfall. A gut feeling. Cop's instinct. Or maybe just wishful thinking. Whatever, he simply knew he'd better be back at his post once the sun set.

When darkness fell, the night came alive, and Darby's true nature stirred to life.

She would show Graham what she was really made of then, and he would see her behind bars, and his own conscience would be cleansed.

He knew it wouldn't bring Linda back. But it would be the next best thing. Justice. Sweet, vengeful justice. Better than sex, even to a man who'd always been after the sweetest piece.

Much better.

Later that afternoon, Darby pulled into the parking space in front of her motel room. Her gaze went to the empty space next to hers, the dark window in the unit just to her left.

She glanced in the rearview mirror, noted the police car just across the street, and wondered what had happened to watchdog Tucker. He should have been the one on duty instead of the cops.

Relief, she told herself. She should feel relief that he wasn't the one following her anymore. Not because of his threats, but because a part of her feared for him should she turn out to be a cold-blooded killer.

Still, despite her fear, knowing he was close was oddly comforting. The blackout terrified her, but at the same time, she felt relieved to know that Graham had seen her. She hadn't gone on a killing spree, taken another victim. She'd simply driven back here to the motel.

A shiver raced along her nerve endings. She'd actually behaved in a normal fashion, even driven a car. That knowledge only added to the clues mounting against her.

What if all the times she'd passed out drunk in the past hadn't really been passing out at all, but having a blackout like the one she'd had last night? What if instead of sleeping off the booze, she'd gone hunting, scouting for a victim, finding and killing one—

Stop it!

She had to think about the slumber party. Nothing else; otherwise she would have a nervous breakdown before she ever remembered anything.

The slumber party, she reminded herself again as she climbed from the car, a white sack containing a burger and fries from the diner clutched in one hand. When she reached the door to her unit, she slid the key in the lock and tried to turn the metal. Stuck.

". . . but I have to find her," came the woman's voice from the open doorway of Pinky's office a few units down.

"Look, lady. I don't know what you want with that blasted mutt. You still got three more where she came from."

"I have to find my baby," came the frantic voice.

"All right, all right. If I see her, I'll give you a holler. That's the best I can do."

"Can't you call the police or something?"

She jimmied the key and tried the lock again. And again.

"Listen, sweet thing, Maggie Cross would have my ass if I busied up her guys trying to find some customer's mongrel dog."

Finally the lock clicked and Darby gripped the doorknob.

"She isn't a mongrel. She's a thousand-dollar purebred poodle, jet black, with a bright red collar."

Darby froze, visions of the dream replaying in her head.

A few practiced movements of the knife and he relished the sight. . . .

Her hands started to tremble and she closed her eyes,

feeling the heat on her skin, smelling the bittersweet aroma.

. . . empty, bloody eye sockets, red tears trailing down the furry face, the blood the same vivid crimson as the collar around the animal's neck.

Her stomach somersaulted and she swallowed against the vomit that rose in her throat. The slumber party, she told herself. Just the slumber party.

". . . whatever, lady. I told you we don't allow no goddamn pets here, pure-bred poodle or not. If you were gonna break the rules, you should've at least kept the mutt on a leash. It ain't the damned pound here."

Somehow, Darby managed to get her trembling fingers to turn the knob. She stumbled inside, the door slamming, blocking out the voices from Pinky's office.

She collapsed on the bed, the burger and fries a mashed bundle next to her. The greasy scent drifted through her nostrils, making her stomach jump, and she tossed the bundle at the nearest trash.

The shaking in her hands spread, gripping her entire body, and she hugged her arms about her. Her mouth turned to cotton, her head pounded and she knew she had to have a drink. Just one tiny drink.

She snatched the bottle of Johnnie Walker from the dresser and slumped back to the bed. Unscrewing the top, she downed most of the mouthful that was left. Then the liquor was gone, the bottle empty. Tears burned her eyes and she blinked frantically.

No, no, no.

She held the opening to her nose and took a deep, desperate breath. The liquor smell curled up into her nostrils, spiraled through her senses like a spider weaving a silken web.

And she was the frantic fly. Caught. Trapped. Waiting for annihilation.

No! Not yet.

Suddenly, the glass seemed to grow hot to the touch, scorching her fingertips. She threw the bottle across the room, watched, both horrified and relieved as it smashed into the wall. Shards of glass rained to the floor, a few pieces landing on top of her inch-high manuscript sitting on the edge of the dresser. Or was that an inch and a quarter? It seemed bigger, the stack growing page by page. As if it mattered.

All that mattered was Darby's pounding heart, the itching deep in the pit of her stomach. She watched as the small amount of liquor that had been left in the bottle slid in whiskey rivers down the dingy wallpaper to pool on the floor. The sight beckoned Darby closer, offering the taste she so desperately needed.

Just a quick lap of her tongue and she could function again, feel like her old self—

Escape her surroundings.

A vision of her mother worked its way into her mind and giant fingers of grief gripped her heart. She forced her gaze away from the shattered bottle, from that little puddle of herself staining the floor.

She clutched the edge of the bed and hauled herself up. Then she curled on her side, hugged the pillow and gave in to the tears burning her eyes. Tears for the dog, the DA's dead daughter back in San Francisco, and the faceless others from her dreams.

When those tears were spent, she cried even more. For her dead mother, for Linda, for the other dead girls, for Katy Evans, for Graham and his family.

But most of all she cried for herself, her soul, because deep down, Darby knew she was going to burn for what she'd done that Halloween night.

Burn, baby, burn . . .

I've never been much of a disco fan, but the phrase sort of fits, don't you think? Though as bad as Darby's been behaving, I don't think she deserves anything quite as good as a fire.

To hear her tell it, she's got much worse coming to her. Darby's one of a kind. Those innocents you don't meet every day. She actually feels bad for all the shit she's done.

Even the shit she only *thinks* she's done.

Classic guilty conscience.

Hell, I can relate. Had a conscience myself. Once. The only thing about a conscience is, it gets in the way. There's no room for guilt or second thoughts, or anything except the fantasy. That's the only way to make it better the next time. And the next.

Darby's conscience always worked to my advantage. Until now.

You'd think the splinter thing would have done the trick, but hell no. And then the dog. Jesus, that was a beautiful piece of work, pardon my blasphemy. A beautiful friggin' piece of work.

Not enough.

I knew I should have stopped her from coming back home, but I'm a sucker for memories, you know? Besides, as screwed up as Darby's always been, I have to admit I was curious as hell to understand why.

Now I know. Her old man was a bastard with a capital B.

I can relate. Had one hell of an old man myself, or so my Granny says. Never really saw him very much. A few times when I was still pissin' the bed at night.

He would come by occasionally, real late at night. He'd come roaring up on this big metal monster of a motorcycle, though it wasn't nearly as big or as bad as I thought at the time. Just a pissant Honda. Not a Harley or any other badass machine. But when you're small, everything's bigger than you, and to me it was like one of the demons straight out of Reverend Masters's fire-and-brimstone services.

Seemed only fitting that my daddy rode one of those bitches, since my Granny used to call him the Devil's child. He'd ride into the yard, cussing and spitting, kill the engine of his demon machine, and stagger up onto the porch, pass out in one of Granny's lawn chairs. On those nights, I couldn't wait to get up the next morning. I would lie awake at night, just waiting for five A.M. to hit. Then I'd pull my clothes on real fast and go out on the porch and wait for Daddy to wake up.

"What the hell are you staring at, kid?" He always said that when he managed to pry open one of his eyes. I didn't say anything. I knew better. I'd just watch him drift in and out of sleep. He was a good-looking man. Tall, with white-blond hair and really intense blue eyes. Those mornings he always smelled like beer and urine and that musty smell—perfume and pussy.

The smell of fornication, my Granny called it. She could smell that a mile away.

She would come out onto the porch, hollering and telling my daddy he was going to hell for his wicked ways.

He'd sit there, legs propped up, pocketknife in hand, scraping at the grease beneath his fingernails, just listening to the old woman.

I loved watching him with his knife, working at the grease, every once in a while digging a little too deep. A drop of red would appear, gliding down his skin, and I couldn't help but wonder what it felt like. That warm drop sliding down . . .

I could have watched Daddy forever, but after a while, Granny's hollering always got to him. Finally, he'd throw his feet on the floor, fold the knife and shove it into his pocket, and turn on her. He would holler at her, tell her he couldn't wait for hell because he'd get to see my momma, and he was in the mood for a good lay. She was the best piece he'd ever had, and he'd had her plenty. Everywhere. In the shed. The barn. Granny's kitchen.

That kind of talk always pissed Granny off. She'd turn this reddish purple, get out her shotgun, the long arm of Jesus, she called it, and threaten to blow him to hell a whole lot sooner than the Devil expected him.

He'd stagger out toward the shed, take a quick piss, not bothering to put his back to her, as if he got off on her seeing his private parts. Then he'd shake his dick, zip his fly, climb onto his demon bike and ride away.

I was always crying by this time. And mad.

"Why do you always make him leave?" I would scream.

That turned Granny an even deeper shade of purple. She'd prop the arm of Jesus against the screen door, grab the nearest fly swatter, and redden my ass, and my legs, and my face, and with each hit she'd tell me what trash I was and how I'd dirtied up my mother. Killed her.

Just like my daddy 'cause he'd been the one to stick his dick into her, knock her up with me, and then she'd died squeezing me out.

Hell, when Granny went to town on me like that, I think she believed I *was* my daddy. I had his eyes and all. His ways, she said so many times I had to shut her up eventually. Like father like son.

She was wrong. Dead wrong about so many things, pardon my phrasing.

My pissant daddy was a con man. Small-time compared to me.

I wondered why he ever bothered to come around at all, especially since he knew it pissed Granny off. At first, I thought he came because Momma had this insurance policy and Granny and me were the beneficiaries. And drinking and fucking required a little cash, and since Granny hated having him around, I always figured he showed up for money. To let her know why she was paying him to stay away. I got my balls up and asked him one morning, after he asked me what the hell I was looking at.

He said screw the cash. He could cop a few bucks anywhere. He came to see me. His son.

Liar. Nothing but a two-faced, goddamned liar!

Oh, he saw me all right. That last time, he saw me real good. Right up close. I hadn't waited for morning to come. I'd gone out onto the porch while it was still dark and slid the knife out of his pocket.

He woke up then, startled, but this time he didn't ask me what the hell I was looking at. He was too busy look-

ing at me, at the knife in my hands. Too busy watching
Death lean closer to him, aiming straight for those lying
blue eyes.

But enough about me. It's Darby I'm worried about.
She isn't acting like herself. I can't remember the last
time she went twenty-four hours without a drink.

And she wants it. She wants it bad, though she's lying
to herself about it.

I expected more of Darby. So innocent. So afraid. So
honest.

Damn, but I expected more.

Not that I'll let Darby's lying interfere with things. I'll
just have to set my sights on a different course of action.
Find another innocent.

Then, of course, I'll have to punish Darby for her lies.
For spoiling my plans. And for lusting after Graham
Tucker. I don't like whores. Never did. Granny can tell
you that.

Oh, well, I guess she can't. You see, Granny turned out
to be even more of a whore than my mother. And, of
course, I had to punish her.

Not that it's too late for Darby. I do have a soft spot for
her, and she's not beyond redemption if she mends her
wicked ways. Then I'll only have to punish her a little. I
hope she wises up. We've been beautiful together. Just
the two of us.

Maybe . . .

But if she doesn't, I'll be ready. I'm always ready, always smart, always one step ahead. Always.

Chapter Fourteen

After the run-in at the diner with Mary Lou Wallis, Darby decided to stock up on snacks and nonperishables, and avoid eating out altogether. It was a coward's move, she knew, but smart, as well. Darby had no doubt Maggie Cross had meant every word she'd said about not pouring salt on open wounds. Darby had no intention of being run out of town before she'd managed to recover those few hours in the attic.

Nostalgia had managed to keep out the large chain grocery stores, and offered only one choice for its inhabitants' culinary needs. With old-fashioned cash registers—forget the electronic bar code scanners—a candy counter where a kid could still get a sackful of penny candy for a quarter, and brown grocery crates instead of plastic bags, Proctor's Grocery and Feed, like the rest of Nostalgia, seemed caught in a perpetual time warp.

Darby cruised down the aisles, dropping items into the small basket hooked in the crook of her arm. The entire act felt so familiar, she half expected to glance up and see her mother behind her, shopping list in hand, searching for dinner items for that night.

Dead.

Even though Proctor's hadn't changed physically, it felt different. Colder. More sterile. The only thing even remotely warm was the tall teenage girl, apron tied around her waist, stocking a shelf near the front of the store. She was so tall, in fact, that she towered over Darby by a good foot.

The girl paused in front of the pyramid of canned cream-style corn and cast warm, welcoming blue eyes on Darby.

"Hey, you're new in town."

"Just got in yesterday," Darby replied, picking up a nearby bag of chips.

"I'm Deana." The girl pointed to her nametag. "Welcome to Nostalgia. There isn't much to see or do, except for Blue's house, that is. If you can get close. The TV people are here doing a live broadcast. Hey, you one of 'em?"

Darby shook her head and watched the girl's excitement fade into disappointment. Still, her blue eyes twinkled.

"Oh, well, enjoy your stay anyway." She glanced at her watch. "Ooohh, I'd better hurry. I'm gonna be late for my class." She glanced up. "I'm a senior at Nostalgia High. Center for the girl's basketball team. We're two-time state champions," she proudly declared. "I work here on weekends, lunch breaks, after school. Doesn't pay much, but it's enough to keep me in panty hose and eyeshadow, that's what my daddy says." She topped off the pyramid with the last can of corn, then pulled off her apron and tossed it behind a nearby counter. Her nametag followed. Then she pulled out a stack of schoolbooks and her purse. "I'm heading out, Mr. Proctor," she called toward the back of the store. "See you after basketball practice to finish those meat specials for tomorrow."

After the clerk left, Darby resumed her shopping, cruising down the aisles, grabbing bread, peanut butter, cookies, instant coffee—

"Your body is a temple of the Lord." The soft voice came from behind.

Darby turned to see Katy Evans, who stood a few feet away. She wore the same ugly skirt and blouse from yesterday. From the dark brown stains on the fabric, Darby suspected she hadn't changed at all. One whiff confirmed it.

"Your body is a temple," Katy mumbled again. She carried a small old-fashioned glass bottle of Coke in one hand, and the ever-present Bible in her other. "A house of the Lord."

A shiver crawled down Darby's spine. She pushed the feeling away and tried to keep her heartbeat from speeding up. There was just something about the words that stirred an uneasiness deep inside.

A memory?

Had someone spoken those words that night in the attic, or was Darby simply thinking back to one of Reverend Masters's sermons?

She didn't know. She only knew she'd heard those words before. Somewhere.

Forcing the strange melancholy aside, she focused on Katy.

"My body's more like a house of punishment," she said jokingly, fingering a box of chocolate cupcakes. "There's overcrowding in the fat cell population, and my poor arteries are this close to a riot." She'd hoped to coax a smile from Katy and break the ice. But the effort seemed lost.

The woman still hadn't met her gaze. Her gaze darted nervously around, at Darby's basket, at the shelves surrounding them. Anywhere but directly at Darby. Yet she didn't turn away, and Darby had the distinct impression Katy had approached her for a reason. Maybe to tell her something.

The woman stared a minute more, then shook her

head, as if clearing out whatever thoughts cluttered her mind. Then she started to back away.

"Wait," Darby said. "Let's go get a cup of coffee or something. Talk. What do you say?"

Another step back, then another.

"Please, Katy. Wait." Darby reached out. Her fingers closed around Katy's wrist.

Katy's frantic brown eyes jerked up and Darby glimpsed the same fear she'd seen outside the piss yellow trailer.

"Katy, it's all right. I'm not going to hurt you. I just want to talk."

The woman shook her head frantically, tearing her gaze away to fix on the point of contact where Darby's fingers gripped her arm.

"A temple of the Lord," she said to herself, the words rushing out, tumbling over one another as if she recited some desperate prayer. "Temple of the Lord. Temple of the Lord. Temple of the Lord . . ."

"Calm down," Darby said. "It's all right—"

Katy jerked away. Her bottle of Coke sailed to the ground, the glass clinking, then rolling, still intact. Bubbling brown soft drink spewed from the mouth, spreading over the tiled floor.

"Katy, wait!" Darby called after her, watching her flee down the aisle. Two seconds later, the door at the front of the store jingled, and Darby knew Katy had left.

Goose bumps crawled up and down her arms and she rubbed her hands over her skin, trying to dispel the sudden coldness. Okay, Katy had changed a lot. One hell of a lot. They all had. That night had destroyed everyone in one way or another.

Darby pushed the thoughts away and dropped to her knees to retrieve the now empty Coke bottle.

". . . floor is a mess."

The voice drew Darby to her feet. Bottle in hand, she walked to the end of the aisle and peered around a Doritos display to see Lyle Proctor, his brown hair now streaked with gray, his beard completely white. He wore his usual snowy button-down shirt and bowtie, white apron tied around his waist, white hat perched on top of his head in a first-class impersonation of the Good Humor man.

Except for his expression. Black eyes narrowed. A frown wrinkled his forehead as he stared down at a spilled container of milk, then at a young girl, maybe ten or twelve, who held a mop.

"Didn't I tell you to get this mess cleaned up?"

"I am," the girl said in a small, trembling voice.

"Well, you're doing a piss-poor job of it, Elsa. Just like your mother. The woman never could keep a neat house or make a decent meatloaf. You're just like her. Just as lazy and slow and . . ."

The words faded into a rush of memories that swamped Darby. Her father's voice bellowed at her.

Good-for-nothing bitch! Just like your mother. Good for nothing. Good for . . .

"But I'm trying, Daddy," Elsa Proctor said. "I am. It's not me. It's the mop. We need a new one—"

"Don't sass me, young lady. This one's just fine if you put a little backbone into it."

"The strands are frazzled. It won't soak up anything—"

The smack of Proctor's hand against the girl's cheek echoed down the aisle, and vibrated through Darby's body like the screech of nails across a chalkboard.

"Don't you ever raise your voice to me. You hear?" He glanced around, as if to make sure no one was watching him.

Just as his narrow black gaze passed her way, Darby ducked back behind the chip display.

He turned back to his daughter and Darby peered around the corner to watch him again.

Throwing the sponge at Elsa's feet, he gripped her by the hair and shoved her down on her hands and knees in the puddle of milk. "Now you put a little backbone into it until you soak up every drop, you hear?"

"My skirt, Daddy—"

"Do it! And I mean, you soak up every last drop, by dammit!" He shoved her down until her face was inches from the milk puddle. "You shouldn't have spilled it in the first place, clumsy, good-for-nothing girl! Just like your ma. She was all thumbs, always screwing things up for me. I always had to come along behind her and fix things or else this store would have gone to the Devil like everything else in this town."

"But my clothes," she whimpered, and he delivered another vicious slap to her other cheek, the sound drawing Darby a few steps closer, the girl's pitiful "Please" ringing in her ears.

"I won't be back-talked, girl. Ever! You do as I say and think twice about being so clumsy again. And hurry it up. I won't have you being late for school."

"How can I go like this?" she asked, the words quavering from her lips.

It was as if the sound of her voice set him off. It didn't matter what she said. All that mattered was that she kept talking, whether she begged or pleaded or damned him to hell, the result would have been the same. He caught her by the hair and yanked her head back.

Darby's feet and hands seemed to move of their own accord. She rushed forward, raised the Coke bottle and cracked it over Lyle Proctor's head.

With a surprised cry, he let go of his daughter and whirled. Black eyes riveted on her, the depths filled with coldness, rage. A tiny drop of leftover Coke trickled down his forehead.

Her heart stopped beating as time sucked her back, to the kitchen, her mother's blood pooling at her feet, her father towering over her, the knife in her hands instead of a broken Coke bottle.

The glass cut into her hand. A liquid warmth filled her palm. Her hand trembled, lifted, as her gaze riveted on the rise and fall of Lyle Proctor's chest. His vicious words echoed in her ears in unison with her father's.

Good-for-nothing bitch! Good-for-nothing . . . bitch!

"Holy shit," Lyle muttered. His eyes widened, filling with fear as Darby raised the piece of Coke bottle threateningly.

"Please, no." The girl's small voice pushed through Darby's thoughts, yanking her back to reality.

Darby stared into Lyle Proctor's eyes, saw the blood dripping from the wound at his temple where she'd hit him. Her gaze went to the frightened girl, skirt soiled with milk, standing a few feet away, then to her own raised hand, the jagged piece of bottle. In a rush of panic, she realized what she'd been about to do.

Her fingers opened. The glass fell to the ground.

"I—I'm sorry," she murmured, her gaze riveted on the little girl. "I. . . ." The words stalled in her throat as she stumbled backward, blood dribbling down her palm.

Darby bolted from the store, her father's face in her mind.

Good for nothing . . .

The face faded into Lyle Proctor's, the voice changing into the grocer's.

Inside her car, she shoved the key into the ignition, peeled out of the gravel driveway and swerved onto the main intersection, heedless of the cars that slammed on their brakes to avoid her. She even left the patrol car sitting back at the red light, stuck behind two cars who'd been slow to move out of her way.

Blood eased from the cuts on her palm, filling the car with the sickeningly sweet scent of death.

It wasn't the blood that sent her speeding down the highway for Poppy's icehouse out on I-45. It was the knowledge of what she'd been about to do. What she would have done had Elsa Proctor's soft voice not penetrated the bloodlust clouding her thinking.

She'd been about to kill Lyle Proctor. Stab him with the broken bottle.

Worse, she'd wanted to do it.

She forced the man's image away and grasped onto the

picture of Elsa Proctor, the bruises on her arms and legs, the loneliness and fear in her wide green eyes. Darby knew what the girl felt. She'd felt it every day of her life until she'd shoved the knife into her father and ended his sorry existence.

And she'd been about to do the same to Elsa's father.

She'd wanted to.

She still wanted to, she realized, staring down at her trembling hand, which grasped the steering wheel already smeared with red heat.

God, she'd wanted to, and she could have. Just one quick motion—

No!

She slammed on the brakes outside of Poppy's and bolted from the car. A pay phone stood to one side of the entrance to the bar and Darby rushed into the booth, slid the door closed and searched her purse for a quarter. Then she dialed 911.

"Nostalgia Police Department. Emergency line. May I help you?"

"I'd like to speak with someone in children's protective services. I need to report an episode of child abuse."

For the next few minutes, Darby relived the scene in Proctor's store while a woman named Mrs. Langley took notes on the other end.

Moments later, Darby hung up and stumbled from the phone booth. The noonday sun spilled over her, temporarily blinding her as she entered the dark coolness of the bar, the sign above the door blinking a neon WELCOME Y'ALL.

A cloud of cigarette smoke and the sweet smell of liquor swallowed her up as the door rocked shut behind her. Daylight ceased to exist as Darby focused her eyes on her surroundings.

This was reality, she told herself as she glanced around, the neon beer signs twinkling. Welcoming. She collapsed on a bar stool.

"What'll it be, hon?" A chubby, middle-aged woman

stood behind the bar, a tube top stretched tight over her double-D breasts and soft middle. Her red lips parted in a smile. Her eyes crinkled and made the surrounding wrinkles even deeper. "Happy-hour special today is long-necks, ninety-nine cents."

"Isn't it a little early for happy hour?"

"Hon, every hour's happy around here. Try a couple of them longnecks, and I guarantee you'll be smiling till sunset."

"Double shot of tequila," Darby said. "And I'll have a bottle of bourbon to go. I intend to be smiling long after sunset."

"Looks like it," the woman said, red-tipped pudgy hands disappearing behind the bar. She pulled out a shot glass and a bottle of clear gold liquid.

Salvation, a small voice whispered inside Darby's head.

But it wouldn't save her. Her brain knew that. Still, she couldn't make herself turn away and walk out.

Maybe the booze was only a distraction, but she needed one, no matter how temporary.

"Nasty cut there on your hand," the bartender observed, setting the glass down in front of Darby before pouring the shot.

The drops splashed into the glass and Darby licked her lips, focusing on the sight in front of her rather than the images rolling through her mind.

Her father. Lyle Proctor. Elsa Proctor.

Good-for-nothing bitch!

"Leave it," she said when the bartender turned to put the bottle away.

"Whatever you say, hon." She turned, pulled a bottle of bourbon off the shelf.

Darby reached out, but the woman held out an open palm. "You want to drink here, you pay up front."

Slapping a credit card down on the bar, Darby gripped the bottle of bourbon, shoved it down deep into her purse, then turned back toward the tequila shot.

"Cash only," the woman said sliding the credit card back to Darby, who hurriedly pulled out a wad of bills.

Red-tipped nails closed around the money and the woman smiled. "Enjoy, sweetie."

But Darby wasn't out to enjoy anything. She just wanted to forget for a little while. Escape.

All the things the booze offered her.

A chip off the old alcoholic block.

She was. As much as she hated the way her fingers reached for the glass, the way her throat welcomed the sting of the liquor, she couldn't help herself.

With each drink, a small part of her rejoiced, while another part damned her for being so weak. And the fight was on, her newfound sobriety battling the craving inside of her in an age-old war. Good against evil. Life against death. And despite the liquor-induced peace stealing through Darby's senses, she couldn't help but wonder which would win.

Then again, deep, deep inside, she already knew the answer to that, and so she drank shot after shot, as if the liquor could blur the truth.

And, as always, it eventually did.

"I want that bitch picked up *now*!" Lyle Proctor glared at the desk sergeant, his face an angry, puffy red, dried blood caked at his temple.

"Now, now, Mr. Proctor. I can't rightly do that without proper cause."

"You have proper cause. Look at my damned head!"

"Yes, but the forms have to be signed by Chief Cross before I can put out an APB on her."

"Then get Cross to sign the damned papers and issue the warrant," Lyle thundered.

"She's on her lunch right now. As soon as she's finished—"

"Lunch! I'm attacked in my own store by a crazy woman and she's eating lunch! Screw her damned lunch!"

"Now, now, Lyle. I know you're upset, but there ain't no need to use that kind of language. You just have a seat and cool down, and the chief'll be done before you know it."

"Like hell I will. I want this woman arrested. Right now, by dammit. Now!"

"No problem, Lyle. I'll have her picked up just as soon as I have your ass hauled in for assault," came the distinct female voice from the end of the corridor.

"What?" Lyle whirled to see the chief of police standing in her office doorway.

Maggie barreled down the hall, hips swaying in her tight black regulation trousers. "You heard what I said. You want me to book you first, or you want to give Milton Prescott a call? Wouldn't want you to say anything that might be incriminating without your lawyer handy."

"What the hell are you talking about?"

She came right up to him, stared him square in the eyes. "I'm talking about assault on a twelve-year-old child. Your child, understand, Proctor? A call came in a little while ago and it seems you weren't being very fatherly to that young'un you got at home. A shame, too. Mabel would turn over in her grave if she knew what she'd left her daughter to."

"You're crazy."

"And you're in deep shit, unless you want to lower your voice and come on into my office where we can talk about this with a civilized tongue. Otherwise, you'll be spending the afternoon behind bars. Your choice." She turned to head back down the hall to her office.

Lyle glared at the desk sergeant, then started after Maggie.

After a fifteen-minute talk, Lyle stomped out of Maggie's office, his face still beet red. He shoved past Graham Tucker, who had just walked into the station.

"What happened to Lyle?" Graham asked a few minutes later as he sank down on the chair opposite Maggie.

"I thought the Lone Ranger was on self-appointed baby-sitting duty?"

"I had some things to do and I thought I'd let your boys handle the situation for a little while."

"You picked a fine time to hand over the reins to Tonto," she muttered. "You missed seeing Lyle Proctor get his head cracked open."

"Darby?" he asked, all the while wondering why he felt so shocked. He knew what she was capable of. He knew. "She hit Lyle?"

"With a Coke bottle. Bopped him right over the head."

"Then why don't you have her picked up?"

"Because Lyle Proctor isn't going to press charges."

"You're kidding."

"He's got a temper, but he isn't dumb. He's already in enough hot water, without drawing more attention to himself by pressing charges. That would mean a trial to sort out the whole story of what happened, a trial with Lyle's peers, and he doesn't want his dirty laundry aired in public. Folks around here don't like child abusers, and Lyle would lose a helluva lot of business to that new Piggly Wiggly in Crocket, even if it is a good twenty miles away."

"Child abuse?" Graham asked, incredulous. "You're kidding, right?"

"Darby called in to the station. It seems Proctor was beating up on his daughter, not anything out of the ordinary, come to find out. I gave Doc Waller a call, put on a little pressure, and learned that Elsa Proctor has had a broken arm, a fractured jaw and two broken ribs—all in the past year, though Waller insists the injuries *could* have resulted from normal child behavior—bike accidents, roller-skating. The funny thing is, Elsa Proctor doesn't own a bike, and she's never been within a mile of the roller-skating rink. Lyle keeps her busy in the store every minute she isn't in school. Doesn't even let her go on any of the church outings. About the only place the child goes is to youth prayer meetings three times a week, and that's probably just Lyle's token gesture to keep himself from frying in hell when Judgment Day comes."

Anger boiled through Graham, making his blood pump faster. "Why didn't you do something sooner?"

"I told you, I just talked to Doc Waller. Never had any complaints before Darby's."

"The guy's been hurting his little girl. How can a whole town of people miss something like that?"

"You've been living big-city life too long," Maggie told him. "Nobody missed it, Tucker. Folks around here are just as smart as those in Dallas. It's just that they're a mite more loyal. Doc Waller's part of the same lodge group as Proctor, and ninety-nine percent of the men in this town. They stick together. The good-old-boy mentality at work."

"That's friggin' crazy."

"I agree, but turning a blind eye is pretty damned tough to prove in court. Besides, most of those good old boys are the backbone of this town. Salt of the earth types. Nearly untouchable when it comes to proving any kind of wrongdoing."

"They're a bunch of ignorant sons of bitches."

"They're just scared is all. They don't want to think stuff like that goes on here, much less admit it, and neither do I. Elsa Proctor is an isolated incident. Most of the people in this town are good, solid folk, and I want it to stay that way."

"Hell, Maggie, you might as well strap on a dick and join the club."

Maggie frowned. "Make no mistake, Lyle will get what he deserves, but he'll get it quietly, without a big ruckus. I don't want to feed the press any more than they've already chomped down on with this Blue anniversary hoopla."

"So what exactly happened at the store?"

"It seems Proctor cut loose on Elsa while she was home from school during lunch break. Place was empty, except for Darby, but Lyle didn't realize anybody was around. Darby saw him, of course. She freaked, or so Lyle says, and went after him with a Coke bottle."

Anger licked at Graham's senses and he wondered why the hell the idea of Darby facing off with Lyle Proctor bothered him. Darby deserved to face a hell of a lot worse.

Or did she? The question tore at him, throwing a dense gray shadow over everything that had once seemed so black-and-white.

"Where is she?" he asked.

"Long gone from here and out of my hair, for the moment. Which is more than I can say for you." She gave the folder under his arm a pointed look. "I hope that isn't one of my case files, or your ass is going to be in a sling. I don't recall signing any release form, and you aren't a member of this department."

"Don't get all hot and bothered. It's a case file, but not one of yours. A friend of mine in Dallas just faxed it to me. Since Pinky hasn't come into the modern age and installed fax machines at the Tropicana, I had the info sent here to the front desk."

"That's taxpayers' money."

"So bill me for the ink and paper," he said.

Her frown turned to an outright glare. A warning flashed in her eyes. "I'd advise you not to start digging up a bunch of stuff better left buried. This town deserves a little peace."

But Graham wasn't worried about the town's peace. He was more concerned with his own, and he wouldn't have a moment of it until he saw justice served.

"That's good advice, Maggie," he said. "Food for thought."

"I mean it, Tucker. Let things alone. I've got enough to contend with as it is. Every newspaper across the state has sent someone to cover this anniversary. And there are national publications as well, TV shows—you name it. Everybody wants the dirt on what happened, and I won't have you shoveling anything their way, you hear? I just have to keep law and order around here another four days, until this broadcast is over; then I'm home free."

He nodded and left the police station, Maggie's warning quickly forgotten. He wouldn't let things alone. He would find his sister's killer, no matter how much he had to dig.

But first, he had to find Darby Jayson.

Chapter Fifteen

The sun had already set by the time Graham found Darby. Her car sat outside of Poppy's, about six miles outside the city limits. The building, sheet-metal walls and a flat tin roof, housed a jukebox, a pool table, and a wall-to-wall bar. Tables were few, yet the parking lot was full. The clientele consisted primarily of blue-collar workers on their way home to the neighboring towns from a huge paper mill just up the interstate, and, of course, there were the women. Any place that attracted a lot of men had a group of female regulars—those out to make a few extra bucks in exchange for their company, toss down a few free drinks, and have a good time. And Poppy's was the place for that, all right, if the noise spilling from inside was any indication.

It took a full minute for Graham's eyes to adjust to the foggy interior, and half that time for him to figure out what all the hooting and hollering was about.

He stared through the smoky neon haze at the woman standing by the jukebox, her body sandwiched between two men.

We're not in Kansas anymore.

The phrase popped into his head as he fixed his gaze on Darby. *Not* the Darby who'd fended off his advances in the ladies' room yesterday when he'd been so bold as to touch her.

This was the Darby he'd seen outside of Samuel Blue's that night, her smile firmly in place as she sweet-talked the security guard, her eyes dark and smoky and filled with unspoken promises.

Her eyes were closed now, but the unspoken promises were there in her body language. Her head tilted back as she gyrated to a Brooks and Dunn song blaring from the jukebox. Her arms were above her head, her breasts thrust tight against the white tank top she wore. Half a tank top. It was one of those cutoff shirts that dropped just below her breasts, exposing a dangerous portion of smooth skin, her belly button peeking over the top of her jeans. A fine sheen of perspiration covered her skin, the interior of the bar warm with so many bodies squeezed in.

Undoubtedly Darby was warm with those two men so close, Graham thought, his fingers tightening around the truck keys in his hand. The one in front of her stood barely inches away, rocking his pelvis along with hers, a smile on his face as his gaze feasted on her breasts. The man in back had his hands on her hips, his touch occasionally drifting down to trace the curve of her shapely ass. And with every suggestive touch, the audience let loose a roar of approval.

Graham was instantly reminded of a bachelor party he'd gone to for one of his fellow officers on the force last year. There had been two female strippers, and the bachelor had been in the middle. The women had practically peeled the guy's clothes off and gone down on him right then and there, to the encouragement of a rowdy bunch of horny cops.

The guy in front of Darby reached out, his palm going

to the side of one breast, and anger rolled through Graham.

Before he could deny the feeling, his legs were eating up the distance through the crowd, to the swaying threesome.

"We need to talk." At the sound of his voice, Darby's eyelids lifted lazily, revealing her wide, chocolate-colored eyes. Bloodshot eyes, he quickly noted, and he knew in that instant she was three sheets to the wind.

A slow smile spread across her face, her full lips curving just enough to send a pang of longing through him to keep the anger company.

"Hi," she said, as if they'd just bumped into each other outside the laundromat, or at a Friday-night football game.

"Hey, buddy." The guy in front of Darby turned a glare on Graham. "Find your own dance partner."

"Yeah, Tucker," said the man in back of Darby.

"Hey, Sullivan." Graham gave the familiar man a pointed stare. "Don't you have a wife and kids waiting at home for you?"

A red stain crept up the guy's neck, and his dancing, if the awkward movements could be called dancing, stopped. "Just taking a breather before I head home," he said defensively.

"Some breather," Graham grumbled before fixing his stare on Darby. "We need to talk," he said again.

Anyone else would have turned tail and run at the sound of Graham's voice, so low, so calm, so damned furious, but Darby seemed oblivious. Her hips didn't miss a beat.

"Talk?" She stared at him as if he'd grown another head. "Tired of talking. Wanna dance."

At that moment, the record changed and a faster song blared from the speakers. Darby quickened her pace, undulating to the new beat, faster and faster. Sullivan, the guy in back of her, threw his hands up in surrender.

"I'll sit this one out," he said, but the guy in front of

Darby—the patch on his chest said Will—obviously had no intention of losing what ground he'd gained. Especially since Darby was the hottest thing to come through Poppy's since the place had started serving jalapeno peanuts at the bar.

"That's it, baby," he crooned, inching in closer. "Just like that."

His pelvis bumped hers. Darby lost her footing and stumbled backward. The guy tried to grab her, to pull her closer, but Graham was quicker. His fingers closed around her wrist and he jerked her from Will's grasp.

"Oops," she said, coming up hard against Graham's chest, his arm locking around her waist. Unlike in the rest room when she'd been as nervous as a wild colt, now she sagged against him, fitting her body to his.

"What the hell do you think you're doing?" Will demanded, hands on his hips, obviously not ready to give up without a fight.

"Talking," Graham said. "You have a problem with that?"

They stared each other down for a long second, the only sound that of the music blaring. Finally the man threw up his hands. "Ain't met a woman yet worth this kind of trouble. Talk away."

"But I don't want to talk," Darby said as Graham led her to a darkened corner of the bar and pushed her down on a vacant stool.

She closed her eyes, swaying back and forth to the music as he sat down beside her.

"So you like this song?" It wasn't one he recognized. Some country cheating-and-drinking song with a fast tempo.

She cast a sideways glance at him. "Well, it ain't the Smashing Pumpkins, but it's not bad for redneck central here. It's got a good, fast beat you can dance to. I give it an eight."

"Redneck central, huh? Forgetting where you came from?"

She stopped swaying and plopped her elbows on the bar. "Unfortunately, that I remember all too well." She signaled to the waitress, who quickly appeared, bottle and shot glass in hand. "I think I'm ready for the rest of that bottle now."

"The rest?" Graham asked incredulously. "It's half empty."

"I was thirsty." She nodded and the waitress moved to pour a shot glass full. Graham's hand darted out.

"I think she's had enough."

"Who're you?" the woman asked. "Her daddy?"

"He's nobody." Darby pushed his hand away. "Go on and pour."

The waitress glanced from Graham's furious expression to Darby's expectant one. "Looks like a family squabble to me, and I ain't of a mind to butt my nose in where it don't belong. Pour it yourself, lady," she said, leaving the bottle.

Darby reached for it, only to have Graham's hand close over hers. "An anonymous call came in about Lyle Proctor today."

"That's nice." She worked at pulling the bottle toward her.

"Seems he beat up his little girl right in front of a customer."

"That isn't so nice. Do you mind?"

Reluctantly, he released her and watched her pour a drink. She filled the shot glass with a surprisingly steady hand that told Graham she'd done it before. Many times.

"So what do you know about the call?"

"Nothing."

"You weren't in Proctor's store today?"

She gave him a pointed stare. "You know I was, so why are you here giving me the third degree? I was the customer, I reported him. End of story."

"And it shook you up so bad you're here getting plastered."

"I'm not plastered. Not yet." She downed another drink.

"Slow down," Graham said, covering the glass when she tried for another.

"Why don't you leave me alone?" she grumbled, her other hand coming up to try to pry his loose. That was when he noticed the makeshift bandage tied around her palm, the white material stained a dark red.

"So that's what happened to the rest of your T-shirt."

"I cut myself," she said defensively.

"How?"

"On a Coke bottle." She fell silent for a moment, her gaze fixed on the bandage. "In Lyle Proctor's store," she finally added before burying her face in her hands.

Graham had the insane urge to reach out, to touch her and ease the sudden trembling that gripped her shoulders.

Any other time he would have called himself every name imaginable and fought the urge, but something about the way she sat there, shoulders slumped, defeated almost, crumpled his hard-ass resolve. At least for the moment.

His hand reached out, closing over her shoulder. "I know that what happened at the store gave you quite a scare."

She moved her hand aside and peeked at him with one eye. "Why the hell did you come here, Graham? To gloat? I almost killed a man today, and I bet it's eating you up that I didn't go through with it."

"Killed him?" Graham's mind traveled back to the police station. Proctor had looked a little bloody, but nothing close to death. "Jesus, I didn't know it was that bad."

"Oh, it was bad, all right. Proctor was beating up on his little girl, so I stepped in." Her hands fell to the countertop and she stared straight ahead, as if contemplating her reflection in the smudged mirror above the bar. "I didn't mean . . . I mean, I didn't even know what I was going to do, I just knew I had to do something. When I

206

saw him hit her, it—it brought back so many memories, and then after seeing Katy again—"

"Katy was there?"

"Aisle nine, right before it happened. She was in the store shopping, I guess, and drinking a Coke. That's where the bottle came from. Anyway, I'd bumped into her and I was a little shaken up."

"Why?"

"Because she kept reciting these biblical verses. It gave me the creeps."

"Your guilty conscience rearing its ugly head?" It was a low blow, but he couldn't resist.

She shook her head. "Just get away from me."

"I'm sorry."

"Yeah, I bet."

"I am," he pressed, surprised to realize he actually meant it. The wall between them was thick enough without him fortifying it with cheap shots. "Now tell me what happened with Proctor."

She didn't say anything for a long moment, just stared straight ahead, then down at her hands. "Like I said," she finally went on. "I saw him hit his little girl." She closed her eyes, as if seeing those memories, reliving the past right there with the music and lights swirling around them. "I couldn't just stand there and do nothing." She fell silent then and Graham knew that for a few seconds, the old Darby, the one who'd been so frightened around him, who'd stared up at him with a mixture of fear and desire bright in her doe eyes, still lived and breathed inside the confident, sexy woman who'd been dancing with Sullivan and Will.

Her gaze captured his. "I really didn't mean to hurt him." Then she shook her head. "No, I did mean to hurt him and that's the problem. I meant to hurt him, to do worse than what I did." Her gaze dropped to the bloodstained bandage covering her hand. "It's crazy. For those few seconds, I wasn't watching Proctor. I was staring at my father, at myself." She grabbed the bottle of tequila, not bothering with a shot glass this time. Instead, she touched the rim to her lips and took a long drink.

When she finished, Graham watched as a drop of gold liquid trickled from the corner of her mouth, down her chin. The urge to reach out and taste the tequila for himself, to taste *her*, was nearly overwhelming.

"I wasn't standing in the middle of that grocery store," she continued, "I was back home. Just me and my old man. That same rage I'd felt the night I watched him hit my mama for the last time swept through me. I wanted to kill the son of a bitch." A hysterical laugh bubbled on her wet lips. "I would have."

"Except?"

The laughter died and she closed her eyes, staring at some unseen nightmare. "Except Elsa Proctor picked that moment to say something." She turned to Graham. "It wasn't much. A *please*, or a *stop*, I don't know. It wasn't really what she said, but the sound of her voice, so desperate. She didn't want me to hurt the bastard, even though he was using her for a punching bag. Stupid." She shook her head. "Funny thing was, I knew what she was feeling. It was the same way I'd felt every time the cops came out to my house, when my daddy had been hollering and beating on my mother. I would cry and beg them not to take him away. My feelings changed the night he killed her, or maybe they'd changed long before then and I just never admitted it. Anyhow, when I heard Elsa's voice, my anger slipped away. In came the fear, of myself, of the bottle in my hands, of what I'd been about to do, and I got the hell out of there." She traced her finger over the label on the bottle. "I guess all that sounds pretty crazy to you, being a cop and all. You probably don't give a shit about motives, just the facts."

"You're wrong about that, and what you said didn't sound crazy at all."

She cut him a glance. "I know I'm drunk, but I could have sworn I heard a note of sympathy in your voice, Tucker. You going soft on me all of a sudden?"

"Not soft, just honest. Nobody faults you for what happened with your old man, Darby. You gave him what he deserved, what somebody else should have given him a helluva lot sooner. He was a mean bastard."

"I know." Her voice was soft, quiet, without a trace of bitterness or anger, only resignation, and Graham wondered for a fraction of a second how in the world he could think her guilty of murder.

Because she was, he reminded himself. It didn't matter how calm and cool and scared she looked now. How sorry. Killers like Darby felt no remorse, and their rage was controlled. So tightly controlled that they fooled everyone around them.

Ted Bundy—the good-looking, intelligent college-boy type.

John Wayne Gacy—business owner and pillar of the community.

Samuel Elijah Blue—the soft-spoken, blue-eyed boy next door who could sweet-talk a woman into slitting her own throat.

Still, when Graham tried to sum Darby up as easily, he couldn't. There was so much about her that fit the typical psychopath profile, and so much that didn't. And with her so close to him, so warm, so open and honest, or so it seemed, he couldn't quite shove her into the monster category. Not now, not yet.

"I shouldn't have hit Proctor," she said. "I should have called the police, yelled at him, something besides what I did, but I couldn't help myself. The bottle was in my hands, and I had the insane notion it was him or me. I just kept picturing my dad. I went out to my old house last night, and it just brought everything back."

"Don't beat yourself up because you reacted the way you did. It stands to reason, after living through hell with your old man, you would react the way you did. It was normal."

"Now I know you're going soft," she said, downing another drink. "What happened to the guy who wants to see me go to the electric chair?"

"No electric chairs in Texas. We're civilized now. It's the needle."

"I stand corrected." She gave him a sideways glance. "So what happened to the guy who wants to see me get the needle?" She half turned, her arm bumping into the tequila bottle.

"Oops," she murmured as a puddle of liquid spread across the bartop before Graham could right it.

"Now I know you've had enough."

"You're avoiding the question."

"I thought we called a truce yesterday."

"You blew the truce, remember? With all the potshots you've been taking."

"I stand corrected." He mopped up the spilled liquor with a stack of cocktail napkins.

"So?"

She was pushing him for an answer, but Graham wasn't of a mind to give her one. Hell, he didn't have one, and he wasn't quite ready to sort through the conflicting feelings swirling in his gut. She'd been right about the sympathy, but he felt a multitude of other things, as well. Compassion, anger, respect, hate—too many things for him to sort through at the moment.

"*So,* I think you've had enough to drink for one night," he said. "Let me give you a ride back to the motel. I'm going that way anyway."

"Yeah, I bet you are. The watchdog back on duty?" He smiled and she took another long drink before adding, "I don't think I'm quite ready to call it a night yet. It's early and I'm in the mood for a little fun."

Anger hit him like a fist to the chest as his gaze swiveled to Will and Sullivan playing a game of pool in the corner. Sullivan kept his eyes glued on the shot he was about to make, but Will made no pretense of hiding his interest in Darby.

Graham could feel his gaze.

"You up for a little more *dancing*?" he said, his voice laced with sarcasm.

"As a matter of fact, I am." She closed her eyes and swayed to the slow song that drifted from the jukebox.

"Then I'm sorry I broke up your little party." He glared at Will for another long minute, then turned back to find Darby staring at him.

"Don't you like to dance, Graham? Don't you ever loosen up enough to have any fun? You used to be a lot of fun, if memory serves me. Graham Tucker—teen heartthrob, star quarterback and personal sex instructor for half the girls at Nostalgia High."

He smiled. "That was a long time ago. I'm all grown up now. Traded in my helmet for a bad haircut and a pension, and all my students have graduated."

"All of them?" When he nodded, she added, "And to think I had you pegged for the wife and 2.3 kids kind of guy. In fact, I think every mother in Nostalgia did."

"I had the wife and kids potential back then, but no more." Images from that night nagged at his conscience, desperate to creep in, but he pushed them back, needing a few minutes away from the guilt, the anger, the hatred. . . . Away from everything and everyone, except the woman sitting a few inches from him.

"My life now doesn't exactly lend itself to the domestic bliss thing. When I'm on a stakeout or an undercover investigation, I can go days, weeks without setting foot in my apartment. I eat in the middle of the night, sleep when I get a few minutes, and I barely make enough to feed myself, much less a family. Not exactly a good catch."

Darby took another drink, her gaze riveted on the liquid in her glass. "I live alone, work alone. Not much different from how I was when I lived here. Still a loner."

"No significant other?" he asked.

She shook her head. "Never. Don't get me wrong; I've had my share of lessons." She stared straight ahead, that faraway look creeping back into her eyes for a long moment. "But never the same teacher more than once."

"It's easier that way," he said. "No ties. No complications. No distractions."

"I agree. My lifestyle doesn't exactly lend itself to domestic bliss either. My column requires me to be up half the night, cruising nightspots, checking out local bands. It would be kind of hard if I had to worry about someone waiting at home for me." She glanced down and studied her bandaged hand. "Kind of hard, but kinda nice, too."

Despite the noise of the bar, a peaceful pause settled between them.

"Yeah, I know what you mean," he finally admitted, damning himself all the while.

"But no use dreaming." She signaled the waitress for another bottle. "Not when there's good music and good whiskey."

"Tequila," he corrected. "And you keep downing that stuff and you won't be able to walk, much less dance."

"I could down two more bottles and still dance circles around you." She tried to get to her feet, only to sway backward toward the bar stool. "Okay, forget the dancing. But I've only finished one bottle and I can still see one of you."

"That's not good?"

"Terrible. When there's three of you staring back at me, I'll be done. Until then, I'm sitting right here." She grabbed the new bottle and tilted it toward him in salute. "Cheers."

From the amount she'd already consumed, Graham knew he was sitting next to a pro. Nearly a full bottle of tequila and she could still think straight, or semistraight. There was no telling how long this would take, but he didn't intend to walk out of Poppy's without her. He settled in and ordered a beer.

They talked a little while longer, about her life in San Francisco, his life in Dallas, exchanging stories, mainly about work and their combined endless string of one-night-stands. As the night wore on, he could almost forget the reality that waited for them outside the bar.

The murders. Her guilt.

Almost, but Graham hadn't had nearly *that* much to drink. Unlike Darby. Slowly but surely, drink by drink, her words slurred. Her eyes drifted closed, until he knew she was ready to fall over.

The bartender issued the last call and Graham, pulled out his truck keys.

"I think it's time to go."

"Go?" She forced her eyes open, swaying on the bar stool. She would have keeled over right then if Graham hadn't reached out a steadying hand.

"But istill eary. Mean, er—ly." She sounded out the word with thick lips. She held up two fingers, indicating about a quarter of an inch. "I think I'm l'il bit drunk." When he stood up beside her, she took one look at him and burst into a fit of giggles. "A lot," she managed after several gulps of air. "There's sree of you."

"Come on. Me and my two buddies will give you a ride home." He helped her to her feet, holding her close when she lost her balance.

"Whew, ishotinhere." The words ran together in an indistinguishable mumble and she fanned herself frantically.

"Outside will be better."

"Don' feelso good," she said once they'd pushed their way through Poppy's and out into the parking lot. She touched her temples and leaned against him. "Stop," she said.

"What?"

"Movin'. Stop movin' the ground."

"Open your eyes and it'll stop."

She tried, pushing her eyes wide, but then the effort seemed too much for her and her eyelids drifted closed. Graham scooped her up, her small frame light in his arms, and carried her the rest of the way to his pickup.

The ride back took less than fifteen minutes, but Darby

was out cold by the time they pulled into the motel parking lot.

Graham found her keys in her purse, hefted her slight weight into his arms and headed for her motel room. Inside, he eased her down onto the bed and slid her boots off. He grabbed her nightgown, which sat folded on the dresser. Leaning down, he tossed the nightgown beside her and went to work on her jeans. He slid the denim down her legs, his eyes feasting on the sight of so much smooth, creamy flesh.

He pulled the jeans free and threw them over the back of a nearby chair. He moved to her T-shirt, then decided against it when he accidentally brushed the side of one breast. Her nipples pebbled beneath the thin material.

She wasn't wearing a bra, and though he'd vowed to be her watchdog and nothing more, at the moment, he felt more like a bulldog. A horny bulldog. The sight of her bare breasts while he put her into a nightgown would definitely be his undoing.

His gaze moved lower, to the thin triangle of white lace that covered a thatch of dark brown curls. His hand trembled, his fingers eager to reach out, to stroke, to push the lace aside and slide deep into her—

He yanked the covers up over her before he could complete the thought and tossed the unused gown back onto the dresser. So much for chivalry. His attention went to the bandage wrapped around her injured hand and his thoughts traveled, not to Lyle Proctor, but to her father, her childhood.

The whole town had known about her old man, and when she'd killed him, not one person had blamed her. Vince Jayson had been an embarrassment to the town. Just another piece of poor white welfare trash, not some pillar of the community like Lyle Proctor.

Had Darby enjoyed killing her father so much that she'd gone on to bigger and better things? To cold-blooded, calculated murder?

Yes.

Most likely.

Since when had *yes* turned to *most likely?*

It hadn't, he told himself. She was guilty. Either killer or accomplice. Either way, blood dripped from her hands. He knew that. He simply had to remember that all-important fact and not underestimate her.

He studied her, from the tips of her blanket-covered toes, to the top of her head. She hadn't moved a muscle since he'd set her on the bed. Not even a twitch. Her breaths came slow and deep, her mind lost somewhere in a liquor sleep that would have her knocked out all night, probably even a good part of tomorrow.

At least he wouldn't have to worry about getting up early, he thought a few minutes later as he collapsed on his own bed and picked up a manila folder full of faxes— the case file on the slumber-party killings a friend of his had sent over from the Dallas PD.

When the murders had occurred, Maggie had had sense enough to know she was in way over her head. She'd called the Dallas Homicide division to help in the investigation. Graham didn't have access to Nostalgia records, and he knew getting the case file from Maggie would be like shoving a cow off ripe grazing land.

Fortunately, the Dallas PD had accumulated their own thick stack of information, complete with copies of most of the information from the Nostalgia file, all of which Graham had read through again and again.

But this time he was looking for something. He didn't know what, just *something*. Something to clue him in to whatever it was Darby had been looking for when she'd tried to break into Blue's house. *If* she'd been looking for anything and not simply trying to relive old memories, as she'd put it.

He only wished he had the pictures that went with the file, but those would be here by tomorrow morning. He'd pulled in at least a handful of favors for that. He started reading, trying his damnedest to concentrate.

Darby was dead to the world next door, her car miles

away at Poppy's. He knew she wasn't going anywhere. Still, he kept the drapes open, and every once in a while his gaze strayed from the case file in front of him to the window. Years as a cop had taught him to expect the unexpected. It wouldn't surprise him in the least to see her walk past his window.

At least he told himself that.

Then she strolled past a few hours later, and Graham felt as if he'd been blindsided by a John Deere.

He blinked, wiping his tired eyes before staring at the window again. Gone. He shot a glance at the clock. Four A.M. He'd been up reading for three hours, or trying to read. He must have dozed off.

Stifling a yawn, he focused his blurry gaze on the page in front of him. He still had some reports to get through.

He'd barely made it through the first line, when the slow creak of the door jerked his head up.

"Holy shit," he muttered, staring at the woman who appeared in the doorway. He slapped the case file down on the bed beside him. "It was you I saw just now."

Just to make sure, he wiped at his eyes again. She didn't disappear this time. June bugs bumped and buzzed around the bare bulb behind her. Pale yellow light caressed her curves, outlining the smooth lines of her thighs, the flare of her hips, the indentation at her waist, the rounded fullness of her breasts, and higher to the graceful slope of her neck.

Her pale skin glowed in the darkness, along with her white panties and T-shirt. She'd shed the blanket, damn her.

"My, my, you look good enough to eat," she murmured, trailing a fingertip along her bottom lip, her gaze devouring his bare chest, down to one hell of an erection that strained painfully against his faded denims.

"But you passed out," he said accusingly. "You drank nearly two bottles of tequila." Impossible. This couldn't be happening. She couldn't be real.

Could she?

She wet her lips and Graham could almost feel the stroke of her tongue. It had to be real. No dream could feel this good. This painful.

"What are you doing in here?" he asked.

"What do you want me to do?"

A dozen answers swirled through his head, skimming over his senses to shout very loudly in the direction of his cock. "You should go back to your room," he managed with tight lips.

"That's not what you want, Graham. Not really. I can see the truth right there." Her gaze dropped to his pants, then lifted, locking with his. "And in your eyes. That's not what you want at all. You want me here. You want this." She cupped her breasts, pulling the T-shirt material tight over the twin globes so that the fabric molded to her nipples. "You want to touch me," she stated, as if she were reading every thought racing through his head.

As if she felt the frantic thud of his heart, heard the roar in his ears from the rush of blood through his veins.

"You want to touch me here." She wet the tip of her finger and circled her nipple. Her lips parted invitingly. "And here." She trailed the same fingertip down, over the tight skin of her belly, her navel, to dip below the waistband of her skimpy panties. "Ah, yes," she said, smiling as her fingers disappeared beneath the lace. "You definitely want to touch me here."

Her head tilted back, her eyes closed, and she stroked herself. It was all Graham could do to keep from coming up off the bed, snatching her hand away and replacing it with his own.

That was what he wanted to do. What he ached to do, yet something held him back.

"You want me," she said.

And despite the heat that fired his veins, a chill swept over his skin as she stared at him, her eyes a bright, vivid blue.

No!

He rubbed his eyes, forcing the sleepy fog away. When

he stared at her again, she was smiling. Her eyes were once again a deep, intense brown.

Not blue.

That had been a play of the light, or simply his imagination, or . . . whatever. But not reality.

"Yes, you want me, Graham," she said. "You know you do."

"I want you to get out."

Her smiled widened. "Liar," she said, the word a seductive whisper that crossed the distance to him and brushed his lips. "You're lying. And I don't like liars. . . ."

". . . dammit, Melba. I said I was sorry!" Pinky's familiar voice cut into Graham's thoughts and shattered the image of Darby.

Graham's eyes snapped open just in time to see the maid push her cart past his window, Pinky hot on her heels.

"I didn't mean to be so rough. I'll watch it next time," Pinky promised.

"It ain't the rough that bothers me, Pinky. Cain't you just keep your zipper up long enough for a little foreplay? Jesus, I barely start to feel good, and—bam—you're done. . . ."

Graham stared at the closed door, then down at the open case file resting against his chest, papers spread across his lap and the bed beside him. He'd fallen asleep, and he'd had a dream.

As the knowledge sank in, he smiled. Just a dream.

He rubbed his eyes, wiping sleep away as he climbed to his feet and went to the doorway. Locked.

His smile widened as relief swept through him.

A dream. A fantasy. A chilling, strangely erotic fantasy. He was definitely suffering from lack of sleep. And horny, he added, glancing down at the bulge in his jeans.

He opened his door and stared down the walkway. Pinky and the maid were just rounding the corner, their voices fading. A quick peek in Darby's window and he saw her blanket-clad form. Still passed out.

Back in his room, he slid off his jeans and stepped into a cold shower.

He needed to cool off in the worst way. His body, that is.

The chill that had spread through his insides still hadn't faded. He felt that deep in his bones.

Fear. Dread.

And he knew down deep in his gut that something was going to happen.

The trouble was, he didn't know when, and he didn't know what.

But something . . . Another chill went through him. Yes, definitely something big. Something bad. Something deadly. Soon.

Chapter Sixteen

He didn't mean to cut out her eyes.

They sat so warm and bloody in his palms and a rush tingled through his veins, sending the blood zinging straight to his private parts. He let the girl's slack body slide to the ground. She collapsed in a heap, head lolling, eye sockets empty and bloody, chest rising and falling to a ragged rhythm.

Still alive.

A giggle vibrated between his lips, but he caught the sound before it burst forth. An old habit. He knew there was no one to hear him in the dark alley that ran behind Proctor's Grocery. Not a soul.

The notion stirred another giggle and this time he didn't hold back, though he was careful to keep his voice low. He lifted his palm and stared at his treasures. The eyes were light blue, the color of a cloudless summer sky at high noon. So soft and gentle and deceitful.

Kneeling down beside the dying girl, he touched his lips to her ear. "Welcome to Nostalgia," he whispered.

THE HOMECOMING

No flinch. No movement. She was unconscious. Shit!

Rage swept through him. She was young, strong. She shouldn't have conked out after the first cut! Sure, it happened sometimes. The pain overwhelmed them and they simply slipped away. But he was usually very careful, his cuts precise, so that they stayed conscious, fighting to the very end, feeling every spasm of delicious agony.

"Bitch," he said with a hiss, slicing her throat with one deft motion. Then again, back and forth as if the knife were the bow of a violin and he was playing a fast country two-step. She'd spoiled his fun, but at least he had the blood. That was almost as good as the pain.

Almost.

A gusher spewed from the gaping slashes at her neck. Red heat flowed over his fingers, between them, like warm sunshine spilling over a frost-covered ground.

He closed his eyes, feeling the response down in his groin—the rush of sensation as the anticipation in his body broke, crested, and he climaxed.

Panting, he slumped back against the wall for a few long seconds, until his breathing had returned to normal.

"Quite a welcome," he said, smiling at the young woman's mutilated body. He raised the knife and slammed the blade down on her wrist, just above the masking tape he'd wound around both hands to keep her nice and co-operative. The same tape he'd used at her ankles and mouth.

He sawed through tissue and cartilage, first one wrist, then the other, just in case she might have scratched him. Her hands amputated, he leaned down and kissed her cheek before wiping the knife on her jacket.

Back and forth, he rubbed and polished. When not a smudge remained on the murder weapon, he dropped the knife—one of Proctor's sharpest slicing knives straight from the butcher section—in her blood-soaked lap and stood.

On silent footsteps, he went inside, made his way through the storage room into the main part of the grocery *store. His gaze lit on the meat department, where a large, glass-enclosed counter stood.*

Rounding the counter, he found the meat grinder, turned the machine on, and dropped his treasures into the vat, along with her hands and a pound or so of raw beef he retrieved from the fridge.

Flipping on the switch, he whistled a little tune while the machine hummed and crackled. A full minute later, he turned the machine off, wrapped the ground meat in white freezer paper and popped it into the walk-in freezer in the rear of the store next to similiar packages containing tomorrow's special—ground chuck.

He had to smile at that one.

The girl had stayed late at the store to finish packaging the last of the meat special. Little did she know, she'd actually be the special, or part of her, at least.

He grabbed several paper towels and began wiping the machine, the butcher paper dispenser, the counter—everything he might have touched. He never left any evidence behind.

Ever.

Outside, he took one last look at his handiwork—the milk-white corpse, a bloody river running from her neck and face.

"Ah, parting is such sweet sorrow," he whispered, leaning down for another kiss, this one on her mouth. He tasted the delicious crimson heat and licked his own lips. "Definitely sweet." But not as sweet as he'd hoped, of course.

It never was.

There was always something missing, something wrong. Tonight, the bitch had lost consciousness before he'd finished his business. That, of course, had pissed him off. To add to that, he'd promised himself he'd leave the eyes alone. He had to be careful, to make sure that this crime's MO didn't resemble that of any of the others. But it was getting harder and harder.

He could only chop off a head so many times—talk about messy work—dismember the body and scatter the parts—too much legwork on his part—cut the face beyond recognition until no one even realized it had once belonged to a person, much less the all-important fact that the eyes were missing.

He always promised himself he would cut off the ears, or the nose, or something—anything besides the eyes. But once the knife was in his hands, his victim staring back at him with those lying blue eyes, he couldn't help himself.

Like tonight.

Not that it really mattered. So what if the cops recognized the MO? They would never in their wildest dreams figure out that it was him. He was much too clever for that.

He always had been. Even when the cocky sons of bitches thought they'd fucked him over, they'd been wrong.

Dead wrong, and so damned stupid. He'd been calling the shots the entire time, even when he'd been behind bars, strapped to the table. Even when the needles had slid into either arm.

He'd been in control.

As always.

Like now, Death thought, casting one last look at tonight's masterpiece. He smiled, smacking his lips, which still tasted of her succulent red heat. Then he turned to disappear down the alley.

The sight of her, eyes wide and frightened and so blue, just begging for his knife, lingered in his mind. His smile widened. A giddiness filled him, a euphoric rush that swept through him from head to toe. But not because of what he'd just done.

No, he was already anticipating the night to come.

Yet another chance to perfect the fantasy.

Darby's eyes snapped open, her heart pounding a frantic rhythm.

Fantasy, fantasy, fantasy . . . The word blared through her head, over and over like a broken record.

She glanced down at her hands. No blood, she saw, yet they burned, trembled. Frantically, she wiped them on the blanket, eager to erase the strange sensation.

A dream, she told herself. *Another goddamn dream.*

She took a long, calming breath, her senses clearing, tuning in to her surroundings as she pushed the nightmare away and tried to fix herself in the here and now.

The ugly time-warped motel room. The air conditioner chugged freezing air. The radio on the bedside table played a local AM station.

". . . you're listening to Nostalgia's KGOD. Before we get into our next song, I would like to send my prayers out to Mr. and Mrs. Charles Mills. We're with y'all in this terrible time of sorrow. . . ."

Darby reached for the off button and her gaze lit on the time display.

Four P.M. . . . Four P.M.!

It couldn't be. The last time she'd seen the clock, she'd been staring above the bar at Poppy's. It had been a little past midnight and she'd been working on her first bottle of tequila.

"A special church service is planned at five o'clock this afternoon. I'll be signing off shortly so that I can attend. The station will play a special gospel hour at that time in memory of Deana Mills, beloved daughter of Charles and Wanda."

She *had* slept the day away. Not that it should surprise her. She'd slept days away before, when she'd had too, too much to drink.

So why the hell did it bother her so much now? Her life was no different . . . but she was different. Since she'd come home to Nostalgia.

Actually, before then. When she'd stared at that girl's face on the television back in San Francisco, something had shifted inside her. She wasn't the same alcoholic she'd been before.

Right. If she was so different, why had she drunk herself into a stupor and passed out, and right in front of Graham Tucker?

"You made one hell of an impression," she told herself

as she crawled from the bed. A cold blast of air hit her. She glanced down, realized she was completely naked.

Goosebumps danced along her bare flesh, quickly chased away by an embarrassed heat that started in her toes and worked its way up, until her face felt hot enough to burst into flames.

What had happened to her clothes?

Fragments of memories swam in her head. Graham's smile. His voice. His touch. The liquor burning her throat. The cool glass of her second bottle.

Things got fuzzy after that. Very fuzzy.

Had she . . . ? Had they . . . ?

Of course not. He hated her. He wouldn't touch her with a pitchfork, no matter how willing she was, and from the amount she'd consumed last night, she'd no doubt been very willing. Unless, of course, she'd passed out first.

Even then . . . Some guys weren't the least bit put off by an unconscious woman. A woman was a woman. . . . But Graham?

"That was our local choir's version of 'Amazing Grace,' a special dedication going out to Mr. and Mrs. Charles Mills. May the Lord bless you in your time of need. . . ."

But what if she hadn't passed out? What if she'd been conscious and she'd simply forgotten what they'd done, if they'd done anything?

That possibility sent her staggering into the bathroom, her hands trembling. What if she'd been fully awake, as far as Graham had been able to tell, and she just didn't remember, like the blackout episode at Samuel Blue's house?

A dozen other questions pounded through her brain, made her grip the edge of the sink and grapple with the cold-water handle. She turned the knob, all the while wishing she were holding a shot glass. A drink could relax her, relieve some of the stress she was feeling. Then she could think. She could—

She saw the tiny drop of blood on the edge of the sink

225

and her thoughts slammed to a halt. Her mind rushed back to the dream she'd just had.

There had been so much blood.

. . . like warm sunshine spilling over a frost-covered ground.

But this was just a drop. One tiny drop. It could have come from anywhere.

She glanced down at her hand. A pink line jagged its way across her palm where she'd cut herself on the bottle in Proctor's store. It could be her own blood.

Yet the cut was already starting to heal, and she had no memory of being in the bathroom last night. Still . . .

Even as denial raged through her, the DJ's voice blared the truth from the nightstand radio.

"Once again, Deana Mills, daughter of Mr. and Mrs. Charles Mills, was found murdered this morning. Deana, a part-time clerk at Proctor's Grocery and Feed, was found in the alley behind the store. Police are searching for clues as to the murderer, but at this time there are no suspects. Let us join in prayer for Deana and her family, that God's blessings will see them through this tragic event."

Her legs buckled and she hit the cold tile of the bathroom floor. When she came to, her gaze riveted on the blood.

Could it be the grocery clerk's blood? Or was it Darby's?

Tremors gripped her body and her teeth chattered, her mind scrambling for answers.

Her head throbbed and she closed her eyes, quelling the nausea in her stomach. A hangover, she told herself, but it was more than that. Despite her queasiness, she needed another drink. Just a sip. To think, to make sense out of all this.

She scrambled to her feet, rushed back into the bedroom and reached in her purse for the bottle of bourbon she'd bought at Poppy's last night. The liquor burned its way down her throat, drink after drink, until she'd consumed half the bottle.

Only it wasn't enough. She would run out soon, and then she'd be desperate for more. Screwing the lid back on, she plopped the bottle down next to her unfinished novel, the stack of pages a neat white square on the dresser. For the space of a heartbeat, her gaze lingered. The stack seemed higher.

She shook her head. The liquor blurred things.

Not nearly enough, she realized, staring down at her trembling hands. She needed to be calm, steady, plastered.

And the rest of that bottle wouldn't come close to accomplishing that. Grabbing blue-jean shorts and a white blouse, she dressed, then headed outside, only to find her car missing. A cab. She would call a cab.

Good idea, or so she thought until the driver decided on a scenic route through town. They passed by the church and Darby saw the group of children filing inside for the nightly prayer meeting. Her gaze riveted on small, blond-haired Elsa Proctor, and time sucked her back to Proctor's Grocery. An image of Deana Mills, alive and smiling, rose in her mind, only to be replaced by the image from the dream, the girl dead and bleeding.

Darby shook like an addict gone too long without a fix by the time she climbed out of the cab outside the bar and paid the driver. She glanced at her car, still in the same spot she'd parked it in the night before. Not that she could use it to get back to the motel. She didn't have her keys. Either Graham had them, or she'd lost them.

It didn't matter. The only place she needed to be was here. Inside.

Inside a bottle. Then she wouldn't have to think at all.

". . . police have no leads to the brutal slaying of Nostalgia resident Deana Mills. Details have not yet been released due to a pending autopsy. All that we know at this time is that the victim is an eighteen-year-old senior at

Nostalgia High School, an honor student and captain of the girl's basketball team, who worked part-time at Proctor's Grocery. It seems she was the night clerk scheduled to close the store. When she failed to return home, her family became worried and called local authorities. The body was discovered this morning by Mr. Proctor. Now we go to Chief of Police Maggie Cross, who has agreed to give us a statement. . . ."

"Damn sons of bitches," Maggie hissed, staring at her own image on the TV screen as she rushed through a crowd of reporters clustered outside the police station. "Statement my ass. I told that TV woman I wouldn't make any kind of statement until all the facts had been gathered."

"And?" Graham asked, downing a Styrofoam cup full of black coffee in three quick gulps.

"And," she said, opening the manila folder on her desk and pulling out a stack of photos. "The fact is that we have a murder on our hands, and not a trace of evidence. No fingerprints, no clothing fibers, no sperm, not a shittin' thing." She stared at the photos before tossing them to the scarred desktop. "Elvis's ghost could've done it, for all we know. Hell, he's as likely a suspect as anyone right now."

"Or Samuel Blue's ghost," Graham said, glancing at the photos one by one before picking up the investigation report.

"You don't believe all that cockamamie nonsense about a ghost, do you?"

"A ghost didn't do this," he said, remembering his words to Darby that day outside of Blue's house.

Maggie gave him a pointed stare. "What about your girl? You think she's guilty, maybe she decided to really relive old times?"

For the first time, Graham shoved his personal prejudice aside and let his police know-how kick in. "Darby's barely five feet, a hundred and ten pounds." He shook his head, the realization sending an odd tremor of relief through him. "She's not nearly strong enough for something as vicious as this."

Maggie gave him a pointed stare. "But she was strong enough to slice up your sister and the other two in Blue's attic?"

"That's different."

"Is it?" Maggie raised one eyebrow.

"Yes." Conviction rang in his voice. "My sister and her friends were small, each one about Darby's size. Deana Mills was six feet tall and over a hundred and fifty pounds. An Amazon compared to Darby."

He studied the investigative report. The sheet detailed the crime scene, who, when and where in regard to the body, the information sketchy compared to that of a typical homicide compiled by the Physical Evidence Unit and Forensics in Dallas.

"The eyes were cut out," he mused. "Where did you find them?"

"We haven't yet. The hands either." Maggie unwrapped the hamburger on her desk, the aroma drifting up. Unease slithered up Graham's spine.

"Dinner?"

"Yeah. Stress makes me eat and I'm addicted to cheeseburgers on Wednesdays. The church has their evening prayer meeting for the kids, so the ladies here pull overtime, finish up paperwork, stuff like that. We all get together and cook up a little dinner in the kitchen out back. Somebody brings chips, somebody else sodas or meat, and we all have a burger fest. I had meat duty. That's how I found out about the girl. I stopped to pick up a package of ground chuck at Proctor's this morning on my way in, and damned if I didn't get there five minutes after him. Squad cars hadn't even arrived yet." She shook her head, adding salt and pepper to the meat patty. "Hell, that was the last thing I expected to see. Her folks didn't even know until this morning that she hadn't come home last night. They found her bed still made, then called the station. Even then they weren't really worried. They figured she'd slept over at a girlfriend's and simply forgot to call." She slapped a bun on top of the meat patty. "Dammit, this sort of thing doesn't happen, not around here."

"I think you'd better get over the denial phase, Maggie. This stuff happens everywhere. Especially here."

"What's that supposed to mean?"

"The circus surrounding Blue's anniversary." He plopped the preliminary report down on Maggie's desk. "This is Blue's MO, Maggie. Haven't you read the old case files?"

"Of course I have," she huffed, snatching the report and scanning the page. A few minutes later, she glanced up at Graham, her eyes narrowed. "Are you trying to tell me Samuel Blue killed Deana Mills? I suppose you believe all that ghost nonsense about the house being haunted."

"Not a ghost, a copycat killer. I think all this media attention has sparked a copycat killer. And, if so, you'd better get on the ball, because you're liable to have a bloodbath on your hands before it's all over."

"You're jumping to conclusions."

"I'm reading facts," he replied. "It's all there in the report. No sperm, hands cut off. He always cut the hands off."

"And so do a dozen other killers."

"There's no sperm," Graham pointed out.

"He wore a rubber," Maggie explained.

"She wasn't penetrated," Graham countered. "But you can bet he got off while he was killing her. When he cut out her eyes, and slashed the shit out of her neck. Yeah, he got off all right. You should call the Dallas PD in on this, Maggie, and the FBI. You don't have the staff to deal with a serial killer."

"We don't know it's a serial killer. It could be an isolated incident. Maybe she had a fight with her girlfriend, or her boyfriend—"

"Get real! This wasn't the result of a disagreement, for

Christ's sake! This was cold, calculated, bloody murder. The guy who did this is smart, and strong, and one helluva sweet talker. There's no sign of struggle in the store, and the back door is never used. This guy talked her from the store, out into the alleyway—"

"All the more reason it could be someone she knew."

"Dammit, Maggie, this isn't the work of an angry boyfriend, and definitely not a woman. The strength it would take to cut through bone with a slicing knife is incredible. It even dulled the blade, but that didn't stop our boy. He put a hell of a lot of weight into it."

"A male friend, then."

"The person who did her in isn't her friend. You're going to have bloody fucking Apocalypse on your hands unless you call in the big guns, Maggie. Now, before anybody else gets killed. Let the FBI and the Dallas PD send in reinforcements, help you nab this guy, or at least scare him away from here."

Maggie shook her head. "I don't want a bunch of outsiders in on this. We've got enough press with this anniversary coming up. That's the cause of all this mess in the first place. I won't make it a bigger circus than it already is." She lifted the burger and took a big bite. "No," she said between chews. "I'll check out all the local leads; then if I come up empty-handed, I'll bring Dallas in, but it'll be after next week and all those nosy press people pack it in and hightail it back to wherever they came from. Until then"—another bite and another quick shake of her head—"I'll head up the investigation myself." She stabbed the intercom button. "Art, you get on over to Proctor's and keep the press away. I want the scene completely secure; then I want you to get Hank and Earl to do a thorough search of the store for the hands and eyes. Maybe there's blood and skin tissue under the fingernails. Why else would he cut them off?"

"Probably," Graham said. "What about the eyes?"

"That I haven't figured out."

"And you won't, not unless you get more people working on this. Experts who know how to deal with this kind of a killer."

"The men in my department are good at their job."

"And not a one of them has ever worked a serial killer. Hell, everyone who worked the slumber-party killings has retired or moved on. Hank's the only one still on the force, and a lot of help he is. He makes a mean cup of coffee, but as for a detective—"

"I don't need your smart-ass insight," she cut in. "You are not a member of this department, so I suggest you get your ass out of here."

"I see I'm wasting my time," he said, watching her attack the cheeseburger for another bite.

His stomach did an unexpected somersault, the aroma of cooked meat crossing the room to swirl around him, and he turned for the door, suddenly desperate to get out of there before he puked.

The pictures, that was what had caused the reaction.

But he'd seen crime-scene photos before. Hell, he'd been the officer in charge, staring at the carnage firsthand too many times to count. It couldn't be that.

"Call in one of your FBI buddies," she finally mumbled.

Graham nodded and left the office, feeling little victory at Maggie's words. His stomach swirled too furiously. He needed to get out of there before he chucked up his breakfast.

He stalked down the hallway, shoved open the doors and walked out into the noonday sunlight. Fresh air filled his nostrils, his lungs, chasing out the strange odor of the meat that had tickled his nostrils.

Find the eyes and hands. Good fucking luck. Maggie would need it, because Graham knew firsthand that the murderer who'd done this job was a pro. A psychopathic pro, cold and careful. Maggie could look until doomsday and she would never find the hands, or the eyes, even if they were right under her nose.

* * *

At five forty-five in the afternoon on a Thursday, Poppy's was nearly empty. The evening shift at the local paper mill didn't let out until seven. Not that Darby minded drinking alone.

She didn't mind anything as long as she had a drink in her hand.

Nursing her fourth drink, she trailed her fingers up and down the condensation on the glass, watching the drops chase each other down the glass. Her hands still trembled, but her muscles weren't as tight. This was better. Much better.

"Do they go away?"

She turned at the sound of Graham's voice. "Does what go away?" she asked.

"Your problems. Does the booze chase them away?"

"Eventually," she lied.

He stood next to her, so close, his nearness overpowering the alcohol's numbing effect. She closed her eyes, willing herself to forget him, to forget everything. But the nightmare lit the blackness of her mind, taunting her.

"Are you okay?" he asked.

She covered her face with her hands, unable to look him in the eye. "No, I'm not okay," she whispered. "And no, they don't go away. Not far enough. I . . ." Her words trailed off when she felt his touch on her shoulder.

"You shouldn't be doing this after last night. You're going to kill yourself."

"I hope so," she said, forcing her gaze to meet his. "You were right about me, Graham. I—I am a killer. I have to be. I saw that grocery clerk murdered. I can't remember anything else about last night, but I remember the dream—I mean, what I did."

"What are you talking about?"

"The nightmares I mentioned to you. I've been having them for a long time. I dream about this killer. I can't see him, but I can feel him." She shook her head. "I can really *feel* him, because it's not someone else. It's me. It has to be. It's too much of a coincidence that Nostalgia has been quiet and peaceful, murder-free, then, boom, I come home and someone is killed. I—I think I killed Proctor's clerk."

There, she'd said it. He could arrest her, turn her over to the cops. At least then she'd be in jail, unable to hurt anyone, or to numb herself and escape her conscience with the booze.

"You didn't kill Deana Mills."

"How can you be so sure?"

"Because you drank nearly two bottles of straight tequila. You were passed out cold the entire night. I tucked you in myself."

"Then you undressed me," she said accusingly.

"Only to make you more comfortable. Though I needn't have bothered. You were sleeping like a baby when I left."

"So we didn't . . . I mean, we . . ."

"We didn't." His gaze caught and held hers, and though he didn't say the words, she knew then that Graham had thought a lot about what they didn't do. That he felt the heat between them, even though he'd been denying it to himself.

For good reason.

"Still, I could have done it," she said.

"Darby, you couldn't wake up long enough to remember your own name, much less drive to Proctor's Grocery, subdue and slice up Deana Mills. The girl was nearly six feet tall, over one hundred and fifty pounds. You might be a murderer, but you aren't Deana's murderer. It's not physically possible." He pulled out his wallet and tossed several bills onto the bartop. "Come on. We're not doing a repeat of last night. You're going to get some food into your system and get to bed early. You look like hell."

"Thanks a lot," she said, but her voice wasn't filled with sarcasm. Relief, yes. Maybe he was right.

As she followed him back to town, his words played

over and over in her head. He was right. She'd seen Deana Mills herself. The girl was big, and Darby had trouble twisting the lid off a jar of peanut butter. She couldn't have killed her.

Okay, so maybe she wasn't Deana's murderer, but as Graham had pointed out, she could still be a killer. The truth lay somewhere in her mind, in the part tucked so far away she couldn't quite reach it. But she would.

She would forget all about the nightmares, the strange cuts, the blackout, the drop of blood, and she would simply remember.

Then she would face the consequences and pay for her crimes.

God help her, but she would.

Her renewed determination scared her, but not half as much as the change in Graham Tucker.

Graham—a man who had vowed to hate her, who had proclaimed that hate to God and everybody.

He seemed nicer, but it was more his eyes that clued her in to the change. Those bluer-than-blue eyes had softened somewhat. It didn't matter that he referred to her as a possible murderer; there wasn't the same hatred when he used the word, or the same coldness in those icy eyes. Something had changed between them.

Softened.

She remembered bits and pieces of their conversation last night, and even though she'd forgotten some of it, she felt close to him. He made a pretense of wanting to keep an eye on her, but she knew there was more to it when he seemed reluctant to leave her motel room later that night, after they'd opened cans of soup and eaten their fill.

They sat in front of the TV both seemingly engrossed in whatever flashed on the screen. There were no words between them, just the knowledge that the other person was there. And the heat. A thin wisp of fire flowed between them, around them, drawing them closer together despite their best efforts to resist.

And that scared her more than anything else. She didn't want to be close to Graham, to depend on him, to want him, for heaven's sake. That clouded her purpose in Nostalgia and made her fear the truth for the first time. What if her memories revealed the worst?

That she really was a killer.

His sister's killer.

He would hate her then, and she didn't know if she could bear it. It was one thing to face her own conscience for better or for worse. But it was quite another thing to face Graham Tucker and be held accountable for her actions. To see her guilt in his eyes, to feel his hatred bite through her heart, and to carry that to the grave and beyond.

It was better not to get too close to him, she told herself. Then it wouldn't matter what he thought of her. He wouldn't matter.

But that was easier said than done. Especially when she dozed off later that evening and awoke to find herself leaning against him, her head cradled in the crook of his shoulder. His scent filled her nostrils. His heartbeat, so clear and distinct against her ear, sent an echoing pulse through her body.

Yes, much easier said than done.

Chapter Seventeen

God, how she wanted to kiss him.

To tilt her head back just so, feel his breath on her lips, his tongue stroking hers. She wanted to nibble and suck and taste him.

Get real. She wanted more than that.

She wanted to strip off her clothes and press herself against him, feel his heat on every inch of her skin. She wanted to open her legs, to feel him thrust inside and end the ache that gripped her entire body.

He wanted the same. She could see it in those brilliant blue eyes of his, a hunger that mirrored her own.

He was hungry.

She was hungry.

He leaned down, so close, and she wet her lips nervously. She'd kissed men before. More than she could remember. Many more. But she'd never done it stonecold sober.

The realization sent an icy draft through her. She couldn't do this. It was wrong. They were wrong. He was who he was, and she was . . .

A killer.
Maybe. Probably.

She moved her hand up, to push him away, she told herself. The moment she felt his heartbeat against her palm, his heat scorching her fingertips, every reason *why not* slipped away.

She closed her eyes. A mixture of fear and anxiety and desperation churned in her stomach.

His lips closed over hers and he kissed her, his tongue stroking her mouth, dipping inside to taste her.

She felt his hand on her arm, stroking down. His fingers skimmed her rib cage and the underside of her breast.

Her nipple hardened, thrusting against her shirt, begging for the wet heat of his mouth. But he was busy kissing her, holding her captive while his tongue worked its magic against hers.

Her arm snaked around him. The back of her hand brushed the shoulder holster draped over the nightstand, the butt of his gun cold against her feverish skin.

Then his fingers found the tip of her nipple and heat spiraled through her, dispelling any cold. She groaned into his mouth.

That seemed all the encouragement he needed. He tore his mouth from hers to lick a delicious path down her neck. Then she felt a warm rush of breath through the fabric of her blouse, and she knew he was about to suckle her. To close his mouth over the thinly clad nipple and give her the heat she craved.

A tremor of excitement rolled through her, followed by a rush of cold dread as the TV announcer's voice pushed its way past the frantic beat of her heart.

". . . is a rebroadcast of tonight's ten o'clock news. On the local scene, Deana Mills, a senior at Nostalgia High School, star of the girl's basketball team, was found brutally murdered this morning."

The television announcer's words were like a freezing

wind that blew through the room, right between Darby and Graham.

The warmth faded and her eyes snapped open to find him staring at the television set, an undefinable expression on his face.

"Oddly enough her death comes while Nostalgia is gearing up for the tenth anniversary of the execution of notorious serial killer Samuel Blue. His home was also the sight of the brutal slumber-party killings that took place nearly ten years ago, the night he was lethally injected."

"You really don't remember anything, do you?" He stared down at her, into her, as if he could see the truth, no matter what words came out of her mouth.

She shook her head. "No, I don't."

"Despite best efforts, the slumber-party killer has yet to be apprehended—"

Graham stabbed the off button. The screen flickered, then went black.

"It's late," he said, the words cold and distant. If only the eyes reflected the tone of his voice. They still blazed with hunger, burning through her clothing, making her feel self-conscious and frightened and excited all at the same time.

Crazy. Insane.

Of all the men in her past, men who'd come on to her, men who'd wanted a relationship, she'd never burned for any of them. Never. Not like this.

"You don't have to run off," she said, surprised at the boldness in her own voice. Afraid of it. Especially when she wanted him to go more than she wanted him to stay.

Her body wanted him to stay.

Her brain knew better.

So why wouldn't her mouth cooperate?

"I could make some coffee," she offered.

"Sorry, I need to get going. I've got work to do."

Yes! her mind screamed. Distance was better. She couldn't afford to get close to Graham Tucker.

She almost wept with relief when he stood. She wrapped her arms around herself, eager to hide her aroused nipples while he moved about the room, gathering up his jacket and gun holster.

"Sleep tight," he said before slipping outside, his hungry gaze everywhere, anywhere but on her.

She closed her eyes. Tears spilled past her cheeks as she listened to his footsteps, the slow creak of his door as he entered the room next to hers.

So close, yet Graham Tucker was miles away.

Good.

So why the hell was she crying? Her throat closed around a sob and she turned, burying her head in the pillow.

She felt as if she were being pulled in two different directions. As if a Dr. Jekyll and Ms. Hyde lived and breathed inside her, battling for control.

Dr. Jekyll—the rational, thinking side of her, knew that any intimacy would be a bad idea. There were too many things standing between them. A past full of hurt, an unpredictable future. But Ms. Hyde—the hormone-driven, lustful side of her—couldn't forget the hunger in his eyes, the heat in his body, or the prominent bulge she'd seen in his jeans.

She strained her ears, listening to him walking around the room. The pipes rumbled as he turned on his shower.

Darby buried her head beneath the pillow and tried to ignore the quivering of her unsatisfied body.

This was better, Jekyll whispered. Graham was far away from her, locked in his own room. Safe. And that was all that really mattered. Not her aching heart, her burning body, the desperate loneliness eating away inside her.

Those things she could handle, on her own, or with a bottle in her hand. She didn't need Graham Tucker, Jekyll maintained, nor did she want him.

If only Hyde didn't keep insisting otherwise.

* * *

He didn't want her. Dammit, he *didn't*.

Graham stood under a cold shower and recited the words over and over with the hope that his throbbing erection would get the point. Soon.

He needed a few hours of sleep before he had to pick up Sully, the FBI's top crime-scene profiler, at a nearby airstrip tomorrow morning. And horny and sleepless wasn't going to put him in top condition, that was for damned sure.

Closing his eyes, he ignored Darby's image, her eyes so full of passion and vulnerability, and forced his mind farther back. To his sister's mutilated body, the anguish gripping his heart.

Empty, bloody eye sockets stared up at him. Blood soaked the white sheet covering the stretcher, her skin ice beneath his hands. His own hollow voice rang in his ears. . . . "Linda, don't do this. Don't leave me! Please. I didn't mean to leave you. I didn't mean to!"

He slammed the water off. He was cooler, but not nearly cool enough. After slipping on a pair of jeans, he walked back into the bedroom and collapsed on the bed. Killing the light, he lay there, his gaze fixed on the open window.

At least Darby wouldn't be going anywhere without his knowledge. Her car was parked right next to his truck, and he had full view of the vehicle from any spot in his motel room. That should make him feel better.

It didn't. The only thing that would make Graham feel better was to pull her beneath him, slide into her—

No! The only thing that would make him feel better was to uncover the truth about his sister's murder. Whether that truth revealed Darby as the killer, an accomplice, or an innocent amnesia victim—

Wait.

She might be many things, but innocent wasn't one of them. She'd been there, inches from the mutilation. She'd had blood all over her. If she truly was an innocent bystander, why in the hell hadn't she been killed, as well?

She'd survived. So had Katy, but she'd run away from the scene to a nearby farmhouse for help. Darby had simply sat there. So if she wasn't the killer, why hadn't she been killed right alongside Linda and the others?

Had the killer shown her a little mercy? Or been scared off before he could finish his gruesome work?

Or was Darby really guilty?

Guilty or innocent?

The question followed him into oblivion, stirring strange dreams, erotic dreams of Darby and all the things he wanted to do to her. But his sister was there, as well. Her empty eye sockets watching him, seeing his betrayal.

He awoke an hour later bathed in a cold sweat, the hair on the back of his neck standing on end.

Guilty or innocent? The words pounded through his head.

Not that it mattered, not when Graham had been the one responsible in the first place. Linda had been at the slumber party because of him. It didn't matter who did the deed. Graham had left her there. Left her to die.

Her death was on his conscience, and no amount of vengeance would wash the blood from his own hands. Deep down, he knew that. But Graham Tucker was a hard-ass, and when he set his mind on something, he didn't give it up.

No matter how much he wanted to fuck Darby Jayson, he wouldn't until he uncovered the truth. If guilty, she would wind up sitting on Death Row down in Huntsville. If innocent, she would end up beneath him, around him, and Graham would satisfy them both. Then he would spend the rest of his life searching for the real killer.

Later that day, blood spilled over Darby's fingers and she tried to swallow the wave of nausea that rolled up her esophagus.

She dropped to her knees in the motel parking lot and

leaned down over the injured dog, her body blocking out the bright noon sunlight.

"Come on, boy, it's okay," she whispered, turning to glance frantically around the parking lot. "Help!" she screamed at the cluster of reporters and concerned citizens who'd gathered outside her motel door after the reverend had proclaimed at last night's prayer meeting that there was a killer among them, namely Darby. "One of you, please help me!"

Only no one was the least bit concerned about a helpless animal. They looked on, the reporters snapping pictures, rolling videotape while Darby sat on her knees next to the wounded animal. Tears rolled down her cheeks, mingling with the blood gushing from the animal's shattered leg, exactly where her back tire had made contact with it.

"I'm so sorry," she whispered. "So very sorry."

"What the hell . . . ?" Graham pushed through the cluster of people. Fresh from a shower, his dark hair dripping, his tanned skin glistening, he wore only a pair of jeans, zipped but not buttoned. No shoes or shirt or modesty, despite the frenzied cameras at work.

Despite the terrible situation, she noticed him. But her attention shifted only briefly; then she was staring down at the bleeding animal once again.

"I was backing out and he must have been behind my wheels. I didn't even see him. I just heard a yelp. I slammed on the brakes but it was too late. We have to do something! He's going to die."

"Told you she was a killer!" came the taunting comment.

The crowd quickly echoed the sentiment.

"Killer!"

"Murderer!"

"Don't you people have any heart?" Graham said, turning a fierce glare on the crowd. No one moved, much less budged to help, and the cameras showed no mercy. "Fucking vultures," he muttered.

"Forget them," Darby said, grasping at his arm. "We've got to get this dog some help."

He turned his full attention back to her and nodded. Then he stood, shoved his way past several reporters and went to rummage in the bed of his truck. He returned with a small sheet of wood, only slightly larger than the dog's body.

"We'll slide him onto this, then head for the vet's."

"It's okay," Darby crooned to the dog as Graham began to move the animal's body.

The dog whimpered as the slow, agonizing seconds ticked by, until finally he was off the ground and secure on the board.

"Come on," Graham said as he hefted the board up, slid it into the bed of the truck. Darby climbed in after the animal, her small hand stroking its brown-and-white snout.

After Graham retrieved his boots, a shirt, and keys from the motel room, they were on their way. The vet was about three miles away, the small animal hospital situated right in the middle of at least fifty acres of land.

"What do we have here?" Janice Wilder, Nostalgia's only single thirty-year-old, and the town vet, walked out of the barn.

"I—I hit him with my car." Darby gestured wildly toward the injured animal.

The vet tossed her feed bucket to the ground, yanked off her gloves and rushed toward the wounded animal.

"How long ago?"

"Maybe ten minutes." Darby moved aside as the woman climbed into the bed of the truck to inspect the animal. "I didn't mean to. One minute he was nosing around on the motel porch, and the next thing I knew, I felt the car jump, heard a yelp." She stroked the animal with trembling, bloodstained fingers. "Can you help him?"

"It looks like his leg is broken in a few different places.

He's got a large wound on his shoulder; that's where all this blood is coming from. He's lost a lot, poor thing." The vet turned to Graham, who stood near the tailgate. "Help me get him inside, into the surgery, and I'll see what I can do."

"Can I come with him?" Darby asked as they burst inside the small hospital, nothing more than a converted two-story house.

"I think it would be better if you wait in the waiting room." The vet pointed to the living room which held two yellow plastic chairs and a daisy-print sofa, before turning to lead Graham down a long hallway.

Darby sank into one of the chairs, her hands trembling, the smell of blood and death smothering her.

Her gaze fell to her bloodstained hands and her stomach jolted. She was on her feet and running in that next instant. She found the bathroom a few doors down the hallway and sank down beside the toilet just as her breakfast—black coffee and dry toast—came back up. After several painful heaves, she cradled her head in her hands, her stomach roiling.

That was how Graham found her.

"What's wrong?"

"I . . ." Her voice failed as she glanced down at her blood-soaked shirt. "I hate blood. The sight makes me sick. It always has."

He shoved a handful of paper towels under the faucet, turned on the cold water and soaked them. Then he hunkered down beside her and handed her the cold compress.

"Thanks." She cast a sheepish smile at him. "I guess I seem pretty silly, considering what I did to my father. . . ." Her words faded as she swallowed against the bile in her throat. "I mean, it seems almost ironic."

"Yeah, ironic." He was looking at her, staring at her, an unreadable expression on his face.

Suddenly self-conscious, she pressed the cold compress to her lips. "I'm sorry. I guess that's twice I've dragged you into the ladies' room. I was just sitting there, and I could smell it on me, feel it burning into my clothes." A shudder rolled through her. "I guess that's hard to understand, considering your line of work. You've probably seen it all."

"And so have you," he said, but his voice was gentle. He shoved a strand of hair back behind her ear. "You just don't remember."

The statement fed her desperation and she begged the past forward. She saw Katy, the flash of blue in her eyes, then . . . She fought for the memory, an invisible tug-of-war that brought tears to her eyes.

"Dammit," she cried, her fingers gripping the toilet bowl. "Dammit it all to hell."

"It's all right," he said, pulling her to her feet and into his arms, a move that startled them both.

Warmth seeped into her, along with the knowledge that she wasn't alone. Guilt and innocence aside, now, Graham at least believed the fact that she truly didn't remember.

The realization sent a surge of heat through her that chased away the cold loneliness and gave her a comfort she craved as much as the alcohol.

More, in fact, only she hadn't admitted it. Until this moment with Graham.

Jekyll pushed her way in, reminding Darby of the mounting clues against her. Now didn't matter. All that mattered was the outcome—her guilt, the condemnation in Graham's eyes, the renewed hatred. *That* mattered.

She should tell him about the clues. That would push him away, put the barriers back up between them.

As much as she wanted to, Hyde reared her ugly head at that moment, the exact moment Graham's fingers slid up her spine to cradle her neck. Heat whispered along her nerve endings.

She shook her head, forced the sensations aside and pushed away from him.

"I . . ." *I think we should stop this before it goes any fur-*

ther. I think we should think about the consequences, about who we are, what we want, what is going to happen when the truth comes out. She wanted to say all of those things, but the words wouldn't come.

"How's the dog?" she managed.

"He's going to make it." He glanced at his watch. "But I can't say the same for me. I was due at McMillan's airstrip fifteen minutes ago. An FBI friend of mine is flying in from the Dallas field office today to help out on the Mills murder. I was supposed to pick him up."

"I'll see you later, then."

"Why don't you come with me?"

"Thanks for the offer, but I've got plans."

"To keep the bar stool at Poppy's warm?"

"No, smart-ass. I was going to go out and have a look around at Jane's house, then Trish's, and yours."

Black fury crept across his features but she rushed on. "I wasn't planning on talking to anyone's parents or anything, just looking around. Maybe it'll trigger something."

"I'll go with you."

"But what about your FBI friend?"

"We'll go after we pick him up. We'll even swing back by here later on and check on the dog."

"Thanks, but no thanks."

"I'm not asking." He dangled his keys in front of her. "And I'm driving. Your car's back at the motel, remember?"

"You just want to keep an eye on me," she said, pushing open the door. He followed her.

"Smart woman," he murmured.

"So tell me about this friend," she said once they were in the pickup, pulling out of the vet's drive.

"He profiles for the FBI and the local Dallas police when they get a tough homicide case."

"Did he do a profile on Linda's killer?"

He shook his head. "No. He's studied the case file, but

he can't seem to get a handle on it, other than the fact that whoever did it was really pissed off. There was no rhyme or reason to the murders. No distinct pattern. The case didn't match up with anything in the computers. Just a random act of violence. No, make that rage." He cut her a sideways glance. "Were you angry at my sister that night?"

"I was never angry at Linda. At least, not during the time I remember." She closed her eyes tight. "I don't know. Maybe I did get angry. Maybe I did . . ." She couldn't make herself say the word, not out loud though every ounce of her screamed it.

Kill!

"I don't know. I wish I did."

"You will," he promised them both. "You will."

The police station was swarming with people when Darby, Graham and FBI agent Mitch Sully arrived. A local group of concerned citizens, led by none other than Lyle Proctor, crowded into the front lobby. The media clustered outside. And every uniformed officer in town packed into the small meeting room where Maggie gave her daily briefing.

"That's her!" Proctor said when Graham ushered Darby past them. "It's because of her all the killing's started up again." His voice set off an echo of agreement.

"Yeah," came another voice. "She was there that night."

Then another. "She killed those girls."

"Murderer!"

Graham turned on Proctor. "Don't you have enough to worry about, or do you intend to add harassment to it?"

The man turned beet red, before muttering, "That's a lie."

"Now, now." The desk sergeant pushed his way through the crowd, clearing a space for Graham and Darby to get by. "You folks move aside."

"We want our grievances heard!" a woman protested.

"Yeah! Where's the chief?"

"Maggie's responsible!"

"She'll see justice is done."

"We had a peaceful town before that Jayson woman came back."

"She's to blame."

"This isn't such a good idea," Darby said, her heart pounding. "Maybe we should go."

"It's a damned good idea," Graham said through clenched teeth. He pushed his way through, his body shielding Darby from the group of angry citizens who leaned in to give her a piece of their mind.

They left the rowdy crowd behind and headed toward a section of the station that allowed police personnel only.

With Graham's hand on her arm, no one said a word to her. A few men nodded in greeting, and Maggie Cross herself glared, but otherwise no one paid much attention to them. They squeezed into the back row just as Maggie took the podium.

"Okay, everybody. We called the big guns up in Dallas in on this one, and they sent down one of their top investigators, agent Mitch Sully."

Sully, a middle-aged man about six feet tall, with dark brown hair and warm brown eyes, looked more like a high school football coach than a tough FBI agent. He had a bulky build, a little extra mileage around the middle, and a tanned complexion. He'd said little during the ride over except to tell them, in a distinct Texas drawl that revealed he was definitely homegrown, that the Bureau was prepared to help in any way to close this case.

"First things first," he began. "Based on the evidence gathered at the crime scene, as well as the autopsy results on the victim, the Bureau has come up with a profile of the killer. Remember, this is just a profile. There are variables, but overall, we're looking for a young white male, approximately twenty to thirty years of age, well built and very strong, based on the victim's size, and very charming. There were no signs of a struggle prior to the attack. This guy charmed his way into this girl's confidence, talked her out into the alley, then slaughtered her."

With each word, relief seeped through Darby. Her hands relaxed, her stomach quieted. She'd considered Graham's words last night, but she hadn't really believed them. After all, he didn't know about the drop of blood she'd discovered. Or the other clues—the footprint, the small cut on her finger. And, of course, he didn't live through her dreams.

Clues or no clues, the profile didn't come close to describing a five-foot-tall female, barely one hundred and ten pounds, falling-down drunk at the time of the victim's death. Darby didn't know much about police work, but she did know the FBI considered profiling somewhat of a science and they prided themselves on the accuracy of their work.

"Overall," Sully went on, "this guy is a very organized killer, given the lack of evidence at the crime scene. No prints, no blood or tissue samples, no semen. Nothing. This guy is very smart, and very precise. The cuts made to the eye area to remove the eyeballs were extremely skilled and practiced. According to the autopsy report, the eyes were gouged out while the victim was still alive. The fatal wound was a slash to the throat. In this case, forty-three, to be exact. This guy isn't conflicted at all. He knows exactly what he's doing and chances are he's done this sort of thing before. He more than likely works in some sort of technical position where accuracy and precision are mandatory. And he's strong. Very strong. The hands were cut off clean through muscle and tendon and bone."

By this point, Maggie Cross's usually ruddy complexion had turned considerably pale, her hands white as they gripped the clipboard on her lap.

"I know what some of you all are thinking," Sully went on, drawling his Texas best. "We've heard this profile before. Yes, we have. In fact, this profile helped catch and convict the notorious killer Samuel Blue, nicknamed 'Old Blue Eyes.' Convicted of killing twenty-nine people and executed down in Huntsville nearly ten years ago."

"How can that be? Blue's dead," one of the officers blurted out.

"Yes, and his tenth anniversary is being hyped from here to the Rio Grande. With the resurgence of interest in the Samuel Blue killings, fueled by the upcoming television broadcast, it's no surprise. What we have on our hands is a copycat. A very smart, very accurate copycat of this town's very own Samuel Blue."

Silence fell over the group for a long moment as Maggie got to her feet and replaced Sully at the podium.

"Er, thank you, Detective. That's it, people. Everyone pick up a copy of the profile on the way out, study it. I want this guy caught. And when you hit the streets, keep your eyes open and your mouths shut. I don't want this all over every newspaper in the state."

Maggie's warning came much too late, however.

Every newspaper, magazine, radio station and television station was broadcasting the news of the copycat. The local station in Dallas that planned to do the Halloween walk-through of the Blue house had already joined with a major network to run a national broadcast, the selling point, of course, the copycat killer roaming the streets of Nostalgia.

Murders were commonplace in big cities like Houston and Chicago, New York and L.A. But in places like Nostalgia, Texas, cold-blooded killings just didn't happen.

Not in the past ten years, that is.

But Darby Jayson was home now, and so was Death.

Chapter Eighteen

"There's a whole goddamn group of vigilantes out front," Graham said, striding into Maggie's office several minutes later, after the meeting had dispersed. He glared at her. "What are you going to do about it?"

"Well, if I had the sense God gave a goose, I'd arrest Darby Jayson and get this whole damned town off my back."

"You know she didn't do anything."

"Damn, but you have to muddy up things with the truth." She took a bite of a chocolate cupcake. "Yeah, yeah, I know she didn't. That's why she's not locked up." She tossed a stack of papers at him.

"A petition?"

"Started by Reverend Masters himself, and signed by almost two thousand of Nostalgia's two thousand, three hundred residents—all showing their support for keeping murderers out of their town. The reverend delivered it to me this morning."

"What are you supposed to do with this?"

"I know what I'd like to do with it, but I doubt the reverend will bend over long enough." She rubbed at her tired eyes. "The petition says the town wants Darby out of Nostalgia. I figure I've got two options. I can run her out of town, or arrest her. The problem is, I don't have basis for either one, and frankly I'm too damned tired to make anything up. Any idea how long she plans on staying?"

"A few more days, at least." He stared at the television behind her, saw Reverend Masters standing in front of the church talking to a reporter.

". . . daughter of Satan. We don't need her in our town, her evil infecting our children, not to mention endangering the life of each and every God-fearing citizen. . . ."

"Jesus, the bastard's going too far," Graham muttered. "He's ready to crucify her."

"Him, and the rest of this town, especially Lyle Proctor and his little group of concerned citizens."

"That's interesting."

"What?"

"Proctor and Masters. I can see why Proctor would want to stir things up. Hell, it keeps everybody's attention away from him and what he's been doing to his little girl. And it gets back at Darby in the process. Lyle's a slimy son of a bitch, but the reverend . . . I would have expected more from him."

"Why? Because he's a man of God? That's the very reason, Tucker. Darby was his one failure. He doesn't want her around to make him look bad. It shakes people's faith," Maggie said. She stopped chewing the cupcake for a long moment.

"You're not thinking what I think you're thinking?" Graham asked her. "What I'm thinking?"

"Hell no," she muttered.

But he knew she was. "A setup," he mused out loud. "I'll be damned. This whole damned murder could be a setup to frame Darby. Bam, she's back in town and some sweet young girl gets sliced up. So friggin' convenient."

"Horseshit. Proctor might be an asshole, and the reverend not too far behind him, but neither one of 'em's capable of doing what was done to Deana Mills."

Graham thought about that for a long moment, his mind filing back through the crime-scene report, the pictures. "Why not? John Wayne Gacy had neighbors who thought the world of him. Pillar of the community. And Bundy was Mr. Charm. What makes you so sure Proctor and/or the reverend don't have a dark side?"

"I ain't so sure," Maggie replied. "The cop part of me knows all the stats just like you. But my gut says those two are innocent. Troublemakers, but innocent. They wouldn't dirty their hands like that."

"So maybe they hired someone."

"I doubt it," she said, "though I ain't saying it's out of the question." She wiped a speck of chocolate from the corner of her mouth. "But to go to all that trouble, and expense, to frame her? It's out of character, not to mention just plain stupid how they went about it. They have to know that Darby isn't physically capable of what happened."

"Do they? They're not cops, Maggie. They don't think like we do. They want Darby out of town, locked up. She won't leave, so they go for the second option. They want her arrested. What better way to ensure that she never comes back than to have her arrested for murder? The more brutal the better, as far as they're concerned."

"Those are serious allegations, and we don't have a shred of evidence to prove anything."

"There's motive, and that warrants at least some investigative attention." At her doubtful expression, he added, "Look, I'm not saying either one of these guys did anything. I'm just saying you can't rule out the possibility, not when they both have very clear motives for wanting Darby out of here. Just keep an eye on them."

Maggie nodded. "All right. But don't you go leaking your ideas to the press. My ass is already in a sling, as it is. How long do you think I'll keep my job if the people of this town see me trying to pin a murder on the reverend? He's the closest thing to God around here. And Proctor's the damned trumpet blower. Would you believe, word leaked about the child abuse allegations, and they've already started a fund for him at the church? Just in case he needs legal counsel to defend himself against these 'false and slanderous accusations made by a daughter of Satan.' It's ridiculous."

"Just keep an eye on them," Graham said, staring through the window at Darby, who sat in a chair in the hallway. She looked so small, so damned vulnerable just sitting there, as if she carried the weight of the world on her shoulders. Oddly enough, he wanted to ease some of that weight.

Ridiculous. But then his dick had a way of forcing those ridiculous thoughts into his head.

And that was all it was, he convinced himself. His damned greedy dick.

He didn't feel anything for Darby Jayson. Certainly not compassion, or sympathy, or anything except lust.

"And you keep an eye on your girlfriend," Maggie said, a knowing expression on her face when he turned back to her. "I haven't completely ruled her out." When he started to protest, she held up a hand. "I know what the FBI says, but I'm no federal agent. I'm a cop and I work on instincts, and something tells me your girl out there isn't quite right."

"We'll see."

"I hope we see soon. A few more nights like this and the city council won't have to fire me; I'll die of exhaustion," Maggie muttered, eating the last bite of cupcake and turning back to her work.

Two suspects, Graham thought as he walked out into the hallway. Two long-shot suspects, but then those often turned out to be the ones.

Hell, he didn't know anymore. He only knew, unlike Maggie, how exact the FBI profiles could be, and he, too, had a hunch. But it didn't tell him Darby was guilty. It told him she was innocent.

"Finished?" Darby asked, getting to her feet.

"Yeah." He glanced toward the front of the station, before grabbing her hand and pulling her in the opposite direction.

"Where are we going?"

"Out the back way. Then we're going to see about recovering your memory."

"So?" Graham killed the pickup truck's ignition and turned to stare at Darby as they sat outside his mother's house.

"So I can't remember anything with you staring at me."

"Okay." He turned, his gaze directed at the white gingerbread house, complete with latticework shutters and a white picket fence.

Darby tried to block out his presence and concentrate. She fixed her attention on the porch swing. The wind rustled and she could hear the slow creak of hinges as it swung back and forth.

They were too far away, several yards from the house, but Darby heard the sound in her mind.

She closed her eyes, her mind going back to that night. She'd walked over from the reverend's and settled into the porch swing to wait for Linda, who, as usual, was still changing.

"Would you like a glass of lemonade, Darby?" Mrs. Tucker, an attractive brunette, hair perfectly coiffed, ducked her head out from behind the screen door, a smile on her face.

"No, thank you, ma'am. I'll just sit out here. It's a nice night." Her gaze spanned the porch, from the carved jack-o'-lantern, the candle flickering in the breeze, to the black and orange streamers wrapped around the porch posts like Halloween candy canes.

"I could bring it out here to you, and a caramel apple,

too. I've got a whole batch ready for the trick-or-treaters tonight."

"I think I'll pass. But thanks again."

"Well, I'll go see if I can hurry Linda up." She smiled, then disappeared inside the house.

"Linda, Darby's here! Graham, would you knock on Linda's door and tell her to hurry it up?"

"Sure," answered the deep voice that never failed to send a spiral of heat through Darby's young body, straight to her newly developing breasts. Her nipples tingled, not from the breeze, but from the sound of that voice.

Darby closed her eyes and leaned her head back. Pushing the floor with her foot, she set the swing to rocking, the slow creak hypnotic.

"Linda, forget all the war paint and get out of that bathroom. It doesn't help anyway." A pounding followed Graham's voice.

"Hold on to your jockstrap," Linda replied.

"Now, now, Linda. You watch your mouth," Mrs. Tucker called from the kitchen.

"Yeah, twerp. Watch your mouth," Graham said, pounding on the door again.

"Cut it out, I'm coming," Linda replied. A lock clicked, a door opened. "And you can go take a flying leap straight into a pile of cow manure, Graham Tucker. Whew." A loud sniff. "You smell like you already did."

"That's my new aftershave," answered his defensive voice.

"Where'd you buy it? The feed store?"

The voices trailed off, doors slammed, and Darby relished every sound. It was the closest she came to a normal life. Standing on the outside, looking in at Linda and her family.

God, how she envied her friend. Linda had it all. The perfect "Ozzie and Harriet" parents—the homemaker and the local bank president. And, of course, the big, strong, popular older brother. They were the classic all-American family.

Everything Darby would never have.

"Boo!" *Linda's voice startled Darby several minutes later and she jumped, only to smile when she turned to find her friend wearing a gorilla mask.*

"Where did you get that?"

"Graham. He wears it on his dates. A definite improvement, huh?"

"I heard that," *said the deep voice from inside the house.*

"Good," *she called over her shoulder.* "You sure you don't want me to leave the mask? Aren't you getting together with Claire tonight? You wouldn't want to scare her showing up au natural, now, would you?"

"Funny," *he grumbled and Linda and Darby burst into a fit of giggles.*

"Come on," *Linda said, dangling her father's truck keys from one hand, the mask in the other.* "We'd better hurry. We still have to pick up Jane and Katy and Trish."

"You sure they won't mind me coming?" *Darby asked.*

"Of course not. We're the five musketeers, aren't we?"

Darby nodded, but she felt more like the fifth wheel, rather than a musketeer. The odd man out. The story of her life.

"Come on," *Linda said again, an encouraging smile on her face.* "Let's get going."

The minute they climbed into the truck, Graham stuck his head out the front door, giving Darby a glimpse of blue eyes and dark, silky hair.

"Where are you going?"

"Excuse me, but I could have sworn my daddy was much older, and better-looking," *Linda called through the open truck window.*

"Older, yes, but nobody's better-looking. Now where are you going?"

"I already told Mom and Dad."

"So tell me."

"Reverend Masters is having an all-night youth prayer meeting."

"Right."

"Really, Graham. Call if you don't believe me."

"I just might."

"Good." Linda slammed on the gas and backed out.

His "Be careful" followed them down the driveway.

The moment they hit the road, Darby turned worried eyes on her friend.

"What if he calls the reverend?"

"He won't."

"But what if he does? Won't you get in trouble?"

"He won't. He's a bully, but he wouldn't rat on me. Not with the shitload of stuff I've got on him. Lighten up, silly. It's Halloween. Let's have some fun." She pulled the gorilla mask down over her head and Darby couldn't help but laugh.

Flipping up the volume on the radio, Linda turned the truck toward town, and sang along with a chorus of "Werewolves of London" that blared from the truck speakers.

Darby forced her thoughts farther, to that night, the Ouija board, the execution play-by-play on the radio.

She saw Linda and Jane and Trish gathered around her. And Katy.

Her wide, frightened brown eyes fired a bright, vivid *blue*. Then . . .

"Well, lookee what we have here." Katy spoke the words, but it wasn't her voice. It was deeper. A man's voice. A *man*.

Darby's eyes snapped open and the image shattered.

"What is it?" Graham turned those all-seeing blue eyes on her, his gaze piercing her, pushing inside her mind to see what she'd seen.

But what had she seen?

Eyes that changed colors?

No, it couldn't have been. That had been her imagination. A play of the candlelight.

And the *man's* voice?

"I . . ." Her own voice failed her and she clutched trembling hands in her lap.

"Did you remember?" He reached out, large hands closing over her shoulders. "What did you see? Tell me, dammit."

"I—I don't know." She shook her head. "I saw Katy, but it wasn't really Katy. She looked funny, and her voice . . ." She wiped at a tear that had trailed down her cheek. "Her voice was different. Deeper. A man's voice."

"There was a man in the room?"

"I don't know. Katy spoke the words, but it wasn't her voice. I—I didn't see anyone else. I guess there could have been." Another frantic shake of her head. "I just don't know." She slammed her fist into the seat next to her. "I have to remember, dammit. I *have* to." She raised tear-filled eyes to him. "What if I did do it, Graham? We know I'm capable. What if I did murder Linda and the others? What if the dreams aren't dreams but actual experiences? *My* experiences. What if I've been killing ever since—"

"Stop it, Darby!" His fingers clamped around her wrist, his other hand forcing her to look at him. "You didn't kill Deana Mills."

"But I saw the murder. I *saw* it. How do you explain that?"

"I don't know. What if you're having some weird psychic experience?"

"Do you believe that?"

"I don't know." He let go of her and ran a hand over his face. "It's possible, I suppose. I've certainly seen stranger shit since I joined the force." He captured her gaze. "I don't know why you're having the dreams, or what the hell they mean, but I do know you didn't kill the grocery clerk. A Samuel Blue copycat did that."

"And Linda?" The question hung between them for several long moments, the truth echoing in the silence.

Killer, killer, killer.

"Look," he finally said. "All this visiting different houses and people isn't getting you anywhere." He turned toward her, resting his arm across the back of the seat. "You don't remember anything more than when you came here."

"If I could just get into the attic. Maybe then."

"And maybe not." He ran stiff fingers through his hair. "Besides, I've already contacted the station. They refuse to allow anyone, even the police, inside. Short of getting a warrant, which a judge isn't likely to issue without probable cause, there's no way the television station is going to let us inside."

"What if we talked to the judge and explained the situation? Surely if he knew how important this was, he would issue the warrant. . . ."

Her words faded as she watched him shake his head. "I've already talked to Maggie, and without her support, the judge won't give us the time of day, and she's set on keeping this anniversary thing as low-key as possible. A warrant would draw too much attention."

"Damn." She touched her aching head and closed her eyes. What happened after the voice? And whose voice had she heard? Someone else in the room? The killer? Who?

"But I do have an idea."

Her eyes opened and she turned toward him. "What?"

"It's a long shot, but have you ever thought of hypnosis?"

"I tried it once."

"When?"

"Right after the murders. The court appointed a psychiatrist to counsel me during the investigation. He put me under one time, but it didn't work."

"You could try again. It's been a long time. Maybe you were too traumatized immediately after the murders to remember anything. But now you've had time to heal. . . ." He slid his hand down to close his fingers around hers. "I have this friend in Dallas, a staff psychologist with the department who works with a lot of violent-crime victims, counsels them, helps them give descriptions of their offenders—that sort of thing. There have been a few cases where the victims were so traumatized they couldn't remember anything. Hypnosis actually helped us get a description and catch the offenders. If you want to try, we could drive up to Dallas this afternoon."

She stared into his deep blue eyes and saw her own desperation mirrored there. He wanted her to remember, not simply because he wanted to prove her guilt. It wasn't vengeance at stake here. There was something else, a need. Graham needed to know the truth, to ease his own guilt.

The knowlege hit her like a fist to her chest. The air bolted from her lungs and she simply sat there, staring into his gaze, really seeing his pain for the first time. The urge to reach out, to run her hand over his stubbled jaw and ease his hurt, nearly overwhelmed her. He looked so much older now, worn, though he was only thirty. And he looked lost. So damned lost. As lost as she felt at times.

He sat beside her, a grown man, his body better developed, muscles thicker, his voice deeper, his gaze so much more experienced, yet beneath it all, she could still sense the nineteen-year-old he'd once been. The boy she'd lusted after, loved . . .

She shoved the thought away.

The murders. She had to keep her mind on the murders, and remembering.

"Let's go," she said, turning to stare out the window rather than at him.

Distance, she told herself.

Distance would keep them both safe.

"Okay, Darby. When I snap my fingers, you'll wake up."

A snap echoed. Darby opened her eyes expectantly and stared up at Dr. J. C. Reynolds.

The doctor looked like a *Playboy* centerfold, with dark green eyes, deeply tanned skin and platinum blond hair. A figure-hugging emerald green suit accented her curves, and an ivory silk blouse draped over her perfect breasts.

Darby herself was no slouch when it came to figures, but everything about her was small. Small build, small breasts, no matter that they were perky and quite substantial for her small frame. She was still small.

A shadow of the woman who sat on the edge of her desk and crossed mile-long legs before picking up her notepad.

"So?"

"So nothing," Graham said, his figure sprawled in a chair across the large office.

The office looked more like a living room, with a cream-colored sofa and chairs, a Queen Anne table covered with a collection of porcelain bells of all sizes and shapes. The hutch that sat against one wall sported more of the porcelain collection. On either side, large walnut bookshelves held volumes of leather-bound medical texts, the only indication that Darby was sitting in a doctor's office and not in someone's living room. To celebrate the fast-approaching holiday, a ceramic jack-o'-lantern smiled from a small table near the doorway.

"You didn't find out anything?" Darby asked, disappointment coursing through her.

"I'm afraid not." Dr. Reynolds walked around the sofa, to another Queen Anne table situated against the far wall that served as her desk. She picked up her glasses, then turned back to Darby, a notepad in her hand. "It's there," she said, with peach-tinted lips, "but it's so deeply buried. It's as if your subconscious doesn't even want to remember."

"Damn," Darby said, touching her throbbing temple. "What's wrong with me?"

But she knew the answer. As much as she told herself she wanted to remember, she was afraid. Afraid of the truth. Afraid because she'd killed Linda and Jane and—

"Nothing's wrong with you," Dr. Reynolds said, her honeyed voice scattering Darby's damning thoughts. The woman sashayed back over to the sofa and sat down, her skirt hiking up to reveal a tanned expanse of thigh as she crossed her long legs. "Some people just aren't good candidates for hypnosis." She reached out and took Darby's hands in her own, her fingers strong and comforting. "Graham tells me you've been having dreams."

Darby nodded, giving in to the urge to talk to this woman despite the jealous part of her that didn't want to like Dr. Reynolds. "I think they're dreams. I'm not really sure. I mean, they started a long time ago. Just visions where I saw women killed, but the images were so fuzzy. I figured it was my subconscious remembering what had happened in the attic. But then the dreams started to get clearer." She swallowed, afraid to continue. Yet she knew she had to.

"Last week, in San Francisco," she went on, "I had another dream, only this time I saw a face. Later, after I woke up, I saw the face on television. It belonged to a real woman who'd been murdered the night before." She closed her eyes, frustration and fear bubbling inside her, like hot lava in a volcano. "I knew then that they were more than dreams. I saw her die. It was like I was inside the killer's head."

"And you saw the recent murder in Nostalgia, as well?"

Darby opened her eyes and nodded.

Dr. Reynolds let go of Darby's hands to flip through the notebook on her lap. "You're right. It seems to me that what you're dealing with aren't dreams."

"Darby thinks she might be having some sort of psychic experience," Graham said, arms folded, a skeptical look on his face.

Dr. Reynolds nodded. "It's possible, though my colleagues would probably shoot me if they heard me admit such a thing."

"Why?"

"Because psychologists don't believe in psychic phenomenon. They believe everything can be explained by parapsychology."

"What's parapsychology?"

"Well, for instance, I think it's quite possible you're empathic."

"Empathic? That's feeling another person's feelings, right?"

"Yes, but I'm not talking your normal degree of empathy. You see, every action, every thought, uses electrical energy. Some people are sensitive to this energy. You could be one of those people. The killer is emitting electrical energy with his actions and thoughts, and you're tuning in. Just like tuning in to a radio station." She glanced at her watch. "I hate to cut this session short, but I have another appointment."

Graham stood. "Thanks, J. C."

"No problem. I wish I could have done more." She went over and slipped her hand into his, a softness in her eyes. "Why don't you stick around? I'm free for dinner once I finish with my next patient." She glanced back at Darby. "Unless you two have something planned?"

"No. There's no 'you two,'" Darby said, gathering up her purse, her gaze anywhere but on Graham, or the point where the good doctor's hand held his arm. "Thanks, Dr. Reynolds." She walked out of the office in the next instant, leaving Graham to say his good-byes and make his dinner arrangements in private.

"Wait up." Graham caught her a half minute later at the elevator. "What's wrong?"

"I'm just tired, and disappointed." She wiped her eyes, refusing to meet his gaze. And jealous, a voice chided silently.

"I'm sorry the hypnosis didn't work. I was hoping." He stuffed his hands into his pockets. "But at least we've got more of a handle on this psychic thing."

"Empathy," Darby corrected.

"Whatever. At least we know it's not you."

"Do we?"

"I do. Don't you?"

She nodded, all the while desperate to blurt out the information about the clues she'd been finding. The small cuts, the blood. Real clues that pointed to her as the killer.

"You don't know—" she started to say, her gaze colliding with his, and the rest of the confession died on her lips. Trust blazed in his eyes, and she couldn't make herself say the words that would dampen that emotion, turn it to something cold and hard.

"I don't know what?"

"You don't know how much I appreciate your help. Thanks."

The elevator dinged, and the doors slid open, waiting. She turned. His hand on her arm stopped her, his other hand punching the button on the elevator to hold the door.

"Look, I need to check in with my captain and update him on what's going on down in Nostalgia in case Maggie asks for some help. My place is a few blocks over. You can crash there until I finish; then we can head back."

At that moment, Dr. Reynolds appeared in the doorway, and the full meaning of his words sank in.

Finish. Until he finished with the good doctor.

Darby shook her head, anger and jealousy and hurt swimming inside her, making her hands tremble and her feet long to turn and run. "No, thanks. I'd really like to head back now." She was thankful she'd insisted on driving her own car, following him up to Dallas, rather than riding next to him. She'd needed some time alone, but most of all, she'd needed out of that truck, to be a safe distance from him.

"Will you be all right by yourself?" He glanced toward the windows. "It's still daylight, but—"

"Fine." A sad smile tugged at her lips as she spoke the words. "I've been by myself for a long time. I like it that way."

Liar. She knew she was. She was pushing him away, building up her defenses, fortifying the paper-thin wall that stood between them.

His gaze caught and held hers, a strange expression in

the deep blue depths. Regret? Disappointment?

Ridiculous, she decided as her gaze went past him, to Dr. Reynolds, who stood in the doorway. Waiting. There was no mistaking the female interest in her eyes, the familiarity in her gaze as it traveled over Graham. Darby knew beyond a doubt that this wasn't just a friend. This woman was much more to him, and *dinner* would be feeding a different sort of appetite.

He shifted then so that his body blocked Darby's view and drew her attention back to him. "Then I'll see you later tonight." The words sounded more like a promise.

"Yeah. See you." She walked into the elevator and turned for one last look at him before the doors swished shut.

He seemed hesitant, his hand holding the elevator button as if he didn't mean to let it go. Then he pulled back.

For a wild second, she panicked.

She was leaving again. Leaving the past behind, leaving Graham behind. Running away.

But she didn't want to. She didn't want to run, to be alone anymore.

Her hand moved for the DOOR OPEN button, then froze an inch away.

Move, she ordered, but her hand wouldn't cooperate. Then the doors closed, the elevator dropped, and her chance was lost.

She was leaving. Running. Alone. Again.

Chapter Nineteen

I never did like shrinks.

Always poking and prodding, sticking their noses into everybody else's business.

Of course, none of them ever looked quite as good as Dr. Reynolds. I'd like to stick my nose into her business, that's for damn sure.

It looks like Tucker already beat me to the punch, though, the two-timing bastard. Imagine, him upsetting Darby like that. She's sweet on him. I know she is. I know everything about Darby.

I wouldn't even mind it, except Tucker's starting to hang around too much. Sticking his nose where it doesn't belong.

I mean, if Darby wants to drink the whole fucking bar out at Poppy's, it's her business, right? And mine, of course.

She doesn't make one move without me. I'm always there. The trouble is, I don't make one move without her. When she was drunk as a skunk, it didn't matter. She didn't remember what she'd seen when we were together. What I'd done.

But now . . .

The damn bitch is watching me again.

Of course, I wanted her to initially. I wanted to teach her a lesson, but it didn't quite turn out the way I'd hoped. She ran to the bar, like I knew she would if pushed far enough. If she got a good eyeful. But that damned Tucker was there, driving her home, playing the hero and keeping her from drinking herself into a damned coma.

That's not the way it was supposed to be.

Darby should have run straight to the bottle, scared shitless after what she'd just seen.

She will. Tonight. She'll run right into a bottle before the night's over, while Mr. Hero spends his time screwing the shrink with the big tits.

Otherwise, I'll have to put Plan B into action.

I can't have Darby ruining things for me. As much as I love her, I'll slit her throat before I let her do that.

Of course, if I implement Plan B, that's exactly what I'll be doing.

The smell of urine and dog food permeated the air, teasing Death's nostrils as he waited beside the back door. He could hear the animals barking, alerting the woman inside to his presence.

Not that he cared.

There was no one around to hear the blasted animals, or her, once the fun began. Only a pasture out back for the horses, at least ten acres on either side to the nearest neighbors. Plenty of room to nurse sick animals back to health, and to keep the dozen or so personal pets he'd seen earlier.

Animal heaven.

He smiled at that. It would be hell before he finished here. Hell . . .

"Here, Sugar. Momma's got a treat for you." The back door opened. The woman walked out onto the porch, a

*bowl of cat food in her hand. A jack-o'-lantern glowed with
a fierce scowl from the window, pushing back the shadows
a fraction with its eerie orange light.*

*He slipped up behind her, so close he could feel her body
heat, practically hear the blood pumping through her veins.*

*"Sugar? Come here, baby. Here, Sugar. Here." She took
a few more steps, one hand on her hip. "Now where did
you run off to?"*

Just a couple more steps, he urged silently. One, yes
that's it. Now another . . .

*"Sugar—" The word died in her throat when she saw the
cat's mangled body, the eyes resting on its chest like mis-
placed marbles. Her fingers went limp. The bowl of cat food
crashed to the ground. She sank to her knees beside the
dead animal and held a hand to her mouth.*

*He reached out, the surgeon's scalpel he'd snatched from
one of her operating rooms gripped tightly in his hand. He
gripped a handful of her hair, jerked her head back. The
scalpel pressed to her throat, stifling the scream she'd been
about to let loose.*

*Fear glittered hot and bright in her eyes as she stared up
at him.*

*"Say a word, and I'll kill you," he said. "Slowly, very
slowly. Understand?" She nodded jerkily and he smiled.
"Good girl," he whispered, patting her on the head before
getting on with his business.*

*He was quick and efficient with the supplies he'd picked
up in one of her operating rooms. He leaned forward, jerked
her hands behind her back and secured them. Next he
stuffed a large surgical sponge into her mouth. Finally he
moved around, the scalpel tip trailing down the front of her
blouse to the valley between her breasts where her heart
pounded. Then he worked on her feet.*

*She whimpered once, her chest heaving, and he pressed
the scalpel deep, watching the dark red stain appear on her
white shirt. A warning.*

*He liked giving them warnings. They were always quiet
then. Scared. Complacent. Long enough for him to secure*

them. Then the real pain would start, and the fight, and, of course, the fun.

"Perfect," he said, checking his handiwork. He stood and walked around behind her. He gripped a handful of her hair again and jerked her head back, her throat arching, convulsing as the sponge strangled the scream in her mouth.

"Here, sugar," he whispered, trailing the tip of the scalpel up the side of her tear-streaked face. A crimson path marked his progress, the scalpel point stopping at the corner of her eye. "Daddy Death's got a treat for you."

Darby opened her eyes to sunlight streaming through the parted blinds. Several flashes blinded her and she quickly realized it wasn't the sunlight, but a camera clicking away.

"Shit," she muttered, struggling to a sitting position. She reached for the blanket to cover herself, but a quick glance down revealed that she was fully dressed, her jeans and shirt rumpled, her boots still on.

She'd staggered in last night after the drive back, collapsed on the bed and fallen asleep.

"Miss Jayson," the reporter started, shooting several more pictures as Darby stumbled over to flip the blinds closed. "Just a few questions."

"No comment," she mumbled, fighting with the plastic cord on the drapes.

"Come on. Just a few. Where were you last night?"

"No comment."

"Are you aware that the citizens have banded together to form a local coalition against violent crime?"

"No comment." Dammit, she would string Pinky up the next time she saw him. She yanked on the cord, but it was stuck.

"Are you aware that they plan to make you a prime target?"

"No comment."

"Are you aware that another murder took place last night?"

Ice water flowed through her body, freezing her to the quick. "Another one?"

"Janice Wilder, the town vet." He snapped several pictures of Darby's pale face. The flashes stirred a blur of white spots, but that wasn't what sent Darby to her knees.

In her mind's eye, she saw the vet's face tilted up, eyes wide with fear and desperation and disbelief.

"Daddy Death's got a treat for you."

"Word is that you're the murderer, Miss Jayson. Considering your past." The reporter fired the remarks at her. "Did you do it? Did you slice up the grocery clerk night before last, then the vet again last night?" Another click, another blinding flash. "Did you, Miss Jayson? *Did* you?"

She gripped a nearby chair, forced herself to her feet, and stumbled into the bathroom. Her stomach jumped, whirled, like a gymnast trying out for the Olympics.

"Did you?" The words followed her into the bathroom.

She slammed the door and sank to the tile floor, holding her stomach, trying desperately to calm herself.

Did you? The question screamed at her, and an echoing shiver rolled through her.

Yes, she wanted to respond. *Maybe.* She didn't know. That was the kicker. She didn't damn well know!

Ah, but she did. She glanced down at the thin line of newly healed flesh she'd discovered three days ago on the plane. Proof of Rudy's and Jan's murders.

Next, she stared at the fast-healing spot on the tip of her finger where she'd picked up the splinter. Proof of the little dog's murder.

Her gaze scoured the bathroom for the tiny drop of blood she'd found yesterday. It was gone now, wiped away in a panicked horror. But she knew exactly where it had been, could still see it in her mind's eye. Proof of the clerk's murder.

And what about proof of this latest death?

In a frenzy, she ripped off her clothes, combed over her body, searching for any damning sign of anything out of the ordinary. A cut. A bruise. Anything.

Nothing. She found nothing.

Frantically, she crawled around the bathroom, shoved towels aside, searching, searching. . . .

For a drop of blood. A dirty footprint. Anything.

Nothing.

She put her clothes back on and went back in the bedroom. She yanked the drapes closed, blotting out the blinding camera flashes, and tore through the room.

Searching, searching . . .

An hour later, she slumped back against the bed, her hands sore from ripping open drawers, digging through clothes, beneath the bed, everywhere.

Relief crept through her, and hope. Other than the fuzzy, distorted dream, there was no real evidence that she'd been at the murder scene, witnessed the carnage, committed the violent act. Not this time.

Graham's words came back to her, his explanation about the copycat killer, and she clung to the hope.

She could be having some sort of psychic connection with the copycat killer; she could be linked to him somehow, some way, so deeply that she actually got inside his head, saw through his eyes, felt what he felt.

Maybe she truly was empathic, as Dr. Reynolds had suggested. That was why she felt this guy's feelings, as intensely as if they were her own. The excitement, the delight, the rage, the blood. So much rich, sweet blood . . .

Her stomach jolted and she forced aside the images swimming in her head.

The empathy would certainly explain why the dreams were from a male point of view. If they'd been *her* dreams, her actions, wouldn't they have been from a female's perspective?

But if she really was empathic, why only with the copycat killer? She'd never had extraordinary talents with anyone else, in any other situation.

The damning questions pounded through her head,

but at the same time, hope sparked, grew, seeping through her.

Empathic. It was possible. Bizarre, yet possible.

Only, the good people of Nostalgia weren't as open-minded, she realized several minutes later when she heard the pounding on her door, then the reverend's booming voice from the other side.

"Open up, Darby! We've come to see that you get out of town and stay out!"

Darby peeked past the drapes to see the reverend and a handful of others crowded outside her door. The press surrounded them like vultures circling a fresh corpse. Obviously they didn't want to miss any juicy detail of what was about to happen.

"Open up!" The reverend's words echoed through the crowd.

Her hands trembled and she thought again of a good shot of whiskey. Or beer. Or anything that could help her through this.

But nothing could. She had to help herself.

And fast, she realized when she chanced another peek and saw one of the citizens waving a crowbar. The reverend took the bar, raised it.

"Hold on!" Pinky Mitchell shoved his way through the crowd and grabbed the tool from the reverend's hand. "What you're about to do is against the law, and preacher or no preacher, I ain't about to let you do it."

"This is none of your business, Pete Mitchell. We've come to do God's work," the reverend said solemnly.

"I don't know much 'bout God, but if you bust down that door, you're making more work for me, and that makes it my business. That's why I called the cops. Maggie's sending a few men over right now, so you people had better get on home unless you want to spend the night in jail."

The reverend was clearly flustered by the turn of events, as were several of his crowd. They looked to him for guidance.

Pinky tapped the reverend's chest. "Listen up, preacher. Maggie said to tell you if you don't want to be the first one booked, she better not find you when she gets here."

The reverend's face turned beet red, his eyes flashed outrage, but he said nothing. "Come on," he finally grumbled, leading his flock away.

The reporters moved in, snapping pictures of Pinky and firing questions at him.

"What is your relationship with Darby Jayson?"

"Do you think she committed the murders?"

"How do you feel about harboring a possible murderer?"

"Y'all settle down now and I'll be happy to answer all your questions." Pinky pointed to a video camera. "That thing on?" At the reporter's nod, he adjusted his pink flamingo-print shirt and pasted on his best smile. "Uh, Darby and I go way, way back." He launched into a very fictitious recount of a shared past. Not that Darby cared. She could have kissed him for getting the reverend away from her door.

Grabbing her purse, she headed for the bathroom, climbed up onto the toilet seat and slid the window open.

The glass didn't even squeak, but slid easily. Shoving her bag through, she listened for the thunk, then hooked a leg over the ledge and climbed through. It was an easy squeeze for someone her size.

Outside, she headed around the building, her gaze casing her surroundings for any lingering reporters. Peering around one corner, she spotted her car. Pinky had led most of the reporters away from her door. Now the group spilled from Pinky's office out onto the walkway, their attention fixed on the man behind the registration desk.

Ducking, she hurried to her car, climbed inside and started the ignition. With a quick peek in her rearview mirror as she drove away, she realized a few reporters had caught her flight. She didn't care.

With any luck, if everyone really believed her to be a

murderer, they might think she'd skipped town.

But Darby wasn't going anywhere. She'd come back to remember the truth—for better or for worse—and she wasn't leaving until then. And after that, she would face the consequences and pay for her sins, if any. Life or death.

First things first, however. She needed to understand what was happening to her. Since Nostalgia wasn't exactly overflowing with supernatural gurus, Darby headed for the one person who might be able to give her a little more information on empathy.

She turned down a dirt road, her gaze fixed on the purple hand outlined in green neon that rose in the distance. The sooner she understood why she was crawling inside this guy's head during the killings, the sooner she could crawl out, and get on with her quest for the truth.

While Darby was trying to crawl out of the killer's head, Graham was desperately trying to crawl in.

Bright and early, he strolled into the Homicide department of the Dallas PD, took the elevator up to the fifth floor, and headed for his captain's office.

"You'd better have a damn good reason for dragging me into work at six A.M., Tucker." Captain Ron Diego shoved a hand through his salt-and-pepper hair before pointing an accusing finger at Graham Tucker, who sat in the desk opposite him. "I've got a noon luncheon with the mayor's representative, and I don't need bags under my eyes."

Graham shifted in his seat and leaned forward. "I need to talk to you about Samuel Blue. You worked the investigations on the two Dallas girls he was convicted of killing. I thought you could give me some insight into this guy, something more than what's in the case files."

The captain shook his head and passed a hand over his sleepy-looking eyes. "Dammit, Tucker. The guy's been dead for nearly ten years. I know this anniversary thing in your hometown's put a bug up your ass, but the Blue murders are history—"

"There's a Blue copycat operating in Nostalgia. A girl was murdered night before last. Eyes cut out, throat slashed. No evidence."

"Are you sure this guy's copycatting Blue and not someone else?"

"Sully flew in yesterday to lend the FBI's support. The profile he put together based on the crime scene could be a carbon copy of Blue's."

"Shit," the captain muttered, reaching for the steaming Styrofoam cup sitting on his desk. He took a sip and frowned. "Why didn't the local chief call us in?"

"She wants to fly solo on this one. The town's already getting too much publicity because of that TV station and the anniversary of Blue's execution day after tomorrow on Halloween."

"And the tenth anniversary of those slumber-party killings," the captain pointed out.

"That, too," Graham added. "She doesn't want to draw even more attention. Hell, you don't know what it took to get her to call the FBI in to consult."

"With your charm? I'm sure she nearly tossed your ass in jail."

"She let me call Sully."

"So where do I come in?" the captain asked, taking another sip of coffee. "You know Nostalgia's out of my jurisdiction. I have no authority, and unless she asks for help, I have to keep my nose clean."

"You got closer to Blue than anyone else. Tell me something about him. Maybe if I can figure out how he worked, I can second-guess the guy who's out there right now."

"Let's see," the captain started. "Blue came from a dysfunctional family. Mother died giving birth to him. Father was a drug addict, alcoholic, rarely at home. Blue was raised by his grandmother, a religious woman who took the 'spare the rod and spoil the child' verse to extremes. He was beaten, punished repeatedly, all in the name of God. It turns out the grandmother let loose on him so often because he looked so much like his father, who she was convinced was Satan's own son. A sinner. She blamed the bastard for her daughter's death, because he knocked her up. Because of Blue's relationship with his grandmother, he grew up with a very distorted view of women. But this is all documented in the files."

"I know," Graham said, "but talk it out with me. Maybe I'll learn something that wasn't mentioned."

The captain shook his head. "You owe me for this, Tucker," he said, taking two more sips of his coffee and settling back in his chair. "Let's see, Blue committed his first murder in seventy-six when he was twelve, on Halloween. The victim was his father. The guy was found the next morning by the grandmother, his throat slit, eyes gouged out. The police investigation concluded the killer was some drug dealer the father owed money to, though no conviction was ever made. No one even suspected Samuel. He was too young, and he had an alibi. The grandmother said they'd spent the entire evening at church, then gone home straight to bed. Though I think the old lady knew a helluva lot more than she let on at the time."

"You think she knew Blue killed the father?"

"I think so," the captain replied. "Maybe that's why she was his next victim. He killed her exactly one year later on Halloween; then he went on to more victims. He had a fascination with blue eyes, his own and anyone else's. Told a shrink one time that even though people lie, the eyes always tell the truth."

"Windows to the soul," Graham murmured, thinking of Darby's wide, innocent eyes. Then the strange flash of blue. He shook the thought away. "Go on."

"Anyhow, with his first victim, his father, Blue was inexperienced. That killing was probably more anger-motivated than any of the others. He wanted the guy dead, period. He slit the throat first. He was just a kid.

Tall, but still scrawny. His father was a bear of a man. He had to slice the throat first, otherwise he would have had a hell of a struggle on his hands. He cut the eyes out afterward. But he didn't get much satisfaction from that."

"What do you mean?"

"Blue was a control freak. He never had any control. He was forced into submission by his grandmother, he did what she said, when she said. It seems his father would come by for a little while, wiggle some money out of the old lady, then take off again. Samuel wanted him to stay. When the father didn't, Samuel begged to go with him. The father refused, so Samuel killed him. Apparently, Samuel liked it a lot more than he bargained for."

"How so?"

"Well, he killed his dad out of anger, to get rid of him. If the dad stopped coming around, maybe the beatings from his grandmother would stop. He simply wanted to eliminate his father. But when he killed him, he realized there was much more to death. There was power. The act gave him a rush, a power high. For once, Samuel was in control, not his father. He was calling the shots, and his father was the one obeying. Still, his father's murder wasn't quite as good as Samuel expected because the father didn't really see Samuel's power, not for longer than those few seconds of realization. That started Blue to thinking. He spent the next year thinking of ways he would improve, *if* he ever did it again."

"And he did it again exactly one year later," Graham said.

"Yep. On Halloween. He spent the year thinking about death, and wishing for it. The grandmother made his life hell. She kept him confined to his room, or in church. Beat the shit out of him because she knew he'd killed the father. You would think she'd have been scared of the little bastard, but she wasn't. She thought her faith could save her and redeem Samuel. Maybe so, but hers was a twisted sort of faith, rooted in violence. That's what she taught her grandson, and he learned well.

"Anyway," the captain went on, "she was his second victim. Tortured her in the kitchen, then moved her up to the attic to finish her off. He left Nostalgia right after that, moved up into Dallas, killed four girls, though we only got a conviction for two. Went on to Lubbock and Houston and San Antonio. Left victims behind everywhere he went. There was no rhyme or reason to his victims. No specific requirements, other than the fact that most were women, with the exception of the security guard he sliced up down in Houston, but he claimed that was self-defense, not premeditated. I think he was right. The throat was sliced before the eyes, and by that time, Samuel got his rocks off by inflicting pain. The guard wasn't a joy killing like the others. The women could be blondes, brunettes, old or young, any race, any religion. The only characteristic they had in common was their eyes."

"Blue eyes."

"Exactly. Samuel traveled around, working here and there as a pharmacist's assistant. He was very smart. He never graduated high school, but he certainly could have. In fact, he was brilliant. Put that together with his good looks and a shitload of charm, and he was dangerous. Very, very dangerous. More so than Bundy. Fortunately, like all psychopaths, the bloodlust eventually got the better of him. He got sloppy."

"His fortieth victim?"

"Off the record, yes, though he was only convicted of twenty-nine deaths. He was in El Paso. He befriended a pretty young schoolteacher—blond, blue eyed—talked her into his car. They went for a drive. When he got her on the outskirts of town, away from everybody, he moved in for the attack. What he didn't know was that one of the children back at the school had seen him. The child had gone back inside to pick up her coat. When she came out, she saw the teacher getting into Blue's car. The school had had a 'Don't Talk to Strangers' campaign going that week and so, like they'd been taught, the child took a good look at the car, the license plate number, and the man. She was able to give the police a description of the vehicle, not the exact make, but she picked out similar pictures, and helped with a sketch of the man. That information went out immediately and the police picked Blue up the next day at his job at a local pharmacy. Too late to save the teacher, but who knows how many others that ten-year-old saved? The director of the Bureau flew to El Paso and gave the child a personal recognition and thank-you on behalf of the FBI.

"Blue went to prison," Captain Diego went on. "He was sentenced to die by lethal injection and spent three years sitting on Death Row."

"I heard he waived his right to an appeal," Graham said, and the captain nodded.

"Never could figure out why he did that. He never did say, but from the profile done on him by the Bureau, Blue was a sadist and a masochist. He was into pain, fascinated with death. He lived vicariously through his victims, inflicting pain that he himself wanted to feel. He wanted death. He had it built up in his mind as the ultimate high. Where he couldn't quite get it right with each victim, his own death would be the perfect fulfillment of the fantasy."

"And?" Graham prodded.

"I don't know about perfect, but it was long overdue. He's rotting in hell now, like he should be."

Graham didn't say anything for a long moment. He just sat there, staring out the window.

"He is dead," the captain added. "I was at the death house myself, sitting in the witness chamber. I saw the needles in his arm, saw him die. He's dead."

"I know that. I'm just trying to figure out what's going on with the killer in Nostalgia." And how he was connected to Darby.

Could it be someone she knew?

Someone they both knew?

"So what did Blue do those three years in prison?" Graham asked. "Besides anticipate death."

"Nothing much. Smoked a lot of cigarettes, burned himself repeatedly." At Graham's raised eyebrows, the captain added, "I told you he was a sadist and a masochist. Anyhow, he spent the rest of his time reading his Bible and writing in that blasted diary of his."

"A diary," Graham muttered. His mind quickly singled out the memory of Darby and her laptop computer, her manuscript. A diary?

He forced the thought away. He was going overboard. Darby was a writer. Hundreds of people kept diaries. That didn't make them all killers. Besides, Darby didn't fit the copycat's profile. Not by a long shot.

The captain downed his last sip of coffee. "The creepiest thing you ever read," he went on. "There was an entry for each victim, a play-by-play account of their deaths. That's how we got a good idea about the number of victims, though guilt was never established in a good third of the cases due to lack of evidence."

"Couldn't the diary be admitted into evidence?"

"We didn't find the diary until after the execution. Too late then." The captain folded his hands on top of his desk. "So you've got one victim with Blue's MO?" he asked, a skeptical look on his face. "That's not much to conclude you've got a copycat serial killer working the town. In my professional opinion, I'd say it's an isolated incident. Because of all the hoopla."

"It was too clean to be a novice. This person's done it before."

"Even so, there's no guarantee this guy will hit again. Maybe he'll move on, pick a new city, a new victim, a new killer to emulate."

"Maybe."

"Just to be sure I'll have a friend of mine at the Dallas Bureau feed the information on this death into VICAP and get you a listing of any homicides with a similar MO."

"Thanks," Graham said, pushing to his feet. "I'm sorry I got you up so early."

Graham left the office and headed downstairs and out the front double doors. All the while, his brain sorted through all the information he'd gleaned about Samuel Blue.

Nothing he didn't already know.

Maybe Diego was right, he thought as he climbed into his car and headed for I-45. Maybe it was an isolated incident, spawned by the fanfare surrounding the anniversary. Perhaps Deana Mills would be the only victim, and after Halloween, the day after tomorrow, Nostalgia could start recovering from its latest tragedy.

Maybe not, he admitted an hour later when he stopped at a convenience store just five miles outside of Nostalgia, picked up the Saturday morning paper and read the headline: COPYCAT KILLER CLAIMS SECOND VICTIM.

A wave of nausea hit him as he stared at the vet's picture. In his mind, he saw the mess that would have been left once the killer finished.

He scanned to the bottom of the page and saw a picture of Reverend Masters, and the bold claim that Nostalgia had to rid itself of a killer. A sinner.

There, next to the reverend's angry face, was a picture of Darby. Doe-eyed, frightened Darby.

A victim herself, or a killer?

Not this killer, he reminded himself. Despite what Reverend Masters claimed, and the coincidence that the murders started once Darby had come home.

Someone else was home, as well.

Someone who'd been in the attic that night.

Someone who could have killed his sister as easily as Darby.

Katy Evans.

Denial raged through him, trying to push the thought

aside, but Graham clung to it and refused to let it go so easily this time. The slumber-party scene had clearly been the work of a very disorganized killer. Someone deeply troubled. Katy certainly fit that description. Now. But then?

Graham had considered Katy as a possible suspect several times, but seeing her at the sanatorium, the way she'd turned from vivacious and strong to slovenly and hysterical, had only furthered his assumptions that Darby—or someone else—had done it, and Katy had witnessed it. Then, when the results of the lie-detector test had confirmed Katy's wild story, not to mention the crucial fact that she'd run for help, Graham had been convinced she hadn't been crazy at all that night, just lucky she hadn't been killed, as well. What she'd witnessed before running, however, had sent her over the edge.

Or what she'd done.

Even more incriminating, the recent murders came so soon after her release from the sanatorium.

She *was* a likely suspect.

Relief battled with the doubt inside him.

Katy would be such a logical answer, to solve the slumber-party case and soothe his guilt. He wouldn't feel like such an asshole for lusting after Darby, the woman who could be the very person who'd murdered his sister. If Katy were guilty, that would answer everything, tie it all up nice and neat, and Graham could get on with forgetting.

And he could give in to the want that made him hard every time he glanced at Darby.

If only everything were that simple. Black-and-white instead of a thousand shades of gray.

The trouble was, he couldn't quite convince himself of Katy's guilt. When he pictured poor, frightened Katy, he couldn't see her as a killer. Nor could he summon any anger toward her, or stifle the thought that there had been four victims that night instead of three. Katy had lost herself, the wonderful girl she'd once been. Her fun-filled adolescence had been traded for the inside of a sanatorium. He could still see her that night, fighting with the paramedics as they led her away, pleading with them to believe her.

"It was the devil!" she'd cried. *"The devil!"*

Now she was too far gone to be a cold, methodical killer. She wasn't in full control of her faculties, and that meant she wasn't the copycat killer. No way in hell would she be able to perform such an "organized" crime, leaving no clues, nothing.

Unless she'd been faking all these years.

Maybe she was still the same Katy beneath the slovenly appearance, the psychosis. Psychopaths were good at hiding their dark side. That was what made them so elusive. And so deadly.

But was Katy *that* good? Had she given up years of her life, biding her time inside an insane asylum so she could strike now?

He couldn't believe it. But then four days ago he never would have believed he could see Darby Jayson as anything more than a cold-blooded killer.

Now he saw a woman.

He felt a woman.

And God, he wanted that woman.

The truth be damned.

Chapter Twenty

Graham headed back to the motel to find Darby and see how she was holding up after the news this morning. He also wanted to apologize for not driving back last night. Damn, he should have made her stay in Dallas with him.

But he'd seen the stubborn expression in her eyes, the hurt.

Hurt?

That didn't make any sense. He had to have been reading her wrong. She'd been tired, just as she'd said.

He wondered how in the hell she'd managed to sleep with all the chaos going on, with Reverend Masters, and Lyle Proctor, and every fucking newspaper in Texas giving her a hard time.

When he got to the motel, Graham pushed his way through the crowd, only to discover that she wasn't in her room. He climbed back in his truck and resisted the urge to bang his head against the steering wheel. Damn, but he wanted to talk to her.

To see her.

He closed his eyes, the realization weighing heavily on him. For the first time, he admitted to himself that the attraction to her went beyond the physical.

Shit. He didn't need the complication, couldn't afford it right now. Shoving his thoughts on the back burner, he concentrated on the task at hand. One that didn't involve Darby, or his damned lust or whatever it was he was starting to feel for her. The most important thing was finding this killer, and right now, he had a hunch to check out.

Ten minutes later, Graham pounded on the door to Katy Evans's trailer, then rattled the screen door. No answer. Another long knock; then he pulled open the door and peered inside.

No one.

The moment he stepped inside, he was even more convinced that Katy wasn't the killer. The killer they were after was very organized, and no one was more disorganized than the woman who lived here.

He remembered her bedroom. Hell, he'd seen it one night. So damned neat and tidy. Pink everywhere.

This place was a pigsty. Three or four litterboxes filled the kitchen, the damn things overflowing. A dozen or so cats milled about the place. Cat hair covered the old sofa, the stuffing coming out in several places. And the smell . . .

He shook his head. She'd always smelled so sweet. Good enough to eat. The scent burning his nostrils now made him want to puke.

Only God knew what the bathroom would look like, if there even was a john. The trailer was so small, he had to duck to walk through. The kitchen and living room were about the size of his motel room, barely large enough for the tiny table and small sofa and TV that crowded inside. He glanced around for another doorway, and saw one partially open. He stepped closer, the stench of urine and shit assaulting him. From the looks of things out here, and the smell, he figured maybe Katy herself was using one of the damned litterboxes on the floor.

A paper mâché Jesus hung above the small sink. On every other wall, fire-and-brimstone pamphlets had been taped up. Graham took a deep breath, ducked his head inside the bathroom for a quick look. He saw two more overflowing litterboxes, several pieces of shit scattered across the floor, a stopped-up toilet, and a single shower stall dripping yellow water into a dingy basin.

Nothing incriminating.

Disappointment flowed through him as he walked through the kitchen and living room, looking.

He rummaged on the countertop, going through a stack of unpaid bills. An electricity bill, a water bill, an old grocery receipt, a receipt from the Harmony Pet Clinic for treatment of one of Katy's cats, several mailings from local evangelists, mail-in coupons and a sweepstakes notice. Nothing.

With every glance, he knew in his gut Katy wasn't the one. She was sick. But she wasn't a murderer—

The thought slammed to a halt the moment he turned. Sunlight streamed through the part in the dingy drapes, hitting the wall next to the television set.

That was when he saw the newspaper clippings. He stared into the smiling face of Deana Mills, then at the picture next to it from her funeral. At least a dozen other articles about the murder had been clipped from newspapers all around. There were more clippings about the vet's recent murder.

A showcase of the killer's handiwork.

Katy's handiwork.

"It's not enough evidence," Maggie said, climbing out from behind the wheel of her police car.

"Just take a look."

"Not without a warrant. I'm not in any hurry to lose my badge, and you shouldn't be either."

"There's a whole goddamn wall in there screaming

guilt, and you're too worried about procedure to check it out. Dammit, Maggie, you know as well as I do that killers like this often keep track of their murders with clippings, souvenirs. You *know* that."

"And I also know you were inside that girl's trailer without a warrant. The judge would throw any evidence you found right out of court."

"So get a warrant, and tear the place apart. There's got to be more."

"I'll see what I can do." She shook her head, her aviator sunglasses reflecting the afternoon sunlight. "But the judge ain't likely to issue a warrant when I ain't got a scrap of evidence for probable cause."

"Then put a tail on her."

"Hell, Graham. I'm using all the manpower I've got keeping tabs on Lyle and the reverend."

"Take them off and put them on Katy."

"You're so sure?"

He nodded. "I've got a feeling about this, Maggie."

"A feeling? Or are you just desperate to pin this on somebody other than Darby?" She shook her head. "Seems mighty convenient if it does turn out to be Katy. That would make her a likely suspect for the slumber-party killings."

"That's not it." He stared at the trailer. "Something's not right."

Maggie stared at him several long seconds. "Amen to that," she finally said. "Okay. I'll take Murdock off Proctor's tail and put him on Katy Evans. I was going to anyway. I know for a fact Proctor and the reverend were both at an Elks meeting last night while the vet was getting sliced up. Solid alibis."

"All the more reason Katy's the one. Damn, why didn't I see it before? She was there, at Proctor's Grocery the afternoon before the killings. Darby said she ran into her. What if it wasn't a chance meeting? What if she was casing the place? Planning the murder?"

"It's possible, I suppose."

"It's more than possible, Maggie. It's likely as hell."

"What about the vet?"

"She has an entire trailer full of cats. I saw a receipt from Harmony Pet Clinic dated day before yesterday. She was there," he said. "Dammit, Maggie. You have to issue an APB on her."

"I hope you're right," she said, picking up the mike for her radio. "Tillie, this is Maggie. Get Murdock on the wire and tell him to get his ass off Proctor and head on over to Katy Evans's place. Pronto."

"You endin' the surveillance on him?"

"Yeah, and issue an APB on Katy Evans. I want her picked up as soon as possible."

"A suspect?"

"Maybe. I just want her for questioning." At Graham's incredulous look, she added, "Right now. Then we'll see."

"How 'bout the reverend? You want the tail pulled off him, too?"

"Leave things for now. I want to know what he's up to."

"Yes sir, boss," came the slow drawl over the speaker.

Seeing Graham's raised eyebrows, Maggie explained, "He's not a suspect. Every damn Elk in this town will vouch for that. But he damn sure knows how to stir up trouble. Would've caused a riot outside the motel yesterday, probably burned and lynched that girl of yours if Pinky Mitchell hadn't called me."

"You're kidding."

"Hell, no. Thankfully the Good Book talks about respecting authority. I gave him a warning and sent him back to the church, but he left some of his congregation. Peaceful demonstrating, he called it. Peaceful, my ass. They're his watchdogs, so I got my own keeping an eye on the whole lot of them. I don't intend to give those nosy reporters any more shit to shovel up to their newspapers. Things are bad enough." She stared up at Graham, pulling her glasses off. "Speaking of which, your mama's decided to leave. She's headed down to Galveston to visit your great-aunt."

"I know. She told me this morning."

"Damn good idea. One less we got to worry about."

Graham nodded. "That's what she should have done in the first place."

"Besides," Maggie added, "she didn't take it too well when she heard Darby was back in town, and that you were, er, baby-sitting."

"Darby isn't a murderer."

"Your mother isn't as convinced."

"Mom blames God and everybody for taking Linda. Hell, she even shot at Dad with a BB gun because he'd been out of town that night on business, instead of at home keeping an eye on Linda."

"So she was a little out of it with the BB gun incident, but maybe she has a point about the Jayson woman."

He frowned. "I thought you didn't care whether Darby was guilty or innocent, as long as she let sleeping dogs lie?"

"Your mother's my friend. I don't like to see her suffer because she thinks her son has a major hard-on for her daughter's killer."

"*Alleged* killer, and I don't have a hard-on for anyone." He wiped a frustrated hand over his face. "It's good that Mom's leaving. She should have hightailed it out of here right after Linda died."

"Then you wouldn't have come back here," Maggie pointed out, shoving the police car into reverse and backing out of the driveway.

But he would have come back, he thought as he watched the police car disappear down the road. More than his mother, it was the town itself that had called Graham home. Despite what Maggie had said about Nostalgia healing and forgetting, Graham knew different. As long as a killer walked free, the people would never completely forget, or heal.

And his sister would never stop calling to him, crying out for vengeance.

A vengeance he was more than ready to hand out, he thought as he cast one more look at the piss-yellow trailer.

But first he had to find Katy Evans.

"Let's see," Myrna Evans said, shoving a pair of bifocals onto her nose and flipping open the monstrous book. "Empathy." She rested the book on her kitchen table, took a sip of iced tea and scanned the index. Then she flipped to the appropriate page. "Here it is. Empathy—capacity for participating in the feelings or ideas of another." She stared up at Darby. "You're empathic, you say?"

"I think so." Darby sank down into a kitchen chair opposite Myrna and leaned her elbows on the daisy-print tablecloth. "I'm not really sure. I've been having these dreams. At least, I think they're dreams."

Myrna sipped her tea and listened intently as Darby described the earlier nightmares—the faceless bodies, the fuzzy glimpses of death.

"At first, I thought they were some sort of flashback experience," she said, "from the slumber party, but then they started to get more vivid, until I finally saw a face." A shiver rolled through her as she pictured the DA's dead daughter. "Now I see everything, and I feel it—the knife in my hands, the blood on my skin." Another shiver rippled through her and she bolted to her feet, pacing.

"So why come to me, dear? If you wanted your palm read, or your chart done, I'm your woman, of course. But this is way out of my league."

"You're psychic. You can see things, feel things other people can't."

"You believe that?" She smiled. "If so, you're probably the only person in this town who does. Most people think I'm a fake."

"Katy always said you were for real."

A wistful smile touched her lips. "Katy never cared what other people said. I know the kids used to give her a hard time. 'Your mama's a witch, a crackpot.' But my Katy never listened to anyone. She knew my psychic abilities were real."

"I need to understand what's happening, to stop it. Can you help me?"

"I can try." Myrna turned her attention back to the book, drinking in several more lines of information. "First, let me try to explain empathy. You see, every action, every thought, uses electrical energy."

"And this energy is detectable," Darby finished, remembering what Dr. Reynolds had said. "In varying degrees."

"That's what some people think." Myrna pulled her glasses from her face and held them in her hands. "Can you feel what I'm feeling right now?"

Darby closed her eyes and clenched her fingers, but she felt nothing. Only her own palm, cold and damp from nervousness. "I can feel physical objects through him, and only him. It doesn't work with anyone else. Just him. The killer." Her throat closed around the word, but she forced herself on. "It's the copycat killer, the one who murdered the grocery clerk and the vet."

"You're kidding."

"I wish I were." Darby turned to stare out the window, away from Myrna's incredulous gaze. "I saw the murders. I was there, inside his head, seeing and feeling everything he did."

Myrna shook her head and shoved her glasses back onto her face. "But that's not right." She read a few more paragraphs. "Darby, if your extrasensory ability is so great that you really *felt* this guy, you wouldn't be able to function. It says so right here." She held up the book. "Those who have a high degree of empathy, the truly rare ones—they call them receptors—can hardly function in everyday life. They drive down a crowded street, and—bam—they're bombarded with feelings from all directions, like a blend of screams, some static, at mega volume. There's no way you could go all this time and not know you're empathic to such a high degree." She shook her head. "No, in order to function in a normal, everyday capacity, you would have had to learn to control your ability, to block out everything around you. Did you ever learn to block?"

"Are you kidding? I didn't even know what empathy was until yesterday."

"That's what doesn't make sense." Myrna looked thoughtful for several long moments. "Darby," she finally said. "I don't think you're the one with the extrasensory talents."

"Meaning?"

"You don't consciously tune in to this guy, right? You don't pick and choose when you focus on him?"

"Of course not. I can't close my eyes, picture this guy and project myself into him. It just happens. I have no say-so."

"That's my point. I think this guy is the one with the powers and he's reaching out to you, rather than you tuning in to him."

"I don't know if I'm following you."

"It's like making a phone call. I think this guy has your number, he punches it in when he wants to contact you, and all you do is pick up the phone. That would explain why you don't have any extrasensory ability in your everyday life."

"So this guy is the empath."

"No. I'm sure you're empathic, to a mild degree, otherwise he couldn't connect with you. Everyone has some extrasensory ability. Haven't you ever had a hunch about something? That's empathy, but on a much lower level." She pulled the glasses off again and stared up at Darby. "The killer is the powerful one. He's telepathic. He reaches out to you with his mind, communicates his feelings to you. That's where your empathy comes into play."

"But why me?"

"That I don't know."

But Darby knew. Her nightmare had started that night in the attic. What if she really hadn't killed anyone?

"What if it was him?" she said out loud, her mind racing with possibilities.

"Who?"

"The copycat killer. What if he was at the slumber party that night? What if he murdered Linda and the others, and I saw him do it?" She stopped pacing, her gaze catching Myrna's. "What if he killed them right in front of me, and meant to kill me, as well. Katy, too, but for whatever reason, he couldn't."

"I'm not sure I'm following you. Why use his powers to contact an eyewitness? Someone who could identify him? And why just you? Why not Katy?"

"Because what Katy saw pushed her over the edge. He didn't have to worry about her fingering him to the police, because she was too hysterical that night."

"And as time passed, she got worse," Myrna chimed in. "At first, she kept telling me she wasn't crazy, insisting that I had to get her out of Point Bluff before it was too late. She was so agitated during those first visits, violent even, insisting she wasn't crazy, that the Devil had killed those girls. After the first year, she started to calm down. Drug therapy, the doctors told me. She stopped talking, started staring off into space. She was like that for several years, until she started meeting with some Christian group they have inside the sanatorium. That became her entire focus. The doctors thought it was good therapy, a way for her to work through her trauma."

"And you? What did you think?"

"Well, she started talking again, but not like my old Katy. She was different. Still, it was better than catatonic."

"But she never changed her Devil story," Darby said, remembering her conversation outside the piss-yellow trailer.

"No. All that religion only reinforced it." Myrna's gaze

locked with Darby's. "So Katy's not a threat to the killer."

"Right. But I am. I have been ever since that night. I blocked out the murders, but the memory is there somewhere in my mind. He's there. He doesn't want me to remember him. That's why he's calling out to me, forcing me to watch what he does. He hopes he'll drive me insane. He's taunting me, showing me his bloody work, trying to push me over the edge. He's been doing it since that night." She sank down into a kitchen chair.

Her mind scrambled, trying to fit all the pieces together. That still didn't explain the bloody footprint in her apartment, the cuts. . . . Coincidence. Yes, they could all be coincidences. Strange, of course, but still purely chance. She latched onto the explanation the way a drowning man clutches a life preserver.

"Oh my God," she mumbled. "That's it."

"Jesus," Myrna said, her voice incredulous.

Desperation burned through Darby, like fire sweeping over a rain-starved prairie. She had to know the truth. Today. She turned to the woman who sat across the table, her face considerably paler. "Myrna, you have to help me get my memory back. If I can remember that night, what this guy looks like, then I can go to the police and give them a description." And ease my own conscience, she added silently. "Please."

"I . . ." The woman swallowed. "I'm not sure about all this." She walked to the cabinet and retrieved a bottle of sherry.

Darby licked her lips, her nerves coming alive. One drink, her body begged. Just one.

"It fits," Darby said, her throat aching with each word. "It all fits so perfectly."

Myrna didn't even bother with a glass. She took a long gulp. "I know, that's what's so overwhelming. I—I always thought . . . I mean, in the beginning, I was convinced some freak had broken in and done those horrible things, and something had scared him away before he'd gotten to you and Katy. I thought the police were just too clumsy to find the clues. When they pinned it on you, I didn't even consider it, despite what you did to your daddy. You were just a little thing, Darby, so small and quiet as a mouse, as harmless as a fly. I know you didn't do it, and I knew my Katy didn't. Then later on, after I saw Katy, how she wasn't herself what with spouting all that nonsense about the Devil and everything, I thought maybe she really had. . . ." Her voice trailed off. "I mean, I never thought she could be violent, but on one of my visits to the hospital, she begged me to bring her home. I said no, and she attacked me." She closed her eyes, her hands clutching at her throat. "She was so strong, I couldn't believe it. She had her hands around my throat and she just kept squeezing. . . ."

Finally her eyes opened and she stared at Darby. "There's no doubt in my mind. She would have killed me. She could have, if the nurses hadn't pulled her off me."

"She didn't kill Linda and the others," Darby said. She didn't know how she knew. She just felt it. Not Katy. Even the Katy she'd seen outside the trailer, in Proctor's store.

"Part of me knows that. Hell, most of me. But there's this little tiny piece that isn't quite sure."

"That's what this guy wants you to think."

"It's a pretty far-fetched theory," Myrna said after a quiet moment. "Are you sure?"

"It all fits, but then I could be grasping at straws." Darby took a deep breath and summoned her courage. "I don't know. That's why I want to find out what really happened that night. Katy always believed you were real, Myrna. She always said you had psychic abilities."

"You want me to pull out my crystal ball and tell you what I see?" Myrna said, her words dripping with sarcasm. Then a sad look crossed her face. "Katy always liked my crystal ball. She would dust it, sit it up on the mantel and open the curtains so that the sun would reflect off it just so. . . ." Her words trailed off. "You know what she calls me now? A devil-worshiper."

Tears swam in her eyes and Darby reached across the table and placed a comforting hand atop hers.

"Crystal balls don't really work," Darby said with a gentle pat. "Or do they?"

Myrna managed a smile. "Maybe for some, but not me. Mine's just for show. But if you're serious, I do know something that really does work."

"If it's hypnosis, forget it. I've already tried, and failed. Twice."

"Not hypnosis, dear. That's in a psychologist's bag of tricks, not mine. I'm talking about a séance." She took another long drink of sherry. "I have to admit, I've thought about it before, about calling Linda or one of the others to find out what really happened. But I was always afraid I would find out something I'd rather not know."

Darby shook her head. "Katy didn't do it. I knew her. She wasn't capable of murder."

"She wasn't, before that night. But it changed her. She's different now, or maybe she was different then and I just didn't see it." She pounded a clenched fist against the countertop. "I just wish I knew the truth."

"So do I." Darby said, ignoring the smell of sherry that crossed the room, teasing her senses, making her hands shake. "Do you really think this séance thing will work?"

"If the vibes are right." She stared Darby squarely in the face. "No skepticism. I need you to believe, Darby. The energy has to be strong, welcoming, if we want to call one of them here to talk to us."

Doubts pushed and pulled, playing tug-of-war with Darby's desperation. A séance? Ludicrous, yet she'd run out of options. It was the end of the line. She nodded. "When?"

"Tonight. Here. Midnight. The spirits will be most active then."

Chapter Twenty-one

"Do we have to have all these candles?" Darby swept her gaze around the small bedroom, bare except for a single wooden table and two chairs. Black curtains obliterated the room's sole window. Short, stubby candles lined the baseboards, lit the dark corners. Wax drizzled down the sides, spilling onto the hardwood floor in glittering pools. "They're everywhere."

"Mediums often work in full light, but I work better this way. It's a softer light, natural. Easier on the eyes." She lit the large candle that sat at the center of the table, her hands visibly shaking. That was when Darby noticed her red-rimmed eyes, her slightly smeared black mascara.

"Ms. Evans, what's wrong?"

The woman sank down into the chair and buried her face in her hands. "The police came here today."

"What for?"

She looked up, tears swimming in her eyes. "Looking for Katy. They think she might know something about the murders." A sob shook her body. "My God, what if she does? What if the worst is true and she did kill the others that night? That she's a . . ." She couldn't seem to make herself say the word.

Darby's mind traveled back, to the day at Proctor's Grocery when she'd run into Katy. Had Katy been there scoping out the store so she could—

She killed the thought. There were enough maybes swimming in her brain as it was; she didn't need to add more.

"Do you really think Katy could have done something so terrible?" Myrna asked.

Darby grabbed Myrna's hands. "No. And don't you even consider it. Not right now. We have to hold on, be strong, and get through this. I'm not saying it's impossible, but there's no sense in breaking down over assumptions. Katy is innocent until proven guilty." And so am I, she told herself, clinging to the thread of hope that kept her from falling apart and climbing back into a bottle. "We simply have to concentrate on uncovering the truth. Then we can worry."

Myrna wiped at her watery eyes. "You're right. I know you are." She sniffled and reached for the book of matches to light another candle.

The flame flickered and a shiver rippled through Darby.

"Don't worry about the candles," she said, managing a smile. "They're perfectly safe, honey."

But it wasn't safety Darby was concerned with. She felt as if she'd stepped back in time, into Samuel Blue's attic. This place was as small, as barren.

She rubbed her arms, a sudden chill whispering over her skin.

"Get comfortable," Myrna said, settling herself in her chair.

Darby sat in the chair opposite Myrna, who reached across, bloodred nails glittering in the candlelight, and grasped Darby's hands.

An image flashed in her mind, brown eyes changing to blue.

No. She forced the thought aside and concentrated on Myrna. But for all her determination, another chill still rippled over her, coaxing the hair at her nape to attention.

"Loosen up," Myrna said, giving Darby's stiff fingers a squeeze. "We haven't even started yet. First off, close your eyes and try some deep breathing. In," she demonstrated, "and out." When she noticed Darby wasn't following, she added, "Come on now. It'll relax you."

"Forget the breathing. Let's just get on with this, please."

Myrna gave her a pointed stare. "You're full of negative energy, Darby. I need your complete focus and faith. No skepticism. Promise?"

Darby nodded her head. Desperation had won out hours ago as she'd waited for midnight and paced the old abandoned house where she'd grown up, her nerves alive, anxious.

She'd tried to go back to the motel, but the swarm of reporters on her doorstep had sent her searching for some solitude. A private place where she wouldn't have to face anyone, not the press, the concerned citizens of Nostalgia, or Graham Tucker.

If he'd even come back to Nostalgia at all.

She'd waited up last night, trying to stay awake, as much to keep the dreams away as to listen for him. But exhaustion had finally gotten the best of her. She couldn't remember anything once her head hit the pillow. Until the dream, that is.

Dozens of images had plagued her throughout the day. Graham and Dr. Reynolds. Graham naked. Dr. Reynolds naked. The two of them naked together.

What bothered her most of all about those images was that they shouldn't bother her. She'd vowed to keep her distance from him. She shouldn't care one way or the other whether he was naked, or who he was naked with.

She did.

Add to that her anxiety about tonight, and she'd been a nervous wreck all evening. Her thoughts had ping-ponged back and forth between Graham and the séance, and she'd nearly paced a hole in the front porch of her old house.

She didn't want to see him again.

She did.

She didn't want to do this.

She was.

"Okay, Darby. Now I want you to close your eyes and picture Linda in your mind."

Darby did as the woman asked, opening the door to her past. She saw Linda wearing the gorilla mask, heard her voice as she sang along with the radio. . . .

"That's good," Myrna said, as if she were inside Darby's head, seeing her thoughts.

"Linda, we see you," Myrna said, her voice clear and distinct in the dead silence of the room. "We see you in our memory, but we know you're more than a memory. You're still with us, close by. We need you to talk to us now, Linda. Help us uncover the truth."

A ribbon of wind whispered by Darby and her eyes snapped open, killing the vision of Linda.

She stared down, saw her skin turn to gooseflesh, felt the unmistakable draft of air. Her glance shot to the window. The curtains didn't stir. Next, she stared at the air-conditioning vent overhead. A ribbon hung limply from the vent slats. The door was closed. The candle flames burned brightly. No flickers. No indication that anything moved in the room.

Yet there was wind. Circling her, touching her . . .

"We call on you, Linda Tucker. Come back to us, come talk to your friends. We miss you, Linda. We welcome you back with us. Can your hear me? Linda, are you here?"

The wind grew stronger, fiercer, filtering beneath the ends of Darby's hair, whipping several strands about her face. Still the candle flames burned brightly, all except for the flame at the center of the table. It flickered, died, smoked, then sparked again.

"Linda?" Myrna's eyes were closed, but she wore a smile on her face, as if she'd seen the candle flame and knew what it meant. "I knew you would come, Linda. I welcome you. Join with my spirit, Linda. Speak to me. Darby is here and we need to know about that night. We need to see the truth. Show us, Linda. Show me. . . ."

Her voice fell silent. The smile disappeared. The hands went slack.

"Myrna?" Darby grasped the woman's fingers, shook them. "Are you all right? Are you—"

Myrna's fingers started to pulse, tingle, the sensation seeping through Darby's fingertips like pinpoints of electricity.

"What the hell . . . ?" She started to snatch her hands away, but Myrna's tightened about her own.

Panicky thoughts tumbled through Darby's mind. Her head jerked up, her gaze colliding with Myrna's.

The woman was now fully alert, sitting erect in the chair, eyes wide.

"Hi, Darby," she said, yet it wasn't Myrna who spoke the words. Her mouth moved, but it wasn't her voice. It came from Darby's past. It came from Linda.

"It can't be."

"It is. Don't be such an old fuddy-duddy, Dar."

"It really is you."

"Of course it's me, silly."

The words registered, dispelling the shock and drawing a hot bout of tears to her eyes.

"It is you." The tears slipped free, trailing in hot rivers down her cheeks. "Linda, I've missed you so much. Things were so awful after that night. I . . ." She swallowed and forced herself to go on, her voice shaky. "I know I was there, but I can't remember what happened after we started playing with the Ouija board. I remember the candles flickering, the stroke of midnight when they started Blue's execution, but everything after that is a blank. I . . ." She took a deep breath and tried to calm her pounding heart. "I need to know who killed you and the others. Tell me. Please."

"I thought Katy was a nutcase with that Ouija board, but she was right. It was a channel into the other world. A doorway." Myrna's eyes closed and Darby knew Linda herself was remembering. "I never thought Katy could really do it."

"You mean Katy was the one who—"

"She contacted someone on the other side," she continued as if Darby hadn't spoken. As if she were watching the scene in her head. "She—" The voice died as Myrna's eyes snapped open, her gaze riveted on Darby.

But it wasn't Myrna looking back at her. It was Linda. A wide-eyed, frightened Linda.

"*He* did it. He's the one. He used her, just like he's using—" The words caught on her lips, her eyes widening.

The candle flame flared brighter, until Darby had to close her eyes against the sudden glare. When she opened them, Myrna was still staring at her. But there was no trace of Linda in the dark, frightened depths of her eyes.

"My God." It was Myrna's voice this time, and Darby knew Linda was gone.

"Linda!" she begged, clutching Myrna's hands tight, begging for her friend to return. "I need you to talk to me." Her voice rose to a high pitch. "Please! Tell me what happened. Help me remember!"

Nothing. Not a whisper of wind marking her friend's presence. Nothing. Just Myrna staring at her as if she faced the very Devil himself.

"You saw, didn't you?" Darby gripped the woman's hands tighter. "Talk to me, Myrna. What did you see? *Who* did you see?"

Myrna wrenched her hands free and bolted from the room before Darby could finish. The door slammed back against the wall, rocked, as the woman fled down the hallway. Another door slammed. A lock clicked.

"Myrna?" Darby followed her, flying down the nearly pitch-black hallway to pound on the door. "Please talk to me. I need to know what you saw. Please!"

She pounded until her hands ached, begged until her throat burned. Finally she gave up, trudging down the stairs and out into the night. She climbed into her car and sat there for a long moment, her tear-filled gaze fixed on the house.

If only Myrna would come out and talk to her. Maybe she would, if Darby sat there long enough.

Myrna never came out. At one point, Darby thought she saw movement downstairs, the shifting of the blinds, but once she'd blinked the tears away to really focus, whoever had been peeking out at her had gone.

If there had been anyone there in the first place.

Much later, she drove through town, tears blinding her as she tried to sort through what had happened. Myrna knew the truth, yet she refused to share it with Darby. Why? Surely if she'd seen the man, she would tell Darby so they could go to the police and give a description.

Unless she'd seen someone else. Katy? Was she trying to protect Katy with her silence? Were the police really on to something? Was Katy the murderer? Had Myrna seen her own daughter with the knife in her hands?

Or had she seen Darby?

The possibilities beat at her brain as she rounded the corner toward the motel. The cluster of reporters had thinned, only a handful camped out on her doorstep. A few of Reverend Masters's devoted congregation kept their vigil, as well, most of them leaning against the brick, dozing. Signs proclaiming A KILLER WALKS AMONG US! and MURDERERS BURN IN HELL! rested on the pavement at their feet.

She drove past the motel and parked around the corner behind the feed store. Walking back, she circled around to the alley and climbed in through the bathroom window, pausing only to stare at the room next to hers. Graham's bathroom.

The shower was on, and in her mind's eye she saw him—gloriously nude, water dripping down his body, making furrows in the dark fur that covered his chest, his legs. . . .

The image made her body ache for him, and her heart ache because she couldn't have him. There were too many things between them, too many unresolved questions, not to mention a certain doctor with fabulous legs and centerfold breasts.

Inside her room, she tiptoed through the darkness, not chancing a light for fear the crowd outside would be alerted to her presence. After a quick check to make sure the door was still securely locked, she yanked off her clothes and collapsed on the bed. The bottle of bourbon sat on her dresser, catching occasional winks of light from passing cars. For the first time, she didn't have to fight the urge to down the whole damned thing. Her mind was too preoccupied to pay any mind to her body's weakness.

She closed her eyes and clutched the pillow to her chest. "What were you trying to tell me, Linda? What?"

The question followed her into a restless slumber, and as expected, *he* came, calling to her, sucking her into his thoughts until she didn't have a mind or will of her own.

Her mind was his mind. Her will his own.

They were one and the same for those long, bloody moments that followed.

I didn't want to let her watch this time. *Really* watch, but I had no choice. It's over between me and Darby. It was great while it lasted, but things are getting too hot. I have to move on, and sweet Darby has to pay the fiddler.

It's time.

Ah, but parting is such sweet sorrow. Darby has been my only true friend for so long, I don't know how I'll get along without her.

Okay, so I know I'll get along fine. Better than fine. Plan B is already in motion. I've taken care of every detail, as usual. I'm so meticulous. Always have been. Except that one time, of course. I knew that damned kid had seen me driving away from the school with the teacher. I knew. I should have gone back and picked the kid up, had a little ménage à trois.

But I so like to focus myself, to really get into what I'm doing, and two at a time is simply too distracting. I could have made an exception. I should have, but we all make mistakes once in a while.

Or rather, once. My one real mistake, not that it proved as disastrous as I'd originally thought. In the end, I came out ahead, as usual.

I'm still here. Still living and breathing and plotting. If only the bastards knew.

But Darby knows. Yes, now she knows.

As much as I'm going to miss her, I'm looking forward to a change. A nice, healthy, young change. Ah, the future looks bright with blood, and sweet, indeed.

Don't get me wrong. I will miss Darby. I love her. I always have, since the first moment. So sweet and in-nocent and vulnerable.

It's not my fault she's changed. We could have gone on forever, she and I. She messed things up. The bitch.

Not that I'll let her simply walk away from me. No, I've got a parting surprise in store for my sweet Darby. Some-thing for her to remember me by.

•

"Our featured story today: Nostalgia resident Myrna Evans was found murdered in her home. A statewide manhunt begins today for Myrna's daughter, Katy Evans, former patient at Point Bluff Hospital, a mental facility just outside of Dallas. . . ."

"Holy shit," Graham said, staring at the television. The police station hovered in the background, behind Maggie Cross. Dozens of reporters clustered around her.

"Yes, we do have evidence linking Katy Evans to her

mother's killer," Maggie was saying. "Though I'm not at liberty to release that specific information at this time."

Myrna was dead, and Graham had been right. Katy was the copycat killer. Possibly the slumber-party killer, as well.

To hell with possibly. She was as good as guilty.

He picked up the phone and tried Darby's number for the tenth time. Busy signal. She probably had it off the hook.

Pulling on jeans and a T-shirt, he walked next door and pounded on her door. Obviously, the news about Katy had spread. The reporters were gone. Even the reverend's congregation had dispersed.

"Darby?" Nothing. "Open up." More pounding.

It was barely a quarter to nine, but maybe she'd already left. She could be at the diner right now having breakfast, or out driving around, simply relishing her clear conscience now that Katy was wanted for the murders.

Maybe . . .

He leaned down and stared through the window, past the half-inch part in the drapes.

Relief crept through him when he saw her curled up on the bed, sound asleep. She looked so tired and vulnerable, and something inside him twisted. Probably those bastard reporters had kept her up all night, knocking on the door, begging for an interview until they'd found out about Katy.

Hell, he'd barely gotten any sleep himself. He'd been too busy thinking. About Katy. About his sister. About Darby, so close next door. Her phone had been off the hook all night, and she hadn't answered his knocks. But he'd known she was there. He'd heard her moving around when he got out of the shower last night. Yes, she'd been there. So close.

So damned unreachable.

Like now.

A spurt of hungry desire went through him as he drank in the sight of her. She wore nothing but a pair of white lace panties and a white tank top that barely covered her breasts. She breathed and her chest rose, quivered.

He felt an echoing thrum go through his body, to that part of him that never failed to rear its head at the worst possible moment. Like now.

The urge to force open the door and join her there on the bed swamped him. He wanted to lie down beside her, over her, thrust sure and fast and deep. . . . God, he wanted her so much.

Too damned much.

It wasn't healthy.

More importantly, it wasn't smart.

He had very little time to spare. Katy Evans was out there somewhere, on the run, and with each moment that passed, the chances of finding her narrowed considerably. Graham hadn't come this close to nabbing his sister's killer, just to let her slip through his fingers.

Hell no. Not even for Darby.

Not yet.

He would come back later. Then they would set things straight between them. Later.

Chapter Twenty-two

". . . once again, Katy Evans is wanted for questioning in the murder of her mother, Myrna Evans, as well as two recent victims."

The voice pushed through the blackness where Darby nestled, safe and secure, and pulled her back to reality.

She forced her eyes open to the blurry images flashing on the television screen. The electricity hummed, breathing frigid air over her flesh. She lay on top of the covers, clad only in panties and a tank top. A shiver rolled through her and she forced herself up onto her elbows.

"A statewide manhunt has begun for Evans, who should be considered armed and dangerous. Please contact law enforcement officers in your area if you should see this person."

Katy's image flashed across the screen as the reality of what was happening crystallized in Darby's mind.

Katy was wanted for murder. *Murder.*

Darby forced herself to her feet, staggered to the bathroom as she'd done so many times in the past, and sank down over the toilet bowl just as the first cramp hit her.

Her stomach spasmed, the vomit rising up her throat. But not because of what she'd just heard.

Because of what she'd seen.

Somewhere in the distance, she heard the pounding on her motel room door, followed by the sound of Graham's voice. But she could no more answer than she could have stood on the witness stand and proclaimed her innocence. The images rolled through her head, demanding her full attention.

She closed her eyes. Myrna's face flashed in Darby's mind and time sucked her backward, into the woman's dark living room where Death waited for her.

Moonlight spilled past the slats in the blinds, cutting through the darkness a few feet before absolute oblivion took over. The woman stumbled through the house, crying Katy's name over and over. When she reached the bathroom, she flicked on the light, leaned over the sink and turned the faucet on full force. With a shaky hand, she grabbed the cup on the counter, filled it with water and gulped greedily before sagging against the countertop.

The soft creak of floorboards brought her whirling around. The cup dropped from her hands, clattering to the tiled floor.

"You scared me," she said softly. Relief swept her features for a brief moment as she realized who stood behind her. Then her gaze dropped and horror crept across her face. Her head started to shake frantically. "But it can't be you. You weren't the one I saw. It wasn't you!" she cried.

Then the knife lunged out, the blade cutting fast and deep into her throat, turning her expulsion of breath into a choked gurgle.

Blood flowed, sticky and sweet and tempting over his fingers, the sensation almost making up for the fact that he had to kill this one quickly.

Time was of the essence and people were watching. He'd seen the police watching this house, waiting for Katy. He should have turned back, but there was something exciting about killing with the Big Bad Cops right outside the door.

If only they knew that Death was right under their fucking noses. If only they knew . . .

Myrna slumped back over the sink, her blood gushing, bleeding to death. She wasn't dead yet. Not yet. If he hurried, she would feel the knife at her eyes. The pain would bombard her, clamp around her brain, and she wouldn't be able to say a word because he'd cut through her vocal cords already.

And she certainly couldn't fight him. The blood was gushing too fast, too furious. She was already weak.

The tip of the knife pierced the edge of her eyelid. She jerked, her hands clawing weakly at him. Little resistance. Soon he held the treasures in his hand. Warm tissue and sweet, sweet blood.

A giggle bubbled on his lips. Closing his eyes, he raised anxious fingertips to his nose and inhaled, the scent better than any crack rush. His lips split into a smile and he opened his eyes to catch his reflection in the mirror above the sink.

Darby stared down into the toilet bowl, but she didn't see all that her stomach had just heaved up. She saw her own reflection, her hands coated with blood, the sick smile on her face, her eyes a bright, unfamiliar blue with no remorse at what she'd done. What *he'd* done.

She knew then that it wasn't Katy who'd committed the murders. Nor was it some copycat of Samuel Blue. No, it was Blue himself. Somehow, some way, he was inside of her. His spirit filled her, his mind commanded her, his strength became her own.

No! her mind screamed.

Wildly, she stared down at her hands, saw the truth staring back at her in the dried blood that creased her skin.

Myrna's blood.

She struggled to the sink, shoved her hands beneath

the faucet. Frantic, she scrubbed and scrubbed until her skin was raw.

Even then, she felt the warm heat on her fingertips. She could still smell it, and the scent fed the desperation inside her.

She really was a murderer.

". . . dammit, Darby. Open up. You got off easy this morning. I let you sleep, but it's already sunset. I need to see you." Graham's voice filtered through her head, but she didn't really hear him.

The words didn't register above the truth blaring in her head.

Killer, killer, killer . . .

Somehow, she'd thought the knowing would ease her fear. That there would be some comfort in being certain, one way or another. But she'd never in her wildest dreams imagined something like this.

She shook her head, stumbling back into the bedroom, tears streaming down her face. *No.* It couldn't be true—

"Darby, open this door. Right now!" Knuckles pounded wood. The door vibrated. "I need to see you!"

No!

Her knees buckled and she clutched the edge of the dresser.

"Dammit, Darby. I can hear you in there! Open up. We need to talk."

Her hands trembled, the smell of blood pungent in her nostrils, suffocating her. She slammed against the wall, sliding to the floor. The dresser rocked. The half-empty bottle of bourbon crashed to the floor.

Liquor spilled, spread, seeping toward her like a golden wave lapping onto the shore. Broken glass littered the floor near her feet, the pieces catching the last rays of sunlight streaming through the bathroom window.

"Goddammit! What the hell's going on in there?" Wood creaked, cracked, and she knew he'd hit the door, desperate to get inside. To her.

To the real killer.

As the truth raged inside her, the answer to all her problems winked back at her.

She reached for the glass. The edge cut into her palm as she scooped up a piece and moved trembling fingers toward her wrist.

The door crashed open, and Graham appeared. He dropped down beside her, snatched the glass from her hands.

"What the hell are you doing?"

"I . . ." She stared up at him, her body trembling. "It's him."

"What the hell are you talking about?"

"The murders." She stared down at her hands, denial raging through her. Yet it was there. She could see it. These were the hands of a killer. Blue's hands. Her hands.

"They found Katy's prints all over Myrna's house," he said, relief in his voice.

Her head jerked from side to side. "No, no. It isn't her. It's . . ." She closed her eyes and gulped for air. "It's me," she finally said.

"Darby." He shook her at the same time he said her name. "Snap out of this and listen to me. I know you're in shock. After what you've lived with all this time, wondering if you were guilty, trying to remember, I can understand. But listen—you aren't guilty. You didn't kill anybody. Not that night at the slumber party, and not here in Nostalgia."

"But I saw it. I saw *me.*"

"It's the empathy. Katy was the one you were tuning in to—"

"No!" She wrenched away from him and crawled across the floor a few feet. Distance was better. Distance would keep him safe.

From her.

"Oh, God." She hugged herself, fear coursing through her. Fear of herself, of what lived and breathed inside of her.

Who lived and breathed inside her.

"You had another nightmare."

"Not a nightmare." Her eyes snapped open. "I was there, Graham. I killed Myrna, and the vet, and the grocery clerk, and who knows how many others."

"That's bullshit—"

"I have proof." She stared down at her hands. "I—I didn't tell you before because I was afraid. I wasn't really sure, not dead certain, and I was so damned afraid." She glanced up. "When Deana Mills was killed, you were so convinced of my innocence. You believed the FBI. You believed in me. For the first time, someone believed in me." She shut her eyes, seeing the drop of blood staining the lime-green tile in the bathroom. "I did it. I know I did. There was a drop of blood in the bathroom the next morning, and before that, there were other clues—proof that the dreams were real." She told him about the small cuts and scratches in her past, the splinter. "I really did black out at Samuel Blue's house," she went on. "But you saw me walking and talking and driving, and I didn't remember any of it. Don't you see? That's proof that I was out there, killing those girls, then blocking it out."

Her fingers closed around a nearby piece of the broken bottle. The sharp edges bit into her thumb, cutting deep as she gripped the bottle fragment. "The blackout, like everything else, is proof," she said, aiming for her wrist again.

Before the glass cut into her tender flesh, Graham grabbed her. One strong hand ripped the glass from her, while the other snaked around her waist. She struggled, pushing against him, crying and pleading for him to get away, to leave her alone, to let her die.

"I can't," he managed, through deep gulps of air. "Listen to me. Really *listen*. This whole idea of yours is ludicrous. You're not a murderer, Darby. I know killers. I make my living crawling inside their heads, tracking them down, getting them off the streets. And I know in my gut you aren't one."

"Liar," she sobbed. "You saw me for what I am. You saw when everyone else turned a blind eye—"

"Dammit, I saw what I wanted to see," he thundered. "I wanted you to be guilty, because then I could catch you. I could end years of wondering and blaming and hating."

"Hating *me*."

"Hating myself," he corrected. "And blaming myself."

The confession stilled her movements. She stared up at him. "But you didn't do anything."

Where all his words hadn't been enough to pierce the fear and revulsion wrapped around her, the pain in his eyes reached inside and touched the part of her that was still her and her alone.

"I left her there that night," he said, the words filled with anguish. "I left her there so that I could go screw in the backseat of some cheerleader's car." He closed his eyes. "Jeez, I'm a bastard. I was out *fucking*, for Chrissake, while my sister was being slaughtered."

"You couldn't have known."

"But I did." He stared at the images flashing on the television screen, as if seeing that night. Reliving it in those few moments. "When Paul and I drove up, I felt it in my gut. I knew something wasn't right, even before I realized Linda was there. I *knew* it, yet I drove away and left her there."

She touched his face, forced him to meet her gaze. "It wasn't your fault, Graham. She wanted to stay."

"I could have made her leave. I *should* have."

"Maybe so. Maybe you could have saved her, and maybe not." She closed her eyes and shook her head. "I blamed myself so many times for Mama's death. I should have killed my father sooner, just a few more minutes, and she would have survived. I thought about that a lot. Going over it in my mind, choosing the moment I should have acted. But I'd know in my heart, even if my head didn't want to believe it, that I couldn't have changed anything. Maybe Linda would have died anyway, even if you were there."

"And maybe I just fucked up." He turned away from her, refusing to consider her words.

Not that she blamed him. She stared at his profile, the strong slope of his nose, the jut of his chin, and her heart crumbled into a thousand pieces because she'd caused his pain, his guilt, his sister's death.

She broke then. Tears fell down her cheeks; her body trembled. "I'm sorry," she said, sobbing. "I'm so sorry, Graham. For taking Linda from you and causing all this pain."

"It's not your fault."

"It is." Her head bobbed as she nodded fiercely. "I did it. That night was my fault."

"That's bullshit," he exploded. But his anger wasn't geared at her. No, he raged on her behalf, and that made her cry harder, fiercer, because she knew the truth. "Linda and the others had multiple knife wounds—deep, angry wounds. You were weaker than my sister, Darby. You couldn't have done it. I see that now."

"But the cuts and the scratches and the drop of blood—"

"—could have come from any number of sources." He shook his head. "You didn't do it, Darby. Christ, you're lucky to be alive after what happened. Katy could have killed you, too."

He reached for her, but she scooted back.

"Please, Graham. Don't." She tried to push him away. "Th-there's more. You won't want me. Not when you know everything."

"I know all I need to." His lips closed over hers, his mouth hot and moist and so damned overpowering.

But not enough to override her fear.

After a few tearful moments, she summoned her resolve and tore her mouth from his.

She pushed away from him, scooting back, inch by precious inch. When he tried to pull her back, she held up her hand. "No. I *did* commit those murders," she rushed on. "It was me. My hands, my body, but not my spirit." She clamped her eyes shut. "Somehow, some way, Samuel Blue's spirit is inside me, like some sort of split personality. I'm me during the day; then he takes over when I'm asleep, or passed out, or whenever he wants to."

Graham's blue eyes were incredulous. "That's crazy. You didn't—"

"I *did*." Her gaze met his, trust so hot and bright in the deep blue depths. For a heartbeat, she hesitated. She wanted to crawl over to him, into his arms and forget everything. But she couldn't.

For better or for worse.

The *worse* was here. Her attention was riveted on the gap in his denim jacket, where the butt of his gun protruded from his shoulder holster.

"Dammit, it's me! *Him*." She made a frantic grab, her hand sliding beneath the jeans material, closing around the gun handle.

A move he didn't expect.

With determined fingers, she managed to get the holster flap unsnapped, the weapon in her hands, before he even realized what was happening.

His fingers latched around hers as she grappled for the safety switch.

"Darby." His voice was calm, despite the struggle between them. "Don't do this. Let's talk. Please." Despite every soothing word, her determination blazed hotter and brighter.

She was possessed by a murderer.

She *was* a murderer.

Killer, killer, killer . . .

Images flashed in her brain—faces of past victims, the feel of the blood on her hands, the excitement rippling through her. So damned sick, yet *he* enjoyed it all. Relished it. The blood, the death, the pain . . .

The safety clicked off.

"Dammit, Darby!" Graham was frantic now, his fingers digging into hers, around hers, prying and pulling. "Let go! This is dangerous!"

But it was too late.

Her fingertip touched the trigger, pressed, and the gun exploded.

"*Fuck!*" Graham's vicious epithet rang out as the bullet smashed into the ceiling. Plaster rained down on them. Then silence closed in.

Shocked, Darby stared at the gun in her hands. The shot echoed in her head, keeping time with the frenzied beat of her heart.

Fire spread through her, revving her pulse and making her tears flow faster. Dammit, the bullet should have hit *her*. Killed her, and ended Samuel Blue's reign of terror.

Yet as much as she regretted that it hadn't, she also felt relieved. Despite what she'd done—what he'd done, she didn't want to die. She wanted to live, and that realization sent a shudder through her and sent her scrambling away from the gun, from death.

"What the hell were you doing?" The moment of shock had passed. Rage glittered in Graham's eyes and Darby scooted backward, scrambling to her feet.

Graham followed her, closing in on her as she backed away from him.

Her entire body was shaking from how close she'd come to death. He was shaking, too, she suddenly realized, for the very same reason.

Crazy.

As the word pounded through her head, he touched her, his strong hands pulling her hard against him.

"You scared the shit out of me," he murmured, his voice so shaky Darby knew she had to be imagining things.

He shouldn't feel afraid *for* her.

She'd admitted her guilt.

She'd murdered his sister.

He should be afraid *of* her, angry with her, ready to

kill her himself, rather than have her do it for him.

Yet for all his initial hatred where she'd been concerned, he seemed hell-bent on refusing the truth.

Killer, killer, killer . . .

And as his hands, so hot and desperate and alive, roamed over her, Darby refused it, as well. She needed to feel his mouth on hers, breathing life into her. His body plunging into hers, filling her with a vitality to mock the death stalking her, living inside her, fighting for control.

There was but one truth at that moment. She wanted him, and he wanted her, and everything else slid into the darkness that hovered around them.

There was only him, his mouth on hers, his tongue deep in her throat, coaxing and stroking, and she wrapped her arms around him, afraid to let him go lest reality push its way back in.

Fear fed her desire, and she met his tongue thrust for thrust, her hands moving over his broad shoulders, the rock-hard muscles of his arms.

He urged her backward, until the backs of her knees hit the edge of the bed. But he didn't lower her down, climb over her and do what they both wanted. Not yet.

His eyes blazed, but still he managed to pull away from her, as if he'd just shoved on the brakes to his pent-up desire.

But it was only a temporary halt. Just long enough for him to pull his shirt over his head and work at the button on his jeans. He opened the zipper and shoved the denim down his thighs. His erection sprang free, a hard and eager heat that reached for her.

Grasping her panties, he stripped the lace down her long legs in one swift motion. He didn't bother with her tank top, not that the soft cotton was much of a barrier against his chest.

He kissed her then, and when he finally pulled his mouth free, he turned her in his arms, pulling her up hard against him so she could feel his erection press into the cleft between her buttocks. His hands gripped her waist, slid up under her top to cup and massage her breasts, stroke her nipples with his fingertips.

Delicious sensation assaulted her senses, but it wasn't enough. She didn't want to be stroked and petted and seduced. She wanted him inside of her. She needed him. Now. This very second.

"Please—" But the word faded into a groan as he slid his hand down her abdomen, between her legs.

"I know," he said, his voice rough, and Darby knew then that he felt the same impatience. The same frightening desperation.

Then he bent her over, thrust deep into her, and a wave of electricity swept over her nerve endings.

The next few moments were fierce, savage. It was sex in its basic, most primal form. No tender words or delicate touches. Graham wanted to lose himself inside her, and Darby welcomed him, as if he could push out the death that dwelled within and fill her with his vitality.

He rode her hard, plunging deep until she all but exploded from the intense pleasure. Then he pulled away, prolonging the sweet pain and making her all the more anxious. She cried out, begged, and urged him back inside. Her body milked his, coaxing every sweet drop of life.

Another fierce stroke and a wild cry burst from her lips. She came apart in his arms, dissolving into a thousand specks that whirled and scattered.

He joined her two strokes later, hands tight around her waist, anchoring her against him while he spilled every drop of himself deep inside.

He stripped her tank top free; then they collapsed on the bed. Graham turned onto his side, pulling Darby back against him. Their hearts beat a frantic rhythm, their breath coming in frenzied gasps.

Darby held her eyes tightly shut, focused entirely on the clenching and unclenching of her body. It was delicious, the small, lingering spasms that still rocked her. Sensations she'd never felt before.

She fought back the tears, but they came anyway. Hot drops rolled down her face, and her cheeks heated with embarrassment. It was crazy for her to cry over sex. Silly, yet she couldn't seem to help herself.

"What's wrong?" Gentle fingertips touched her face, wiped the tears away, his voice so deep and rough against her ear. "Tell me."

"I . . ." She swallowed. "Maybe this wasn't such a good idea."

"This was the best idea I've had in a hell of a long time." He gripped one of her shoulders and forced her to face him. Dark blue eyes, like vivid blue neon, glittered down at her. "Was it so terrible, being with me? Is that what the tears are about?"

She shook her head. "No. It—it was wonderful. It's not that. . . ." She fell silent, closing herself off and blinking back the tears. She didn't want to be this way with him, with anyone. No emotion. That was better.

Her head knew that, but her heart didn't want to listen. Especially when he kept staring at her with those deep eyes that begged her to talk. Compelled her to feel.

"It's all so new. You and me and what just happened." The words tumbled from her lips before she could stop them.

"New? You're not a virgin. . . ." The words trailed off, and then a thought seemed to strike him. "You mean you've never had an orgasm before?"

"Of course I have. At least, I think so." She turned away to stare at the ceiling. "I don't really remember."

"You're kidding!" He shook his head. "How the hell can you have an orgasm and not remember? Did you block it out? Like the slumber party?"

She shook her head. She should tell him to mind his own damn business. To get away from her. To stay away. But her mouth didn't want to cooperate. "No, I . . . I was drunk at the time."

"How many times?"

"Every time," she admitted after a long moment of silence. More tears welled in her eyes, spilling over, as if the wetness could wash away her sins.

"How many?" he pressed, his hand cradling her cheek, forcing her gaze back to his. "How many?"

"I . . . Too many." Her voice caught on a sob. "I don't have any diseases or anything like that. I've been checked and rechecked during my paranoid sober moments."

"You don't even remember the *first* time?"

"Kind of. It hurt. I remember that, but it was a dull sort of hurt."

"I'm sorry." His lips were on her shoulder. "I'm so sorry." The words rumbled against her skin, sending shivers over her.

"It's no big deal." She wiped at her eyes. "It wasn't anyone special. Nobody I should remember."

"You'll remember this," he promised, leaning back to stare deep into her eyes. "You're going to remember every moment with me, Darby. I swear it. Every moment tonight, and all the nights to come."

No, I'm not a virgin by any means, Darby thought.

But neither was she experienced. She'd never really felt a man's gaze on her, mentally caressing her before his hands took over. Never felt that nervous flutter of anticipation in her stomach.

Sex had always been like the booze. A temporary feel-good. She could project herself into the act, the sensation, and forget everything else, even her partner. She'd never been acutely conscious of who or where or when. Hell, sometimes she was so drunk, she doubted she stayed awake longer than thirty seconds into the act itself.

"What about Dr. Reynolds?" she blurted out, hating herself for asking, as if his answer would make any difference. They'd already done the deed.

"What about her?"

"Don't you think she might prefer a little monogamy?"

323

It was ludicrous to be having this conversation. Here she was debating over the other woman when death hovered so close. It was ridiculous, yet a small part of her wanted to know. Wanted him to be different from all the others in her past. She'd never cared before. Never bothered to ask.

"I don't think she prefers monogamy. I know she does."

She closed her eyes, guilt swamping her, and jealousy. But then why should this be any different from the rest of her life? One big mistake after another. Bad decision after bad decision. "And you don't care?" she asked him.

"Why the hell should I?"

"Because she's—I mean, the two of you are . . ."

"The two of us are what?"

"You know." She stared away from him, watching the television's colorful play of shadows on the dingy wall. "Involved."

"In what way?"

"In *that* way."

He forced her gaze back to his, his hands on either side of her face. "If *that* refers to a professional relationship, then you're right. If it's anything else, then I'm afraid you're mistaken."

"You aren't involved?"

"Not like that."

"But you said she was into monogamy—"

"She is, at least that's what her boyfriend, George, says, and he knows her better than anybody."

"So you've never . . ."

"Once," he admitted. "We did once, a long time ago; then we decided not to again. It complicates matters. Do you want me to confess my entire past to you right here and now? I think it might take the rest of the night, and there are other things I'd rather be doing."

His gaze dropped, roving over her; then his hand followed. He touched the nest of curls between her legs, parted her slick folds, and slid one long finger deep inside her.

She gasped, arching up off the bed against his hand, taking all of him and wanting more.

"So are we done talking?" he asked, bending to close his lips over one ripe nipple.

"Mmmmm," she moaned.

"Is that a yes?" He pulled away, his warm breath brushing her wet nipple, making it swell and harden.

"Yes," she said.

"Good, because I'm going to give you a night to remember, Darby Jayson," he promised. "Tonight there's only you and me."

And there was only the two of them, for the next incredible few hours as Graham brought her to climax after climax. They drifted off to sleep in each other's arms, the rest of the world locked safely outside the warm haven that engulfed them.

But no matter how she ignored the truth, it wouldn't go away.

An evil lived and breathed deep inside her.

An evil that craved blood, lusted after the kill.

An evil that could rise up and take control when she least expected it.

Chapter Twenty-three

Death slipped free of the muscular arm draped about his waist and slid from the bed. The mattress creaked, shifted; then he was standing beside the bed, staring down at the man sprawled naked on the sheets.

Hatred boiled fast and deep, spewing through his veins. His skin prickled, burned, and he rubbed his arms. The ache between his legs intensified as he turned to move about the room, a constant reminder of the filthy thing Darby had done.

Whore! She was a filthy whore who liked spreading her legs, for me and anybody else with a dick! His father's words thundered through his head and nausea rolled through him.

Whore, whore, whore!

The creak of bedsprings filled his ears and he froze. Shit, he didn't need Tucker waking up. Not now! The bastard would stick his nose in where it didn't belong, and he would have to teach him a lesson for that.

For everything he'd done. For sullying Darby. For giving her a reason to fight.

Yes, he would teach him a good lesson.

He relished the notion, but he couldn't afford to linger here in this filthy motel room, the smell of sex all around him, creeping over his skin to make it itch.

A bath. Sweet Jesus, he wanted a bath.

He usually indulged himself. Darby was right: she wasn't a virgin, not by a long shot. But the sex had always been brief, the men faceless, and afterward she'd gone home, straight to a shower to scrub away her sin.

She never lingered with anyone. She didn't like that, any more than she liked to feel dirty, and neither did he.

Now was different. That very fact stirred the heat in his body and made him long to reach for the gun on the nightstand and blow Tucker's brains all over the dingy motel room.

That would be too quick. Too painless, and he needed the pain. Tucker would die slowly, feeling every delicious cut, smelling every drop of blood, seeing Death close in on him.

Slowly. Painfully.

He took a deep breath. But not now.

Dammit, he was late!

Slipping into his clothes, he gathered up the car keys and took one last look at the man on the bed.

"Soon," he promised, Granny's words thundering through his head.

Thou shalt not fornicate! Thou—shalt—not—fornicate!

He flinched with each word, feeling the sting of Granny's palm on his bare ass. She hadn't been able to take the pain when it came down to it herself. No, she'd screamed, cried, begged, and then she'd passed out. *Goddamn her.*

She wasn't much on the endurance end, but she could dish it out like a mother. He had to give her that one.

Tucker would be punished, and Darby; oh, sweet Darby would get hers as well.

He rubbed his arms. He felt so dirty. Tainted. The shower called to him, yet he couldn't answer.

If he didn't leave now to take care of his business, he would miss his chance, and then he'd really be screwed.

He had to smile at that one.

Turning, he eased open the door, and headed for the car.

Cool. Calm. Control. The words chased through his head, slowing his heartbeat, soothing the itching of his skin.

Funny how it was so easy to rein in his emotions, to let his head rule when the bloodlust inside him was so very hungry. But then that was why he was so successful, so elusive, so damned good at what he did.

He whistled "Amazing Grace" as he started the ignition and headed through town for the church.

Turning the corner, he spotted the small white building. Only a single bulb burned outside the rear entrance, where the meeting rooms were located. The front of the church that housed the sanctuary was very well lit, complete with spotlights situated throughout the shrubbery. But that part was locked up tight, the lights all off to keep the kids in the back section where they belonged.

The reverend didn't take too well to having the kids rearrange the hymnals or sneak up to the baptismal to make out. He'd gleaned that bit of information from Darby. Nor did the religious old coot like the kids running hell-for-leather out front, trampling his bushes and flowers until their folks picked them up.

His gaze traveled from the lit doorway to the darkened churchfront. He'd been inside the sanctuary. Once. It was pretty, with red carpet and red pews and red velvet drapes. As if the blood of Jesus himself had washed through the place.

Damn, but he'd liked that sanctuary.

Not Darby. She'd thought of it as a prison. But then she'd had the weight of the world on her shoulders, her sins locked up inside her, festering. She'd been so perfect back then.

His eyes watered, but he blinked back the moisture,

surprised at his own melancholy. But then he loved Darby. They'd been together a long time.

Too long.

But then that was why he was here.

And just in time, he thought, noticing the lights that blazed inside the back part of the building.

He eased the car around to the far edge of the parking lot and simply sat there. One minute ticked by, then two, three; then the doors opened, light spilled out onto the walkway, and the youth prayer meeting let out.

About two dozen girls and boys, ranging in age from ten to fourteen, filed out of the building. Some headed for waiting cars; others started the short trek to their homes.

She was the last one out, as always.

His eyes focused on her and he forgot all about Darby. The girl, pale blond hair gleaming white in the dim light, headed for the sidewalk and started across the dark street, toward home.

There was no one waiting for her. No one who cared. Her mother had died long ago, and her father was too busy leading his crusade against Darby Jayson down at the Elks' lodge.

She was alone. As always.

She stayed several yards behind the other children, walking along by herself, her Bible in one hand and her prayer manual in the other. Her step was light, her movements so free and easy, yet her head hung just so.

So sad and unhappy. What a terrible pity.

He smiled, turning the ignition and steering the car out onto the darkened street.

Slowly, the children ahead of her dropped away. She had the farthest to go. Three blocks. Poor thing.

He eased up beside her, rolling down the opposite window.

"Elsa?" Darby's voice floated out into the night and the little girl stopped, turned.

"Hi." Her voice was timid, like her movements, her

eyes. She glanced at Darby once, then stared at her feet.

"Why don't you let me give you a lift?"

Blond hair brushed her shoulders as she shook her head. "I don't think my daddy would like that much."

"No, I guess he wouldn't. But he's at the lodge, right?"

Her head bobbed up and down. "How did you know?"

"Everyone in town knows he and the reverend are rallying to have me arrested or kicked out of town. Either one, as long as I'm gone. Your daddy isn't too fond of me right now."

"Because of me."

"No. Because of me. Because I stood up to him."

"You shouldn't have."

"Maybe not, but I'm glad I did. Aren't you?"

The little girl looked up after a long moment. "Nobody's ever done that for me before."

He smiled as Darby's smooth voice reassured the little girl. "I'm your friend. Friends stand up for each other."

She glanced up and he saw the sparkle of trust in her eyes; then the emotion sank into murky pools of doubt. "I can't be your friend. Daddy wouldn't like it. If he knew, he'd tan my hide for sure."

"He won't know," Darby's smooth voice reassured the child. "We'll be secret friends. Okay?"

The girl looked undecided for a moment; then a timid smile crept across her face. "Okay."

"And secret friends don't let each other walk home when they can easily ride." He leaned over and opened the car door to motion her inside. "I'll drop you off a few houses down and your daddy will never know."

Indecision crept across her features again.

"It'll be our secret," he prodded in Darby's smooth, silky voice. "Promise."

She glanced down the street toward her house. "It's only a little way. I guess a short ride wouldn't hurt." She smiled and stepped into the car, settling herself into the seat.

"Now buckle up," he said, and watched the girl pull the seat belt and lock it into place.

He started the car toward her house. Soon only one stop sign and three houses separated them from Lyle Proctor's two-story house. Easing off the gas, he braked to a stop at the stop sign, took a deep breath and slipped his hand beneath the edge of Elsa's seat belt. Then he switched on his turn signal.

"Hey," she said, when he turned the car and started down the street perpendicular to hers. "Where are you going?"

"Home," he said, smiling into her puzzled face. Then he jerked her seat belt back and up.

The strap caught her under the chin, tightened. Her child's hands clawed frantically at the choke hold.

The car didn't even swerve as he steered with the palm of one hand and gripped the seat belt with the other.

The windows were open. Wind whipped through, catching the sound of her choked gurgles and flinging them into the pitch-black night.

The sound fed his anticipation, and the sight—her wide frightened eyes, frantic fingers, small body arched forward—fed his excitement.

Unfortunately, the child went slack all too soon and he loosened his grip. The fun was over. For now.

After pulling over to the shoulder of the deserted farm road, he stuffed Elsa Proctor's limp body into the trunk of the car, careful to secure her hands and feet, and, of course, her mouth. Not that she would wake up for a while. No, he would probably have to revive her once they reached their destination.

"So sweet and innocent," he said to himself, stroking her delicate forehead, immensely pleased that things were going so well. But then they always did. He was too good for things to turn out otherwise.

As long as they'd been together, it seemed only logical that Darby should have realized that by now. She couldn't push him out if he didn't want out. He could stop her quicker than she could take a breath. He'd done just that the night she'd managed to sneak up to his old house. She'd been so close to opening the window and climbing inside.

But he hadn't wanted that. Not at all. What if she'd managed to get into the attic and really push him out? With no fresh, weak-spirited body there ready for him to take over, he would have been stuck in that dusty old place for who knew how long.

He hadn't been ready then. But he was now, he thought, drinking in the sight of helpless, frail Elsa Proctor, all trussed up like a turkey ready for slaughter.

He had slaughter on his mind, all right. But not his sweet, innocent Elsa. She would be his cover, his security, his shelter from the world. His home away from home.

Yes, he was ready now.

"We're going home, sweet Elsa," he whispered. "Soon." Just as soon as he tied up his last loose end back at that trashy motel.

His and Darby's final performance as a duo.

"It's been great," he said, pulling back his control just enough so that he was certain Darby heard. "But I'm about to trade you in for a newer, cleaner model. Don't worry, though. I wouldn't leave you high and dry. No, sirree. I'm not a love-'em-and-leave-'em kind of guy." He glanced down, saw the rapid rise and fall of Darby's chest. "Well, in this case, a love 'em and leave 'em kind of *girl*." He laughed, Darby's soft voice whispering through his ears. "No, sweet Darby. I'm going to give you a farewell present. Something you'll never forget, even while you're burning in hell."

Like glittering chips of gold, glass littered the floor, reflecting light from the silent television. He picked up one large piece, tested the sharpness on his palm and watched the blood ooze, warm and sweet, from Darby's creamy skin.

Perfect.

A faint snore drifted from the bed, luring him, pumping the excitement in his blood faster.

Tucker was sound asleep, his deeply tanned body a stark contrast to the lighter sheets. He lay on his back, one arm over his head, the other across the indentation where Darby had stretched out beside him just a half hour ago.

He leaned over and touched the glass to Tucker's throat.

No! The cry forced him around. His gaze darted frantically as he searched for the source of the voice.

The room was dark, empty except for Tucker.

Must be his imagination, he thought. He was too excited. He had to calm down, relax. He took a deep breath and turned back to his work. Leaning forward, he touched the glass to Tucker's throat again, just so—

No! The command thundered through his head, *inside* his head, and stopped his hand cold. He urged the glass forward, just a fraction more, rage swamping him, but his fingers wouldn't budge.

"Do it," he murmured, coaxing them on. "Kill," he whispered. *"Kill."*

No, came Darby's insistent cry as her spirit pushed its way forward, fighting Samuel Blue for control of her body. *No.*

The blackness smothered Darby; then, as if a pillow had been lifted from her face, she saw Graham. And she saw the glass in her hand, so close to his throat. Too close.

Her stomach lurched and she swallowed against the vomit rising in her throat. Revulsion rolled through her and she started to shake.

Killer, killer, killer . . .

Samuel was there, inside her head, her body, taunting her.

Against her will, her fingers tightened around the glass

and she moved forward. Closer to Graham and the delicious throb at the base of his neck.

No! She'd battled Samuel for consciousness, and she'd won. She could win even more, too. She had to.

Killer . . .

"No," she whispered. "I'm not. *I'm* not!" Her hand went limp. The glass fell silently to the bed and she scrambled backward, away from Graham, from the sweet heat of his blood calling to her.

To *him*.

A call she wouldn't answer. Just as she'd managed to ignore her body's desperate craving for a drink during the past forty-eight hours, she could ignore Samuel's craving for death.

This time, she promised herself, forcing aside the other images that battered at her. The faceless women from past dreams, the DA's daughter in San Francisco, Rudy and Jan, the grocery clerk, the vet . . . *No*. It was too late for any of them, but it wasn't too late for some unsuspecting someone who might be Blue's next victim, or for Graham.

Despite the life-and-death struggle going on next to him, Graham slept soundly, his bare chest covered with black hair that swirled down his abdomen, into a funnel that dipped below the edge of the sheet that barely covered his nakedness.

Her body tingled. Heat pulsed through her and sent a delicious warmth to her nipples—

Whore! The word roared in her head, and a cramp hit her. She doubled over, as if someone had kicked her in the gut and jolted the air from her body. Crumbling onto her side, she held her stomach and shut her eyes against the sting of tears.

She reached out. If she could just wake Graham up, tell him to leave, he would be safe. If she could just . . .

The thought disintegrated as her hand found the glass again, razor-sharp and ready.

Pick it up.

She shook her head, all the while her brain screaming fierce commands to her hand. Gasping for air, she managed to pull her hand away, to push herself up and away from Graham.

The floor came up to meet her and she slumped there for several breathless moments, her hands trembling, Samuel raging deep inside her, making her heart race.

She fixed her eyes on the steady rise and fall of Graham's chest, refusing to tune in to Samuel's commands. She saw only Graham, felt only him, and slowly Samuel quieted.

She'd won, she realized several calm breaths later. No cramps, no trembling in her hands. Nothing. Samuel had lost his grip and Darby was in control.

But for how long?

The question forced her to her feet. She looked around for her clothes, realizing a heartbeat later that she was already dressed.

She cast one last look at Graham, her gaze drinking in his features, traveling lower to memorize every muscle, every dip and curve. Memories of their time together flooded her, and her body ached. If only she could climb back into bed with him, pull him close, lose herself in his kiss.

She could do none of those things. And she wouldn't do them. She wouldn't ignore the truth, hide from her fear and look for an escape. She didn't have to.

The old Darby would have jumped into bed, and into a bottle, in no particular order, eager to forget. To run away. But she'd stopped running from her past, herself.

She'd come home, remembered the ugliness of watching her mother killed by her father, faced her own feelings when she'd plunged the knife into him and ended his miserable existence. She'd even accepted the fact that she might well be a cold-blooded killer.

Killer. The word sounded in her head, only it wasn't her own voice she heard. It was his.

Just as her body was his.

Not for long.

She touched her lips to Graham's cheek, let them linger for a long moment. Then she pulled away, retrieved his gun from the shoulder holster that lay draped over the nightstand and slipped out of the motel.

Her hand gripped the car door handle and she hesitated.

Don't, a voice whispered, but she refused to listen. All her life she'd been manipulated. First by her father, then by the alcohol and Samuel Blue. No more.

Hauling open the door, she climbed into the car and keyed the ignition. The car lurched into reverse, shot out of the parking lot, then swerved onto the main strip through town, headed for Samuel Blue's house.

She still had one part of her past that remained locked away. Though deep in her heart she already knew the dreadful truth—that she'd killed Linda and the others, with Blue guiding her hands—she still needed to see the scene in her mind. And she would. Tonight. Then she would end Samuel Blue's miserable existence and send him straight to hell where he belonged.

And herself along with him.

Tires skidded and Graham opened his eyes to find the bed beside him empty, and Darby gone.

He shot from under the covers and hauled back the drapes. The car was nothing more than a black flash as it bolted onto the road and disappeared.

"Shit," he muttered, pulling on his jeans, all the while trying to shake his brain awake.

One minute they'd been having incredible sex, the next he'd been sleeping peacefully, and the next?

He dressed quickly, then reached for his gun. The holster was empty. Dammit, she'd taken his gun.

Fear coiled inside him, swirling with his anger, and panic bolted through him. She was going to kill herself.

The realization sent him scrambling for his keys. He left the motel room behind, and headed for his own room. After a quick rummage in the desk drawer he pulled out the .38 he kept for emergencies. Shoving the gun into the waistband of his jeans, he headed for the door.

The shrill ring of the phone stopped him.

He snatched up the receiver. "What?" he growled.

"Hello to you, too," answered his captain's voice.

"I'm in a hurry."

"Cool your heels. This won't take long. I hear there's a suspect?"

"Yeah, Katy Evans. Ex-mental patient and textbook psychotic. Look, I'll call you back."

"Hold it. They catch her yet?"

"Not yet, but there's an APB out from here to Mexico. We'll catch her. Is that why you called? To ask about Evans?"

"Partly. I just got the printout from the Bureau matching similar MOs to the three victims in Nostalgia."

"Fax it to the station."

"I will, I will. But I thought you'd be interested to learn that the same MO, or something very similar, has been reported in nearly two dozen cases across the U.S, all reported at different times, so it could very well be the same killer. That Evans sure knows her way around, and she's a pro. Been doing it a long time. The first murders started nearly ten years ago in Chicago, then there's Denver, Miami, Washington, New Jersey, and the latest reports came in from San Francisco—some third-rate guitar player and his girlfriend, and the local DA's daughter."

The words registered in Graham's head, but it wasn't his captain's voice ticking off the names of the cities. It was his own from that time in the pickup when he'd recounted Darby's actions for the past ten years.

"Impressive, huh?" Her reply echoed in his head, drowning out everything else for a long moment.

". . . okay? Graham?" The captain's voice finally pushed through.

"Thanks for the info," Graham replied, his throat dry.

"Anytime. I'll fax the hard copy to the station and you can pick it up later."

"Fine."

"When can I—"

The receiver fell from Graham's suddenly limp fingers.

The Katy theory had just been shot to hell and back. She'd been institutionalized at Point Bluff for nine of the past ten years, only recently released. Katy wasn't the pro, but he knew who was.

It couldn't be.

Even as denial raged fast and furious in his head, the truth laughed at him, mocking his instincts, taunting him. He'd traded his better judgment for a piece of ass. Again.

He bolted to the door. Great sex or not, it didn't matter. If Darby was guilty—no, *because* Darby was guilty—he was bound and determined to bring her in. To see justice served.

To see the killing end once and for all.

Chapter Twenty-four

Darby pulled onto the shoulder of the road and parked right behind one of the television station's trailers. The lights were off, the place empty, the crew tucked safely away back at the motel, resting up for the big broadcast.

She glanced at her watch. One A.M. It was Halloween. Yes, tonight was the night of the broadcast.

A shiver crawled down her spine and her skin turned to gooseflesh. She rubbed her bare arms and fought back the sensation. No fear, not now. Not when she was so close.

Climbing from the car, she tucked Graham's gun into her back pocket, shoved her keys into her front pocket. Gravel crunched beneath her feet as she made her way to the gate.

"Hold it right there, miss." The security guard walked up to her. "No one's allowed—" He smiled. "It's you."

"Me?"

"From the other night."

The blackout. He had to be talking about the blackout.

"I felt really bad about having to run you off," he said. "Regulations. You understand."

She nodded. "Of course."

"But I'm afraid I still can't let you have a look around. Tune in to channel fourteen tonight, though, and you can look your fill with the thousands of others watching the broadcast."

"Can't I take just a little peek now?" she asked, widening her eyes and giving him her most imploring look. "Just the yard," she added. If she could just get past the barricade, maybe she could persuade him to let her into the house. Or maybe she could slip away from him and climb through a window—

Her vision blurred and the earth seemed to tilt.

My turn, whore. The words pounded through her senses a moment before the darkness closed in, like a grave digger heaping dirt over her. But she wasn't dead yet! She was still alive, still conscious.

You can't do this! I fought you back at the motel and won! I won. Not you!

Only because I let you, sweet Darby. You're nothing without me. Weak, fragile. Nothing!

I fought you. I came here to get rid of you.

I wanted to come here, Darby. So I could get rid of you, my sweet. Not the other way around.

Dread spiraled through her and Darby fought, focusing her energy, pushing him back to the dark pit inside her where he dwelled.

I'm stronger now!

You're nothing, he fired back. *Nothing.*

". . . okay," the guard was saying. "I don't see what five minutes in the yard would hurt. Maybe you can do a little of that stargazing you were talking about the other night."

"I don't think I feel like stargazing tonight." It was her voice, her mouth forming the words, yet they didn't coincide with the frantic thoughts tumbling through her head.

"No?" the guard asked.

"No," she replied smoothly, just as Samuel wanted. "I'm in the mood for something a little more exciting. A real bang to kick off the day. Oops, I seem to have dropped my keys. Could you be a dear and pick them up for me?"

"No problem."

She felt her arm raised, heard the sound of bones cracking as the gun crashed into the back of the security guard's head.

No! Darby's spirit cried, as she fell faster, deeper into the black pit Samuel Blue had called home for the past ten years, her own voice following her down.

"As easy as cracking open an egg. How's that for excitement, huh, Darby?" Laughter followed the chilling question. "But I've got much more planned. You screwed me up back at the motel, but the buck stops here, whore. It's the end of the line for you, and the beginning for me. We're home now. Home . . ."

I can't tell you how it feels to be home again.

This place . . . Well, no words can really describe what these old walls mean to me. I could always close my eyes and see this place—the bare bulb hanging in the kitchen, rocking back and forth on the link chain that had once held a chandelier. Back and forth that light would rock while I lay there on that kitchen table being sorry for every one of my sins, and my Daddy's, too.

Repent, sinner, Granny used to say after she'd fastened my arms and legs to the table. Then she'd slam the switch into me, digging into my skin until I screamed how sorry I was.

I was a tough little bastard. Always determined not to scream. At first I'd shut my eyes real tight and try to pretend I was the one with the switch and Granny was strapped to the table. I was carrying out the Lord's work and she was the sinner.

But after the first few times, the pain grew bearable. I

started to like it, to crave it, in fact. I'd stomp through the house in my muddy two-sizes-too-large tennis shoes the old ladies at the church had taken up for charity. I'd pour vinegar into Granny's homemade biscuit batter. Hell, I even pulled the panties down on one of Granny's old dolls she kept in the attic. I tell you, she didn't like that one. I must have been strapped to the table a good four hours for that one, that switch coming down over and over. Then she'd pour salt water on me and the pain was so fierce it set my teeth on edge.

But I liked it, and I never closed my eyes or said I was sorry. No, I stared straight at Granny. She tried to pretend it was for my own good, but I could see she did it more for herself than anybody else. I saw the look in her eyes as she stared down at me, watching me squirm. The hatred. The power.

She couldn't hide anything from me, 'cause I felt the same things. The only difference was, she was the one trussing me up like a turkey and tearing into me.

Oh, but the times they were a changin', or so the song said. It wasn't too long before Granny was flat on her back, staring up at me, feeling the bite of the switch, then the cut of my knife. But before I carved out her baby blues, I made sure she saw my hatred. My power.

Daddy never got the chance to see how strong I was. I'd killed him too quick, but not Granny.

I was thorough, no sparing the rod and spoiling the Granny. She felt everything, even the salt water, before I was finished.

She was my first true masterpiece.

Ah, memories. Maybe that's why I have such a fondness for this place. So many damned wonderful memories. Daddy on the front porch, Granny in the kitchen and the attic, those three young things up in the attic, as well. And very soon, Darby will have her own place on my fine list of credentials. Another masterpiece for the artist who keeps going and going. . . .

Damn, but I like that commercial. It's so fitting, and

the bunny is kind of cute, too. At least, I'm sure sweet Elsa Proctor thinks so. She's so young, so fragile. She definitely seems like the bunny-loving type.

I'm getting goose bumps just thinking about sinking into all that precious innocence. So refreshing for someone in my line of work. I used to get the same rush with Darby at first, but she'd already been a little soiled when I met her. Not Elsa. She'll be mine to mold and shape. I'll be the first to dirty her fragile little hands, to revive that dark part of her that's in us all.

That was about the only shrink nonsense that I agreed with. They said we all have a dark part of us, but most resist the urge to act on those nastier impulses. Your classic psychopath doesn't resist. He embraces the dark side, cultivates it.

That's what I intend to do with Elsa, and Darby will be our first project. The first kill. I'll make a quick exit from Darby into Elsa. Then the fun begins.

Just as soon as I get my little protégé into the attic and untie her, which shouldn't be long.

"Wake up, wake up, you little sleepyhead."

The child's voice pushed through the blackness for Darby, coaxing her forward, into reality and the dusty attic of Samuel Blue's house.

Darby blinked, her gaze drinking in her surroundings for a long, puzzled moment. Where the hell was—

The thought slammed to a halt when she saw the dusty floor, the lone window. *The attic . . .*

It's almost time! Katy's voice chanted in her head. *Everybody get ready; touch the Ouija.*

"You're awake."

The voice brought Darby's head jerking back. She saw Elsa Proctor leaning over her. The girl still wore her school clothes, a plaid skirt and white blouse. Her blond hair framed her angel's face.

But there was something wrong. Something different. Her gaze clashed with Elsa's bright blue eyes and

Darby knew. Because Elsa Proctor didn't have blue eyes. She had green eyes. Bright, grass green eyes.

"No," Darby said, the word no more than a rush of breath.

"Oh, yes," Elsa said in her child's voice, but Darby knew she wasn't the force behind the words. It was him. His eyes. Death himself stared down at her. "Welcome home, Darby."

Elsa lifted her arm. The knife in her hands caught rays of moonlight filtering in through the sole window. The blade glittered silver fire, the edge razor-sharp.

"It's your turn to feel the knife, Darby. Your turn to relish the pain."

"No," she begged. "Not yet." She'd come so far to uncover the truth. She couldn't die now without ever really knowing what happened that night. She needed to hear the words, see the images, unlock the memories. "Tell me what happened that night. I need to know. Please! Were you inside me? Did you use me to kill Linda and the others?"

"He used *me*," came a familiar voice from the doorway.

Darby pulled her attention from the knife, to stare past Elsa.

"Katy?" Darby's frantic gaze raked over the woman who stood in the doorway. Her short hair was wet, hanging in limp strands around her face. Water beaded her face, drenched her clothes and made the ugly blouse and skirt stick to her skinny body.

"It was me," Katy said, stepping inside the room. Her drenched clothes dripped onto the hardwood floor, funneling wet rivers over the dusty wood. "He was inside me."

Darby's gaze locked with Katy's, the woman's eyes a clear, distinct brown. Darby knew then that it was the real Katy who spoke to her, the strong-willed, popular girl she'd grown up with. No matter what she looked like on the outside, at least for a moment the madness had eased.

"They started the execution and I started calling my grandpa. Only he wasn't the one who answered. It was Samuel Blue himself. I don't know how or why. . . ."

"This was my home, where it all began," Elsa said, but it wasn't her child's voice any longer. It was a man's voice. Blue's voice, the words tinged with a soft Southern drawl. "They wanted to send me to hell, those bastards, but I wasn't about to let them. I didn't want to die. They stuck it to me, so I came home." Elsa smiled, the sight chilling Darby to the bone. Slowly, she inched backward, knowing in her heart there was no place to run. And knowing just as well that she couldn't simply lie there and wait for death.

"And what did I find when I came home?" Elsa went on, the masculine voice prickling the hair at Darby's nape. "Why, I found a damned party, and I hadn't even been invited." He made a *tsk-tsk* sound. "That's not nice, throwing a party in my own place and not even inviting me. That wasn't nice, girls. Not a'tall."

"I knew something was wrong," Katy said. "The minute the lights flickered out, I felt a presence." Her voice was clear, distinct, matching the determination in her eyes. This was Katy, Darby realized, and this was the truth. "It came through the pointer, into my fingers; then something hit me. I felt this rage. I picked up the knife and I started stabbing. Linda, then Jane, then Trish. You were hiding in the corner, crying. I turned to you, walked toward you with the knife. . . ." Her voice faded, her eyes widening slightly, as if seeing Darby for the first time. "But I couldn't do it. I had the knife in my hands, I raised my arms, but then you looked straight at me with your scared eyes and it froze me." She shook her head. "It was like waking up from a bad dream, even though I hadn't really been asleep. During the killing, I knew what I was doing, but I was so mad, so enraged that I couldn't stop myself."

"*I* was mad. Those pissant cops slid that needle into me and cheated me out of my due," Samuel roared.

"Those stupid fuckers! But they couldn't kill me. They didn't have the power. *I'm* the powerful one. *I* call the shots." Elsa's delicate fingers clenched and unclenched around the knife. "I always have. *Me.*" Elsa shook her head. "They made me so mad I didn't even enjoy those three that night. I just hacked away, slicing and slicing, until I saw you. You stopped us."

"I realized what I had done then," Katy said, a tremor making her body shake as she continued to walk, circling them, her wet shoes making footprints in the dust. "I realized that something was inside me and I started to fight. I pushed the evil out."

"She didn't push anything out. I *wanted* to leave her. She put up too much of a ruckus for me to really enjoy myself, the damned headstrong bitch. But you, Darby." Elsa took a deep breath, eyes gleaming a brighter blue. "You were perfect for me. So innocent and weak and scared. Exactly the house that my spirit needed. You see, I needed a body to walk out of here; otherwise I would have stayed in this dusty old attic forever. Just a damned ghost, like half the misguided folks in town already think. I needed a vulnerable spirit to complement mine, and I saw it in you, Darby. You were the one. You were easy pickings for someone as strong as me."

"I knew the moment he left me, like the devil had been exorcised," Katy said. "But the blood was still on my hands." She held her fingers out and stared down, as if seeing the crimson heat. "I mean, I knew it wasn't me, and I tried to tell the police."

"The Devil," Darby said. "You told them the Devil did it." Regret coiled through her. "And you were right."

"But no one believed me. I even took a lie-detector test and it confirmed it, and they still didn't believe." A helplessness filled her eyes, and Darby knew then that what Katy had seen and done that night as Blue's puppet hadn't been the final shove that sent her tumbling into madness. No, it had terrified her, sent her into shock and left her on the edge of insanity, but the years that followed in the sanatorium, the pleading for someone, anyone, to believe her story, had sent her spiraling over that edge. Katy hadn't been crazy then, but she was now. Darby knew that the moment Katy's clear, bright eyes faded back into a murky, dull brown.

"So much blood," Katy murmured, her voice distant, far away now as she walked. Around and around. "It was everywhere. On my clothes, my face. But my hands were the worst. I tried to wash them. Over and over, I tried. . . ."

Darby stared up at Elsa, who held the large butcher knife in her small hands. "When you came into me, why didn't you kill Katy then? She knew the truth. She was a witness."

"A witness everybody thought was crazy. Don't you know I got a kick out of knowing the truth was out there, right under their damned stupid noses, and they couldn't see it?" Elsa smiled. "The killing itself wasn't any fun, but that almost made up for it. The stupid sons of bitches. So ignorant." He started to laugh, a cold sound that sent shivers dancing up and down Darby's spine. "Wouldn't know the truth if it jumped up and bit them on the ass."

"There was so much blood," Katy went on, her eyes cloudy and unfocused. Darby knew then that the small, sane part of Katy had disappeared altogether. It was as if that tiny part had held on, waiting for a chance to confess the truth to someone who would believe. And now that it was done, that part was gone forever, her sanity completely crumbled. "I can see it." Her wild eyes darted frantically around. "Can't you? Can't you see it, too? I asked God to wash it away, but it's still there. I can see it. I used to sit in my room at Point Bluff and stare at my hands, watching the red flood over my skin, trickle onto the floor. Nobody could ever see it, but it was there." Katy nodded, her head bobbing up and down. "It's always there."

Elsa shook her head, her blond hair brushing her small shoulders, her whole image a mockery to the deep voice, the chilling words. "Looks like you're going to have company for tonight's performance, Darby." He closed in on her. "Trying to run? Don't you know you can't run from me, Darby? You never could."

A small clicking sound drew their attention.

Katy had stopped a few feet away, in front of the doorway, inside the puddle her shoes had made. She held a lighter, the single flame flickering.

All too late Darby smelled it. Gasoline. Katy wasn't wet from the weather. There wasn't a cloud in the night sky. She was dripping gasoline, not water.

"No!" Samuel said, the deep command ringing out as he lunged for Katy.

But he wasn't fast enough. Katy brought the flame to her gasoline-drenched clothing. A blaze erupted, sweeping over her from head to toe. The dry wood of the attic quickly flared, until the room lit up with flames. With a horrible shriek, Katy stumbled forward, collapsing into a burning heap.

Darby scrambled to her feet just as Elsa screamed, the flames having caught the sleeve of her blouse where her hand held the knife. The blade clattered to the floor and her pain-filled shriek split the crackling silence.

It was Elsa's voice, not Samuel's.

In stunned horror, Darby watched as Blue's image stepped from the little girl, unfolding to his full height. He looked as he had in all the newspapers—the good-looking, clean-cut boy next door with his blond hair and vivid blue eyes. But the image was a pale, shimmering transparency, the eyes like glittering pinpoints of blue neon. A shadow of the real Blue. His spirit, which had refused to cross over into death.

He whipped around, searching for an escape, but the fire had spread around him, caging him. Samuel Blue had finally met a force that matched his own, even overpowered it.

"Darby?" Elsa's frightened voice drew her closer. She hugged the child to her, the dreaded reality weighing down on her. Samuel was going to face death, but so were Darby and Elsa. They were inside the inferno, as well. Trapped.

Helplessness overwhelmed her as she hugged the child to her, as if she could protect her from Blue's spirit should he try for another possession. He didn't. With the flames surrounding them, Darby and Elsa were as doomed as he was.

Frantically, he lunged forward, trying to break free, only to bounce back to the center. With every lunge, a keening sound, the wail of Samuel's lost soul, echoed through the room.

"Darby." Elsa gasped, clawing frantically at the arm that held her, her eyes wide, puzzled. "What happened? Where are we?" As the girl realized their predicament, tears streamed down her face. "We're going to die!"

"No, no," Darby said, knowing she lied. There was no escape. For Samuel, or any of them.

"Darby!"

At the sound of her name, Darby's head jerked up. She stared through a shimmering wall of orange at Graham, who stood beyond the flames in the doorway.

"You have to run through. Blue can't; without a body he's trapped. But you can, sweetheart. You can!" He motioned her toward him.

The wall of fire flared hotter, brighter, and a lifetime of fear and cowardice spiraled through her. She shook her head. "I can't!" She hugged Elsa, refusing to look at him, to watch him as the fire closed in on her. She was dying.

"Look at me, dammit!" Graham shouted. "Please, sweetheart. *Look at me!*" The desperation in his voice drew her gaze when the actual words failed. "You can do this," he said. "You have to do it. You have to save Elsa and yourself." When she shook her head, he added, "Please! Just grab Elsa and run through. It's the only chance you've got."

"But—"

"You can't tell me you're going to let that little girl burn to death without even trying."

Darby glanced down and saw Elsa, the girl's head buried in Darby's side, her hands clinging around Darby's waist. Elsa wouldn't try it by herself. Darby knew that. She was her only hope. Their only hope.

"I—I don't know. . . ."

"Just do it!"

She wasn't sure what prompted her more—the worry and fear blazing in Graham's eyes, the knowledge that she couldn't let Elsa Proctor burn to death, or her own desperation. Maybe all three.

"Let go of my leg, honey. We have to get out of here." When Elsa refused to look up, Darby pried the girl's small fingers loose and gave her a quick shake. "Listen, sweetie. We're getting out of here, but you have to help me. Okay?"

The girl nodded, tears rushing down her pale cheeks.

"Good. Now I want you to close your eyes and hold my hand. And don't let go of me no matter what. Okay?" The little girl sniffled, nodded.

Darby cast one last look over her shoulder, at Samuel Blue's spirit still lunging at the flames, at Katy's burned body crackling on the floor; then she turned back to Graham and the shimmering wall. She gripped Elsa's hand, closed her eyes and bolted through the fire.

A blazing moment later, she was in Graham's arms and he was slapping at the flames that had caught on their clothes.

Before she could blink, he thrust her away and did the same to Elsa. Then he hefted the twelve-year-old into his arms, gripped Darby's hand and they flew down the stairs and out into the yard. To safety.

Darby pulled Elsa into her arms and collapsed on the ground, Graham beside her. Sirens wailed in the distance, growing louder, louder.

Minutes later, police and firemen swarmed the area under the direction of Chief Maggie Cross, who looked ready to drop from exhaustion. The yard turned into a flurry of activity as hoses were unloaded and hooked up. Police secured the grounds, and Darby simply sat there, staring, unable to move, to pull her mind away from the attic, and the truth.

It had been Katy. Samuel Blue had been inside of her, slicing away at Linda and the others. Katy.

"Let go of her, miss."

The voice pushed its way past the shock holding Darby's brain frozen. She focused on the paramedic leaning over her, trying to pull Elsa Proctor from her arms.

"She's only got minor burns that I can see, but they need to be treated," he told her.

Darby nodded, willing her arms to move. She let go of Elsa, then watched as the paramedics led the girl over to a waiting ambulance.

"They need to have a look at you, too," Graham said, helping her up. His gaze raked over her, searching for any signs of injury.

"I'm fine," she assured him. Her hands trembled despite her words. "Really."

"Clear the path. We've got a critical one!" Darby turned to see a group of firemen carry Katy's limp body from the burning building. In seconds, the paramedics had taken over, hooking up machines, inserting tubes and IVs.

"Where are they taking her?"

"To the hospital," Maggie Cross said as she came up to them. "If she makes it, then eventually she'll come back here and stand trial for the murders of the grocery clerk, the vet, and her mother."

"And my sister," Graham added. "I heard the confession upstairs." He glanced toward the flaming house. "She told all about the slumber party before she set the place on fire."

Maggie looked as though she'd been punched in the stomach. "Well, I'll be damned." She shook her head. "This has turned into one hell of a night."

Darby turned to Graham and stared deep into his eyes, and for the first time, she saw relief.

"You didn't do it," he said. "You really didn't do it."

"One hell of a night," Maggie muttered again, glancing back at the flaming house before stomping away toward her patrol car.

Arm in arm, Graham and Darby turned to stare at the flaming structure. The firemen had pulled back at Maggie's order, despite the head honcho from the TV station, who was stalking Maggie all over the yard, and threatening a lawsuit.

The chief wasn't the least bit intimidated. Of course, the crowd that had gathered at the fence—led by Reverend Masters, who sported a hastily painted sign that read BURN, DEVIL'S HOUSE, BURN!—might have made her a bit bolder and more determined to see Blue's house finished once and for all. Bad press be damned.

"So you heard," Darby said, tightening her fingers around Graham's as they followed a police officer to a nearby squad car. "I'm really not a killer." She closed her eyes for a long moment. "You know, it's funny. Once Katy started talking, everything rushed back to me. But it wasn't her words that forced me to remember. Once Blue was gone, it was like the block that kept me from remembering was gone. I can see everything so clearly now." She shook her head.

"What's wrong?"

"That night is clear in my mind, only now I've got other blanks."

"Blanks?"

"Like the dreams. I know I was having bad dreams. I remember telling you about them at the bar that night, but for the life of me, I can't remember what they were."

Graham gripped her arms and turned her to face him. "You don't remember the dreams?"

"No." She stared up at him. "Should I? Is there something important about them?"

He hesitated, but only a moment, before shaking his

head, as if he'd come to some monumental decision.

"The past is past," Graham finally said. "The dreams aren't worth remembering. Blue's the killer. He has been all along." His voice held such conviction that Darby couldn't hold back the tears that flooded her eyes. "Not you," he added. "Never you." Then he kissed her long and hard and deep.

"Blue is burning now," he said after the kiss had ended. "Like he was always meant to."

Amen, Darby thought, the slumber party vivid in her mind. She could see the knife, the blood, Katy's wild blue eyes—*Samuel's* eyes. And she could hear the screams.

"Please, no!" Linda wailed, inching backward, her hands trying to fend off the knife. But it kept driving down, over and over, turning the hardwood floor to a sea of blood. "Nooooo!"

"You all right?" Graham's voice was low, tender, his fingers stroking her jaw.

"Fine," she said, resisting the urge to clamp her hands over her ears to shut out the voice of her friend.

"It's over," Graham said. "Come on." She let him turn her away from the house, the darkness, toward the pink-tinged horizon. Night had ended. The sun was rising. A new day. A new beginning.

And for the first time in a long while, Darby Jayson felt like smiling. The darkness had left her, taking with it all the ugliness of the past ten years. Her conscience was clear, her soul was free, and Samuel Blue was getting his in hell.

"What have we got?" Dr. Richards rushed into ER room ten and headed for the sink to wash his hands.

"Female," one of the nurses said, clipboard in hand. "Late twenties. Third-degree burns over ninety percent of the body, a collapsed lung, kidney failure . . ." The nurse went on, ticking off the problems as the ER doctor pulled on his gloves and turned toward the gurney, where the trauma team of nurses and technicians worked with the critical woman.

"I haven't got a pulse," somebody called out.

"She's flatlined," came another frantic report.

"Get the paddles," the doctor ordered.

Fifteen minutes later, there was still no pulse, no heartbeat. Nothing. Katy Evans was dead.

"Okay, we're calling it quits on this one," Dr. Richards finally said. "June." He glanced at the nurse who had the clipboard. "Record it. The time is four-fifteen A.M., October thirty-first. One hell of a Halloween," he muttered, stripping off his gloves and turning away.

The frenzy was over. Members of the ER team filed out, headed for room twelve, where a hit-and-run victim was barely hanging on. The nurse with the clipboard stayed behind, unhooking machines, turning them off. Her usual routine when they lost one.

Grabbing the edge of the sheet, she jerked it up over the poor girl's burned body and turned away, her shoes squeaking on the linoleum floor. Halfway to the door, she heard a sound. A gasp.

She froze. Only the steady flow of air from the air-conditioning unit and the distant commotion from the neighboring ER rooms filled her ears. She shook her head, made the last few steps and popped the chart into the plastic holder on the wall for the guys downstairs who would be coming soon.

"You need a vacation, June," she said, shaking her head and rubbing at her tired eyes. "A long, long vacation. You're too young to be imagining things."

She pulled the door open, and the sound came again.

The door swished shut and she whirled.

Forget the vacation. The sound was real, as real as the movement under the sheet that covered the woman's charred body.

The nurse rushed over and yanked the sheet down. The air lodged in her throat as she found herself staring into frighteningly clear blue eyes.

She stabbed the nurses' call button. "Number ten is breathing," she cried. "Get Dr. Richards back in here. Now!"

In minutes, the room had filled with ER personnel.

Dr. Richards leaned over Katy, her breathing little more than wheezing gasps that sailed past her burned lips. He checked her pulse and her vitals.

"It's a miracle," he finally said. "She's very much alive." He stared down into those unflinching blue eyes. "You're a very lucky woman. Looks like somebody upstairs is giving you another chance."

The blue eyes glittered triumphantly.

Yes, a second chance, indeed.

Epilogue

Darby opened her eyes to the darkened apartment and
shot a glance at the alarm clock that sat on the nightstand. Three A.M.

Three A.M. and she was wide awake.

Turning her head, she stared at Graham's face, his expression relaxed, his jaw darkened with three days' worth
of stubble. He looked dangerous even when asleep, and
she could only imagine the impression he made on the
street. If she were a criminal, she certainly wouldn't want
him chasing her.

Not that she objected to him chasing her for an altogether different reason. He'd done that plenty in the last
two months since they'd left Nostalgia and moved in together in Dallas.

She should wake him. He'd told her to whenever she
couldn't sleep, which was often. Not because of nightmares, or anything like that. It was almost as if she'd
spent the past ten years in sort of a sleepy, alcoholic fog.
Now that she was sober, and free of the past, she
brimmed with energy.

Usually, Graham was a pretty light sleeper himself. But he'd just come off of a forty-eight-hour stakeout. Their nightly lovemaking had been fast and furious; then he'd collapsed into a dead sleep. He hadn't even shifted positions. He lay sprawled on top of the royal blue sheets, still naked and slightly aroused.

Sliding free of his bare leg and one muscled arm, she inched over to the edge of the bed and rubbed her arms. December had rolled around, and brought with it one hell of a cold front.

Glancing around, she stared at the boxes stacked in the corners of the new apartment she and Graham had leased in downtown Dallas, just off Commerce Street. Nice, or it soon would be once she finished unpacking. *If* she ever finished. It was one of those chores she dreaded.

After leaving Nostalgia, she hadn't even gone back to San Francisco. There was nothing for her there, so she'd telephoned her landlord, wired him some money, and had all her belongings shipped to Dallas. And Mr. Wilcox had done a piss-poor job of packing. Things had been heaped into boxes in no particular order. Just as Pinky Mitchell had thrown all of her things from the motel into a couple of boxes and shipped them via UPS. Those boxes had joined the others in the apartment.

She cast one lingering glance at Graham, thought about crawling back into bed and waking him. A few kisses here, a few strokes there, and she had no doubt she could revive him from his sleep-induced coma. That was one thing about Graham. No matter how tired, he could always rise to the occasion.

Leaning over, she planted a tender kiss on his cheek, pulled the sheet up over him, then climbed from the bed. He needed to rest, and the clutter called too loudly for her to put off the unpacking any longer.

Pulling one of Graham's T-shirts over her naked body, she headed for the living room to the stack of boxes situated in the area she was going to turn into an office.

She would need one. She'd just landed a weekly entertainment column with the *Dallas News*, a job that had started last night with a movie premiere. If she didn't get her laptop and other essentials unpacked, she'd be turning in her copy in longhand, and that certainly wouldn't gain her any points with the new boss.

She flicked on a nearby lamp, sat down Indian-style and reached for a box.

An hour later, she sat surrounded by books, computer equipment, diskettes, knickknacks, a pair of guitar-shaped bookends. . . .

"Look at this," she murmured, pulling a stack of computer pages from the bottom of one of the boxes. She read the title page and realized this was her beloved Great American Novel. Only her inch-high manuscript looked more like three inches high.

Her mind traveled back to the motel room in Nostalgia, the quick looks when she'd noticed the stack of pages had been growing. Yet she couldn't remember doing any writing.

But then Darby couldn't remember a lot of things.

Unimportant things, Graham stressed whenever she broached the subject of the past, or got frustrated with herself for forgetting. He didn't seem the least bit upset that she couldn't remember the dreams.

No, he seemed as if he wanted her to forget. Not that she could blame him. Graham was doing his damnedest to put the past behind them, the hatred. A fresh start, he'd said. They were making a fresh start. A new beginning. Just the two of them.

They'd cut all ties to Nostalgia. Graham's mother had moved to Houston to be near her only living sister. The family home had been sold. Graham's father lived and worked in Fort Worth.

Katy Evans was in Houston, in the burn unit at Ben Taub Hospital. She was healing nicely, though her body would be badly disfigured from the fire. Not that it mattered what she looked like. Death Row would welcome her anyway as soon as she was well enough to be released from the hospital.

Neither Graham nor Darby had anyone or anything calling them back to Nostalgia. The place was nothing more than a bad memory now.

A new beginning, she told herself. Just the two of them. Together.

Her attention returned to the novel. She pulled the cover sheet off the top of the stack and turned to the first page of text.

A coldness seeped through her, settling into her bones. She quickly forgot all about fresh starts and new beginnings. The past reared its ugly head. Samuel Blue had left her a memento of their days together, she realized, the stack of pages heavy in her hands. A reminder of the time they'd shared.

A memoir of every bloody moment, starting with . . .

I'd always wondered what death would feel like.

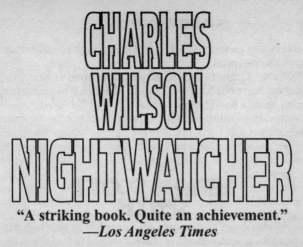

CHARLES WILSON
NIGHTWATCHER

"A striking book. Quite an achievement."
—*Los Angeles Times*

The staff of the state hospital for the criminally insane in Davis County, Mississippi, has seen a lot in their time—but nothing like the savage killing of Judith Salter, one of their nurses. And with three escaped inmates on the loose, there is no telling which of them is the butcher—or who the next victim will be. Even worse, as the danger and terror grow apace, the only eyewitness to the nurse's death—a psychopathic mass murderer—begins to reveal a fearsome agenda of his own.

___4275-4 $4.99 US/$5.99 CAN

WHEN SHADOWS FALL

BRIAN SCOTT SMITH

Martin doesn't believe his aunt's death is an accident, and he and a couple of buddies are determined to find the truth. But when he starts sneaking around the house of his aunt's new "friends," he never expects to witness a blood-drenched satanic ritual. But he does see it, and more important, the witches see him!

Suddenly Martin is in a horrifying race for his life. He has to stop the witches before they stop him for good. And he has to do it before Halloween night, the night of the final sacrifice, the night when the demons of hell will be unleashed on the Earth, the night when shadows fall.

___4313-0 $4.99 US/$5.99 CAN

DRAWN TO THE GRAVE — MARY ANN MITCHELL

"A tight, taut dark fantasy with surprising plot twists and a lot of spooky atmosphere."
—Ed Gorman

Beverly thinks that she has found something special with Carl, until she realizes that he has stolen from her. But he doesn't just steal her money and her property—he steals her very life. Suddenly she is helpless and alone, able only to watch in growing despair as her flesh begins to decay and each day transforms her more and more into a corpse—a corpse without the release of death.

But Beverly is not truly alone, for Carl is always nearby, watching her and waiting. He knows that soon he will need another unknowing victim, another beautiful woman he can seduce...and destroy. And when lovely young Megan walks into his web, he knows he has found his next lover. For what can possibly go wrong with his plan, a plan he has practiced to perfection so many times before?

___4290-8 $4.99 US/$5.99 CAN

ROUGH BEAST
GARY GOSHGARIAN

mommy

Max Allan Collins

"Chilling!"—Lawrence Block, author of *Eight Million Ways to Die*

Meet Mommy. She's pretty, she's perfect. She's June Cleaver with a cleaver. And you don't want to deny her—or her daughter—anything. Because she only wants what's best for her little girl...and she's not about to let anyone get in her way. And if that means killing a few people, well isn't that what mommies are for?

"Mr Collins has an outwardly artless style that conceals a great deal of art."
—*The New York Times Book Review*

THE TAKING

DONALD BEMAN

What could Sean McDonald possibly have done to deserve what is happening to him? He was a happy man with a beautiful family, a fine job, good friends and dreams of becoming a writer. Now bit by bit, his life is crumbling. Everything and everyone he values is disappearing. Or is it being taken from him? Someone or something is determined to break Sean, to crush his mind and spirit. A malicious, evil force is driving him to the very brink of insanity. But why him?

__4202-9 $4.99 US/$5.99 CAN

SHADOWS

Kimberly Rangel

WHERE TERROR RULES...

In the distant past, in a far-off land, the spell is cast, damning the family to an eternity of blood hunger. Over countless centuries, in the dark of night, they are doomed to assume the shape of savage beasts, deadly black panthers driven by a maddening fever to quench their unspeakable thirst. Then Selene DeMarco finds herself the last female of her line, and she has to mate with a descendent of the man who has plunged her family into the endless agony.
_4054-9 $4.99 US/$5.99 CAN